用「進入情境」的觀點，
學習「代表情境」的字根字首字尾；
才能幫助你掌握正確用法，
學習節奏與效率都一氣呵成！

User's Guide

使・用・説・明

會話秘笈 1

情境式的目錄編排，最符合學習效率！

本書打破現有制度，以「情境→情境→情境」的設計，將具有相近意思的字根、字首，以及字尾放置在一起，並特別標示首、根、尾，用最強邏輯學習！

Part1

Unit 02　首 **pre** 之前、預先

🎧 Track 002

情境對話 試水溫

Wendy: It has been a long time since I saw you last time. How's your job going?

Nancy: Pretty good. I'm now taking care of premature infants in a hospital now.

Wendy: Wow. That could be challenging for both you and their parents.

Nancy: Right. Even once they're home from the hospital, it's important to take extra precautions to protect the infants due to the undeveloped immune system. What about you? How's your job search going?

Wendy: I'm still working on it. Applying for a new job can be frustrating when you find out that previous working experiences are a precondition.

Nancy: That's true. Yet, not all interviewers will preview the resume. Compared to a well-written resume, your portfolio is more of a rerequisite when it comes to getting a good job.

溫蒂：自從上次見到妳已經過一陣子了。妳的工作進展如何？

南茜：不錯。我現在在一間醫院照顧早產兒。

溫蒂：對妳和他們的家人而言，我覺得那很有挑戰性。

南茜：沒錯。即使他們從醫院回家後，也必須採取額外的預防措施，保護因免疫系統發育不全而死亡的嬰兒。[……]呢？妳找工作進行得怎麼樣了？

溫蒂：我還在努力。[……]妳意識到工作經驗是個先決條件時，申請一份新工作可能會讓人覺得沮喪。

南茜：真的。然而，[……]不是所有面試官都會先審查履歷表。[……]要找到好工作的[……]對於一份寫得漂亮的履歷表，你的作品集是必需的事項。

　單字解析 零距離

❶ **pre** 預先＋**mature** 成熟
premature [ˌprimə`tjur] 形 太早的、不成熟的
延伸片語 premature infant 早產兒

會話秘笈 2

獨家設計情境對話，單字絕不誤用！

本書除了精心設計的目錄之外，在內容的編排上，也依照範例單字加上精心設計的情境會話，讓讀者可以簡單透過情境對話，掌握單字的使用脈絡！

會話秘笈 3

延伸片語加例句，臨時急用沒問題！

每個單字還搭配一個延伸片語，再以此片語編寫例句，學習者在記下單字的拼法之後便能一併學習該字在句子中的正確使用方法，短時間內惡補也沒問題！

Ch 1

Part 1

表示時間、前後順序

Part 2
Part 3
Part 4

▶ The premature infant was kept in the incubator until he was 2000 grams. 那個早產兒在達到二千公克前一直被放在保溫箱裡。

2 pre 之前 + condition 條件
precondition [ˌpriˈkənˈdɪʃən] 名 先決條件
延伸片語 precondition-based 以先決條件為基礎的
▶ A precondition-based marriage is sad.
一個以先決條件為基礎的婚姻是悲哀的。

3 pre 預先 + caution 謹慎
precaution [priˈkɔʃən] 名 預防措施
延伸片語 precaution against... 預防⋯⋯
▶ The villagers were warned to take necessary precautions against the typhoon. 村民接到採取必要防颱措施的警告。

4 pre 預先 + view 閱覽
preview [ˈpriˌvju] 名 預習
延伸片語 preview of a movie 電影試映
▶ We are invited to see the preview of the movie.
我們受邀欣賞這部電影的試映。

5 pre 之前 + re 再次 + quis 尋找 + ite 形容詞字尾
prerequisite [priˈrɛkwəzɪt] 名 首要事項、前提
延伸片語 prerequisite to... ⋯⋯的先決條件；⋯⋯的前提
▶ Being able to speak more than two foreign languages is the prerequisite to getting this job.
會說兩種以上的外語是得到這份工作的先決條件。

💡 延伸補充自然學

與 pre- 近義的字首：ante、ex、fore、pro

☆ **ante**natal	先前 + 出生的	形 出生前的
☆ **ex-husband**	先前的 + 老公	名 前夫
☆ **fore**head	前 + 頭	名 額頭
☆ **pro**gress	前 + 腳步	名 進展

015

會話秘笈 4

延伸補充一次學，快速擴充單字量！

除了額外的單字，其變化型或是近義、反義的字根、字首，或是字尾也很重要！本書補充大量與該單元主題相關的單字，配上基本拆解，一次學滿學足！

Preface

作・者・序

我在英語教學這個領域已經有很多年的經驗了，但一直沒想過有一天會出一本關於字根字首字尾教學的書，很高興這次有機會跟捷徑出版社合作，希望能用自己累積多年的教學經驗獻給各位學習者一本好的學習教材。

學英文的第一步就是背單字，而公認最好的單字記憶方式當然非字首、字根、字尾的學習法莫屬了。不過，如果呆板地用一個字母一個字母去背，不但速度慢，其實也很容易忘記；若是用字首、字根、字尾的拆解方式去記憶的話，可以更徹底地理解單字的組成方式和原理，如此融會貫通的學習效果也會更好。當背單字就像是玩拼圖一樣，將字首、字根、字尾一塊一塊地拼起來，就會發現其實背單字真的一點都不難。

然而，要怎麼要才能「順利」地把拼圖拼起來呢？你需要的是一個「情境」。本書最大的特色在於擺脫傳統學習字根、字首，以及字尾的編排方法，不僅在目錄的分類上獨具巧思，每個章節內的小節也同樣再細分情境，達到符合思考模式的樹狀圖學習法，讓讀者可以一次掌握具有相近意思的字根、字首，以及字尾，使讀者對該字根、字首，或是字尾的印象大大加深。簡單來說，本書強調的就是生活中的「情境」，因為情境是最容易幫助我們記憶的切入點。

除此之外，每個範例單字都還會再配上一個常用片語以及片語例句，學習者在記下單字的拼法時也能一併學習該單字在句子中的正確使用方法。這樣下來，有了情境，還有解析和補充，還有哪個單字背不起來？除此之外，本書趁勝追擊，在每個章節最後附上該字根、字首，或是字尾的可能變化型，並透過簡單的基本拆解，讓學習者能快速理解各補充單字的意義由來，使讀者可以把同語源或是相近義字根、字首，或是字尾也學起來，快速擴充單字量。

最後，老話仍然是那一句：語言能力的養成必定是長時間的累積，但在這過程當中，如果找到正確且有效的學習方式，便能事半功倍。祝福各位學習之路順利！

Contents

目・錄

Chapter One

Chapter Two

Chapter Three

Chapter Four

Chapter Five

Chapter 1

 根 **tempor** 時間

💬 情境對話試水溫　　　　　　　　　🎧 *Track 001*

Lilian: Do you know that these two artists are contemporaneous?	莉莉安：你知道這兩個藝術家是同時期的嗎？
Melody: Really? Their artworks exhibit very contrasting spatiotemporal settings.	美樂蒂：真的嗎？他們的藝術品展現出差異非常大的時空背景呢。
Lilian: That's because they have different personality, which has something to do with their family background. One is extremely poor, and one is incredibly rich.	莉莉安：這是因為他們擁有不同的性格，且跟他們的家庭背景有點關係。其中一個非常貧窮，另一個則不可思議地有錢。
Melody: I see. This makes me feel like I am just a tiny temporal being, like an ant, in this mundane world.	美樂蒂：明白。這讓我覺得在這個塵世間，我只是個小小的世俗的存在，像一隻螞蟻一樣。
Lilian: Aren't we all? Temporariness isn't entirely a bad thing. It helps us value what we have.	莉莉安：我們不也都是嗎？無法長久並不全然是件壞事。這樣能幫助我們珍惜我們所擁有的。
Melody: True. After all, one's inner knowledge isn't temporary. It lasts and shows itself through one's creations.	美樂蒂：那倒是。畢竟，一個人的內在知識不是暫時性的。它會持續下去，並從一個人的創作作品中嶄露出來。
Lilian: Well said.	莉莉安：說的好。

 單字解析零距離

❶ **tempor** 時間 ＋ **ary** 形容詞字尾

temporary [ˈtɛmpəˌrɛrɪ] 形 臨時的；暫時的

Ch 1

Part 1

表示時間、前後順序

Part 2

Part 3

Part 4

延伸片語 **a temporary job** 臨時工

▶ I found a temporary job at the gas station.
　我在加油站找到一份臨時工作。

- -

❷ tempor 生命 + **ariness** 形容詞轉名詞

temporariness [ˈtɛmpəˌrɛrənɪs] 名 暫時性

延伸片語 **the temporariness of life** 生命的暫時性

▶ I find it hard to deal with the idea of the temporariness of life.
　我覺得要面對生命的暫時性這個想法很難。

- -

❸ tempor 時間 + **al** 形容詞字尾

temporal [ˈtɛmpərəl] 形 時間的；短暫的；世俗的

延伸片語 **a temporal dimension** 時間的維度

▶ We all live in this temporal dimension. 我們都生活在這個時間的維度。

- -

❹ spatio 空間 + **tempor** 時間 + **al** 形容詞字尾

spatiotemporal [ˌspeʃɪoˈtɛmpərəl] 形 時空的

延伸片語 **spatiotemporal background** 時空背景

▶ This painting portrays a very specific spatiotemporal background. 這幅畫展現出了一個非常特有的時空背景。

- -

❺ con 共同 + **tempor** 時間 + **aneous** 形容詞字尾

contemporaneous [kənˌtɛmpəˈrenɪəs] 形 復活、使恢復生氣

延伸片語 **be contemporaneous with** 與～同期

▶ Chopin is not contemporaneous with Mozart.
　蕭邦和莫札特不是同時期的。

延伸補充 自然學

☆ **atemporal**	表否定 + 時間的	形	不受時間影響的
☆ **temporality**	時間的 + 名詞字尾	名	暫時性；時間性

與 tempor 近義的字根：chron

☆ **chronic**	表示時間性的	形	慢性的；習慣性的
☆ **synchronize**	一起 + 時間 + 動詞字尾	動	同步
☆ **chronology**	時間 + 學科（學問）	名	編年史

Unit02 首 pre 之前、預先

情境對話試水溫

Wendy: It has been a long time since I saw you last time. How's your job going?

溫蒂：自從上次見到妳已經過了一陣子了。妳的工作進展如何？

Nancy: Pretty good. I'm now taking care of premature infants in a hospital now.

南茜：不錯。我現在在一間醫院照顧早產兒。

Wendy: Wow. That could be challenging for both you and their parents.

溫蒂：對妳和他們的家人而言，我覺得那很有挑戰性。

Nancy: Right. Even once they're home from the hospital, it's important to take extra precautions to protect the infants due to the undeveloped immune system. What about you? How's your job search going?

南茜：沒錯。即使他們從醫院回家後，也必須採取額外的預防措施來保護因免疫系統發育不全而死亡的嬰兒。妳呢？妳找工作進行得怎麼樣了？

Wendy: I'm still working on it. Applying for a new job can be frustrating when you find out that previous working experiences are a precondition.

溫蒂：我還在努力。當妳意識到工作經驗是一個先決條件時，申請一份新工作可能會讓妳覺得沮喪。

Nancy: That's true. Yet, not all interviewers will preview the resume. Compared to a well-written resume, your portfolio is more of a rerequisite when it comes to getting a good job.

南茜：真的。然而，並不是所有面試官都會預先審查履歷表。如果你要找到好工作的話，相對於一份寫得漂亮的履歷表，你的作品集更會是必需的事項。

單字解析零距離

1 pre 預先 + mature 成熟

premature [ˌprimə'tjur] 形 太早的、不成熟的

延伸片語 premature infant 早產兒

Ch 1
Part 1
表示時間、前後順序
Part 2
Part 3
Part 4

▶ The premature infant was kept in the incubator until he was 2000 grams. 那個早產兒在達到二千公克前一直被放在保溫箱裡。

・・・・・・・・・・・・・・・・・・・・・・・・・・・・・・・・・・・・・

❷ pre 之前 ＋ condition 條件

precondition [ˌprikənˈdɪʃən] 名 先決條件

延伸片語 **precondition-based** 以先決條件為基礎的

▶ A precondition-based marriage is sad.
一個以先決條件為基礎的婚姻是悲哀的。

・・・・・・・・・・・・・・・・・・・・・・・・・・・・・・・・・・・・・

❸ pre 預先 ＋ caution 謹慎

precaution [prɪˈkɔʃən] 名 預防措施

延伸片語 **precaution against...** 預防……

▶ The villagers were warned to take necessary precautions against the typhoon. 村民接到採取必要防颱措施的警告。

・・・・・・・・・・・・・・・・・・・・・・・・・・・・・・・・・・・・・

❹ pre 預先 ＋ view 閱覽

preview [ˈpriˌvju] 名 預習

延伸片語 **preview of a movie** 電影試映

▶ We are invited to see the preview of the movie.
我們受邀欣賞這部電影的試映。

・・・・・・・・・・・・・・・・・・・・・・・・・・・・・・・・・・・・・

❺ pre 之前 ＋ re 再次 ＋ quis 尋找 ＋ ite 形容詞字尾

prerequisite [ˌpriˈrɛkwəzɪt] 名 首要事項、前提

延伸片語 **prerequisite to...** ……的先決條件；……的前提

▶ Being able to speak more than two foreign languages is the prerequisite to getting this job.
會說兩種以上的外語是得到這份工作的先決條件。

💡 **延伸補充 自然學**

與 pre- 近義的字首：ante、ex、fore、pro

☆ **ante**natal	先前 ＋ 出生的	形	出生前的
☆ **ex-husband**	先前的 ＋ 老公	名	前夫
☆ **forehead**	前 ＋ 頭	名	額頭
☆ **progress**	前 ＋ 腳步	名	進展

首 fore 前面、在~之前、先

💬 情境對話試水溫　　　　　　　　🎧 *Track 003*

Kristy:	I strongly recommend Ian's latest novel. Though I only finished the foreword last night, I guess you'll definitely love it!

克莉絲汀：我強烈建議你一定要看伊恩最新的小說。雖然我昨晚只看了前言，但我猜你一定會喜歡！

Molly:	What's it about?

莫莉：內容是關於什麼？

Kristy:	A boy with a lightning-bolt-shaped scar on his forehead has this mysterious power to foresee the future, foretell the results, and know all details about others' foretime.

克莉絲汀：是關於一個額頭上有閃電疤痕的男孩，他擁有預知未來、預言結果，以及了解每人過去的超能力。

Molly:	Harry Potter?

莫莉：哈利波特？

Kristy:	Cut it out!

克莉絲汀：你夠了！

Molly:	Alright, alright! Lend it to me after you finish reading, but no spoilers, ok?

莫莉：好啦好啦！你看完以後借我，但不要爆雷好嗎？

Kristy:	Sure. Now I hope I can foresee if the baseball tournament will take place tomorrow.

克莉絲汀：當然！我現在希望我也能預知明天棒球聯賽會不會舉行。

Molly:	I checked the weather forecast and it said it will be raining tomorrow. I think it'll be postponed to next Saturday.

莫莉：我剛剛看了天氣預報，明天會下雨，我猜比賽會延到下週六。

Kristy:	No way!!!

克莉絲汀：不會吧！！

⚡ 單字解析零距離

❶ **fore** 預先 ＋ **cast** 拋、擲

forecast [ˋforˏkæst] 動 預測、預示　延伸片語 **weather forecast** 天氣預測

Ch 1

Part 1

表示時間、前後順序

Part 2

Part 3

Part 4

▶ According to the weather forecast, it will rain this afternoon.
根據天氣預報，今天下午會下雨。

❷ fore 前面的 **+ head** 頭部

forehead [ˈfɔr.hɛd] 名 前額　　延伸片語 **forehead thermometer** 額溫槍

▶ The nurse used a forehead thermometer to take his temperature. 護士用額溫槍幫他量體溫。

❸ fore 預先 **+ see** 看見

foresee [fɔrˈsi] 動 預知

延伸片語 **foresee the result of...** 預測……的結果

▶ I wish I could foresee the result of the final exam.
我希望我可以預知期末考的成績。

❹ fore 預先 **+ tell** 說

foretell [fɔrˈtɛl] 動 預測、預言　　延伸片語 **foretell the future** 預測未來

▶ The fortune teller foretold the woman's future by reading her hand. 算命師看女子的手相，預測她的未來。

❺ fore 前面的 **+ time** 時光

foretime [ˈfɔr.taɪm] 名 過往

延伸片語 **say goodbye to foretime** 告別過去

▶ We should say goodbye to foretime and look to the future.
我們應該告別過去，往前看。

❻ fore 前面的 **+ word** 字詞

foreword [ˈfɔr.wɜd] 名 前言　　延伸片語 **foreword to a book** 書的前言

▶ I am honored to have my respected teacher write a foreword to my book. 能請恩師幫我的書寫序，我感到很榮幸。

 延伸補充 自然學

☆ **forearm**　　　前面的 + 手臂　　　名 前臂

根 sequ 追隨其後

🎧 *Track 004*

情境對話試水溫

Natalie: You know the consequences of breaking the school rules, right?

娜塔莉：你知道打破校規的後果，對吧？

Laura: I know, but I believe it's the right thing to do. I hate seeing those obsequious people who always try to flatter the greedy principal.

蘿拉：我知道，但是我相信這是對的事情。我討厭看到那些奉承的人總是試著要討好貪心的校長。

Natalie: But you have to know that this issue is bred by a sequence of previous events. It's not that simple.

娜塔莉：但你必須知道，這個議題是由先前一連串事件所導致的。事情沒有那麼簡單。

Laura: So it's wrong for me trying to correct this subsequent outcome, which has already become a burden for the students?

蘿拉：所以我想要解決這個隨之而來的後果是錯的嗎？這早已變成學生們的負擔了。

Natalie: That's not what I meant. But I don't see how painting an ugly graffitti is going to help the issue you're talking about.

娜塔莉：我不是那個意思。但是我不是很清楚畫一個醜陋的塗鴉可以怎麼幫助你正在說的問題。

單字解析零距離

❶ **con** 共同 ＋ **sequ** 跟隨 ＋ **ence** 名詞字尾

consequence [ˈkɑnsəˌkwɛns] 名 結果

延伸片語 **of no consequence** 無足輕重

Ch 1

Part 1

表示時間、前後順序

Part 2

Part 3

Part 4

▶ He is only a man of no consequence.
他只是個無足輕重的小人物。

❷ **ob** 到 ＋ **sequ** 跟隨 ＋ **ious** 形容詞字尾

obsequious [əbˋsikwɪəs] 形 奉承的

延伸片語 **obsequious flattery** 阿諛之詞

▶ Jack's obsequious flatteries make his boss overwhelmed with joy.
傑克的阿諛諂媚之詞讓他老闆樂不可支。

❸ **sequ** 跟隨 ＋ **ence** 名詞字尾

sequence [ˋsikwəns] 名 接續

延伸片語 **a sequence of** 一連串的……

▶ After interviewing a sequence of applicants, the interviewers were all tired.
在面試了一連串的應徵者後，所有面試官都累了。

❹ **sub** 在……下面 ＋ **sequ** 跟隨 ＋ **ent** 表示性質

subsequent [ˋsʌbsɪkwɛnt] 名 後繼

延伸片語 **subsequent to** 在……之後

▶ On the day subsequent to their divorce, he married another woman.
就在他們離婚的第二天，他就娶了另一個女子。

延伸補充 自然學

sequ的變化形：secu、sec、sue

☆ **consecutive**	共同 ＋ 緊跟的	形 接續的
☆ **second**	跟隨的 ＋ 性質	形 第二的
☆ **ensue**	加強 ＋ 跟隨	動 接踵而來

首 **post** 之後

情境對話試水溫

Marvin: I heard that you're now a postgraduate student.

馬文：我聽說你現在是一名研究所的學生。

Linda: Yes. I'm now focusing on post-modern cultural theories.

琳達：是的。我現在正專攻後現代的文化理論。

Marvin: Wow. Sounds deep. How many people are there in your class?

馬文：哇，聽起來很深耶。你的班上有很多人嗎？

Linda: It depends. But I'm so fed up with my team partner postponing her part of the project. It's so annoying.

琳達：要看情況。但我真的受夠我的組員一直在拖延繳交她作業的部分。真的很煩。

Marvin: You should notify your professor. Write a postscript on your report.

馬文：你應該要告知你的教授。在你的報告上做個附錄。

Linda: I wish it is that easy. Her report always came posterior to mine! Then I became the telltale!

琳達：我希望這有那麼簡單。她的報告總是比我晚交！這樣我就變成抓耙仔了！

Marvin: She's the one that hasn't done things right. Why do you have to feel guilty about it?

馬文：她是那個沒把事情做好的人。為什麼你要為此覺得自責？

單字解析零距離

❶ **post** 後面的 ＋ **modern** 現代的

postmodern [post`madən] 形 後現代的

延伸片語 postmodern theory 後現代理論

Ch 1

Part 1

表示時間、前後順序

Part 2

Part 3

Part 4

▶ This professor is well-known for his in-depth grasp in postmoder theories. 這位教授以他對後現代理論深度的理解而出名。

. . . .

❷ post 後面的 ＋ pon 放置 ＋ e

postpone [post`pon] 動 延期、延遲

延伸片語 to postpone a meeting 延後開會

▶ The manager requested to postpone the meeting to the afternoon. 經理要求將會議延遲到下午。

. . . .

❸ post 後面的 ＋ e ＋ ior 形容詞字尾

posterior [pas`tırıə] 形 後面的 名 後部；臀部

延伸片語 the posterior side 後面的部分

▶ The posterior side of the building is out of use now.
這棟大樓的後部已沒有在使用了。

. . . .

❹ post 後面的 ＋ gradu 一步一步 ＋ ate 表示群體

postgraduate [post`grædʒuɪt] 名 研究生 形 研究生的；大學畢業後的

延伸片語 to study as a postgraduate 讀研究所

▶ I studied hard in order to get into that famous school and study as a postgraduate.
我認真讀書只為了進入那間有名的學校讀研究所。

. . . .

❺ post 後面的 ＋ script 書寫

postscript [`post͵skrıpt] 名 附筆；附錄

延伸片語 to add a postscript 加上附註

▶ I added a postscript in my report, hoping that I could get extra credits. 我在我的報告加了附錄，希望可以得到額外的分數。

延伸補充 自然學

| ☆ post-war | 後面的 ＋ 戰爭 | 形 戰後的 |
| ☆ postlude | 後面的 ＋ 演奏 | 名 後奏曲 |

首 **en** 入、向內、使進入

情境對話試水溫   🎧 *Track 006*

Ethan: Why did I ever want to enroll in this class at the first place?

伊森：我當初到底為什麼會想要註冊這堂課？

Mary: What happened?

瑪莉：怎麼了？

Ethan: I feel encaged in all these theories. They're so unpractical.

伊森：我覺得好像被這些理論困在籠子裡一樣。它們好不實用。

Mary: Well, once you absorb them and transform them into a form of mindset, you won't feel entrapped again.

瑪莉：這個嘛，一旦你把他們吸收進去，並將他們轉換成一種心態，你就不會覺得被騙了。

Ethan: I'm just very lost in this course. The professor just sent the files to us and provided no explanations.

伊森：我只是在這堂課覺得很迷惘而已。教授只把檔案寄給我們，然後沒有提供解釋。

Mary: Okay. Now, I know why. You didn't notice that the handouts were enclosed in the email, right?

瑪莉：好的。我現在知道為什麼了。你沒有注意到講義被附在信裡面，對不對？

Ethan: Oh my god...

伊森：我的天。

Ch 1

Part 1

Part 2

Part 3

Part 4

表示方位、方向、地點

單字解析零距離

1 **en** 向內 ＋ **roll** 名單

enroll [ɪnˋrol] 動 註冊、登記

延伸片語 **be enrolled for military** 應召入伍

▶ Sam was enrolled for military service as soon as he graduated.
山姆一畢業就應召入伍了。

• •

2 **en** 入、向內 ＋ **cage** 籠子

encage [ɛnˋkedʒ] 動 關進籠子

延伸片語 **feel encaged** 感覺被囚禁

▶ Many women feel encaged in their marriages.
許多女人感覺自己被囚禁在婚姻中。

• •

3 **en** 使進入 ＋ **trap** 陷阱

entrap [ɪnˋtræp] 動 使……陷入圈套

延伸片語 **entrap... into...** 誘騙……做……

▶ Those teenage girls were entrapped into prostitution.
那些少女被誘騙來賣淫。

• •

4 **en** 入、向內 ＋ **close** 關閉

enclose [ɪnˋkloz] 動 圈住、關住

延伸片語 **enclose herewith** 隨函附上

▶ A recent photo of me is enclosed herewith.
隨信附上一張我的近照。

延伸補充自然學

| ☆ **entomb** | 入 ＋ 墓地 | 動 埋葬 |
| ☆ **encase** | 入 ＋ 事例 | 動 包裝 |

首 trans 穿過、橫越、轉變

情境對話試水溫

🎧 *Track 007*

Mario: Are the goods ready for transport?

馬立歐：貨品都準備好運送了嗎？

Phoebe: Yes, but I want to remind you that they also need to be transferred to another company for quality inspection during the shipment.

菲比：是的，不過我想要提醒你，這些商品在運輸途中也需要被轉運到另一間公司做品質檢查。

Mario: I know. Do transmit the required files for the examination first.

馬立歐：我知道。請先將檢測需要的文件發送出去。

Phoebe: Copy that. I'll also transcribe the information we need here, just in case.

菲比：收到。我也會把我們這裡需要的資訊謄寫下來，以防萬一。

Mario: You are very thoughtful. By the way, how long will the goods arrive at the destination?

馬立歐：你真的想得很周到。對了，商品多久會到達目的地？

Phoebe: Just a couple of days.

菲比：大概幾天。

Mario: Wow. Logistics is really transcending, huh?

馬立歐：哇。物流業真的不斷在超越，是吧？

Phoebe: You bet.

菲比：當然。

單字解析零距離

❶ trans 穿過 **+ port** 運送

transport [`trænsˏpɔrt] 名 運輸

延伸片語 **ready for transport** 準備運輸

▶ The merchandise is ready for transport. 商品已準備送運。

Ch 1

Part 1

Part 2

表示方位、方向、地點

Part 3

Part 4

❷ **trans** 橫越 ＋ **fer** 攜帶

transfer [træns`fɝ] 勔 轉移；調動；轉運

延伸片語 to be transferred 轉往、調往

▶ I had been, unfortunately, transferred to the department that has to constantly work overtime.
我很不幸地，已經被調往需要常常加班的部門了。

⋯⋯⋯⋯⋯⋯⋯⋯⋯⋯⋯⋯⋯⋯⋯⋯⋯⋯⋯⋯⋯⋯

❸ **trans** 從一端到一端 ＋ **mit** 傳送

transmit [træns`mɪt] 勔 傳送；發射；傳染

延伸片語 to transmit disease 傳染疾病

▶ Some animals may transmit disease.
有些動物可能會傳播疾病。

⋯⋯⋯⋯⋯⋯⋯⋯⋯⋯⋯⋯⋯⋯⋯⋯⋯⋯⋯⋯⋯⋯

❹ **tran** 轉移 ＋ **scribe** 寫

transcribe [træns`kraɪb] 勔 謄寫

延伸片語 to transcribe a letter 抄寫一封信

▶ I transcribe the letter in case the original one goes missing.
我把信抄寫了一遍，怕原本的不見。

⋯⋯⋯⋯⋯⋯⋯⋯⋯⋯⋯⋯⋯⋯⋯⋯⋯⋯⋯⋯⋯⋯

❺ **tran** 橫越 ＋ **scend** 爬

transcend [træn`sɛnd] 勔 超越

延伸片語 to transcend the boundaries 突破疆界

▶ Some artworks can truly transcend the boundaries between dream and reality.
有些藝術品真的能夠超越夢與現實的疆界。

延伸補充 自然學

☆ **transfix**	穿越 ＋ 固定	勔 使驚呆
☆ **transform**	轉移 ＋ 形狀	勔 改變形態
與 trans- 近義的字首：dia		
☆ **diameter**	穿越 ＋ 測量	名 直徑
☆ **diagonal**	穿越 ＋ 角度	形 對角線的

 根 **medi** 中間

情境對話試水溫

🎧 *Track 008*

Amber: This painting gives me an immeidate sense of sadness. How weird.

> 安柏：這幅畫給了我立即的悲傷感受。好奇怪。

Miriam: I felt the same way, too .This one is from the medieval age, and it's not the mediocre kind of production, but a creation made from a true craftsman.

> 米莉安：我也這麼覺得。這幅畫是來自中世紀，而且不是一幅平庸的作品，而是來自於真正工藝家的創作。

Amber: I appreicate how he utilizes sunlight as the medium to portray the relations among the people in it.

> 安柏：我欣賞他利用太陽的方式，用來作為展現畫中人物關係的媒介。

Miriam: Yes. I guess the painter wanted to show how mother nature and human beings mediated a balance between the two sides.

> 米莉安：是的。我猜，這位畫家想要展現的是大自然如何和人類協調出一種雙方之間的平衡。

Amber: You have such wonderful interpretations of this painting.

> 安柏：你對於這幅畫真的有很棒的詮釋。

Miriam: I'm flattered.

> 米莉安：過獎了。

單字解析零距離

❶ im 表否定 ＋ **medi** 中間的 ＋ **ate** 形容詞字尾

immediate [ɪˈmidɪt] 形 立即的；即刻的

延伸片語 an immediate feedback 立即的回饋

▶ The speaker received an immediate feedback from the guests.
講者立刻得到了聽眾的回饋。

Ch 1

Part 1

Part 2

表示方位、方向、地點

Part 3

Part 4

② **medi** 中間的 ＋ **eval** 形容詞字尾

medieval [͵mɪdɪˋivəl] 形 中世紀的

延伸片語 **medieval architecture** 中世紀建築

▶ Henry has been studying medieval architecure for over ten years.
亨利研究中世紀建築已經超過十年了。

. . . .

③ **medi** 中間的 ＋ **ocre** 狀態

mediocre [ˋmidɪͺokəͺ] 形 平庸的

延伸片語 **a mediocre performance** 平庸的演出

▶ The actress only gave a mediocre performance in this movie.
這位女明星在這部電影裡的表現只能算是平庸。

. . . .

④ **med** 中間的 ＋ **ium** 名詞字尾

medium [ˋmidɪəm] 形 中間的；平庸的 名 中間；媒介

延伸片語 **a medium of** 作為……的媒介

▶ Nature is ususally the medium of expression for artists.
大自然對藝術家來說通常都是表達的媒介。

. . . .

⑤ **medi** 中間的 ＋ **ate** 動詞字尾

mediate [ˋmidͺet] 動 調停；調解 形 居中的

延伸片語 **to mediate between** 在……中協調

▶ The dean of our department had to intervene in the issue now and mediate between teacher and the student.
我們系的院長現在必須介入問題，並於老師和學生之間進行協調了。

. . . .

延伸補充 自然學

☆ **midterm**	中間的 ＋ 結束	名 期中
☆ **mediator**	中間 ＋ 表示人	名 居中協調者
☆ **intermediate**	之間 ＋ 中間 ＋ 形容詞字尾	形 中間的；中等的

首 inter 在～之間

Petty: 2019 SPH International Baseball Summer Camp will take place at Taichung Intercontinental Baseball Stadium this July.

佩提：2019年SPH國際棒球夏令營七月要在台中洲際棒球場舉行耶！

Nelson: You mean the one at the intersection of Chongde Rd. and Huanzhong Rd.?

尼爾森：你是説崇德路跟環中路十字路口那一個棒球場嗎？

Petty: Yes. Intermediate school students from all over the world will gather and join the summer camp. It aims to improve not only baseball skills but interpersonal skills. They're recruiting translating and interpreting volunteers. Are you interested? You can fulfill the online volunteer sign-up sheet.

佩提：對呀！全世界的中學生都會聚集在一起參加這個夏令營，目標不只是提升他們的棒球技能，也希望提升他們的人際間的技能。他們正在招募翻譯的志工，你有興趣嗎？只需要上線填妥報名表單。

Nelson: Count me in! First, I need to find an internet café to fulfill the online sheet because my computer is so laggy!

尼爾森：我要參加！但首先我要先找間網咖填表單，因為我電腦跑超慢！

單字解析零距離

❶ **inter** 在……之間 + **continental** 洲的

intercontinental [ˌɪntɚ͵kɑntə`nɛntl̩] 形 大陸之間的、洲際的

延伸片語 **intercontinental flights** 洲際航班

▶ The airport has direct intercontinental flights from most major cities around the world. 該機場有直飛世界主要城市的洲際航班。

❷ **inter** 在……之間 + **mediate** 中間

intermediate [ˌɪntɚ`midɪət] 形 居中的

Ch 1

Part 1

Part 2

表示方位、方向、地點

Part 3

Part 4

延伸片語 intermediate school 初級中學
▶ He went to a local intermediate school before he entered high school. 他在進入高中之前，唸的是本地的一間初級中學。

- -

❸ inter 在……之間 **+ national** 國家的

international [͵ɪntə˙ˋnæʃən!] 形 國際的
延伸片語 International Date Line 國際換日線
▶ Greenwich is a town that lies on the International Date Line.
格林威治是個位於國際換日線上的小鎮。

- -

❹ inter 在……之間 **+ net** 網

internet [ˋɪntə͵nɛt] 名 網際網路
延伸片語 internet café 網咖
▶ Eric spent the whole day in an internet café playing online games. 艾瑞克一整天都泡在網咖裡玩線上遊戲。

- -

❺ inter 在……之間 **+ personal** 個人的

interpersonal [͵ɪntə˙ˋpɝsən!] 形 人際之間的
延伸片語 interpersonal intelligence 人際智能（人際溝通智慧）
▶ An exceptional publicist should possess outstanding interpersonal intelligence.
一個優秀的公關人員必須擁有出色的人際智能。

- -

❻ inter 在……之間 **+ section** 部分

intersection [͵ɪntə˙ˋsɛkʃən] 名 十字路口
延伸片語 intersection theory （數學）相交理論
▶ The math teacher is explaining the intersection theory to the students. 數學老師正在對學生解釋相交理論。

延伸補充自然學

☆ **inter**link   在……之間 + 連結   動 連接
☆ **inter**marry   在……之間 + 婚姻   動 通婚

首 e 出、以外、加強語氣

情境對話試水溫 🎧 *Track 010*

Jennifer: Ben and I file for divorce. My love and sympathy for him has totally evanished into the air.

珍妮佛：我跟班訴請離婚，我對他的愛跟同情已經蕩然無存了。

Olivia: What about your two little boys?

歐莉薇亞：那你兩個孩子怎麼辦？

Jennifer: I'll try to get full custody of my sons with all strength. The lawyer suggested that I should elaborate the whole thing to prove that I am the only one qualified to get full custody. Ben never cares about the children but he pretended that he couldn't live without us in court! That was disgusting!

珍妮佛：我會盡全力爭取所有監護權，律師建議我詳細說明所有事件，以證明我才是有資格取得所有監護權的人。班從來就不在乎孩子，卻在法庭上裝得好像沒有我們他活不下去，真的太噁了！

Olivia: The fact is sure to emerge eventually. Let me know if there's anything I could help.

歐莉薇亞：真相一定會水落石出的，有任何需要幫忙的地方一定要讓我知道。

Jennifer: All I want to do now is eject that odious man from my house! I'm evaluating the possibility of emigrating to Canada with my kids.

珍妮佛：我現在只希望把那可憎的男人趕出我家，我也正在評估帶著孩子遷到加拿大的可能性。

Olivia: True. Start a new life with a new environment.

歐莉薇亞：嗯，到了新的環境開始新的生活。

Ch 1

Part 1

Part 2

表示方位、方向、地點

Part 3

Part 4

單字解析零距離

❶ e 出 ＋ ject 噴射

eject [ɪˈdʒɛkt] 動 趕出、噴射　　延伸片語 eject sb from... 將某人趕出……

▶ The restaurant manager ejected that rowdy man from the restaurant. 餐廳經理將那搗亂的男人轟了出去。

❷ e 加強語氣 ＋ labor 勞作 ＋ ate 動詞字尾

elaborate [ɪˈlæbərɪt] 形 精心製作、策劃的

延伸片語 elaborate on 詳細說明

▶ The police asked the witness to elaborate on the incident. 警方要求該目擊者詳述案發經過。

❸ e 以外 ＋ merge 融合

emerge [ɪˈmɜdʒ] 動 浮出、顯現　　延伸片語 emerge from 從……中顯露

▶ More and more political scandals emerged from the investigation. 越來越多的政治醜聞在調查中被揭露出來。

❹ e 出 ＋ migr 遷移 ＋ ate 動詞字尾

emigrate [ˈɛməˌgret] 動 遷出（國外）

延伸片語 emigrate from 從……遷入

▶ Sam emigrated from Japan to Belgium. 山姆從日本移居到比利時。

❺ e 加強語氣 ＋ valu 價值 ＋ ate 動詞字尾

evaluate [ɪˈvæljuˌet] 動 評估　　延伸片語 evaluate performance 績效評估

▶ Our manager evaluates each employee's performance carefully. 我們經理謹慎地評估每個員工的表現。

❻ e 加強語氣 ＋ vanish 消失

evanish [ɪˈvænɪʃ] 動 消失　　延伸片語 evanish into thin air 消逝無蹤

▶ My remaining respect for him has evanished into thin air. 我對他僅有的尊敬已經消逝無蹤了。

情境對話試水溫

🎧 *Track 011*

Emily: I witnessed Abby's ex-husband exclaimed in anger that he would never give up two daughters' custody. Abby was arguing with him, but made a quick exit after spotting me standing right next to them.

艾蜜莉：我昨天目睹艾比的前夫大聲嚷嚷説他不會放棄兩個女兒的監護權。艾比跟他吵得正兇，但發現我就站在他們旁邊後就馬上離開了。

Cody: I've never heard that she had a husband!

寇弟：我從來不知道她有老公耶！

Emily: Her ex-husband was an ex-soldier, now working for an international trading corporation, in charge of exporting industrial products to Australia.

艾蜜莉：她前夫是個退伍軍人，現在在國貿公司上班，負責出口工業產品到澳洲。

Cody: You know all the details!

寇弟：你知道得好詳細。

Emily: I extracted these from Abby's colleague. You know, break room chatting.

艾蜜莉：我從她同事那裡得到的消息，你知道的，茶水間八卦嘛！

單字解析零距離

❶ **ex** 前面的 ＋ **husband** 丈夫

ex-husband [ɛksˋhʌzbənd] 名 前夫

延伸片語 **dead ex-husband** 死去的前夫

▶ She admitted that her dead ex-husband was the only one who treated her well. 她承認死去的前夫是唯一善待她的人。

表示方位、方向、地點

❷ ex 向外 + **claim** 説明

exclaim [ɪksˋklem] 動 （由於情緒激動）叫嚷

延伸片語 **exclaim against** 大聲抗議；強烈譴責

▶ Everyone exclaimed against the erroneous judgement.
所有人都對這起誤判予以強烈譴責。

- -

❸ ex 向外 + **it** 走動

exit [ˋɛksɪt] 名 出口、通道

延伸片語 **make one's exit** 退出

▶ Please sign out before you make your exit. 離開前請先簽退。

- -

❹ ex 向外 + **port** 運輸

export [ɪksˋport] 名 輸出品

延伸片語 **export promotion** 出口鼓勵；外銷推廣

▶ The policy of export promotion has greatly improved the economy of the country. 出口鼓勵政策大大地改善了這個國家的經濟狀況。

- -

❺ ex 前面的 + **soldier** 軍人

ex-soldier [ɛksˋsoldʒɚ] 名 退伍軍人

延伸片語 **employment of ex-soldier** 退伍軍人就業

▶ The government should bring up strategies to increase the employment of ex-soldiers.
政府應該提出一些能增加退伍軍人就業率的政策。

- -

❻ ex 向外 + **tract** 拉

extract [ɪkˋstrækt] 動 用力拉出、萃取、提煉

延伸片語 **extract... from...** 從……提取……

▶ The reporter extracted some insider information about the election from the campaign staff.
記者從助選員那得到了一些選舉的內幕消息。

延伸補充 自然學

☆ **exotic**	外面的	形 外來的
☆ **exogamy**	向外 + 婚姻	名 異族聯姻
☆ **expose**	向外 + 放置	動 暴露

首 over 超過、過度

情境對話試水溫

🎧 *Track 012*

Chloe: It was a nightmare traveling with Ruby! I'm not gonna do this AGAIN!

克羅伊：跟露比一起旅行是個惡夢！我再也不幹了。

Ollie: What happened? It seems that your anger is overflowing…

奧莉：怎麼了？感覺你的怒氣已經滿溢出來了。

Chloe: We planned to fly to Hong Kong and transferred to Dubai. We decided to meet up at 10 a.m. at the boarding gate, but she didn't show up until 9:20. At 9:30, I had no choice but to get on board myself.

克羅伊：我們預計飛香港之後轉機到杜拜，我們約好十點在登機口見，但她到了九點二十都還沒出現。沒辦法，我只好在九點半自己先上飛機了。

Ollie: Then, why didn't she show up?

奧莉：那她為什麼沒出現？

Chloe: The reason was so ridiculous! She overslept. She missed my 36 phone calls because she put it on the silent mode.

克羅伊：理由超荒唐！她睡過頭！她把手機調成靜音模式所以沒聽到我打了36通電話。

Ollie: It was really hard to overlook the stupid fault.

奧莉：這種低級錯誤真的很難讓人原諒耶。

Chloe: You won't believe that her oversleeping was just the overture to my terrible and long journey. She took another flight to Dubai. During the trip, she lost her phone, kept complaining about the food and weather, unwilling to walk under the sun, and only wanted to dine in high-end restaurants.

克羅伊：你不會相信她睡過頭只是我這趟可怕又漫長的旅行的序曲而已。她搭了另一個班機，在旅行中她把手機搞丟了，還不停地抱怨食物和天氣，拒絕在太陽下走路，而且只想去高級餐廳吃飯。

Ollie: You really overworked yourself for traveling with her.

奧莉：跟她一起旅行真是讓你過度勞累。

表示方位、方向、地點

⚡ 單字解析零距離

① over 過度 + flow 流

overflow [ˌovəˈflo] 動 溢出

延伸片語 overflow with joy 洋溢著喜悅

▶ Holding the baby in her arms, her heart overflowed with joy.
她懷裡抱著嬰兒，心中洋溢著喜悅。

② over 超過 + look 看

overlook [ˌovəˈluk] 動 俯瞰；忽視

延伸片語 overlook one's fault 原諒某人的錯誤

▶ Don't expect him to overlook your fault. 別期待他會原諒你的錯誤。

③ over 過度 + sleep 睡覺

oversleep [ˈovəˈslip] 動 睡過頭

延伸片語 oversleep oneself 睡過頭

▶ Set the alarm clock in case you oversleep yourself tomorrow.
先設定鬧鐘，以免明天睡過頭了。

④ over 過度 + ture 行為

overture [ˈovətʃur] 動 主動提議

延伸片語 the overture to ... ……的開端

▶ The dancing performance was the overture to the ceremony.
舞蹈表演揭開了典禮的序幕。

⑤ over 過度 + work 工作

overwork [ˈovəˌwɜk] 動 太過操勞

延伸片語 overwork oneself 過度勞累

▶ The doctor warned the woman against overworking herself.
醫生警告婦人不要過度勞累。

Unit 13 首 hyper 在～之上、過度、超過

Track 013

情境對話試水溫

Laura: Life is so hard. I have to deal with hypersensitive children in the child-care center, and at night, I need to take care of my father-in-law. He has hypertension.

羅拉：人生好難。我要在幼稚園照顧過動的孩子，晚上還要照顧我的岳父，他有高血壓。

Mavis: Hang in there. Things will get better!

梅維思：撐著點。事情會好轉的！

Laura: It's not that I want to complain. I love all of them. It's just that all these stress has made me hypersensitive sometimes.

羅拉：不是說我想抱怨。我很愛他們。只是這些壓力讓我變得有點過敏。

Mavis: I understand. Well, let me show you a website. It teaches people with similar conditions like you to relax.

梅維思：我懂。這樣吧，我給你看一個網站，它教導和你擁有類似情況的人如何放鬆。

Laura: Okay. Please show me now.

羅拉：好的。請給我看。

Mavis: Check this hyperlink.

梅維思：點這個超連結。

Laura: Let me see… Well, it's full of the usual hyperbole. I guess I'll just rely on my own.

羅拉：讓我看看⋯⋯嗯，這充滿了常見的浮誇語。我還是靠我自己好了。

單字解析零距離

❶ **hyper** 過度 ＋ **act** 動作 ＋ **ivity** 名詞字尾

hyperactivity [ˌhaɪpərækˈtɪvətɪ] 名 活動過度；過動症

延伸片語 the treatment of hyperactivity 過動症的治療

Ch 1
Part 1
Part 2
Part 3
Part 4

表示方位、方向、地點

▶ More and more children are receiving the treatment of hyperactivity nowadays. 現今越來越多小孩在接受過動症的治療。

② **hyper** 過度 ＋ **tens** 緊張 ＋ **ion** 名詞字尾

hypertension [ˌhaɪpɚˈtɛnʃən] 名 高血壓；過度緊張

延伸片語 the symptom of hypertension 高血壓的症狀

▶ The symptom of hypertension includes chest pain, blurry vision, and irregular heart beat.
高血壓的症狀包括胸腔疼痛、視力模糊以及心跳不規律。

③ **hyper** 過度 ＋ **sens** 感覺 ＋ **itive** 表示性質

hypersensitive [ˈhaɪpɚˈsɛnsətɪv] 形 過於敏感的；過敏的

延伸片語 a hypersensitive personality 過於敏感的性格

▶ Having a hypersensitive personality may lead to interpersonal issues. 過於敏感的個性可能會造成人際關係上的問題。

④ **hyper** 超過 ＋ **link** 連結

hyperlink [ˈhaɪpɚˌlɪŋk] 名 超連結

延伸片語 to attach a hyperlink 附上超連結

▶ Please attach the hyperlink of the website in the email.
請將網站的超連結附在電子郵件裡面。

⑤ **hyper** 過度 ＋ **bole** 扔

hyperbole [haɪˈpɝbəlɪ] 名 修辭的誇張法；誇張的語句

延伸片語 to be filled with hyperbole 充滿誇飾法

▶ As usual, the cover of the book is filled with those commonly-used hyperbole. 一如往常，這本書的封面充滿著常見的誇飾法。

延伸補充 自然學

與 hyper- 近義的字首：ultra-

☆ **ultrasonic** 超過＋音波的 形 超音波的

與 hyper- 具相反之意的字首：hypo-

☆ **hypotension** 低＋緊張＋名詞字尾 名 低血壓

Unit 14 首 sub 下面、在~之下、次、分支

情境對話 試水溫

Kyle: I heard that in this subtropical region, there's a tribe that uses a type of herb to penetrate one's subconscious mind.

凱爾：我聽說在這個亞熱帶地區，有一個部落會使用一種草藥來侵入人們的潛意識心理。

Charlie: And do what?

查理：然後要做什麼？

Kyle: To cure any subnormal symptoms.

凱爾：治療任何異常的症狀。

Charlie: That sounds like an uncivilized subculture.

查理：那聽起來很像是不文明的次文化。

Kyle: Well, maybe you should stop subdividing everything you see. No wonder you are so pessimistic. You observe all phenomena as fractures.

凱爾：這個嘛，也許你應該停止把你看到的所有事物都再分割。難怪你這麼悲觀。你把所有現象都視為斷裂的事物。

Charlie: There's nothing wrong with that. I'm just trying to say that the ritual you mentioned is very traditional and should be gotten rid of.

查理：這樣沒有錯啊。我只是想要試著說明，你提到的儀式非常傳統且需要被淘汰。

單字解析 零距離

1 sub 下面 + conscious 意識

subconscious [sʌbˈkɑnʃəs] 名 潛意識

延伸片語 subconscious behavior 潛意識行為

▶ Sleepwalking is a subconscious behavior.
夢遊是一種潛意識行為。

Ch 1

Part 1

Part 2

Part 3

Part 4

表示方位、方向、地點

② sub 次 ＋ culture 文化

subculture [ˌsʌbˈkʌltʃɚ] **名** 次文化

延伸片語 youth subculture 青年次文化

▶ Otaku is one of the youth subcultures in modern Japan.
御宅族是現代日本的一種青年次文化。

③ sub 分支 ＋ divide 分割

subdivide [ˌsʌbdɪˈvaɪd] **動** 細分為

延伸片語 be subdivide into... 被再分割為……

▶ The apartment was subdivided into four independent suites.
這間公寓又被分割為四個獨立套房。

④ sub 次 ＋ tropical 熱帶

subtropical [ˌsʌbˈtrɑpɪkl] **形** 亞熱帶的

延伸片語 subtropical air mass 亞熱帶氣團

▶ According to the meteorological map, there is a subtropical air mass formed near the island.
根據氣象圖顯示，該島的附近形成了一個亞熱帶氣團。

⑤ sub 在～之下 ＋ normal 正常

subnormal [ˌsʌbˈnorml] **形** 水準之下的

延伸片語 subnormal intelligence 智力偏低

▶ It's quite rude to call a person of subnormal intelligence a retarded.
以白痴稱呼一個智力偏低的人是相當無禮的行為。

延伸補充 自然學

與 sub 近義的字首：suc、suf、sup、sus

☆ **succumb**	躺＋下方	**動** 屈服
☆ **suffuse**	下方＋溶解	**動** 充滿
☆ **suppress**	下方＋壓力	**動** 壓制、壓抑
☆ **suspect**	表面底下的想法	**動** 猜疑

首 **para** 在～之旁、違反

🎧 *Track 015*

情境對話試水溫

Teresa: I noticed several paradoxes in this paragraph. They made this article illogical.	泰瑞莎：在這個段落我有注意到一些矛盾之處。它們讓這篇文章很沒有邏輯。
Laura: Really? Let me see.	羅拉：真的嗎？讓我看看。
Teresa: Here. I know the author is trying to paraphrase what he had mentioned in the previous sections, but the attempts apparently failed.	泰瑞莎：這裡。我知道這位作者試著想要將他在前面部分說的話重新敘述，但這些嘗試很顯然地失敗了。
Laura: Well, in terms of the writing methods, he surely couldn't parallel others, but his insight is quite ingenious.	羅拉：嗯，在寫作方法上，他當然無法和其他人相比擬，但是我覺得他的洞見蠻創新的。
Teresa: How so?	泰瑞莎：怎麼說？
Laura: See how he compares capitalists as social parasites? How audacious!	羅拉：看到他如何將資本主義者比喻為社會寄生蟲了嗎？超大膽！

單字解析零距離

❶ para 相反 ＋ **dox** 意見

paradox [ˈpærəˌdɑks] 名 自相矛盾的情況；似非而是的說法

延伸片語 **to be shown in paradox** 以矛盾的情況呈現

▶ Truth may sometimes be shown in paradox.
事實有時可能是矛盾的。

Ch 1

Part 1

Part 2

表示方位、方向、地點

Part 3

Part 4

❷ **para** 在～之旁 + **graph** 圖表

paragraph [ˋpærəˏgræf] 名 段落；節

延伸片語 in the ~ paragraph 在第～段

▶ In the second paragraph, we read that the earth will perish in no more than 20 years.
在第二段落中，我們讀到地球再不到二十年就會滅亡。

• •

❸ **para** 在～之旁 + **phrase** 用……方式表達

paraphrase [ˋpærəˏfreɪz] 動 意譯；解釋；改述

延伸片語 to paraphrase one's words 重述某人的話

▶ The reporter paraphrased the president's words in the news article.
這位記者在新聞稿裡重述了總統的話。

• •

❹ **para** 在～之旁 + **llel** 表示性質

parallel [ˋpærəˏlɛl] 動 使成平行；與……平行；比較 形 平行的；同方向的

延伸片語 A parallels B A與B呈平行

▶ The park actually paralleled the train station.
公園其實與火車站同方向。

• •

❺ **para** 在～之旁 + **site** 位置

parasite [ˋpærəˏsaɪt] 名 寄生蟲

延伸片語 to suffer from parasites 患有寄生蟲而受苦

▶ Most animals suffer from parasites and die of relevant disease.
大多數的動物都受寄生蟲之苦，並且死於相關疾病。

💡 延伸補充**自然學**

☆ **paramedic**	在～之旁 + 醫療相關的	名 醫護人員
與 para- 具相近之意的字根：later-		
☆ **bilateral**	雙的 + 邊長	形 雙邊的；雙方的
☆ **collateral**	相等的 + 邊長	形 附帶的；次要的

尾 **ward(s)** 往～方向的

💬 情境對話試水溫

Melissa: My grandfather really believes in feng shui, so he's looking for a house faced northward. He said it will help lay aside the fortune.	瑪莉莎：我爺爺真的很信風水，所以他現在正在找朝北的房子，他說可以聚財。
Paige: I've never heard of that. What other changes do your family need to make?	佩吉：我從來沒聽過耶，你們還需要做什麼其他的改變？
Melissa: In order to go for upward mobility, we need to put crystals at the certain directions of the house. Also, for not having downward spiral of misfortune, we have to change the layout of the kitchen so it won't face the main gate.	瑪莉莎：為了要提升社經地位，我們必須要在房子的特定方位放上水晶。而且為了不讓我們一直被厄運纏身，我們必須改變廚房的格局，所以廚房才不會面對大門。
Paige: Those really sound like hard works. I don't believe feng shui at all.	佩吉：聽起來就很麻煩，我根本不信風水。
Melissa: Me neither. But my grandfather is very wayward to make some changes, so I just look forward to any miracles happening to change our family's fate.	瑪莉莎：我也不信啊，但我爺爺非常剛愎想要做改變，所以我只好期待奇蹟發生可以改變我們家的命運。

⚡ 單字解析零距離

❶ **north** 北方 + **ward** 方向的

northward [ˋnɔrθwəd] 形 朝北的

延伸片語 migrate northward 向北遷移

Ch 1

Part 1

Part 2

Part 3

Part 4

表示方位、方向、地點

▶ The migrant birds will migrate northward again after winter.
候鳥在冬天過後又會向北遷移。

. . . .

❷ up 上方 **+ ward** 方向的

upward [ˋʌpwəd] 形 朝上的、往上的

延伸片語 upward mobility 提升社會和經濟地位的能力

▶ He will go to every expedient for upward mobility.
他將不擇手段提升自己的社經地位。

. . . .

❸ down 下方 **+ ward** 方向的

downward [ˋdaʊnwəd] 形 往下的

延伸片語 downward spiral 惡性循環

▶ It is an institution that helps drug addicts to combat the downward spiral of drug.
這是一個幫助癮君子與毒品之惡性循環搏鬥的機構。

. . . .

❹ way 路、習慣 **+ ward** 方向的

wayward [ˋwewəd] 形 剛愎的，反覆無常的

延伸片語 wayward and difficult 倔強的

▶ She is so wayward and difficult, so she never listens to what her mother says. 她是如此倔強，所以她從不聽她媽媽的話。

. . . .

❺ for 前面 **+ ward** 方向的

forward [ˋfɔrwəd] 形 往前的

延伸片語 look forward to 期待

▶ I am looking forward to the summer vacation.
我很期待暑假的到來。

延伸補充 自然學

與 -ward 近義的字尾：wide、wise、bound

☆ **world**wide　　世界 + 方向的　　形 全世界的

☆ **clock**wise　　時鐘 + 方向的　　形 順時針方向的

☆ **home**bound　　家 + 方向的　　形 回家鄉的

首 **mon(o)** 單一

🎧 *Track 017*

情境對話試水溫

Margaret:	I love the monologue made by the protagonist. He truly manifested the misery and hopelessness of being born in an era of monarchy.	瑪格莉特：我喜歡那個主角的獨白。他真正地展現了生存在君主國家的悲慘與絕望。
Megan:	Not to mention how the verses also hinted at the economic monopoly at that time. The country was one of the giant powers globally.	梅根：更別說詩句是如何反應出當時的經濟壟斷。那個國家在當時是全球的經濟巨頭之一。
Margaret:	The only downside of the play was that some of the scenes were basically read in a plain monotone. The performers seemed amateur.	瑪格莉特：這齣劇唯一的缺點就是，有些場景基本上都是用平淡的音調朗誦的。演員們看起來是業餘的。
Megan:	I agree. But I also think it's because the lines they were responsible of were mostly monosyllable. So, it's hard to blame them.	梅根：我同意。但我同時也認為這是因為他們負責的台詞都是單音節詞。所以，很難責怪他們。
Margaret:	Well, a professional one will…	瑪格莉特：這個嘛，專業的演員就會……
Megan:	Stop it, will you? Let's not argue about this.	梅根：停了，好嗎？我們就別爭論這個了。

單字解析零距離

❶ **mono** 單一 ＋ **archy** 統治

monarchy [ˋmɑnəkɪ] 名 君主國

延伸片語 constitutional monarchy 君主立憲制

▶ Norway, Spain and Belgium are all constitutional monarchies.
挪威、西班牙及比利時都是君主立憲制的國家。

Ch 1

Part 1

Part 2

Part 3

表示數量

Part 4

② **mono** 單一 + **logue** 說

monologue [`manl͵ɔg] 名 獨角戲

延伸片語 interior monologue 內心獨白

▶ This familiar essay is filled with the author's interior monologues.
這篇小品文充滿了作者的內心獨白。

③ **mono** 單一 + **syllable** 音節

monosyllable [`manə͵sɪləbl] 名 單音節的字詞

延伸片語 divine monosyllable 神聖的單音節字

▶ "OM" is a divine monosyllable which symbolizes Brahman in India. 「阿曼」在印度是一個代表婆羅門的神聖單音字。

④ **mono** 單一 + **tone** 音調

monotone [`manə͵ton] 形 單調的

延伸片語 speak in a monotone 說話單調

▶ He was bored of listening to the woman who spoke in a monotone. 那個女人說話單調的聲音讓他感到很無聊。

⑤ **mono** 單一 + **poly** 多數

monopoly [mə`naplɪ] 名 壟斷

延伸片語 monopoly group 壟斷集團

▶ The government used to be the largest monopoly groups in that country. 政府曾經是該國最大的壟斷集團。

延伸補充自然學

與 mono 同含義的字首：uni

☆ **uniform**　　　　將形式變一致　　　名 制服

☆ **unify**　　　　使……單一　　　動 使統一

首 **bi** 二、雙

情境對話試水溫

🎧 *Track 018*

Ricky:	I need to fly to Hong Kong for an international bicycle exhibition this weekend.	瑞奇：我這週末要飛香港參加一個國際自行車展。
Ally:	Again? You were there last year, weren't you?	艾莉：又去？你不是去年才去嗎？
Ricky:	No, it's a biannual exhibition. I went with my coordinators for increasing bilateral trade with our cooperative enterprises two years ago.	瑞奇：不，這是兩年一次的展覽，兩年前為了和我們合作的企業加強雙邊貿易，我和組長們去參加了一次。
Ally:	Cool! I receive your bilingual EDM biweekly! Is Tim responsible for translating the text?	艾莉：酷！我每兩週都會收到你們公司的雙語電子型錄，是提姆負責內文翻譯嗎？
Ricky:	Yes. Oh! Do you know he is bisexual? He has been seeing Bob for around three months.	瑞奇：沒錯。對了！你知道提姆是個雙性戀嗎？他和鮑伯交往三個月啦！
Ally:	You're such a nosy parker!	艾莉：你也太八卦了吧！

單字解析零距離

① **bi** 雙 ＋ **ann** 年 ＋ **ual** 關於……的

biannual [baɪˈænjuəl] 形 一年兩次的

延伸片語 **biannual publication** 半年刊

▶ This journal of medicine is a biannual publication.
這本醫學雜誌是一份半年刊物。

Ch 1

Part 1

Part 2

Part 3

Part 4

表示數量

❷ bi 二 **+ cycle** 圓圈

bicycle [ˈbaɪsɪkl̩] 名 兩輪腳踏車

延伸片語 **tandem bicycle** 協力車（雙人自行車）

▶ The two of them rode a tandem bicycle along the river.
他們倆沿著河騎著協力車。

. . . .

❸ bi 雙 **+ later** 邊 **+ al** 形容詞字尾

bilateral [baɪˈlætərəl] 形 對稱的、雙方的

延伸片語 **bilateral trade** 雙邊貿易

▶ The two countries cosigned an agreement to increase bilateral trade.
兩國共同簽署了一份增加雙邊貿易的協議。

. . . .

❹ bi 雙 **+ lingual** 語言的

bilingual [baɪˈlɪŋwəl] 形 雙語的

延伸片語 **bilingual education** 雙語教育

▶ Bilingual education in Taiwan has become a trend in recent years.
近年來，雙語教育在台灣已經成為一種趨勢。

. . . .

❺ bi 二、雙 **+ sexual** 關於性的

bisexual [ˈbaɪˌsɛkʃuəl] 形 兩性的

延伸片語 **innate bisexual** 天生的雙性戀

▶ Sigmund Freud believed that everyone is innate bisexual.
佛洛依德認為每個人都是天生的雙性戀者。

💡 延伸補充**自然學**

與 bi- 近義的字首：du、twi、di

☆ **dual**	有兩個的	形 雙的
☆ **twilight**	（白天黑夜）兩方的光線	名 暮光
☆ **dilemma**	有兩種選擇	名 困境

首 tri-~mili 三~千

Ethan: Do you want to go to the triathlon with me? It's on this Saturday.	伊森：你想要和我去參加三項全能嗎？在這禮拜六。
Amanda: Nah. I'd pass. I'm going to quartet show in the Art Museum.	亞曼達：不了，我不去。我要去美術博物館看四重奏。
Ethan: I thought it is held in the Pentagon?	伊森：我記得是在五角大廈？
Amanda: Really? Let me check .... Oh my god. You are right! It is the sextet performance that takes place in the Art museum.	亞曼達：真的嗎？讓我看看……。我的天，你是對的。是六重奏才是在美術博物館。
Ethan: Haha. So, you still aren't going with me?	伊森：哈哈。所以，你還是不跟我去嗎？
Amanda: I'd go if it's decathlon.	亞曼達：如果是十項全能我就去。
Ethan: Stop bragging!	伊森：少在那邊吹噓！

單字解析零距離

❶ tri 三 ＋ **athl** 競賽 ＋ **on** 名詞字尾

triathlon [traɪˋæθlɑn] 名 鐵人三項

延伸片語 **to compete in a triathlon** 參加鐵人三項比賽

▶ Our whole family will go compete in a triathlon this Sunday.
這星期天我們全家都會去參加鐵人三項。

❷ quart 四 ＋ **et** 名詞字尾

quartet [kwɔrˋtɛt] 名 四重奏

Ch 1

Part 1

Part 2

Part 3

表示數量

Part 4

延伸片語 **a gospel quartet** 福音四重奏

This church is famous for its gospel quartet.
這座教堂以它的福音四重奏為名。

. . . .

❸ **pent** 五 + **agon** 角度 (=angle)

pentagon [ˈpɛntəˌgɑn] 名 五角形

延伸片語 **to build a pentagon** 蓋一座五角大廈

▶ The government decided to build a pentagon to honor the death of the martyrs.
政府決定蓋一座五角大樓以表示對烈士們殉國的敬意。

. . . .

❹ **sex** 六 + **et** 名詞字尾

sextet [sɛksˈtɛt] 名 六重奏

延伸片語 **a string sextet** 弦樂六重奏

▶ This Orchestra organization is known for its string sextet.
這樂團著名的是他的弦樂六重奏。

. . . .

❺ **dec** 十 + **athl** 運動 + **on** 名詞字尾

decathlon [dɪˈkæθlɑn] 名 十項全能

延伸片語 **to win in a decathlon** 贏得十項全能

▶ The disabled man won in a decathlon and took home a prize of 1 million dollars.
這殘障人士贏得十項全能並抱回一萬元美金。

⚡ 延伸補充 **自然學**

✬ **hept**agon	七 + 角度	名 七邊形
✬ **oct**opus	八 + 腳	名 八爪魚；章魚
✬ **non**ary	九 + 表示與……有關	形 與數字九相關的
✬ **cent**ipede	百 + 腳	名 蜈蚣
✬ **kilo**meter	千 + 公尺	名 一公里
✬ **mille**nial	千 + 年	名 千年

首 semi 一半

情境對話試水溫

Track 020

Nora: Do you know that Andy now works in the semi-conductor industry?	諾拉：你知道安迪現在在半導體產業工作嗎？
Robert: Yeah, I know, and I also heard that the prize his company offers is semiannual.	羅伯特：我知道，而且我聽說他的公司每半年就會提供一次獎金。
Nora: That doesn't sound much.	諾拉：那聽起來不多耶。
Robert: Well, the prize actually amounts to that of other companies offered annually.	羅伯特：應該是說，這個獎金和其他每年發放的獎金數量是一樣的。
Nora: Wow. Also, he got into the semi-final of that international decathlon. He's so versatile.	諾拉：哇。而且，他還打入了那個國際十項全能的準決賽。他真的很多才多藝。
Robert: He's now as famous as anyone successful people that publishes their semi-autobiographical novel and probably a film adaptation later on.	羅伯特：他現在就和那些成功人士一樣有名，會出個半自傳的小說，然後接著被改編成電影。
Nora: I wish I could be like him. Anyone has a semiautomatic gun? I want to...	諾拉：我希望我可以和他一樣。誰有把半自動手槍？我想……
Robert: Hey! Stop saying that! We are all blessed, and the definition of success varies.	羅伯特：嘿！別那樣說！我們都很幸運，而且成功的定義因人而異。

單字解析零距離

❶ semi 一半 + conduct 傳導 + or 名詞字尾

semi-conductor [ˌsɛmɪkənˈdʌktɚ] 名 半導體

延伸片語 to enter the semi-conductor industry 進入半導體產業

Ch 1

Part 1

Part 2

Part 3

表示數量

Part 4

▶ Many engineers wish to enter the semi-conductor industry for high salary. 許多工程師為了高薪期望能進入半導體產業工作。

❷ **semi** 一半 + **annu** 年 + **al** 形容詞字尾

semiannual [ˌsɛmɪˈænjʊəl] 形 每半年的；半年期的

延伸片語 a semiannual journal 半年刊

▶ A Bright Star is a semiannual journal that always surprises people with its amazing content.
A Bright Star 是一個每半年發行的期刊，其出色的內容總是能帶給人們驚喜。

❸ **semi** 一半 + **final** 最後

semifinal [ˌsɛmɪˈfaɪnl] 名 準決賽

延伸片語 a semifinal match 準決賽

▶ My son is having a semifinal match tomorrow. I'm so nervous.
我兒子明天有一場準決賽。我好緊張。

❹ **semi** 一半 + **autobiograph(y)** 自傳 + **ical** 形容詞字尾

semi-autobiographical [ˌsɛmɪˌɔtəˌbaɪəˈgræfɪk] 形 半自傳體的

延伸片語 a semi-autobiographical novel 半自傳體的小說

▶ The Silent Night is a semi-autobiographical novel from the recently deceased French director.
Silent Night為一本最近逝世的法國導演的半自傳體小說。

❺ **semi** 一半 + **auto** 自動 + **matic** 形容詞字尾

semiautomatic [ˌsɛmɪˌɔtəˈmætɪk] 形 半自動的

延伸片語 carry a semiautomatic gun 攜帶半自動的手槍

▶ Some citizens carry a semiautomatic gun on the go for self-defense. 有些市民旅途中會攜帶半自動的手槍以保自身安全。

💡 延伸補充 自然學

✿ **semidiameter**	一半 + 直徑	名 半徑

與 semi- 近義的字首：demi-、hemi-

✿ **demigod**	一半 + 神仙	名 （古代故事中的）半神半人
✿ **hemisphere**	一半 + 球面	名 （尤指地球的）半球

首 multi 多種的

情境對話試水溫 　　　　　　🎧 *Track 021*

Ryan: How are you doing recently, Nick?	萊恩：你最近過的如何，尼克？
Nick: It's great. I'm now working in a multi-national company.	尼克：很好。我現在在一間跨國的公司上班。
Ryan: Wow. That's impressive. What does your company do?	萊恩：哇，好厲害。你的公司是做什麼的？
Nick: We produce multi-functional home appliances, and what I like about my job is our multicultural working environment. I really learn a lot.	尼克：我們製造多功能家電，而且我喜歡我們公司的是多文化的工作環境。我真的學到了很多。
Ryan: Good for you. I guess the work load is pretty heavy, right?	萊恩：很棒呢。我猜工作量應該很大，對吧？
Nick: Yes. You will master the ability to multi-task just within one month!	尼克：對，你會在一個月內就學會如何一心多用！
Ryan: Highly stressful workplace atmosphere, huh?	萊恩：工作環境很高壓，是吧？
Nick: You bet, but that's also why we can release multiple kinds of prototype every half a year and bring in huge profits for our company.	尼克：當然，不過這也是為什麼我們可以每半年就推出多種模型，並替我們的公司賺進大錢。

單字解析零距離

❶ **multi** 多 ＋ **nation** 國家 ＋ **al** 形容詞字尾

multi-national [ˈmʌltɪˈnæʃənl] 形 多國的；跨國的

延伸片語 a multi-national corporation 跨國企業

Ch 1

Part 1

Part 2

Part 3

表示數量

Part 4

▶ Many college students study hard so as to get into this prestigious multi-national corporation.
許多大學生用功讀書就為了進入這家十分有聲望的跨國企業。

. . . .

② **multi** 多 ＋ **function** 功能 ＋ **al** 形容詞字尾

multi-functional [ˌmʌltɪˈfʌŋkʃnl] 形 多功能的

延伸片語 a multi-functional system 多功能系統

▶ Our company is hoping to purchase a multi-functional system from your factory. 我們公司希望能從貴司購買一個多功能系統。

. . . .

③ **multi** 多 ＋ **cultur(e)** 文化 ＋ **al** 形容詞字尾

multicultural [ˌmʌltɪˈkʌltʃərəl] 形 融合多種文化的；多種文化的

延伸片語 a multicultural society 多文化社會

▶ Children raised from a multicultural society are said to be more respectful. 聽說在多文化社會中成長的小孩更懂得尊重他人。

. . . .

④ **multi** 多 ＋ **task** 任務

multitask [ˌmʌltɪˈtæsk] 動 處理多個任務；同時做多件事情；一心多用

延伸片語 to multitask and to prioritize 同時處理多件事物並排列優先順序

▶ Being a president of a country must possess the ability to multitask and to prioritize.
作為一國總統必須擁有能夠同時面對許多事物且能釐清輕重緩急的能力。

. . . .

⑤ **multi** 多 ＋ **ple** 與數字有關的字尾

multiple [ˈmʌltəpl̩] 形 複合的；多樣的 名【數】倍數

延伸片語 a multiple of something 是⋯⋯的倍數

▶ 16 is a multiple of 4. 16是4的倍數。

💡 延伸補充 自然學

☆ **multitude** 多 ＋ 表示動作或狀態 名 許多

與 multi 近義的字首：poly-

☆ **polygon** 多 ＋ 角度 名 多邊形；多角形

☆ **polygamy** 多 ＋ 婚姻；交配 名 一夫多妻（制）；一妻多夫（制）

首 circ 環

情境對話試水溫

🎧 *Track 022*

Rebecca: Don't you think the circles this painter drew are asymmetrical?

瑞貝加：你不覺得這個畫家畫的圓圈很不對稱嗎？

Ray: Well, that's because they are combined by different semi-circles.

瑞：嗯，這是因為它們是由不同的半圓形組成的。

Rebecca: I see. That also explains why their circumference doesn't match with each other.

瑞貝加：這樣啊。這大概也是為什麼它們的圓周都沒有與彼此相符。

Ray: I mean, it's an abstract painting. Don't be too strict about balance and symmetry. It will lose the fun. Try to observe how these circles seem to be circulating in the river instead.

瑞：這樣説吧，這是一幅抽象畫。不要對平衡與對稱這麼執著，這樣會失去樂趣。試著觀察這些圓圈是如何在河流裡循環看看。

Rebecca: Okay... wow. Now they look like a circuit. This painting is full of surprises!

瑞貝加：好的……哇。現在它們看起來就像一個迴路！這幅畫真是充滿驚喜！

單字解析零距離

1 circ 環 **+ le** 名詞字尾

circle [ˈsɝkl] **名** 圓圈；環狀物

延伸片語 to draw a circle 畫圈

▶ Our art teacher asked us to draw a circle and paint it with the color we like.
我們的美術老師叫我們畫圈並塗上自己喜歡的顏色。

表示形狀大小

② **semi** 一半 ＋ **circ** 環 ＋ **le** 名詞字尾

semi-circle [ˌsɛmɪˋsɝkl̩] 名 半圓；半圓弧；半圓形

延伸片語 **combine two semi-circles** 結合兩個半圓

▶ If you combine two semi-circles with the right angle, you can get a precise full circle.
如果你以正確的角度結合兩個半圓，你將會得到一個完美的正圓型。

- -

③ **circum** 環 ＋ **fer** 帶來 ＋ **ence** 名詞字尾

circumference [səˋkʌmfərəns] 名 圓周；周長

延伸片語 **the circumference of** 物體（或圖形）的周邊

▶ The doctor measured the circumference of my upper arms.
醫生測量我上臂的周長。

- -

④ **circ** 環 ＋ **ul** ＋ **ate** 行走；行動

circulate [ˋsɝkjəˌlet] 動 循環，環行；傳播，流傳

延伸片語 **to circulate in the blood** 在血液裡循環

▶ The medicine we take circulates in the blood and cure diseases for us. 我們服用的藥物在血液裡循環並治癒疾病。

- -

⑤ **circ** 環 ＋ **uit** 名詞字尾

circuit [ˋsɝkɪt] 名 環道；一圈，一周 動 繞……環行

延伸片語 **a circuit of** 物體的一周

▶ We ran a circuit of the community to show support toward LGTBQ right.
我們用跑的環繞社區一周，以表我們對同志文化與權益的支持。

延伸補充 自然學

與 circ 近義的字根：cycl、cycle

☆ **cyclone**　　環 ＋ 名詞字尾　　名 旋風、暴風

☆ **cyclical**　　環 ＋ 形容詞字尾　　形 圓的；環式的；循環的

☆ **bicycle**　　雙的 ＋ 環 ＋ 名詞字尾　　名 腳踏車

根 rect 正、直、指導

情境對話試水溫

🎧 *Track 023*

Ellen: The new-elected rector is coming to inspect the preparedness of teaching plans of all departments, and to check if everything is on the correct track next Monday morning.

艾倫：新上任的校長下週一早上會來視察各部門的教學計畫，確認每件事情都在正確的軌道上。

Mina: Monday morning? I have the Monday blues. Do we all need to stand erect in line to welcome him?

米娜：週一早上？！我有週一症候群。我們需要列隊站好歡迎他嗎？

Ellen: No need. Just make sure you finish your teaching plans, rectify errors, make them perfect, and send them to coordinators by 3 o'clock. The rector directed them to collect all documents by tomorrow!

艾倫：不需要，你只要確定你已經完成你的教學計畫，修正完裡面的錯誤，確保它很完美，並且在三點前寄給組長們。校長指示他們明天前要蒐集完所有文件。

Mina: Could you pass me that rectangle candy box right over there? I need some sweets to counteract depression.

米娜：可以把那邊長方形的糖果盒給我嗎？我現在需要一點甜食來抗憂鬱。

單字解析零距離

1 cor 一併 **+ rect** 直

correct [kə`rɛkt] 形 正確的

延伸片語 all present and correct 全體到齊

▶ All present and correct! Now we can take the road.
全體到齊！現在我們能出發了！

Ch 1

Part 1

Part 2

Part 3

Part 4

表示形狀大小

❷ **di** 分開 ＋ **rect** 指導

direct [dəˋrɛkt] 勔 指引 形 直接的

延伸片語 direct action 直接行動

▶ Since the negotiation with the employers came to nothing, they decided to take direct actions.
既然與資方的協商沒有結果，他們決定採取直接行動。

⋯⋯⋯⋯⋯⋯⋯⋯⋯⋯⋯⋯⋯⋯⋯⋯⋯⋯⋯⋯⋯⋯⋯⋯⋯⋯

❸ **e** 往上 ＋ **rect** 直

erect [ɪˋrɛkt] 勔 豎起

延伸片語 stand erect 站得筆直

▶ The soldiers on guard all stood erect. 站崗的士兵們各個站得筆直。

⋯⋯⋯⋯⋯⋯⋯⋯⋯⋯⋯⋯⋯⋯⋯⋯⋯⋯⋯⋯⋯⋯⋯⋯⋯⋯

❹ **rect** 直 ＋ **angle** 角

rectangle [rɛkˋtæŋgl̩] 名 長方形

延伸片語 oriented rectangle 斜置矩形

▶ Being given three coordinates, the students were asked to find the fourth coordinate of the oriented rectangle.
學生們必須以已知的三個座標找出該斜置矩形的第四個座標。

⋯⋯⋯⋯⋯⋯⋯⋯⋯⋯⋯⋯⋯⋯⋯⋯⋯⋯⋯⋯⋯⋯⋯⋯⋯⋯

❺ **rect** 指導 ＋ **ify** 使⋯⋯成為

rectify [ˋrɛktəˌfaɪ] 勔 矯正

延伸片語 rectify a mistake 矯正錯誤

▶ It is more important to rectify a mistake than to punish for a mistake. 矯正錯誤比懲罰過錯來得重要。

⋯⋯⋯⋯⋯⋯⋯⋯⋯⋯⋯⋯⋯⋯⋯⋯⋯⋯⋯⋯⋯⋯⋯⋯⋯⋯

❻ **rect** 指導 ＋ **or** 人

rector [ˋrɛktɚ] 名 教區長

延伸片語 honorary Lord Rector 榮譽校長

▶ They have elected Mr. Robinson as the honorary Lord Rector of the university. 他們已經推選羅賓森先生擔任該大學的榮譽校長一職。

💡 延伸補充**自然學**

☆ **misdirect**	錯誤的＋指導	勔 誤導
☆ **rectifiable**	能夠再被指導的	形 可糾正的

057

根 form 形狀

情境對話試水溫

Kim: You know we have to conform to the regulations, right?

金：你知道我們必須遵守規定的，對吧？

Ada: Yes, I know. But I also feel like certain reforms are necessary.

艾達：是的，我知道。但我同時也覺得某些改革是必要的。

Kim: Like how you try to deform the building?

金：就像你如何毀壞那棟大樓嗎？

Ada: I was just attempting to formalize a way of expression. They are called graffiti, okay?

艾達：我只是想要讓這種表達成為一種正式的方式而已。它們叫做塗鴉，好嗎？

Kim: They are too ugly to be graffiti.

金：它們太醜，不叫做塗鴉。

Ada: That's because you don't know how to appreciate graffiti. They follow a specific formation, okay?

艾達：那是因為你不懂得如何欣賞塗鴉。它們是遵循一種特定形式的，好嗎？

Kim: What I'm trying to say is that you you may get kicked out of school.

金：我想要表達的是你可能會被退學的。

單字解析零距離

1 **con** 一起、共同 ＋ **form** 形狀

conform [kən'fɔrm] 動 遵照、遵守、適應

延伸片語 to conform to 遵守

▶ Students are required to conform to school rules.
學生被要求要遵守校規。

Ch 1

Part 1

Part 2

Part 3

Part 4

表示形狀大小

② re 重新 ＋ form 形狀

reform [rɪˋfɔrm] 動 改革、革新、改良 名 改革、改良
延伸片語 **a reform of** 事物的改良
▶ The protesters are appealing to a reform of the labor system.
抗議者正提出改革勞動系統的訴求。

③ de 反轉 ＋ form 形狀

deform [dɪˋfɔrm] 動 變畸形、變形
延伸片語 **to be physically deformed** 遭受身體上的扭曲變形
▶ The bicyclist was physically deformed in the notorious bomb terrorist attack.
這位腳踏車騎士在一場惡名昭彰的炸彈客攻擊下造成身體扭曲變形。

④ form 形狀 ＋ alize 使……化

formalize [ˋfɔrml͵aɪz] 動 使正式、使形式化、正式化
延伸片語 **to formalize one's idea** 定型某人的想法
▶ My thesis advisor helped me formalize my idea so I can better structure my paper.
我的論文指導教授協助將我的想法定型，讓我能夠進一步架構整個內容。

⑤ form 形狀 ＋ ation 名詞字尾

formation [fɔrˋmeʃən] 名 形成、構成、組成
延伸片語 **the formation of** 事物的形成
▶ We went to Taroko to appreciate the stunning formation of the gorge. 我們到太魯閣欣賞美到令人屏息的峽谷構造。

延伸補充 自然學

與 form 近義的字根：morph
☆ **polymorphous** 多＋形狀＋形容詞字尾 形 多形的、多形態的
☆ **amorphous** 非、沒有＋形狀＋形容詞字尾 形 無定形的
☆ **metamorphosis** 表示變化、變換＋形狀＋名詞字尾 名 變形、質變、（外形等的）完全變化

首 **mini** 小的

情境對話試水溫

Olivia: I went to a miniature exhibition last Sunday. It was mind-blowing.

奧莉微亞：我上週日去看了那個微型展。真的很厲害。

Grace: Oh. I heart that they were all man-made by a Japanese minimalist?

葛蕾絲：噢。我聽說它們是由一位日本極簡主義者手工製作的？

Olivia: Yes. The title of the exhibition is "Minimalism," one simple word that summarizes the essence of the artworks.

奧莉微亞：對。展覽的名字就取名為「極簡主義」，一個總結了這些藝術品之精華的簡單詞彙。

Grace: I adore minimalism. I like to see how the artists try to stick to the minimum of the materials used, but still manage to make the best out of them.

葛蕾絲：我喜歡極簡主義。我喜歡看那些藝術家如何堅守使用材料的最低量度，但仍然能將其最大價質發揮出來。

Olivia: Same here. It's a plus-and-minus process that also displays a perspective toward life.

奧莉微亞：我也有同感。這是一個加與減的過程，同時也展現了一種人生觀點。

 單字解析零距離

❶ mini 小 ＋ **ature** 名詞字尾

miniature [`mɪnɪətʃə] 名 縮樣；縮圖；小型物

延伸片語 **in miniature** 小型的；在小規模上

▶ This place is like Italy in miniature!
這地方像是義大利的縮影。

Ch 1
Part 1
Part 2
Part 3
Part 4

表示形狀大小

❷ mini 小 **＋ al** 表示性質 **＋ ist** 表示人的名詞字尾

minimalist [ˈmɪnəməlɪst] 名 極簡抽象派藝術家

延伸片語 **to become a minimalist** 成為極簡抽象派藝術家

▶ This young architect wishes to become a minimalist like John Pawson.
這位年輕的建築師期許自己能成為像是約翰・波森的極簡抽象派藝術家。

- -

❸ mini 小 **＋ al** 表示性質 **＋ ism** 表示主義或行為的名詞字尾

minimalism [ˈmɪnɪməˌlɪzm] 名 極簡派藝術；極簡派藝術風格

延伸片語 **the trend of minimalism** 極簡派藝術的風潮

▶ The trend of minimalism is coming back.
極簡派藝術的風潮正在回歸。

- -

❹ mini 小 **＋ mun** 名詞字尾

minimum [ˈmɪnəməm] 名 最小量，最小數；最低限度

延伸片語 **keep ~ to a minimum** 保持……在最低限度

▶ The manager was required to keep the budget to a minimum due to the recession. 因經濟蕭條，經理被要求要將預算保持在最低限度。

- -

❺ min 小 **＋ us** 形容詞字尾

minus [ˈmaɪnəs] 形 略差一些的；不利的

延伸片語 **on the minus side** 站在負面或不利的角度

▶ On the minus side, we have less budget.
站在負面的角度來看，我們預算較少。

💡 延伸補充**自然學**

與 mini- 近義的字首：micro-

☆ **microscopic** 小 ＋ 範圍；規模 ＋ 形容詞字尾　　形 極小的；用顯微鏡才可看見的

與 mini- 反義的字首：macro-

☆ **macroeconomics** 大 ＋ 經濟 ＋ 表示學說、知識的名詞字尾　　名 宏觀經濟學

首 omni 全部的

情境對話試水溫

Emily: I truly believe no one is omniscient, even God.	愛蜜莉：我真的相信沒有人是全知的，包括上帝。
Harry: But God is omnipresent.	哈利：但是上帝是無所不在的。
Emily: How do you know?	愛蜜莉：你怎麼知道？
Harry: Because God helps me go through those hard times. He is omnipotent.	哈利：因為上帝幫助了我度過難關。它是全能的。
Lilian: What are you two talking about?	莉莉安：你們兩個在講什麼？
Harry: Oh, we were just rehearsing a play.	哈利：噢，我們只是在演練一齣戲。
Emily: We are omnivorous readers, you know. We are currently emerging ourselves in the books regarding the role of God in the past 100 years.	愛蜜莉：我們是雜食性讀者，你知道的。我們最近沉浸在談論上帝於過去一百年來所扮演的角色之書籍中。
Lilian: Really? Then check Dr. Lee's omnibus of her recently-published trilogy. You won't regret it.	莉莉安：真的嗎？那去看看李博士最近出版三部曲的選集，你不會後悔的。

單字解析零距離

1 **omni** 全部的 ＋ **sci** 表示知道 ＋ **ent** 形容詞字尾

omniscient [ɑmˋnɪʃənt] 形 無所不知的，全知的

延伸片語 **an omniscient narrator** （故事寫作中的）全知敘事者

▶ This classic fiction is told by an omniscient narrator, creating a both subjective and objective immersive reading atmosphere.
敘事者以全知觀點的角度述說這本經典小說，營造出一種主客觀融合且身歷其境的閱讀氛圍。

Ch 1

Part 1

Part 2

Part 3

Part 4

表示形狀大小

❷ **omni** 全部的 ＋ **present** 出席的

omnipresent [ˌɑmnɪˋprɛznt] 形 無所不在的；遍及各處的

延伸片語 **an omnipresent threat** 無所不在的威脅

▶ Global warming is an omnipresent threat, and we should take action immediately.
全球暖化是個無所不在的威脅，我們應該要馬上採取行動。

❸ **omni** 全部的 ＋ **potent** 強有力的；有權勢的

omnipotent [ɑmˋnɪpətənt] 形 全能的；有無限權力（或力量）的

延伸片語 **an omnipotent ruler** 全能的統治者

▶ This dynasty was said to be governed by an omnipotent ruler and lasted for about 1000 years.
據說這個王朝被一位全能的統治者掌管並且延續超過1,000年之久。

❹ **omni** 全部的 ＋ **vorous** 以……為食物

omnivorous [ɑmˋnɪvərəs] 形 無所不吃的；雜食的

延伸片語 **omnivorous animals** 雜食動物

▶ Dogs are omnivorous animals, and so are pigs and chicken.
狗為雜食性動物，豬和雞也是。

❺ **omni** 全部的 ＋ **bus** 公車

omnibus [ˋɑmnɪbəs] 名 【舊】公車、選集；文集 形 總括的；多項的；多種用途

延伸片語 **an omnibus of** 選集

▶ I went to the bookstore and bought Dr. Lee's omnibus of her amazing trilogy on the history of feminism.
我到書局買了李博士赫赫有名的女性主義歷史三部曲。

💡 延伸補充**自然學**

與 omni- 近義的字首：pan-

☆ **pantheism**　　　　全部的 ＋ 有神論　　　　名 泛神論

☆ **panorama**　　　　全部的 ＋ 看　　　　　　名 全景；全貌、概述

根 **part** 部份、分開

Anita: Harper flied to Japan, departing at noon. I heard that she'll stay there for at least five years for her new job. Did you know that?

艾妮塔：哈潑中午離開飛到日本了，我聽說他因為工作要在那邊待至少五年，你知道這件事嗎？

Debby: I haven't heard from her for a while. She grew apart from me after she moved to Taipei few years ago. I kind of missed the good old days when we worked together. Though it was disgustingly busy, we were the best partners.

黛比：我很久沒有她的消息了，自從她幾年前搬到台北之後，我們就漸行漸遠了。我有點想念以前一起共事的美好時光，雖然真的忙到很噁心，但我們真的是最好的夥伴。

Anita: True. You two were exactly the counterparts in personality. Both of you were quite reliable and could always impact positive energy to all team, even the director was partial to you then.

艾妮塔：真的，你兩人很相像，你們都很值得信賴，而且總是能為團隊帶來正面力量，就連主任也偏坦你們呢！

Debby: Thanks for the compliment, but I can't take all the credit.

黛比：謝謝你的讚美啦！但這不全是我的功勞！

單字解析零距離

① a 朝向 ＋ **part** 分開

apart [ə`pɑrt] 形 分開的

延伸片語 **grow apart from someone** 與某人逐漸疏遠

▶ Jenny grew apart from her friends after she got married.
珍妮結婚之後就與朋友逐漸疏遠了。

Ch 1

Part 1
Part 2
Part 3
Part 4

表示形狀大小

❷ counter 相對的 **+ part** 部分

counterpart [ˈkauntɚˌpɑrt] 名 對應的人、物

延伸片語 **overseas counterpart** 境外同業

▶ Peter is in charge of business with their overseas counterparts.
彼得負責處理境外同業往來之業務。

- -

❷ de 轉移 **+ part** 分開

depart [dɪˈpɑrt] 動 離開　　　延伸片語 **depart this life** 離開人世；亡故

▶ Everyone will depart this life one day without exception.
每個人毫無例外地都會在某天離開人世。

- -

❹ im 在……內 **+ part** 部分

impart [ɪmˈpɑrt] 動 告知　　延伸片語 **impart knowledge** 授業

▶ Imparting knowledge to students is the main responsibility of teachers. 老師的主要職責就是傳授學生知識。

- -

❺ part 部分 **+ ial** 形容詞字尾

partial [ˈpɑrʃəl] 形 局部的　　延伸片語 **be partial to sb.** 偏袒某人

▶ That teacher is obviously partial to outstanding students.
那個老師分明就是偏袒成績好的學生。

- -

❻ part 部分 **+ ner** 人

partner [ˈpɑrtnɚ] 名 夥伴　　延伸片語 **partners in crime** 共犯

▶ The police arrested the man as well as his partners in crime.
警方將他以及他的同夥都予以逮捕。

延伸補充自然學

☆ **particular**　　部分＋與……有關＋性質　形 獨有的
☆ **partake**　　部份＋拿　　　　　　　　動 參與

Chapter2

根 anim 生命、精神

情境對話試水溫

Melissa: Have you seen Dr. Satoshi's new animation? It's brilliant.	梅莉莎：你有看了敏教授最新的動畫了嗎？它超棒。
Alice: Of course I have. How he vivified the breeze animating the trees is just mind-blowing.	愛莉絲：當然。他那種將風吹動樹木生動化的手法真的很令人印象深刻。
Melissa: Plus the movement of the animals!	梅莉莎：還有動物的動作！
Alice: I still remembered the animation was screened during the meeting, and it brings the inanimate atmosphere back to life!	愛莉絲：我還記得動畫是在會議中播放的，它簡直讓死氣沉沉的氣氛起死回生！
Melissa: It's really difficult nowadays to see an already well-honored professor insisting on details.	梅莉莎：現在真的很難看到一個早已德高望重的教授仍如此堅持細節。
Alice: True. He literally reanimates everything with his craftsmanship.	愛莉絲：真的。他確實就是用他的技藝讓一切恢復生氣！

單字解析零距離

1 **anim** 生命 + **ation** 名詞字尾

animation [ˌænəˈmeʃən] 名 生氣；活的狀態；激勵；動畫

延伸片語 with animation 充滿生氣的

▶ They discussed the up-coming trip with great animation.
他們起勁地討論著即將到來的旅行。

Ch 2

Part 1
表示生命

Part 2

Part 3

Part 4

❷ anim 生命 ＋ **ate** 使成為

animate [ˋænəˏmet] 動 賦予生命；使有生命

延伸片語 to animate the occasion 使場合充滿活力

▶ The president's presence animated the occasion.
總統的出席使這個場合充滿活力。

∙ ∙

❸ anim 生命 ＋ **al** 名詞字尾

animal [ˋænɪməl] 名 動物 形 動物的

延伸片語 animal courage 蠻勇

▶ Courage in excess becomes animal courage.
勇敢過分即成蠻勇。

∙ ∙

❹ in 表否定 ＋ **anim** 生命 ＋ **ate** 表示性質

inanimate [ɪnˋænəmɪt] 形 無生命的；無生氣的；沒有精神的

延伸片語 inanimate objects

▶ He likes to photograph inanimate objects.
他喜歡拍攝靜止的物品。

∙ ∙

❺ re 再 ＋ **anim** 生命 ＋ **ate** 使成為

reanimate [riˋænəˏmet] 動 復活；使恢復生氣

延伸片語 to reanimate a drowned person 使溺水者復活

▶ How come he could reanimate that drowned person?
他為什麼能讓那個溺水的人復活？

延伸補充 自然學

☆ **magnanimous**	大＋充滿精神的	形 寬宏大量的
☆ **unanimous**	充滿同一種精神的	形 一致同意的
☆ **animalize**	動物的＋動詞字尾	動 使……動物化
☆ **animosity**	精神上呈反對狀態	名 憤怒；敵意

Unit29 根 bio, bi 生命的、生物的

🎧 *Track 029*

💬 情境對話試水溫

Novia: I heard that Prof. Lee has opened several courses in this university.	諾維亞：我聽說李教授在這間大學開了好幾堂課。
Alice: You mean that biologist?	愛莉絲：你指那個生物學家嗎？
Novia: Yes, the one that has not only invented antibiotic but also possessed in-depth knowledge of the earth biosphere.	諾維亞：是的，那個不僅發明了抗生素，還對於地球生物圈擁有深度知識的生物學家。
Alice: Oh, now I know who you are talking about. Come take his class!	愛莉絲：噢，那我知道你在說誰了。來上他的課吧！
Novia: I read his autobiography the other day. I'm just so entralled.	諾維亞：我前幾天讀了他的自傳。我真的好著迷。
Alice: I understand. But I think you better manage to pass your biochemistry class first. His classes are very difficult to enroll in unless you have high academic achievement.	愛莉絲：我明白。但是我想你最好先修過你的生物化學課。他的課很難選上，除非你課業成績很好。

⚡ 單字解析零距離

❶ bio 生命的 **+ logist** 專家

biologist [baɪˋɑlədʒɪst] 名 生物學家

延伸片語 **a famous biologist** 一位有名的生物學家

▶ His father is a famoust biologist.
他的父親是一位有名的生物學家。

Ch 2

Part 1

表示生命

Part 2

Part 3

Part 4

② **anti** 表示相反 ＋ **bio** 生命的 ＋ **tic** 表示性質

antibiotic [͵æntɪbaɪˋɑtɪk] 名 抗生素 形 抗生的

延伸片語 to take antibiotic 服用抗生素

▶ It's not good for your health to take antibiotic constantly.
頻繁服用抗生素對你的健康不好。

③ **bio** 生物的 ＋ **sphere** 球

biosphere [ˋbaɪəˏsfɪr] 名 生物圈

延伸片語 earth biosphere 地球生物圈

▶ We all know that earth biosphere is very versatile and complex.
我們都知道地球生物圈是非常具多樣性且複雜的。

④ **auto** 自己 ＋ **bio** 生命的 ＋ **graphy** 書寫

autobiography [͵ɔtəbaɪˋɑgrəfɪ] 名 自傳

延伸片語 to read someone's autobiography 讀某人的自傳

▶ I take great delight in reading Mark Twain's autobiography.
我非常享受閱讀馬克吐溫的自傳。

⑤ **bio** 生物的 ＋ **chemi** 化學 ＋ **stry** 建造（名詞）

biochemistry [ˋbaɪoˋkɛmɪstrɪ] 名 生物化學

延伸片語 to study biochemistry 讀生物化學

▶ I study biochemistry very hard.
我非常認真讀生物化學。

延伸補充 自然學

☆ **biophysics**	生物的＋物理＋學科	名 生物物理學
☆ **biographer**	書寫生命的人	名 傳記作家
☆ **microbiology**	微小的＋生物的＋學科	名 微生物學
☆ **amphibious**	兩側＋生物的	形 兩棲的

根 **viv** 活、生存

💬 情境對話試水溫

Annie: What interests me here is that the painter, though always wearing a vivacious look, draws really depressing paintings.

安妮：我感到有興趣的是，即便這個作家總是帶有充滿朝氣的模樣，這些畫卻非常陰鬱。

Alice: Indeed. While somehow I can tell that she is trying to embody the recent revival of absurdism, the melancholy vibe is really strong.

愛莉絲：真的。儘管我可以察覺到，她是想要去體現最近荒謬主義的復甦，但是這幾幅的憂鬱氛圍真的很重。

Annie: These paintings surely revived memories of my sad adolescence.

安妮：這些畫確實重現了我悲傷的青春時代。

Alice: I heard that she lost her family during a car accident. They didn't survive. She is the only one left.

愛莉絲：我聽說她的家庭在一場車禍中喪生，沒有人存活，只剩她一個人。

Annie: Oh… that explains why. Anyway, it's a successful exhibition. The convivial atmostphere somehow balances the sadness from the paintings.

安妮：噢……難怪。總之，這是場成功的展覽。歡愉的氛圍莫名地平衡了畫作中的哀傷。

⚡ 單字解析零距離

1 viv 活 ＋ **acious** 形容詞字尾

vivacious [vaɪ`veʃəs] 形 活潑的；有朝氣的

延伸片語 a vivacious look 有朝氣的模樣

▶ His father is an elderly man with a vivacious look.
他的父親是個看起來很有朝氣的老人。

Ch 2

Part 1

表示生命

Part 2

Part 3

Part 4

② **re** 再、又 ＋ **viv** 活 ＋ **al** 名詞字尾

revival [rɪˋvaɪvl̩] 名 復甦；再生

延伸片語 revival meeting 復興佈道會

▶ Mary, a religious Christian, met her significant other in a revival meeting.
虔誠的基督徒瑪莉，在一場復興佈道會上認識了她的另一半。

. . . .

③ **re** 再、又 ＋ **vive** 活

revive [rɪˋvaɪv] 動 復活；重生

延伸片語 revive the dead 使死人復活

▶ The psychic claimed that he had the power to revive the dead. 那個通靈者聲稱他有能使死人復活的能力。

. . . .

④ **sur** 於……之上 ＋ **vive** 生存

survive [səˋvaɪv] 動 生存；存活

延伸片語 survive from 從……倖存

▶ The boy was the only one who survived from the flood.
那男孩是這場洪水中唯一倖存下來的人。

. . . .

⑤ **con** 一同 ＋ **viv** 活 ＋ **ial** 形容詞字尾

convivial [kənˋvɪvɪəl] 形 歡愉的

延伸片語 convivial nature 歡樂愉快的天性

▶ The woman is attractive not because of her beauty but of her convivial nature.
那女子的魅力在於她歡樂愉快的天性，而非她的美貌。

延伸補充 自然學

☆ **vivisect**	活 ＋ 切割	名	活體解剖
☆ **vivid**	活 ＋ 形容詞字尾	形	生動的
viv 的變化形：vit			
☆ **vitamin**	生存 ＋（化學）胺	名	維他命
☆ **vital**	活的	形	充滿活力的；極其重要的

根 **nat** 出生

情境對話試水溫

🎧 *Track 031*

John: Let me tell you something. According to the native eldery, each one of us has a natal star that will guide us to a destined road of life.

約翰：我來跟你說件事。根據當地耆老，我們每個人都擁有一顆生辰的星，它會引導我們走向一個註定好的人生道路。

Jerry: That is so cool. So that star basically determines the nature of your existence?

傑瑞：太酷了。所以那顆星星基本上決定了我們生存的本質？

John: More or less. Therefore, in the old times, some women even shorten or lengthen their prenatal period, like suffering longer pain, to choose a "better" star.

約翰：或多或少。所以，在古時候，有些婦女甚至會簡短或是加長她們的產前時間，像是忍痛久一點，就為了要選一個「更好的」星星。

Jerry: Well, I somehow feel like postnatal care and happiness affects a person's life in more aspects, don't you think?

傑瑞：這樣啊，我總覺得產後照護和幸福會影響一個人人生較多的層面，你不這麼覺得嗎？

John: Uhm… yes. But I still believe each of us has this fate that we couldn't say no to.

約翰：恩……，對。但我還是相信我們每個人都有無法說不的宿命。

Jerry: Be your own master!

傑瑞：要當自己的主人！

 單字解析零距離

❶ **nat** 出生 ＋ **ive** 形容詞字尾

native ['netɪv] 形 當地的

延伸片語 **native speaker** 母語人士

▶ Sally speaks English well like a native speaker.
莎莉的英文說得跟母語一樣的好。

Ch 2

Part 1

表示生命

Part 2

Part 3

Part 4

❷ **nat** 出生 ＋ **al** 形容詞字尾，表……的

natal [ˋnetl] 形 出生的

延伸片語 **natal chart** 個人星盤；本命星盤

▶ The fortune teller foretold Peter's fortune according to his natal chart. 算命師根據彼得的本命星盤預言他的命運。

・・・・・・・・・・・・・・・・・・・・・・・・・・・・・・・・・・・・

❸ **nat** 出生 ＋ **ure** 表示性質

nature [ˋnetʃɚ] 名 自然；本性

延伸片語 **the call of nature** 上廁所

▶ It is not very convenient for girls to answer the call of nature in the woods. 對女孩子來說，要在樹林裡上廁所並不是很方便。

・・・・・・・・・・・・・・・・・・・・・・・・・・・・・・・・・・・・

❹ **pre** 前、先 ＋ **nat** 出生 ＋ **al** 形容詞字尾

prenatal [priˋnetl] 形 出生以前的

延伸片語 **prenatal period** 產前階段

▶ It is normal for an expectant mother to be nervous during prenatal period. 準媽媽在產前階段會緊張是很正常的。

・・・・・・・・・・・・・・・・・・・・・・・・・・・・・・・・・・・・

❺ **post** 在……之後 ＋ **nat** 出生 ＋ **al** 形容詞字尾

postnatal [postˋnetl] 形 產後的

延伸片語 **postnatal depression** 產後憂鬱症

▶ Daisy has been suffering from postnatal depression after giving birth to her first child.
黛西生下第一個孩子後就一直為產後憂鬱症所苦。

💡 **延伸補充 自然學**

nat的變化型：nate

☆ **connate**	伴隨著出生的事物	形 天賦的
☆ **innate**	裡 ＋ 出生	形 與生俱來的
☆ **supernatural**	超越自然的	形 超自然的
☆ **cognate**	共同出生	形 同起源的

根 **mort** 死亡

情境對話試水溫

Milo: I envy the Greek Gods. They are powerful and immortal.

米洛：我好羨慕希臘的神。祂們充滿力量又長生不死！

Annie: What's wrong with being mortal? Eternity isn't necessarily a good thing.

安妮：會死又如何？永恆並不一定是件好事。

Milo: With mortaliy, we suffer pain, we get sick, and we die. Isn't that sad? What's the meaning of being alive then? Look where I am now. I'm poor, and I have tons of mortage to pay.

米洛：在有限生命裡，我們承受痛苦、生病，然後我們會死掉。那不是很悲傷嗎？那麼活著的意義是什麼？看看我現在的處境。我窮，還要付一堆貸款。

Annie: My dad is a mortician. He has seen everything. You should really talk to him.

安妮：我爸是名殯葬業者，他看過生老病死。你真的該和他聊聊。

Milo: Remember where I work? A hospital with a mortuary! Oh, man. How can I get rid of this morbid mindset toward life?

米洛：記得我在哪工作嗎？有太平間的醫院！我要怎麼樣才能擺脫這樣病態的人生觀？

Annie: Come to my house tonight. Maybe you will feel better after meeting my dad.

安妮：今晚來我家吧。也許和我爸見面後你會感覺好點。

單字解析零距離

❶ im 不、否 **＋ mort** 死 **＋ al** 形容詞字尾

immortal [ɪˈmɔrtl] 形 不死的

延伸片語 immortal music 不朽的音樂

▶ Mozart surely created immortal music.
莫札特確實創造了不朽的音樂。

Ch 2

Part 1

表示生命

Part 2

Part 3

Part 4

❷ mort 死 ＋ **al** 形容詞字尾

mortal [ˈmɔrtl̩] 形 致命的

延伸片語 mortal sin 死罪；不可饒恕的大罪

▶ It is believed that people who commit mortal sins will be sent to hell. 人們認為犯下不可饒恕之大罪的人會下地獄。

---

❸ mort 死 ＋ **ality** 名詞字尾

mortality [mɔrˈtælətɪ] 名 死亡率

延伸片語 infant mortality rate 嬰兒死亡率

▶ The infant mortality rate in Africa is rather high. 非洲的嬰兒死亡率相當高。

---

❹ mort 死 ＋ **gage** 抵押物品

mortgage [ˈmɔrgɪdʒ] 名 抵押品

延伸片語 mortgage loan 抵押貸款

▶ Mark works like a dog in order to pay off his home mortgage loan. 為了還清房屋貸款，馬克拼了命地工作。

---

❺ mort 死 ＋ **ic** 屬於……的 ＋ **ian** 人

mortician [mɔrˈtɪʃən] 名 殯葬業人員

延伸片語 nature's mortician 自然界的殯葬師

▶ The sexton beetle is called nature's mortician, for it does the cleanup when a small creature dies. 塞克斯頓甲蟲因為會清理小生物死後的屍體而被稱為自然界的殯葬師。

---

❻ mort 死 ＋ **uary** 表場所

mortuary [ˈmɔrtʃuˌɛrɪ] 名 太平間

延伸片語 mortuary makeup artist 禮儀化妝師

▶ More and more people want to be a mortuary makeup artist because it pays well. 因為薪水高，越來越多人想當禮儀化妝師。

💡 延伸補充 自然學

mort的變化型：morb

☆ **morbid**　　　　死病的狀態　　　形 病態的

☆ **morbidity**　　　死病＋名詞字尾　　名 病態；不健全

Unit33 根 flo(u)r 花、葉

George: Have you ever seen the flora on the island over there? It's really worth visiting.	喬治：你有看過那邊那座島上的植物群嗎？真的很值得去看。
Mary: No, I haven't. But I've heard the locals say that flowers there are one of a kind.	瑪莉：沒有，我還沒看過。但我已經有聽當地人説那邊的花絕無僅有。
George: They sure are, and that's probably why there are many professional florists here in this community.	喬治：確實是，而且這大概也是為什麼這個社區有這麼多專業的花藝師。
Mary: Oh, right! I've seen many beautiful hand-dyed floral patterns.	瑪莉：噢，對！我看到很多很漂亮的手染花朵的圖樣。
George: I know right? We should really protect this special space on earth so that these flowers may flourish forever.	喬治：對吧？我們真的要好好保護這片特別的地方，讓這些花朵可以永遠盛開。
Mary: I feel the same way. See how the scene matches with the florid architectural style here? I'm literally in a paradise!	瑪莉：我認同。看看這景色如何和當地華麗的建築風格相輝映。我簡直就是在天堂！

單字解析零距離

❶ flor 花 ＋ a 名詞字尾

flora [ˋflorə] 名 （某一地點或時期的）植物群

延伸片語 the flora of the Eastern Taiwan 東台灣的植物群

▶ Many foreign visitors came for the flora of the Eastern Taiwan to appreciate its magnificence.
許多外國觀光客來台為了一探東台灣植物的壯麗美景。

❷ **flower** 花

flower [ˋflauɚ] 名 花；花卉；開花植物

延伸片語 **dried flowers** 乾燥花

▶ My mom is good at making dried flowers.
我媽媽很擅長製作乾燥花。

- -

❸ **flor** 花 ＋ **ist** 名詞字尾，通常指人

florist [ˋflorɪst] 名 花商；花店店員；花卉研究者

延伸片語 **to work as a florist** 做花藝師的工作

▶ Many hispsters dream of working as a florist.
很多文青都夢想成為一名花藝師。

- -

❹ **flor** 花 ＋ **al** 形容詞字尾，有……性質的

floral [ˋflorəl] 形 用花製作的；飾以花卉圖案的

延伸片語 **floral patterns** 花卉圖騰

▶ This year's fashion trend is floral patterns.
今年的潮流趨勢是花卉圖案。

- -

❺ **flour** 花 ＋ **ish** 動詞字尾，表示造成、致使

flourish [ˋflɝɪʃ] 動 茁壯成長；繁榮；蓬勃發展

延伸片語 **begin to flourish** 開始成長；盛開

▶ The flowers began to flourish last week.
這些花從上星期就開始綻放。

- -

❻ **flor** 花 ＋ **id** 形容詞字尾

florid [ˋflɔrɪd] 形 過分裝飾的；花俏的

延伸片語 **a florid style** 過於花俏的風格

▶ The writer is known for a florid style of wording and phrasing.
這位作家是以華麗的寫作風格出名的。

延伸補充 自然學

與花相關的字首：herb- 草

☆ **herbal**　　　草 ＋ 形容詞字尾，有……性質的　　形 香草的；藥草的

☆ **herbivore**　　草 ＋ 以……為食　　　　　　　　名 食草動物，草食動物

根 luc, lumi 光亮

情境對話試水溫

Track 034

Melinda: **Luminaries** of theatre came to our school to give a speech yesterday. I really benefited a lot.

梅琳達：劇場名人昨天到我們學校演講。我真的受益良多。

Diane: Wow. In what way?

黛安：哇，在哪方面？

Melinda: They **illuminated** the idea of absurdism through an example of looking at a **translucent** glass.

梅琳達：他們用觀看半透明的玻璃杯的例子來解釋荒謬主義。

Diane: Can you **elucidate**? I'm not following you.

黛安：你可以闡明一下嗎？我聽不懂。

Melinda: There's always a **lucid** part of what we see, but with a turn of angle, it became unclear again.

梅琳達：我們看的東西總有一面是很清晰的，但是角度一轉，它就又變得不清楚了。

Diane: Okay… which is common sense?

黛安：好……但這是常識？

單字解析零距離

1 **lumi** 光 + **n** + **ary** 形容詞字尾，關於⋯⋯的

luminary [ˈlumə͵nɛrɪ] 名 （某一領域的）專家；知名人士

延伸片語 **a luminary in the field of** 某個領域的專家

▶ She is a luminary in the field of astronomy.
她是一位天文學的專家。

2 **il** + **lumi** 光 + **ate** 動詞字尾，表示使成為

illuminate [ɪˈlumə͵net] 動 照亮；照射；闡明

延伸片語 **to illuminate an issue** 闡明一個議題

表示動植物、自然、宇宙

▶ The government is supposed to illuminate an issue when it arouses controversy.
當一個議題出現爭議時，政府應當出面闡明。

❸ trans 穿透 ＋ **luc** 光 ＋ **ent** 形容詞字尾，在……狀態的

translucent [træns`lusnt] 形 半透明的

延伸片語 a transluent characteristic 半透明的特色

▶ The artifect is made of a very special material and hence has a translucent characteristic.
這件手工藝品是用非常特別的材料製作，因此呈現半透明的特性。

❹ e 超出 ＋ **luc** 光 ＋ **idate** 動詞字尾

elucidate [ɪ`lusədet] 動 闡明；闡述

延伸片語 to further elucidate 進一步闡述

▶ The speaker was asked to further elucidate his viewpoint.
這位講者當時被要求進一步闡明他的論點。

❺ luc 光 ＋ **id** 形容詞字尾

lucid [`lusɪd] 形 清楚易懂的；明晰的

延伸片語 to offer lucid guidance 提供清楚易懂的指示或指引

▶ My advisor offered me lucid guidance whenever I felt lost.
我的教授總在我迷失時，給我很明確的指導。

延伸補充 自然學

與光相關的字首：photo-

☆ **photograph** 光＋紀錄；圖示；書寫 　名 照片
☆ **photography** 光＋學問或學科 　名 照相術；攝影術
☆ **photosynthesis** 光＋合成 　名 光合作用

根 **pyr** 火

 情境對話試水溫

🎧 *Track 035*

Lauren: Did you see the news? A pyromania escaped from a psychiatric hospital.

蘿倫：你看到新聞了嗎？有一個縱火犯從精神病院逃跑出來了。

Natalie: What? What are we going to do?

娜塔莉：什麼？我們要怎麼辦？

Lauren: It is said that he carried a pyrometer with himself. I guess that can be a clue to spot him.

蘿倫：據說他隨身帶著一個高溫計。我想這是一個抓到他的線索。

Natalie: I wonder how a person ever becomes pyromanic. I mean, I understand that fire has its fascinating appeal. The ancestor created pyrography, and pyrogen exists in mother nature, not to mention fire makes things edible for us!

娜塔莉：我在想一個人怎麼會變得具有縱火的特性。我的意思是，我懂火具有一種迷人的吸引力。我們的祖先發明了烙畫，然後發熱物質存在於大自然中，更不用說火替我們將事物變得可食用！

Lauren: Well, maybe he has a morbid obsession toward the scene of a flaming house. I mean, this sort of thing is unpredictable.

蘿倫：嗯，也許他對於燃燒中的屋子之景像有一種病態的迷戀。我的意思是，這種事情是無法預測的。

Natalie: I just hope that he can be arrested as soon as possible.

娜塔莉：我只希望他可以趕快被逮捕。

⚡ 單字解析零距離

❶ **pyro** 火 ＋ **man** 瘋狂 ＋ **ia** 名詞字尾，表示疾病

pyromania [͵paɪrəˋmenɪə] 名 縱火癖

延伸片語 the symptom of pyromania 縱火癖的症狀

Ch 2

Part 1

Part 2

表示動植物、自然、宇宙

Part 3

Part 4

▶ He has shown the symptom of pyromania. We should be cautious. 他表現出了可能縱火的徵兆，我們得提高警覺。

❷ pyro 火 ＋ **meter** 測量

pyrometer [paɪˋrɑmɪtɚ] 名 高溫計

延伸片語 to use a pyrometer 使用高溫計

▶ The scientist used a pyromater to detect the temperature of metals. 這位科學家了一個高溫計來檢測金屬的溫度。

❸ pyro 火 ＋ **man** 瘋狂 ＋ **ia** 名詞字尾，表示疾病 ＋ **(a)c** 形容詞字尾常轉作名詞用

pyromaniac [ˌpaɪrəˋmenɪˌæk] 名 縱火狂

延伸片語 to be a pyromaniac 當一個縱火狂

▶ How odd someone wants to be a pryomaniac! 怎麼會有人想要當一個縱火狂！

❹ pyro 火 ＋ **graphy** 名詞字尾，代表學問或學科

pyrography [paɪˋrɑgrəfɪ] 名 烙畫術；烙畫

延伸片語 to utilize pyrography 利用烙畫

▶ Ancient publishers utilized pyrography to complete the making of a book. 古代的出版商都會利用烙畫來製作書籍。

❺ pyro 火 ＋ **gen** 名詞字尾，表示產生跟生成

pyrogen [ˋpaɪrədʒən] 名 致熱物；致熱原

延伸片語 to detect pyrogens 偵測致熱原

▶ The scientist was thrilled to know that he had discovered a pyrogen, and had the chance to name it after him.
當這位科學家得知是他發現了發熱物質並能為其命名時，情緒相當激動興奮。

延伸補充 自然學

☆ **pyrotechnics** 火 ＋ 技能 ＋ 名詞字尾，表示學 名 煙火製造術；煙火使
說或知識　　　　　　用法

Unit36 根 aqua, aque 水

情境對話 試水溫

Track 036

Luise:	Do you want to go to the aquarium with me this Sunday?	露薏絲：你星期六要不要和我一起去水族館？
Victoria:	You mean the one that has a technological aqueduct to reroute the water?	維多利亞：你是說用技術導水管在換水的那家嗎？
Luise:	Wow. You did some research, huh?	露薏絲：哇！看來你有做功課！
Victoria:	Well, I actually have aquaphobia, but aquarium is acceptable for me. I adore those little aquatic animals!	維多利亞：嗯……其實我有懼水症，但水族館我覺得還可以接受，我很愛那些水生小動物。
Luise:	Me too! And I love how the glass reflects slightly the color of aquamarine. It's so beautiful.	露薏絲：我也是！而且我喜歡玻璃輕微反射出海藍色的感覺。好漂亮。
Victoria:	Let's go there then!	維多利亞：那麼我們去吧！

單字解析 零距離

❶ aqua 水 **+ ium** 名詞字尾，代表地方

aquarium [ə`kwɜrɪəm] **名** 水族槽；水族館

延伸片語 an aquarium of 某個東西的水族館

▶ The newly-built building on the corner of the street is an aquarium of subtropical marine animals.
街角的那棟新大樓是一間亞熱帶海洋生物的水族館。

表示動植物、自然、宇宙

❷ aqua 水 ＋ **tic** 形容詞字尾，表示有……性質的

aquatic [əˋkwætɪk] 形 水生的；水棲的；水上的

延伸片語 **aquatic animals** 水生動物

▶ My father is fond of raising aquatic animals.
我爸爸的興趣是飼養水生動物。

- -

❸ aqua 水 ＋ **phobia** 名詞字尾，表示恐懼害怕

aquaphobia [ˏækwəˋfobiə] 名 恐水症

延伸片語 **to have aquaphobia** 患有恐水症

▶ All of my families have aquaphobia, hereditary through generations.
我家族的所有人皆患懼水症，代代遺傳。

- -

❹ aqua 水 ＋ **duct** 輸送管；導管

aqueduct [ˋækwɪˏdʌkt] 名 輸水管；導水管

延伸片語 **an underground aqueduct** 地底導水管

▶ The government announced that they are going to build an underground aqueduct to improve the drainage system.
政府宣布即將建造一個地下導水管，來加強排水系統功能。

- -

❺ aqua 水 ＋ **marine** 海洋

aquamarine [ˏækwəməˋrin] 名 水綠色；海藍色

延伸片語 **the color of aquamarine** 海藍色

▶ I'm fascinated by the color of aquamarine shown slightly through the glow of the diamond.
我完全被這顆鑽石的海藍色光芒給震懾住。

💡 延伸補充 自然學

與 aqua- 近義的字首：hyrd(o)-

✡ **hydrate**	水 ＋ 動詞字尾，表示使成為	動	使成水合物
✡ **hydrophobia**	水 ＋ 名詞字尾，表示恐懼害怕	名	恐水症
✡ **hyrotherapy**	水 ＋ 治療	名	【醫】水療法

Unit37 根 **mar** 海洋的

情境對話試水溫

Megan: Hi, Harry. I heard that you're now a mariner?	梅根：嗨，哈利，聽説你現在是水手？
Harry: Yep, mostly working in a submarine.	哈利：對，大部分時間都在潛艇裡工作。
Megan: How do you like your life on the sea?	梅根：海上生活怎麼樣？
Harry: Well, our country is one of the maritime powers, so I work with a sense of pride.	哈利：我們國家是海上強國之一，所以我與有榮焉。
Megan: Good to know!	梅根：很棒！
Harry: And we have several marine biologists on board. You know how I love sea creatures! They taught me a lot!	哈利：我們也有一些海洋生物學家在船上，你也知道我很愛海洋生物！他們教了我很多！
Megan: Sounds terrific. So, when's your next mission?	梅根：聽起來超棒，那你下一個任務是什麼？
Harry: It's going to be a transmarine one, all the way to the Indian Ocean. It's in June.	哈利：是一個跨海任務，直航向印度洋，六月出發。
Megan: All the best to you.	梅根：祝你好運！
Harry: Thanks, Megan.	哈利：謝謝。

單字解析零距離

❶ **mar** 海 ＋ **ine** 形容詞字尾，與……有關的 ＋ **(e)r** 名詞字尾，表示人

mariner [ˈmærənɚ] **名** 水手；船員

表示動植物、自然、宇宙

延伸片語 to become a mariner 成為一位水手
▶ Both of my brothers wish to become a mariner, and are now under training. 我兩個兄弟都希望能當一名水手，現在正在受訓。

・・・・・・・・・・・・・・・・・・・・・・・・・・・・・・・・・

❷ sub 在……下方 **＋ mar** 海 **＋ ine** 形容詞字尾，與……有關的
submarine [ˈsʌbməˌrin] 形 海底的；水下的 名 潛艇
延伸片語 submarine sandwich 潛水艇三明治
▶ Everytime I go to Subway, I order a submarine sandwich. 我每次去Subway都會點一份潛艇堡。

・・・・・・・・・・・・・・・・・・・・・・・・・・・・・・・・・

❸ mari 海 **＋ time** 時間
maritime [ˈmærəˌtaɪm] 形 海的；海事的；航海的
延伸片語 maritime powers 海上強國
▶ Both Britain and Spain were maritime powers in the 17th century. 英國跟西班牙在17世紀時都曾為海上強國。

・・・・・・・・・・・・・・・・・・・・・・・・・・・・・・・・・

❹ mar 海 **＋ ine** 形容詞字尾，與……有關的
marine [məˈrin] 形 海的；海運的
延伸片語 marine life 海上生活
▶ My grandparents are both experts in the knowledge of marine life. 我的祖父母都是海上生活的專家。

・・・・・・・・・・・・・・・・・・・・・・・・・・・・・・・・・

❺ trans 跨越 **＋ mar** 海 **＋ ine** 形容詞字尾，與……有關的
transmarine [trænsməˈrin] 形 海外的；橫越海洋的
延伸片語 a transmarine voyage 出海的旅程
▶ This trip is going to be an exciting transmarine voyage! 這趟旅程將會是場很刺激的航海旅遊！

延伸補充自然學

☆ **ultramarine** 超越 ＋ 海 ＋ 形容詞字尾　　　　　形 海外的；群青色的
☆ **submariner** 在……下方 ＋ 海 ＋ 形容詞字尾，　名 潛水艇船員
　　　　　　　　　與……有關的 ＋ 名詞字尾，表示人

根 lith 石頭

情境對話 試水溫

🎧 *Track 038*

Larry: Wow. Is this project made by you? I have no idea you are fond of Neolithic and Paleolithic creatures.

賴瑞：哇，這專題是你做的嗎？我都不知道你對新石器時代跟舊石器時代的東西有興趣。

John: It's my hidden hobby. I spend most of my leisure time reading related materials.

約翰：沒有很多人知道，我花了很多空閒時間在讀相關的資料。

Larry: What's this monolith called? The one at the center of this page.

賴瑞：這個巨石叫什麼？在這頁中間。

John: It's called Marvin's Stone. I actually created this by myself. The professor said we must make something memorial for this project.

約翰：我稱馬文巨石，其實是我自己取的，教授說我們都要想方法來記這些東西。

Larry: Is that a requirement? Oh, no. I only did a research on the lithosphere. I thought we only needed to do some compare and contrast.

賴瑞：教授有說嗎？完了，我只研究了岩石圈。我以為只需要研究比較跟對照。

John: Well, it's a lithology class. I'm sure the professor will not flunk you as long as your research is good enough.

約翰：這堂課是岩石學，我想只要你的報告夠好，教授就不會當掉你。

單字解析 零距離

❶ neo 等於**new**，新的 **+ lith** 石頭 **+ ic** 形容詞字尾

neolithic [ˌniəˈlɪθɪk] 名 新石器時代的；早先的；已經過時的

延伸片語 Neolithic remains 新石器時代的遺跡

表示動植物、自然、宇宙

▶ The archeologists found some Neolithic remains on the island.
考古學家在島上發現了一些新石器時代的遺跡。

❷ **paleo** 古代的 ＋ **lith** 石頭 ＋ **ic** 形容詞字尾

paleolithic [ˌpelɪəˈlɪθɪk] 形 舊石器時代的

延伸片語 the Paleolithic period 舊石器時代

▶ The Paleolithic period sounds more fun to me.
我對舊石器時代比較有興趣。

❸ **mono** 單一的 ＋ **lith** 石頭 ＋ **ic** 形容詞字尾

monolithic [ˌmɑnəˈlɪθɪk] 形 獨塊巨石的；整體的石料

延伸片語 monolithic columns 巨大石塊

▶ These ancient monolithic columns were said to be discovered
in 1954. 據說這些巨大石塊是在1954年被發現的。

❹ **lith** 石頭 ＋ **o** ＋ **sphere** 名詞字尾，表示球面

lithosphere [ˈlɪθəˌsfɪr] 名【地】岩石圈；陸界

延伸片語 the hydrosphere and lithosphere 水圈和岩石圈

▶ The hydrosphere and lithosphere are two of the compositions
making up the Earth's skin. 地球表面是由水圈與岩石圈所組成。

❺ **lith** 石頭 ＋ **o** ＋ **logy** 名詞字尾，表示學科

lithology [lɪˈθɑlədʒɪ] 名 岩石學；【醫】結石（病）學

延伸片語 to dig into lithology 鑽研岩石學

▶ My brother was inspired by a film and decided to dig into
lithology. 我弟弟受一部電影激勵而開始鑽研岩石學。

延伸補充 自然學

與 litho- 近義的字根：calc- 石灰

☆ **calcium** 　　石灰 ＋ 名詞字尾　　　　　名 鈣

☆ **calcic** 　　石灰 ＋ 形容詞字尾　　　　形 鈣的；含鈣的

根 **geo** 土地

情境對話試水溫

Jane: Which professor's geography class are you going to take?

珍：你要去上哪一位地理教授的課？

Darcy: I'm thinking Prof. Lee's. It's easier to pass.

達西：我在考慮李教授的，比較好過。

Jane: I thought you want to be a geographer! Don't lower the standard!

珍：我以為你想當地理學家！不要降低標準！

Darcy: I know, but my parents want me to make more money in the future. I'm even thinking dropping the geology class.

達西：我知道，可是現在當地理學家又沒用。我爸媽想要我未來賺多點錢。我甚至考慮要棄修地質學了。

Jane: Then do what?

珍：那你要修什麼？

Darcy: Take a geometry class I guess. They want me to minor in architecture.

達西：改上幾何學吧。他們想要我輔修建築學。

Jane: What a shame. I always thought you have this special aptitude as a geographer. Remember how you memorize all the geographical traits of Mountain Jade all at once? It's so impressive.

珍：好可惜。我一直都覺得你對地理學很有熱忱。還記得你一次背下玉山地理所有的重點嗎？太令人難忘了。

Darcy: I know... I'll talk to my parents tonight.

達西：我知道……今晚再跟我爸媽聊聊吧。

單字解析零距離

❶ **geo** 土地 ＋ **graphy** 名詞字尾，學問或學科

Ch 2

Part 1

Part 2

表示動植物、自然、宇宙

Part 3

Part 4

geography [ˈdʒɪˋɑgrəfɪ] 名 地理學；地形；地勢
延伸片語 **the geography of** 某個地方的地勢
▶ The geography of Taiwan is diverse and stunning.
台灣的地理很多樣化且令人讚嘆。

❷ **geo** 土地 ＋ **graph** 紀錄；圖示；書寫 ＋ **er** 名詞字尾，表示人
geographer [dʒɪˋɑgrəfə] 名 地理學家
延伸片語 **to meet with a geographer** 與一位地理學家碰面
▶ I met with a geographer to gather materials for my geography class. 我拜訪了一位地理學家來收集我地理課的資料。

❸ **geo** 土地 ＋ **logy** 名詞字尾，表示學科
geology [dʒɪˋɑlədʒɪ] 名 地質學；（某地區的）地質情況
延伸片語 **in the field of geology** 地質學領域
▶ I want to level up and become an expert in the field of geology. 我想要提升我自己並成為一名地質學專家。

❹ **geo** 地理 ＋ **metry** 等於**measure**，表示測量
geometry [dʒɪˋɑmətrɪ] 名 幾何學
延伸片語 **a geometry class** 幾何學課程
▶ Do you remember that we went to a geometry class together last year? 你記得去年我們一起去上幾何學課嗎？

❺ **geo** 土地 ＋ **graph** 紀錄；圖示；書寫 ＋ **ical** 形容詞字尾
geographical [dʒɪəˋgræfɪkl] 形 地理學的；地理的
延伸片語 **the geographical features of** 某個地方的地理特質
▶ The team went far into the mountain to study the geographical features of Mountain Jade. 這支隊伍走入玉山去研究深山的地理特色。

延伸補充 自然學

與 geo- 近義的字根：insul-
☆ **peninsula** 近似於 ＋ 島 名 半島

根 lun, sol 月亮、太陽

情境對話試水溫

Laura: Do you know that the name, Luna, refers to the Goddess of Moon?

蘿拉：你知道【露娜】這個名字，指的是月之女神嗎？

Paul: I have no idea. You're so resourceful.

保羅：不知道，你好聰明。

Laura: And that's also how lunar calendar got its name.

蘿拉：而且陰曆也與這個詞有關。

Paul: What about the sun?

保羅：那太陽呢？

Laura: It's S-O-L-A-R. Remember, the solar system? Don't tell me you forgot what we'd learned in Prof. Lee's class.

蘿拉：太陽系，記得嗎？別告訴我你忘記李教授課上教的。

Paul: I do remember, okay? I still couldn't get of that terrible memory when John did this little experiment that tried to solarize a strange pot of liquid under the blazing sun.

保羅：我當然記得，我還沒辦法擺脫關於約翰那段淒慘的回憶，他試圖把一罐莫名的液體放在烈日下曝曬。

Laura: And nothing happened. It was so hilarious.

蘿拉：結果什麼都沒發生，太好笑了。

Paul: Yeah, and that was also when I learned the word "lunisolar" because John kept telling me he did that experiment based on the lunisolar calendar and it was supposed to succeed!

保羅：對，我就是那天學到了「陰陽」這個詞，因為約翰不停告訴我他用陰陽曆的概念做了一個實驗，而且絕對會成功！

單字解析零距離

❶ lun 月亮 ＋ **a** 名詞字尾

luna [ˈlunə] 名 月神；月亮　　　　　延伸片語 the Luna Goddess　月神

▶ In ancient Roman myth, Luna is the epitome of the moon.
在古羅馬神話中，Luna一詞象徵的就是月亮。

. . . .

❷ **lun** 月亮 ＋ **ar** 形容詞字尾，表示狀態

lunar [ˈlunɚ] 形 月的；月球上的　　　　延伸片語 lunar calendar　陰曆

▶ Chinese people hold festivals according to the lunar calender.
中國人照著陰曆舉辦許多節慶。

. . . .

❸ **sol** 太陽 ＋ **ar** 形容詞字尾，表示狀態

solar [ˈsolɚ] 形 太陽的；利用太陽光的　　　延伸片語 solar energy　太陽能

▶ Solar energy is seemed as an alternative to traditional coal-burning. 太陽能被視為傳統燃煤技術的取代方案。

. . . .

❹ **sol** 太陽 ＋ **ar** 形容詞字尾，表示狀態 ＋ **ize** 動詞字尾，表示使成……狀態和使……化

solarize [ˈsolɚˌraɪz] 動 使受日光作用

延伸片語 to solarize sth.　使……受日光作用

▶ Please avoid solarizing the negatives. 請避免讓底片曝光。

. . . .

❺ **lun** 月亮 ＋ **i** ＋ **sol** 太陽 ＋ **ar** 形容詞字尾，表示狀態

lunisolar [ˌlunɪˈsolɚ] 形 日與月的；由於日、月引力的

延伸片語 lunisolar precession　日月歲差

▶ The rotational difference between sun and moon with respect to the Earth is called lunisolar precession.
太陽和月亮相對於地球之間自轉的誤差，稱為陰陽歲差。

💡 延伸補充 自然學

☆ **semilunar**	半＋月亮＋形容詞字尾	形 半月形的
☆ **lunitidal**	月亮＋潮汐＋形容詞字尾	形 月潮的
☆ **antisolar**	反對＋太陽＋形容詞字尾	形 反日的

表示動植物、自然、宇宙

首 astro, aster 星

💬 情境對話試水溫

Melody:	I'm so mesmorized by the astral planets. They are just beyond expressions.	美樂蒂：我完全愛上這些星系，無法言喻。
Bella:	I understand. I guess everyone wished to be an astronaut as a kid.	貝拉：我懂，我猜每個人小時候都夢想當太空人。
Melody:	Not me. In my children, I always hoped to become as astronomer because I preferred close and thorough examination of each star. I didn't really want to stay in a rocket.	美樂蒂：我就不是，我小時候總想當天文學家，因為我比較喜歡貼近並仔細研究每顆星，我才不想住在石頭上。
Bella:	Oh, that explains why you're now majoring in astronomy.	貝拉：哦，難怪你現在主修天文學。
Melody:	You?	美樂蒂：你呢？
Bella:	Nothing serious. I'm now studying economics, but in my spare time, I do some amateur research in astrology.	貝拉：沒什麼特別的，我現在念經濟學，但有空的時候會看一下占星學。
Melody:	Let's meet up some other time and share what we've learned so far!	美樂蒂：我們改天可以約出來聊聊我們學的內容！

⚡ 單字解析零距離

❶ astro 星 **+ al** 形容詞字尾，表示有……性質的

astral [ˋæstrəl] 形 星的；星狀的；星際的

延伸片語 **astral bodies** 星體

Ch 2

Part 1

Part 2

表示動植物、自然、宇宙

Part 3

Part 4

▶ Astral bodies fascinate me with their everlastingness.
星體的永恆性深深吸引我。

- -

❷ astro 星＋**naut** 名詞字尾，表示航行者

astronaut [ˈæstrənɔt] 名 太空人

延伸片語 **to become an astronaut** 成為一個太空人

▶ Every kid wants to become an astronaut in the future.
每個小孩未來都夢想當一位太空人。

- -

❸ astro 星＋**nom** 表示法則；學科＋**er** 名詞字尾，表示人

astronomer [əˈstrɑnəmə] 名 天文學家

延伸片語 **a retired astronomer** 退休的天文學家

▶ My grandmother is a retired astronomer, and I admire her very
much. 我奶奶是一名退休的天文學家，我非常崇拜她。

- -

❹ astro 星＋**nomy** 名詞字尾，表示法則；學科

astronomy [əsˈtrɑnəmɪ] 名 天文學

延伸片語 **to study astronomy under sb.** 在某個人底下研究天文學

▶ I decided to study astronomy under Prof. Lee and contributed
to the society. 我決定上李教授的天文學課，然後把所學回饋社會。

- -

❺ astro 星＋**logy** 名詞字尾，表示學科

astrology [əˈstrɑlədʒɪ] 名 占星術；占星學

延伸片語 **the science of astrology** 占星學

▶ Some claim that there's no such thing as the science of
astrology at all and it is only nonsense.
據說世上根本就沒有什麼占星學，都是無稽之談。

💡 延伸補充 **自然學**

☆ **astrologer** 星＋學科＋名詞字尾，表示人　　名 占星家
☆ **astrophysics** 星＋自然科學＋名詞字尾，表示學 名【天】天體物理學
說或知識

根 cosm 宇宙、次序

情境對話試水溫

🎧 Track 042

Alice: Don't you find it mysterious that the cosmos operates in this way? I mean, if we all die, does it still exist?

愛麗絲：你不覺得宇宙的運行很神秘嗎？ 我是說，如果人類都滅亡了，宇宙還存在嗎？

Melissa: Everything cosmic all leads to one conclusion, which is, STOP THINKING.

梅麗莎：宇宙的一切最終都只有一個結果，就是，你想太多了！

Alice: C'mon. You studied cosmology You know what I'm talking about.

愛麗絲：拜託，你念宇宙學，你懂我在說什麼。

Melissa: Let me explain it in this way. Right now, both of us live in this cosmopolitan. What do you think?

梅麗莎：這樣說好了，此時此刻，我們兩個人都活在這世上，你怎麼看？

Alice: Transient?

愛麗絲：我們只是過客？

Melissa: Yes. We look at this world through our microcosmic perspective, and that's because we are all humane.

梅麗莎：這就對啦，我們只能用微觀的角度看世界，都因為我們只是人類罷了。

Alice: So, what we should do is to deepen and broaden this humane perspective that we have?

愛麗絲：所以，我們應該要做的就是深化和擴張我們所擁有的這個人類視野？

Melissa: Yes. In this case, whether or not the cosmos will exist after we die should cease to matter.

梅麗莎：是的，如此一來，我們死後宇宙是否存在就一點都不重要了。

單字解析零距離

1 cosmo 宇宙 ＋ **s**

Ch 2

Part 1

Part 2

表示動植物、自然、宇宙

Part 3

Part 4

cosmos [ˈkɑzməs] 名（有和諧體系的）宇宙；秩序；和諧

延伸片語 in the cosmos 在宇宙中

▶ Can we eventually find the meaning of life in the cosmos?
我們最終是否能在宇宙中找到生命的意義？

- -

❷ **cosm** 宇宙 ＋ **ic** 形容詞字尾

cosmic [ˈkɑzmɪk] 形 宇宙的；外層空間的

延伸片語 the cosmic system 宇宙系統

▶ The cosmic system is actually beyond human comprehension.
宇宙系統實際上是超乎人類所能想像的範圍的。

- -

❸ **cosmo** 宇宙 ＋ **logy** 名詞字尾，表示學科

cosmology [kɑzˈmɑlədʒɪ] 名 宇宙論

延伸片語 the scope of cosmology 宇宙論的範疇

▶ I'm afraid that this question is beyond the scope of cosmology.
這個問題恐怕已經超出宇宙學的範圍了。

- -

❹ **cosmo** 宇宙 ＋ **polit** 城市 ＋ **an** 形容詞字尾，表示屬於……的

cosmopolitan [ˌkɑzməˈpɑlətn] 形 世界性的；國際性的

延伸片語 a cosmopolitan city 大都會城市

▶ Living in a cosmopolitan city is very different from living in the
countryside. 國際大都市的生活與鄉村裡截然不同。

- -

❺ **micro** 微小 ＋ **cosm** 宇宙 ＋ **ic** 形容詞字尾

microcosmic [ˌmaɪkrəˈkɑzmɪk] 形 小宇宙的；微觀的

延伸片語 a microcosmic version of 微觀版本的……

▶ This village, suffering from famine and corruption, resembles a
microcosmic version of the world.
這個村落飽受飢荒和貪汙，就像世界的縮影。

⚡ 延伸補充 自然學

☆ **microcosm**	微小＋宇宙	名 小宇宙；縮圖
☆ **macrocosm**	大；宏觀＋宇宙	名 大宇宙；大世界；整體

根 **capit** 頭、主要的

情境對話試水溫

🎧 *Track 043*

Mark:	Did you hear the news? A captain of the ship in a harbor small town has been taken away by a group of infamous pirates.
	馬克：你聽說了嗎？ 碼頭小鎮的船長被一群惡名昭彰的海盜綁架了。
Mandy:	Really? You mean Kango? They are known for decapitating captives!
	曼蒂：真的嗎？ 你是指康幗幫？ 他們都以斬首俘虜出名的！
Mark:	It is said that the ship capsized in the middle of the ocean; the captain and his crew thought the pirates were rescuers.
	馬克：據說這艘船在在海洋中翻覆，船長和船員誤以為那群海盜是搜救隊。
Mandy:	What is the government going to do now?
	曼蒂：那政府打算怎麼處理？
Mark:	The officials have no other options but to capitulate. The pirates made it clear that if the ransom were not paid, all the people would be dead.
	馬克：那些官員除了妥協也沒得選擇。這群海盜表明如果沒有收到贖金，船上沒人可以活著回來。
Mandy:	That's terrible. Hope everything ends well.
	曼蒂：太可怕了。希望事情能圓滿落幕。

單字解析零距離

❶ **de** 除去 ＋ **capit** 頭 ＋ **ate** 動詞字尾，表示使成為

decapitate [dɪˋkæpəˌtet] 🔟 斬首；解僱

延伸片語 to decapitate the enemy 斬首敵人

▶ The Queen ordered to decapitated the enemy.
女王要求獵人斬首敵軍。

Ch 2

Part 1

Part 2

Part 3

表示身體

Part 4

❷ **capt** 頭＋**ive** 形容詞字尾，表示有……性質的

captive [ˈkæptɪv] 形 被俘的；受監禁的；受控制的；被迷住的

延伸片語 **to be held captive** 被監禁

▶ The villagers were held captives by the rebels.
這群村民是叛亂份子挾持的俘虜。

• •

❸ **capt** 主要的＋**ain** 名詞字尾，表示與……相關的人

captain [ˈkæptɪn] 名 船長；隊長；領隊

延伸片語 **a team captain** 團長；隊長

▶ A team captain is responsible for leading to team to work together and achieve their goal.
隊長負責帶領團隊，共同合作並完成目標。

• •

❹ **cap** 頭＋**s**＋**ize** 動詞字尾，使……化

capsize [kæpˈsaɪz] 動 傾覆；翻覆

延伸片語 **to capsize in the sea** 在海上傾覆

▶ The report said that the battle vessel capsized in the sea due to the hideous weather.
據報導指出，該戰艦因惡劣的天氣狀況而在海中翻覆。

• •

❺ **capit** 頭＋**ul**＋**ate** 動詞字尾，表示使成為

capitulate [kəˈpɪtʃəˌlet] 動 （有條件地）投降；屈從；停止反抗

延伸片語 **to capitulate to the enemy** 向敵人投降

▶ The Queen failed the assassination, and had to capitulate to the enemy at last.
女王暗殺失敗，因此最後不得不向敵軍屈服。

 延伸補充**自然學**

| ☆ **capital** | 主要的＋名詞字尾 | 名 首都；首府 |

根 **cord** 心臟

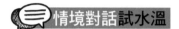

情境對話試水溫

🎧 *Track 044*

Vivian: When are you moving to San Francisco?	薇薇安：你什麼時後要搬到舊金山？
Ann: Maybe next month.	安：大概是下個月吧。
Vivian: Just can't wait to have you as my neighbors! I will definitely give you a cordial welcome then! What about a BBQ party?	薇薇安：簡直等不及跟你成為鄰居啦！我一定給你熱烈的歡迎！烤肉派對如何？
Ann: Hahaha! Do I need to prepare a GoPro to record the red-letter day next month? Tell me more about my new community.	安：哈哈，我需要準備一台運動攝影機來記錄這值得紀念的一天嗎？多說一些有關我新社區的事吧！
Vivian: It's a Chinese community and most of the neighbors live in concord except the Lins. Even petty things could stir up discord between the Lins and others. The Lins are manning battle stations all the time.	薇薇安：他是一個華人社區，大家都和睦相處，除了林家人。任何雞毛蒜皮的小事都能激起他們和其他人的不愉快。林家人永遠處於戰鬥狀態！
Ann: Your description of the Lins is concordant with my cousin's, who is also living in that community.	安：你對他們的描述和我表妹說的如出一轍，我表妹也住在那個社區。
Vivian: Believe it or not, after you move to that community, your attitude toward them would accord with mine!	薇薇安：信不信由你啦，等你搬到那裡之後，你對他們的態度也會跟我一樣！

Ch 2

Part 1

Part 2

Part 3

表示身體

Part 4

單字解析零距離

① ac 朝向 ＋ **cord** 心

accord [ə`kɔrd] 動 與……一致

延伸片語 **of one's own accord** 自動地、出於自願

▶ He helped me of his own accord. 他是自願幫助我的。

② cord 心 ＋ **ial** 屬於……的

cordial [`kɔrdʒəl] 形 熱忱的、真摯的

延伸片語 **a cordial welcome** 熱忱歡迎

▶ We will give you a cordial welcome and reception.
我們會給予您熱烈的歡迎和招待。

③ con 聚合、共同 ＋ **cord** 心

concord [`kɑnkɔrd] 名 協調　　延伸片語 **in concord** 和諧地

▶ The neighbors here always live in concord.
這裡的鄰居們一直都和睦相處。

④ dis 相反的 ＋ **cord** 心

discord [`dɪskɔrd] 名 不一致 動 與……不一致

延伸片語 **discord with** 與……不協調；與……不一致

▶ His view discords with the basic principal. 他的觀點與基本原則不符。

⑤ re 此表示強調 ＋ **cord** 心

record [`rɛkəd] 名 紀錄　　延伸片語 **make a record of** 將……加以紀錄

▶ Please make a record of the important meeting.
請為這次重要的會議加以記錄。

⑥ con 聚合、共同 ＋ **cord** 心 ＋ **ant** 形容詞字尾

concordant [kɑn`kɔrdənt] 形 協調的；和睦的

延伸片語 **concordant music** 和諧的音樂

▶ The band can play concordant music. 這個樂團能奏出和諧的音樂。

根 corpor, corp 身體、團體

Bowen: Do you know the corporal over there? I heard that he is very strict.

博文：你認識那邊的下士嗎？聽說他很嚴格。

Evan: Yes, I know, and he had won many battles. He said in his autobiography that the corpses he had seen were more than the salt he'd ever taken.

伊凡：我認識，他可是戰功赫赫。還在自傳中提到，看過的屍體比吃過的鹽還多。

Bowen: And now his figure can be described as ... corpulent. Do you know why?

博文：但他現在看起來……有點胖。你知道原因嗎？

Evan: He's now in the business industry. I guess all the late hours and social events have brought some negative effects on his body.

伊凡：他現在從商了，我猜應該是長期熬夜跟應酬造成的。

Bowen: Didn't he mention anything about it in his autobiography as well?

博文：他自傳中沒提到嗎？

Evan: A little. He said that he now runs a corporation and intends to incorporate other affiliated firms into his conglomerate.

伊凡：稍微提一些，只說現在正經營一家公司，未來打算將其他相關產業併入他的集團裡。

Bowen: I see. Well, I still prefer to see him in a military uniform though.

博文：我懂了，好吧，我還是覺得他穿軍服比較好看。

單字解析 零距離

❶ **corpor** 身體 ＋ **al** 形容詞字尾，表示有……性質的

corporal [ˈkɔrpərəl] 形 肉體的；身體的

延伸片語 corporal punishment 體罰

Ch 2

Part 1

Part 2

Part 3

表示身體

Part 4

▶ Many parents and teachers are now against corporal punishment. 很多家長及老師現在都反對體罰。

· ·

❷ **corp** 身體 ＋ **se** 名詞字尾

corpse [kɔrps] 名 屍體；殘骸

延伸片語 a corpse of a human body 人類的屍體

▶ The kids were frightened to see a corpse of a human body in the park. 孩子們在公園看見人類屍體都被嚇壞了。

· ·

❸ **corp** 身體 ＋ **ulent** 形容詞字尾，表示充滿

corpulent [ˋkɔrpjələnt] 形 肥胖的

延伸片語 a corpulent old man 肥胖的老人

▶ The police said that a corpulent old man had gone missing early in the afternoon. 警方說有一名肥胖的老人今天下午失蹤了。

· ·

❹ **corpor** 團體 ＋ **ation** 名詞字尾，表示情況或行為

corporation [͵kɔrpəˋreʃən] 名 法人；社團法人；【美】股份（有限）公司

延伸片語 to manage a corporation 經營一家公司

▶ My father said that it is tiring and difficult to manage a corporation.
我父親表示要管理一間公司是很累人又困難的工作。

· ·

❺ **in** 裡面；進入 ＋ **corpor** 身體 ＋ **ate** 動詞字尾，使成為

incorporate [ɪnˋkɔrpə͵ret] 動 包含；加上；吸收

延伸片語 to incorporate A into B 把 A 併入 B

▶ My professor asked me to incorporate this theory into my thesis.
我教授要求我將這個理論併入我的論文。

💡 延伸補充 自然學

✿ **corporeal**	身體 + 形容詞字尾	形 肉體的；物質的
✿ **corps**	身體 + 名詞字尾	名 兵團，軍，部

Unit 46 根 **face** 外表、表面

🎧 *Track 046*

💬 情境對話試水溫

Ellen: Look at your facial expression!

艾倫：你看你這什麼表情！

Ray: Haha. I'm just blown away by the magnificent façade of this castle. Even though some of the stone columns have been defaced by the passage of time. I still want to live in here!

雷：哈哈。我只是被這座城堡宏偉的外觀震懾住了，雖然隨著時光流逝，一些石柱都已經被破壞，我還是想住在這裡！

Ellen: Same here. This castle has multiple facets to appreciate. It is truly a wonder of architecture.

艾倫：我也是，這城堡有好多面可以欣賞。真是一個建築奇蹟。

Ray: Let's hope the government and the conglomerates aren't trying to efface this beautiful phase of human civilization.

雷：希望政府跟企業集團不要毀了這人類文明美麗的階段。

Ellen: Let's pray!

艾倫：祈禱吧！

單字解析零距離

❶ fac 表面 **+ ial** 形容詞字尾

facial [ˈfeʃəl] 形 臉的；面部的；表面的

延伸片語 **facial expression** 臉部表情

▶ One's facial expression is crucial in terms of behavioral interpretation.
在行為解釋方面，一個人的臉部表情相當重要。

- -

❷ fac 表面 **+ ade** 名詞字尾，表示行為、動作或產品

façade [fə`sɑd] 名（建築物的）正面；前面；表面；外觀

延伸片語 **the façade of ~** （某物）的外觀

▶ The façade of the 18th century castle draws millions of tourists annually.
這個18世紀的城堡外觀每年吸引數百萬的觀光客。

- -

❸ **de** 除去 ＋ **face** 外表

deface [dɪ`fes] 動 毀壞……的外貌；損壞；塗汙（使難辨認）

延伸片語 **to deface ~** 破壞

▶ It's illegal to deface books in public libraries now.
現在在公眾場合破壞書籍是非法的行為。

- -

❹ **fac** 表面 ＋ **et** 名詞字尾，表示小的

facet [`fæsɪt] 名（多面體的）面；（寶石等的）琢面；（問題等的）一個方面

延伸片語 **have/ has many facets to ~** 多面向

▶ This film has many facets to religious interpretations.
這部影片在宗教詮釋上有很多面向。

- -

❺ **ef** 向外 ＋ **face** 外表

efface [ɪ`fes] 動 擦掉；抹去

延伸片語 **to efface the memory of** 抹去關於……的記憶

▶ Many sexually-abused victims may spend their whole life trying to efface the memory of the traumatic experiences.
許多性虐待的受害者花了一生的時間，試著抹去關於這些創傷的記憶。

延伸補充自然學

✿ **interface**	在……之間；互相 ＋ 表面	名 界面，分界面；接合部
✿ **preface**	之前（時間／空間）＋ 表面	名 序言，緒言；引語
✿ **surface**	之上 ＋ 表面	名 外表；外觀 動 顯露，呈現

根 derm 皮膚

🎧 Track 047

💬 情境對話試水溫

Alice: The doctor said that I have a serious dermal problem.	艾莉絲：醫生說我有嚴重的皮膚疾病。
Melissa: What is it?	梅麗莎：是什麼？
Alice: Dermatitis. It's killing me.	艾莉絲：皮膚炎，超痛苦的。
Melissa: I know a very famous dermatologist. But it's in Tainan. If you want to go there, I can accompany you.	梅麗莎：我認識一位有名的皮膚科醫生，但他在台南，如果你想要我可以陪你去。
Alice: But the doctor said that it needs a special treatment that deals specifically with hypodermic symptoms.	艾莉絲：但醫生說需要用一種特殊的療程來處理我皮下的症狀。
Melissa: We can still go and consult with him. I guess dermatology trainings are alike. If he couldn't provide the treatment you need, you can go back to the one you're visiting now.	梅麗莎：我們還是可以去諮詢他。我想皮膚科訓練都是一樣的，如果他無法給你需要的治療，我們也可以回來這裡繼續你的療程。
Alice: Sounds like a good idea. Thanks Melissa!	艾莉絲：聽起來不錯，謝謝你梅麗莎！

⚡ 單字解析零距離

❶ **derm** 皮膚 ＋ **al** 形容詞字尾，表示有……性質的

dermal [`dɝməl] 形【解】皮膚的；真皮的

延伸片語 **dermal layers** 真皮層

▶ Damages to dermal layers may require weeks to recover.
真皮層受損可能需要好幾個星期才能復原。

Ch 2

Part 1

Part 2

Part 3

表示身體

Part 4

❷ **dermat** 皮膚 ＋ **itis** 名詞字尾，表示發炎

dermatitis [͵dɝməˋtaɪtɪs] 名 皮膚炎

延伸片語 the contraction of dermatitis 皮膚炎感染

▶ The contraction of dermatitis is sometimes difficult to avoid.
有時候皮膚炎感染是很難避免的。

• •

❸ **dermat** 皮膚 ＋ **ology** 學科 ＋ **ist** 名詞字尾，通常指「人」

dermatologist [͵dɝməˋtɑlədʒɪst] 名 皮膚科醫生

延伸片語 to become a dermatologist 成為皮膚科醫生

▶ My sister has wished to become a dermatologist since she was
a kid. 我姊姊從小就希望成為一位皮膚科醫生。

• •

❹ **hypo** 低 ＋ **derm** 皮 ＋ **ic** 形容詞字尾

hypodermic [͵haɪpəˋdɝmɪk] 形 皮下的

延伸片語 a hypodermic syringe 注射針筒

▶ Hypodermic syringes are used in some special treatment of
dermal problems. 有些皮膚問題的特殊療程會使用針筒。

• •

❺ **dermat** 皮膚 ＋ **ology** 名詞字尾，表示學科

Dermatology [͵dɝməˋtɑlədʒɪ] 名 皮膚醫學

延伸片語 the field of dermatology 皮膚學領域

▶ Many people are now aspiring to enter the field of
dermatology because it is a lucrative business.
很多人現在都渴望進入皮膚學領域，因為利潤很豐厚。

延伸補充 自然學

☆ **epidermis**	在表面＋皮		名【解】表皮；外皮
☆ **dermatic**	皮＋形容詞字尾		形 皮膚的
☆ **hypodermal**	低＋皮＋形容詞字尾，表示有……性質的		形 皮下組織的；皮下的

根 **manu** 手

情境對話試水溫

🎧 *Track 048*

Barney: This suit manufacturer claims that their suits are all handmade.

巴尼：這套西裝的製造商說他們的西裝全都是手工製造的。

Steward: That's why their suits are so expensive and rare. Manufacturing suits by manual labor must take a lot of time to make it delicate and fit.

史都華：難怪他們的西裝這麼貴又這麼稀有。手工製造的西裝必須花費很多時間把它做得很精緻又合身。

Barney: You bet. Only this type of suits can match my status. I can give you my tailor's phone number who is the agent of these suits, so he can definitely make you a man.

巴尼：肯定地，只有這種西裝可以襯托我的身分地位。我可以給你我裁縫師的電話，他也是這品牌西裝的代理商，他一定可以幫你穿得很體面。

單字解析零距離

1 **manu** 手 ＋ **fact** 製作 ＋ **urer** 人

manufacturer [ˌmænjəˈfæktʃərə] 名 製造商

延伸片語 original equipment manufacturer 初始設備製造廠商

▶ The original equipment manufacturer has stopped producing this component.
初始設備製造廠商已經停止生產這個零件。

Ch 2

Part 1

Part 2

Part 3

表示身體

Part 4

② **manu** 手 + **fact** 製作 + **ure** 表動作

manufacture [ˌmænjəˈfæktʃə] 動 製作

延伸片語 of home manufacture 國內製造的

▶ My father only buys products of home manufacture.
我父親只買國貨。

- -

③ **manu** 手 + **al** 形容詞字尾

manual [ˈmænjʊəl] 形 手工的；手的

延伸片語 manual alphabet 手語字母

▶ The deaf use manual alphabets in finger spelling.
失聰者以手語字母做手指拼寫。

延伸補充自然學

☆ **man**icure	手的照顧	名 修指甲
☆ **man**euver	用手操作	動 策劃
☆ **man**acles	把手可移動的範圍縮小	名 手銬
☆ **man**umit	讓手可以移動	動 奴隸解放
☆ **man**ner	手部 + 行為	名 舉止；動作

根 **ped, pod** 足

情境對話試水溫

🎧 *Track 049*

Mark:	I have no idea why you stood on the pedals of your bike to speed up. Don't you know you're also carrying a delicate pedestal?	馬克：我無法理解你為什麼要站在腳踏車踏板上加速？難道你不知道你載著一個精緻的檯座嗎？
Deborah:	It's not for me though. I just want to get back home as soon as possible.	黛伯拉：反正又不是給我的，我只想趕快回家。
Mark:	That's very irresponsible. Also, remember that day when you said you were going to have a pedicure and you rode on the sidewalk? Please don't do that again. You may hit other pedestrians!	馬克：你這樣很不負責任。還記得你說要去修腳趾甲的那天你騎在人行道上嗎？下次不要再這樣，你可能會撞到路人！
Deborah:	I don't care. They should be aware of me too!	黛伯拉：關我什麼事，他們自己也要注意路況才對！
Mark:	Well, then I hope the next time when you go jogging, and you stop to adjust your pedometer, you get hit by someone like you.	馬克：好吧，那我希望你下次出門跑步停下來調整計步器時，會被像你這樣的人撞。
Deborah:	That's very terrible of you to say so.	黛伯拉：你怎麼這樣講話。
Mark:	So is your reckless behavior!	馬克：你魯莽的行為也沒多好！

單字解析零距離

❶ **ped** 足 **+ al** 形容詞字尾，表示有……性質的

pedal ['pɛdl] 名 踏板；腳蹬 形 足的；踏板的；腳踏的

Ch 2

Part 1

Part 2

Part 3

表示身體

Part 4

延伸片語 **the pedals of a bike** 腳踏車踏板

▶ If you want to get extra power, you can stand on the pedals of a bike to speed up. 如果你想要增加動力，可以站在腳踏車踏板上加速。

· ·

❷ **pedes** 行走 ＋ **tal** 站立

pedestal [ˈpɛdɪstl̩] 名 【建】柱腳；（雕像等的）墊座；臺座

延伸片語 **to fall from a pedestal** 從檯座上掉下來

▶ The vase fell from a pedestal during the earthquake.
地震時花瓶從檯座上掉下來。

· ·

❸ **pedes** 行走 ＋ **tr** ＋ **ian** 名詞字尾，表示人

pedestrian [pɛˈdɛstrɪən] 名 步行者；行人

延伸片語 **to be aware of pedestrians** 注意行人

▶ When you try to ride a bike on the sidewalk, please be aware of pedestrians and get off it as soon as possible.
當你試圖在人行道騎腳踏車時，請隨時注意行人並盡快離開。

· ·

❹ **ped** 足 ＋ **i** ＋ **cure** 治療

pedicure [ˈpɛdɪkˌjʊr] 名 足部治療；修趾甲術

延伸片語 **to get a pedicure** 修腳趾甲

▶ Many young men are interested in getting a pedicure nowadays. 現今有許多年輕男性對修腳趾甲有興趣。

· ·

❺ **ped** 足 ＋ **o** ＋ **meter** 測量

pedometer [pɪˈdɑmətɚ] 名 步數計；步程計；計步器

延伸片語 **to wear a pedometer** 戴計步器

▶ Wearing a pedometer is a good way to measure the progress you've made for your health.
戴著計步器是檢視你是否有更健康的好方法。

💡 延伸補充 自然學

| ☆ **centipede** | 百＋足 | 名【昆】蜈蚣 |
| ☆ **podiatrist** | 足＋治療＋名詞字尾，通常指人 | 名【美】足科醫師 |

Unit 50 根 grat(e) 高興的、感謝的

情境對話試水溫

Track 050

Linda: This mayor is going to take over the Premier of Executive Yuan shortly after he came in for 100 days.

琳達：這位市長即將在短短上任100天後接下行政院長的位置。

Maze: He is such an ingrate that he once promised the electorate he would revive the city out of gratitude. Nonetheless, He's leaving for greater power.

麥茲：他真是一位忘恩負義之人，當初還感激地承諾選民將會復興這座城市。然而現在為了更大的權力而離開。

Linda: Exactly! He had been being grateful on his drum-up support activities, and even sworn to gratify the voters.

琳達：對啊，他曾經在造勢活動上表現得很感激，而且發誓會使選民滿意。

Maze: Now, this position is just a rebound job, and those political views will be left undone. His ingratitude indeed startles all the city residents.

麥茲：現在這個位置只是個跳板工作，而他會留下政見芭樂票。他的不知感恩確實使市民錯愕。

單字解析零距離

❶ in 否、不 ＋ grate 感謝

ingrate [ɪnˋgret] 名 忘恩負義的人

延伸片語 a complete ingrate 一個純粹的忘恩負義之徒

▶ He is a complete ingrate; I'll never help him.
他是一個徹頭徹尾的忘恩負義之徒，我再也不幫他了。

. . . .

❷ grat 感謝 ＋ itude 表「性質」

gratitude [ˋgrætəˌtjud] 名 感謝；感恩

延伸片語 out of gratitude 出於感激

表示情緒、認知、抽象事物

▶ I believe that the young man did it all out of gratitude.
我相信這那個年輕人完全是出於感激才那麼做的。

❸ grat 高興的、感謝 + **ful** 充滿……的

grateful [ˈgretfəl] 形 令人充滿感激的

延伸片語 an uninhabited island 一個無人居住的荒島

▶ I am grateful to all those who helped me in the past.
我感謝所有曾經幫助過我的人。

❹ grat 高興的、感謝 + **ify** 使……成為

gratify [ˈɡrætˌfaɪ] 動 使滿意

延伸片語 gratify by 對……感到欣慰

▶ The old man was gratified by his son's achievements.
老人對兒子的成就感到欣慰。

❺ in 否、不 + **grate** 感謝 + **itude** 性質

ingratitude [ɪnˈɡrætəˌtjud] 名 不知感恩

延伸片語 repay kindness with ingratitude 忘恩負義

▶ How dare you to repay his kindness with ingratitude?
你怎麼敢對他忘恩負義？

延伸補充 自然學

☆ **ingratiate**	進行希望別人打從內心喜悦的行動	動 迎合討好
☆ **congratulate**	開心的聚在一起從事某項行動	動 恭賀
☆ **gratulate**	開心的進行某項活動	動 歡迎
☆ **gratuitous**	有令人歡愉的特性	形 免費的；無端的

根 **mem(or)** 記憶

情境對話試水溫

🎧 *Track 051*

Daniel: Why are you still commemorating your ex-fiancé by celebrating the anniversary? You have broken up for a year!	丹尼爾：你為何還在慶祝周年慶來紀念你的前未婚妻？你們已經分手一年了！
Marcus: Days with Chloe were such memorable memories. I just can't move on, but immerse myself in the past time.	馬克思：與克羅伊在一起的時光是難忘的回憶。我就是無法忘懷，只能沉浸在過去裡。
Daniel: Well, I can still see you wear the memorial ring with you, and even memorize Chloe's likes and dislikes, preparing brunch for her every day.	丹尼爾：嗯，我仍然看得出來你還帶著紀念信物戒；甚至熟記克羅伊的好惡，每天準備早午餐給她。
Marcus: I just want to win her back. Please help me, Daniel.	馬可思：我只想要贏回她芳心。丹尼爾，請幫幫我！
Daniel: Dream on! She's getting married to Lucifer next Saturday!	丹尼爾：你繼續作夢吧，她下週六將與路西法結婚了！

單字解析零距離

1 **com** 共同 ＋ **memor** 記憶 ＋ **ate** 動詞字尾

commemorate [kə`mɛməˌret] 動 紀念

延伸片語 commemorate victory 慶祝勝利

▶ In order to commemorate victory of the revolution, the new government made the day a national holiday.
為了慶祝革命成功，新政府將這一天訂為國定假日。

表示情緒、認知、抽象事物

❷ memor 記憶 **+ able** 能夠的

memorable [ˈmɛmərəbl] 形 難忘的

延伸片語 memorable event 難忘的事件

▶ Winning the beauty contest is the most memorable event in my life.
贏得選美比賽是我人生中最難忘的一件事。

. . . .

❸ memor 記憶 **+ y** 名詞字尾

memory [ˈmɛmərɪ] 名 回憶

延伸片語 in memory of 紀念

▶ They erected a statue in memory of this national hero.
他們樹立一座雕像以紀念這位民族英雄。

. . . .

❹ memor 記憶 **+ ial** 形容詞字尾

memorial [məˈmorɪəl] 名 紀念物

延伸片語 memorial hospital 紀念醫院

▶ The enterpriser built a memorial hospital in memory of his mother.
該企業家興建一座紀念醫院以紀念他的母親。

. . . .

❺ memor 記憶 **+ ize** 動詞字尾

memorize [ˈmɛməˌraɪz] 動 背熟

延伸片語 memorize a word 背單字

▶ It is easier to memorize a new word if you can use it in a sentence.
將單字使用在句子中能更容易背熟單字。

 延伸補充 自然學

☆ **remember**	再一次＋記得	動 記住
☆ **rememberable**	能夠被一再想起的	形 值得回憶的
☆ **memo**	關於記憶的	名 備忘錄

根 **fid** 信任、相信

情境對話試水溫

🎧 *Track 052*

Kevin: I envy you. You have such a confiant like Mandy.	凱文：我羨慕你。你有像蔓蒂那樣的好朋友。
Lauren: You lack confidence. That's all I can say. You need to be more positive.	羅倫：你缺乏自信。我能說的只有這樣。你要更正向一點。
Kevin: I know, but I've been betrayed by a really close friend before. I now no longer belive in the fedelity of any human relationships.	凱文：我知道，但是我以前曾被一個很親近的朋友背叛過。我現在很難再相信任何人際關係中的忠實了。
Lauren: I understand. But if you want to make more friends, you've got to konow that acts of perfidy are not predictable. You can say for sure who is going to turn his/ her back on you.	羅倫：我懂。但是如果你想要交更多朋友，你就要知道不忠誠的行為是無法預期的。你沒辦法保證說他／她會不會背棄你。
Kevin: So?	凱文：所以呢？
Lauren: Enjoy the moment, and be brave! Change all that diffident manner, and show people what you've got!	羅倫：享受當下，勇敢一點！改變那些沒自信的儀態，然後像人們展現自己！

單字解析零距離

❶ **co** 共同 ＋ **fid** 信任 ＋ **ant** 人

confidant [ˌkɑnfɪˈdænt] 名 好友

延伸片語 good confidant 好知己

▶ Everyone should have a good confidant.
每個人都應該有一個好知己。

表示情緒、認知、抽象事物

❷ co 共同 **+ fid** 信任 **+ ence** 表示狀態

confidence [ˈkɑnfədəns] 名 信任

延伸片語 **give one's confidence to** 信任

▶ You can give your confidence to him, he is nice guy.
你可以信任他,他是個很不錯的傢夥。

· ·

❸ fid 信任 **+ elity** 名詞字尾

fidelity [fɪˈdɛlətɪ] 名 忠貞;忠誠;準確度

延伸片語 **a high-fidelity receiver** 高度傳真收音機

▶ I extremely want a high-fidelity receiver for my birthday.
我生日的時候非常想要一台高度傳真收音機。

· ·

❹ per 通過 **+ fid** 信任 **+ y** 行為

perfidy [ˈpɝfədɪ] 名 不忠實

延伸片語 **act of perfidy** 背信棄義的行為

▶ Only he could do that act of perfidy.
只有他能做出那種背信棄義的行為。

· ·

❺ dif 不 **+ fid** 信任 **+ ent** 的

diffident [ˈdɪfədənt] 形 缺乏自信的

延伸片語 **speak in a diffident manner** 羞怯地說話

▶ Why does he always speak in a diffident manner?
他為什麼總是羞怯地說話?

延伸補充 自然學

☆ **confide**　　　　共同相信　　　　動 託付

☆ **self-confidence**　相信自己的狀態　　名 自信

根 sci 知道

情境對話試水溫

🎧 **Track 053**

Dr. Lee:	Is your patient conscious now after the surgery?	李醫師：你的患者在手術後有意識嗎？
Dr. Wang:	No. Only semiconscious. This surgery was a big one. I'm afraid she can only hear our voices in her subconscious.	王醫師：沒有，是半清醒狀態。這次是大手術，恐怕她潛意識中只能聽到我們的聲音而已。
Dr. Lee:	Well, that's better than being unconscious. Remember last one, there was a patient who underwent the same surgery?	李醫師：好吧，總比沒意識來的好。記得上次也有一個病患做同樣的手術嗎？
Dr. Wang:	You mean Mr. Zhang? Yeah, I remember. How's he doing now?	王醫師：你是說張先生嗎？我記得，他恢復得如何？
Dr. Lee:	He passed away at the end. It was too late.	李醫師：他最後過世了，一切都來不及。
Dr. Wang:	May he rest in peace. I guess being self-conscious, especially one's health problem, is really important.	王醫師：願他安息吧。我覺得特別對身體有狀況的人來說，自我意識真的很重要。
Dr. Lee:	Yep. Prevention is better than cure.	李醫師：沒錯，預防勝於治療。

單字解析零距離

❶ **con** 完全地 ＋ **sci** 知道 ＋ **ous** 形容詞字尾，有……性質的

conscious [ˈkɑnʃəs] 形 神志清醒的；有知覺；覺察到的

延伸片語 be conscious of 意識到

Ch 2

Part 1

Part 2

Part 3

Part 4

表示情緒、認知、抽象事物

▶ One should be fully conscious of one's health condition at all times. 每個人都應該要隨時意識到自己的健康狀況。

. . . .

❷ semi 一半 + **con** 完全地 + **sci** 知道 + **ous** 形容詞字尾，有……性質的

semiconscious [ˌsɛmɪˈkɑnʃəs] 形 半清醒的；半意識的

延伸片語 **to remain semiconscious** 維持半清醒狀態

▶ The old man remained semiconscious after a major operation. 這老人家在結束一場大手術後，一直維持半清醒狀態。

. . . .

❸ sub 在……下方 + **con** 完全地 + **sci** 知道 + **ous** 形容詞字尾，有……性質的

subconscious [sʌbˈkɑnʃəs] 形 下意識的；潛意識的；意識不清的；意識模糊的 名 下意識心理活動；潛意識心理活動

延伸片語 **in one's subconscious** 在潛意識中

▶ The idea of opening my own business has been in my subconscious for years. 創業的想法一直存在我的潛意識中好多年了。

. . . .

❹ un 不 + **con** 完全地 + **sci** 知道 + **ous** 形容詞字尾，有……性質的

unconscious [ʌnˈkɑnʃəs] 形 不省人事的；失去知覺的；不知道的；未發覺的

延伸片語 **to be unconscious of** 沒有意識到

▶ He was unconscious of the potential danger when investigating the crime. 他在調查這個案子時，沒有意識到潛在的危險。

. . . .

❺ self 自己 + **con** 完全地 + **sci** 知道 + **ous** 形容詞字尾，有……性質的

self-conscious [ˈsɛlfˈkɑnʃəs] 形 【心】有自我意識的；自覺的

延伸片語 **be self-conscious about** 對……有自我意識

▶ Women tend to be more self-conscious about their figure than men. 相較於男性，女性通常對自己外表較有自我意識。

延伸補充 自然學

☆ **conscience** 完全地 + 知道 + 名詞字尾 名 良心；道義心；善惡觀念

☆ **science** 知道 + 名詞字尾 名 科學；自然科學

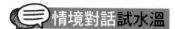 根 **pass, path** 感覺、感受

Brandon: What's your passion in life?

布蘭登：你人生中的熱情是什麼？

Travis: Uhm.. I guess I'm passionate about voluntary works. I especially feel great sympathy toward orphans.

崔維斯：嗯……我想我對志工工作很有熱忱吧。我會特別對孤兒有強烈的同情。

Brandon: I know you're a man of compassion. That explains why you always seem passionate about our community project. When I saw you interacting with the children in the orphanage, I knew instantly that you're a genuine person.

布蘭登：我就知道你是個有同情心的人。難怪你每次都對我們社區的活動這麼有熱情。每當我看到你跟育幼院孩子們互動時，我馬上就感受到你是一個很真誠的人。

Travis: Thanks. Brandon. What about you?

崔維斯：謝謝你，布蘭登。那你呢？

Brandon: All I could feel is this immense sense of apathy. I feel like I don't know what I'm doing here.

布蘭登：我完全沒有感覺，根本不知道我在這裡要做什麼。

Travis: C'mon. You just need time. Don't push yourself too hard. Take it easy, okay?

崔維斯：拜託。你只是需要時間，別給自己太大壓力。放輕鬆，好嗎？

Brandon: Alright. I'll try.

布蘭登：好，我盡量。

 單字解析零距離

❶ **pass** 感覺 ＋ **ion** 名詞字尾

passion [ˈpæʃən] 名 熱情；激情

延伸片語 **to have a passion for** 對……有熱忱

Ch 2

Part 1

Part 2

Part 3

Part 4

表示情緒、認知、抽象事物

▶ My mom has a passion for gardening. 我媽媽對園藝很有熱忱

. . . .

❷ a 無 ＋ **path** 感覺 ＋ **y** 名詞字尾

apathy [ˋæpəθɪ] 名 無感情；無興趣；冷淡；漠不關心

延伸片語 **voter apathy** 選民的冷漠態度

▶ How should we overcome the voter apathy?
我們該如何克服選民的冷漠態度？

. . . .

❸ com 具有 ＋ **pass** 感覺 ＋ **ion** 名詞字尾

compassion [kəmˋpæʃən] 名 憐憫；同情；愛心

延伸片語 **out of compassion** 出於同情

▶ She did that only out of compassion. Don't make too much out
of it. 她只是出於同情才這樣做，別想太多。

. . . .

❹ pass 感覺 ＋ **ion** 名詞字尾 ＋ **ate** 形容詞字尾，和……有關的

passionate [ˋpæʃənɪt] 形 熱情的；熱烈的

延伸片語 **to be passionate about** 對……有熱忱

▶ My sister is passionate about astrology, and she studies our star
signs all the time. 我姐姐對占星術很有熱忱，她總是在研究我們的星座。

. . . .

❺ sym 同一的 ＋ **path** 感覺 ＋ **y** 名詞字尾

sympathy [ˋsɪmpəθɪ] 名 同情；同情心；贊同；一致認同

延伸片語 **to express sympathy for** 對……很同情

▶ I expressed sympathy for your predicament, but there's really
nothing I can do to. 我很同情你的處境，但我真的無能為力。

💡 延伸補充**自然學**

☆ **sympathize**	同一的 ＋ 感覺 ＋ 動詞字尾，使成……狀態	動 同情；憐憫；體諒；贊同
☆ **telepathy**	距離遙遠；在遠處 ＋ 感覺 ＋ 名詞字尾	名 心靈感應；傳心術
☆ **antipathy**	反對；對抗 ＋ 感覺 ＋ 名詞字尾	名 憎惡；厭惡；反感

根 sent, sens 感覺

情境對話試水溫

Linda: So, have we reached a consensus that human sentiments are transient?

> 琳達：所以，人類情緒只是暫時的這部分，我們已經達成共識了吧？

James: Yes, but with a point that our sensory functions play a crucial role in our worldly existence.

> 詹姆士：對，但有一點說我們的感官的功能在這世俗的存在中是重要的關鍵。

Linda: Please specify.

> 琳達：請說清楚一點。

James: Our senses lay the basis of all our experiences, without them, all theoretical analyses are of no meanings.

> 詹姆士：我們的感官是仰賴我們的經歷，沒有這些經歷，各種理論的分析都沒有意義。

Linda: You mean that being sensible is the foundation of everything that we call our own?

> 琳達：你意思是「有所感受」是所有事情的基礎嗎？

James: Yes. To be able to feel is undoubtedly crucial in our living on earth.

> 詹姆士：對，「感受」這件事絕對是我們活在世上最重要的事。

單字解析零距離

❶ **con** 一起；共同 ＋ **sens** 感覺 ＋ **us** 名詞字尾

consensus [kənˋsɛnsəs] 名 一致；合意；共識

延伸片語 **to reach a consensus** 達成共識

▶ We finally reached a consensus on the revonation of the office.
我們終於在辦公室改建這件事上達成了共識。

表示情緒、認知、抽象事物

② sens 感覺 ＋ e 名詞字尾

sense [sɛns] 名 感官；官能；感覺；意識

延伸片語 five senses 五感

▶ It's important to release and open our five senses sometimes.
時不時釋放並敞開我們的五感是很重要的。

③ sens 感覺 ＋ ible 形容詞字尾，表示能夠的；可以的

sensible [ˈsɛnsəbl] 形 明智的；合情理的；意識到的；明顯的

延伸片語 to be sensible of 對……有意識

▶ In an international seminar, you need to be sensible of your own remarks. 在國際研討會中，你需要對自身的言詞有所注意。

④ sent 感覺 ＋ i ＋ ment 名詞字尾

sentiment [ˈsɛntəmənt] 名 感情；心情；情操

延伸片語 human sentiment 人類情感

▶ Human sentiments are the cause of all heartaches.
人類的情感是所有心痛的原因。

⑤ sens 感覺 ＋ ory 形容詞字尾，表示性質的；與……有關的

sensory [ˈsɛnsərɪ] 形 知覺的；感覺的

延伸片語 sensory function 感官功能

▶ Having healthy sensory functions is part of the key to lead a wholesome life. 擁有健康的感官功能是擁有健康人生的關鍵之一。

延伸補充 自然學

☆ consent	一起；共同 ＋ 感覺	動	同意；贊成；答應
☆ dissent	否定；分開 ＋ 感覺	動	不同意；持異議
☆ insensible	無 ＋ 感覺 ＋ 形容詞字尾，表示能夠的；可以的	形	昏迷的；不省人事的；無感覺的；麻木不仁的

根 **psych** 靈魂；心理

Ruby: Remember I told you I wanted to go to see a psychologist? Well, I did last week.	魯迪：你記得我曾跟你說我要去看心理醫生嗎？我上週去了。
Cindy: Good for you! How did it go?	辛蒂：很棒啊！感覺怎麼樣？
Ruby: I didn't like it. The whole psychology thing is just not my cup of tea.	魯迪：我不喜歡。心理學根本就不對我的味。
Cindy: What do you mean? She kept talking about psychoanalysis to you?	辛蒂：什麼意思？他一直在跟你聊心理分析嗎？
Ruby: Sometimes, but I was a bit offended when she asked some really personal questions.	魯迪：偶爾，但有時她問的問題太私人了，讓我有點不舒服。
Cindy: That's necessary! And inevitable!	辛蒂：這是必要的過程！也無法避免！
Ruby: I know... maybe I should go see a psychiatrist instead.	魯迪：我知道……可能我應該去看精神科。
Cindy: I think you should just visit a psychic.	辛蒂：我覺得你應該去找靈媒。

單字解析零距離

1 **psych** 心理 ＋ **o** ＋ **logy** 名詞字尾，表示學科

psychology [saɪˈkɑlədʒɪ] 名 心理學

延伸片語 the study of psychology 心理學研究

▶ I'm interested in the study of psychology, for I yearn to know more about how a mind works.
我對心理學研究很有興趣，因為我很渴望去探索人的思想如何運作。

表示情緒、認知、抽象事物

② **psych** 心理 **+ o + log(y)** 學科 **+ ist** 名詞字尾，通常指「人」

psychologist [saɪˋkɑlədʒɪst] 名 心理學家

延伸片語 **to see a psychologist** 去看心理學家

▶ It's common for Westerners to see a psychologist regularly.
對於西方人來説，定期去看心理醫師是很常見的事情。

- -

③ **psych** 心理 **+ iatr(y)** 醫學治療領域 **+ ist** 名詞字尾，通常指「人」

psychiatrist [saɪˋkaɪətrɪst] 名 精神病醫師

延伸片語 **to become a psychiatrist** 成為一名精神病醫師

▶ Having been troubled by depression once, my sister decided to become a psychiatrist and help more people.
我妹妹因為曾備受憂鬱所苦，而立志成為精神科醫師以幫助更多人。

- -

④ **psych** 心理 **+ o + ana** 再次 **+ lysis** 名詞字尾，表示分解

psychoanalysis [ˌsaɪkoəˋnæləsɪs] 名 精神分析（學）；心理分析（學）

延伸片語 **psychoanalysis theory** 精神分析理論

▶ Many people don't know that the Department of English also offers classes on psychoanalysis theory.
許多人不知道英語系也會開設精神分析理論的課。

- -

⑤ **psych** 靈魂 **+ ic** 形容（名）詞字尾

psychic [ˋsaɪkɪk] 形 精神的；心靈的；超自然的 名 靈媒；巫師

延伸片語 **a fake psychic** 假靈媒

▶ The one murdered in the notorious abduction case was a fake psychic. He was killed because his real identity was discovered.
在那惡名昭彰的綁架案中死者是個江湖郎中，死因是他的身分被揭穿。

延伸補充 自然學

☆ **psychosis** 靈魂；心智 + 名詞字尾 名 精神病；精神變態

☆ **psychopathy** 靈魂；心智 + 名詞字尾，表示疾病 名 精神病態

情境對話試水溫

🎧 *Track 057*

Ellie: Have you ever seen the Statue of Liberty?

艾莉：你看過自由女神像嗎？

Ellen: Of course. You know I'm into everything about liberation.

艾倫：當然。你知道我很熱衷於任何跟解放有關的事。

Ellie: I know. You are one of the most liberal people I've ever known. That's why I hang out with you all the time!

艾莉：我知道，你是我認識的人中最崇尚自由的。我才一直跟你混在一起！

Ellen: It feels just really good to know that the victims, or the minorities, are finally liberated, you know? This fact makes me believe in this world.

艾倫：你知道嗎？當得知那些受害者或少數族群終於得到解放時，感覺真的很棒！這些事情讓我還能相信這世界。

Ellie: Also, there are liberators who set their minds to lead the people. Otherwise, a revolution may fall apart easily.

艾莉：而且，還有一些解放者決定領導百姓。否則，革命很容易就瓦解了。

Ellen: That's very true, and that's why I also love hanging out with you.

艾倫：沒有錯，這也是我喜歡跟你混在一起的原因。

單字解析零距離

① liber 自由 **+ ty** 名詞字尾

liberty ['lɪbɚtɪ] 名 自由

延伸片語 take the liberty of 擅自（主動）做某事

▶ I took the liberty of buying a house for my parents.
我擅自作主替我父母買了一棟房子。

Ch 2

Part 1
Part 2
Part 3
Part 4

表示情緒、認知、抽象事物

② **liber** 自由 ＋ **ate** 動詞字尾，表示使成為

liberate [ˈlɪbəˌret] 動 解放；使獲自由

延伸片語 **to liberate something / someone** 解放某人／某事

▶ The army liberated the captives right after they landed near the center of the city. 這支軍隊降落在市中心時，隨即就解放了俘虜。

- -

③ **liber** 自由 ＋ **at(e)** 動詞字尾，表示使成為 ＋ **ion** 名詞字尾

liberation [ˌlɪbəˈreʃən] 名 解放；解放運動

延伸片語 **to celebrate the liberation of** 慶祝……的解放

▶ Back then, all the people went on the street to celebrate the liberation of Paris. 回顧當時，所有人都上街慶祝巴黎的解放。

- -

④ **liber** 自由 ＋ **al** 形容詞字尾，有……特質的

liberal [ˈlɪbərəl] 形 自由主義的；允許變革的；不守舊的

延伸片語 **to have a liberal mind** 心胸開放

▶ It is nowadays crucial to have a liberal mind; otherwise, you'll certainly be eliminated.
在現今社會中擁有開放的思想非常重要；否則，你肯定會被淘汰。

- -

⑤ **liber** 自由 ＋ **at(e)** 動詞字尾，表示使成為 ＋ **or** 名詞字尾，通常指「人」

liberator [ˈlɪbəˌretə] 名 （民族）解放者；解救者

延伸片語 **to act as a liberator** 擔任解放者

▶ He acted as a liberator in the rebellion that lasted almost half a year. 他在這場叛亂當中擔任解放者，持續了將近半年。

延伸補充**自然學**

☆ **post-liberation** 之後；後來；後面 ＋ 自由 ＋ 動詞字尾，表示使成為 ＋ 名詞字尾　名 解放後

☆ **liberalism** 自由 ＋ 形容詞字尾，有……特質的 ＋ 名詞字尾，表示主義或行為　名 自由主義；寬容；開明

☆ **liberalist** 自由 ＋ 形容詞字尾，有……特質的 ＋ 名詞字尾，通常指「人」　名 自由主義者

根 pac, peac 和平

情境對話試水溫

Matt: Did you know that these two countries have signed a Peace Treaty?

麥特：你知道這兩個國家簽了和平條約嗎？

Bella: Yes, it's on the headline. Finally, the Pacific Ocean can have a long-awaited peacetime.

貝拉：知道，上頭條了。終於，太平洋得到了等待已久的和平時光。

Matt: Well, thanks to the neighboring countries. All newspapers call them "peacekeepers." Otherwise, the war is pretty much impending now.

麥特：這個嘛，也要多虧鄰近的國家。所有報導都稱它們為「和平守護者」。否則，戰爭現在應該就要來臨了。

Bella: True. The last thing we want is a war! Life is already hard enough.

貝拉：真的。我們最不想要的就是戰爭！活著本身已經就夠艱難了。

Matt: The economy is bad, and dictatorship is somehow coming back. I seriously hope we can have a peaceful future.

麥特：經濟很糟，而且獨裁體系似乎又有復甦跡象。我認真希望我們可以有個和平的未來。

Bella: And a bright one for the younger generation.

貝拉：也給下一代一個更明亮的未來。

單字解析零距離

❶ peac 和平 ＋ e 名詞字尾

peace [pis] 名 和平；（心的）平靜；（社會）治安；秩序

延伸片語 to find inner peace 尋找內在的平靜

▶ My yoga teacher said that one should find our inner peace in order to acquire spiritual and physical balance.
我的瑜珈老師說，我們應該要找到自己內心的平靜，來達到身心靈的平衡。

表
示
情
緒
、
認
知
、
抽
象
事
物

❷ pac 和平 **＋ if ＋ ic** 形容詞字尾

pacific [pə`sɪfɪk] 形 和解的；愛好和平的；溫和的；平靜的

延伸片語 **the Pacific Ocean** 太平洋

▶ A war between the two coastal countries has broken out on the Pacific Ocean.
太平洋上的兩個沿海國家爆發了一場戰爭。

- -

❸ peac 和平 **＋ e** 名詞字尾 **＋ time** 名詞字尾，表示時間

peacetime [`pis⸝taɪm] 名 平時、和平時期

延伸片語 **during peacetime** 在和平時期期間

▶ The three countries agreed to remain a certain level of economic collaboration during peacetime.
這三個國家同意在和平時期維持一定程度的經濟合作關係。

- -

❹ peac 和平 **＋ e** 名詞字尾 **＋ keep** 保留；維持 **＋ er** 名詞字尾，表示人

peacekeeper [`pis⸝kipɚ] 名 和平維護者；維和士兵

延伸片語 **to be the world's peacekeeper** 為世界的和平維護者

▶ The United States usually claims itself to be the world's peacekeeper.
美國常自稱是這世界的和平使者。

- -

❺ peac 和平 **＋ e** 名詞字尾 **＋ ful** 形容詞字尾，表示充滿

peaceful [`pisfəl] 形 平靜的；和平的；愛好和平的

延伸片語 **to take part in a peaceful protest** 參加和平抗議

▶ My friends, families, and I decided to take part in a peaceful protest regarding freedom and democracy this Saturday.
我的朋友、家人、跟我都決定週六要去參加自由民主的和平抗議。

延伸補充自然學

☆ **pacify**	和平 ＋ 動詞字尾	動 使平靜，使安靜，撫慰；平定
☆ **peaceless**	和平 ＋ 形容詞字尾，表示缺乏	形 無和平的；不安詳的

根 dyn, dynam 力量

Marvin: Have you ever heard of the Tang dynasty?	馬文：你有聽過唐朝嗎？
Marcus: Yep. I know that it was a rather dynamic era, be it economically or culturally.	馬克斯：聽過，不管在經濟或文化上，都是個很強勢的朝代。
Marvin: The dynasts were open-minded, and comparatively able to embrace multi-cultural interactions. Also, Tang dynasty was known for beauties!	馬文：統治者都很開明，也能夠接受跨文化的交流。而且，唐朝也以美女出名！
Marcus: That I also heard of! Besides, I once read in a book that they liked to use dynamite to demolish old buildings and created new ones.	馬克斯：我也聽說過！此外，我曾經讀過相關記載說他們喜歡用炸藥來摧毀老舊建築再蓋新的。
Marvin: Really? I think we need to do more background research about that.	馬文：真的嗎？我覺得我們需要對這做更進一步的研究了。
Marcus: Anyway, Tang dynasty had already been recognized as a dynastic power that outdid other adjacent countries.	馬克斯：總之，唐朝已經被視為超越其他鄰近國家的統治勢力了。
Marvin: That's for sure.	馬文：當然。

 單字解析零距離

❶ dyn 力量 ＋ **ast** 人 ＋ **ty** 名詞字尾

dynasty [ˈdaɪnəstɪ] 名 王朝；朝代

延伸片語 the XXX ruler of the dynasty 朝代的第X位統治者

▶ His father was the first ruler of the dynasty back in 1920, and was raised and educated well.
回溯到1920年，他父親是當朝第一位首領，所受的教育及教養都很好。

表示情緒、認知、抽象事物

② **dynam** 力量 ＋ **ic** 形容詞字尾

dynamic [daɪˋnæmɪk] 形 力的；動力的；力學的；有活力的

延伸片語 **to create a dynamic atmosphere** 創造一個有活力、有生氣的氣氛

▶ A host is supposed to create a dynamic atmosphere and make sure everything runs smoothly.
一位主持人應該要創造一個活潑的氣氛並確保細節順利進行。

. . . .

③ **dyn** 力量 ＋ **ast** 人 ＋ **ic** 形容詞字尾

dynastic [daɪˋnæstɪk] 形 王朝的

延伸片語 **to witness dynastic changes** 目睹王朝的轉變

▶ My grandparents witnessed dynastic changes and always talked about the good old days.
我祖父母皆目睹了朝代的改變且總是在談論那些美好的回憶。

. . . .

④ **dynam** 力量 ＋ **ite** 名詞字尾，此表示製品

dynamite [ˋdaɪnəˌmaɪt] 名 炸藥；【口】具有爆炸性的事；具有潛在危險的人（或物）

延伸片語 **to blow up sth with a dynamite** 用炸藥炸毀某物

▶ My father blew up the barn at the back yard with a dynamite.
我爸爸用炸藥炸毀了後院的穀倉。

. . . .

⑤ **dynas** 力量 ＋ **t** 名詞字尾，表示做動作的人

dynast [ˋdaɪnəst] 名 統治者（尤指世襲的）

延伸片語 **the (name of the dynasty) dynast** （某朝代的）統治者

▶ The Tang dynast dedicated to broadening maritime trade with neighboring countries. 唐朝的統治者致力於擴展與鄰國的海上貿易。

💡 延伸補充 **自然學**

☆ **dynamics**	力量 ＋ 名詞字尾，表示學科；學術	名 動力學；動力；變遷過程
☆ **dynamo**	力量 ＋ 名詞字尾	名 發電機；電動機

根 **phil** 愛

💬 情境對話試水溫

Oliver:	There are so many people going into the philanthropy business now. Isn't it weird?	奧利佛：現在有好多人都投入慈善事業。你不覺得很奇怪嗎？
Jack:	Weird? How?	傑克：奇怪？怎麼說？
Oliver:	The economy isn't good now; if there are more people living with another identity as philanthropists, that means social classes are diverging wider than ever.	奧利佛：現在經濟不景氣；如果還有這麼多人又同時以慈善家身分在生活；那就代表貧富差距比以前更大。
Jack:	But maybe we should focus on the fact that rich people can be also philanthropic?	傑克：可是或許我們應該把重點放在有錢人也可以有慈善的心？
Oliver:	Trust me. It's a means of evading taxes. To them, it represents a philosophy to make more money.	奧利佛：相信我。這只是逃稅的一種方法而已。對他們來說，那代表賺更多錢的哲學。
Jack:	Wealthy people are supposed to love money, huh?	傑克：有錢人就是愛錢，對吧？
Oliver:	Of course, and we should just continue to be bibliophiles.	奧利佛：當然，我們應該當藏書家。
Jack:	What?	傑克：什麼意思？
Oliver:	That means people who love books!	奧利佛：愛書的人！

 單字解析零距離

❶ **phil** 愛 ＋ **anthrop** 人 ＋ **y** 名詞字尾

philanthropy [fɪˈlænθrəpɪ] 名 慈善事業

延伸片語 **to be known for one's philanthropy** 以其慈善事業聞名的

Ch 2

Part 1

Part 2

Part 3

Part 4

表示情緒、認知、抽象事物

▶ My father not only has a high reputation as a professor, but is also known for his philanthropy.
我爸爸不只是位名望很高的教授，同時也是以他的慈善出名。

❷ **phil** 愛 ＋ **anthrop** 人 ＋ **ist** 名詞字尾，表示人

philanthropist [fɪˈlænθrəpɪst] 名 慈善家

延伸片語 to be funded by a philanthropist 由一位慈善家資助的

▶ This Academy funded by a philanthropist and received the money for the construction. 這個學院得到慈善家贊助因而籌得建造資金。

❸ **phil** 愛 ＋ **anthrop** 人 ＋ **ic** 形容詞字尾

philanthropic [ˌfɪlənˈθrɑpɪk] 形 慈善的；樂善好施的（尤指透過捐款幫助窮人）

延伸片語 to establish a philanthropic organization 創辦一個慈善組織

▶ My mother hopes to establish a philanthropic organization to help more people. 我媽媽想要成立一個慈善機構來幫助更多人。

❹ **philo** 愛 ＋ **sophy** 名詞字尾，表示知識

philosophy [fəˈlɑsəfɪ] 名 哲學；哲理；人生觀

延伸片語 a philosophy of life 人生哲學

▶ Each one of us possesses a philosophy of life that differs from one another, but somehow also merges together.
我們每個人都有不同的人生哲學，但又不知怎麼也都融合在一起。

❺ **biblio** 書 ＋ **phil** 愛 ＋ **e** 名詞字尾

bibliophile [ˈbɪblɪəˌfaɪl] 名 愛書的人；愛收藏書的人

延伸片語 to call oneself a bibliophile 稱自己為愛書的人

▶ My sister always calls herself a bibliophile and enjoys spending time in the library. 我姐姐總是自稱愛書人，享受待在圖書館的時間。

💡 延伸補充 **自然學**

☆ **phil**harmonic　愛 ＋ 和諧 ＋ 形容詞字尾　　形 愛樂的
☆ **phil**ology　　　愛 ＋ 名詞字尾，表示學科、學術 名 語言學；文獻學

尾  phobia 恐懼

情境對話試水溫

Jacob: Do you want to go bungee jumping with me?	雅各：你想要跟我去玩高空彈跳嗎？
Harry: Nah. I'll pass. I have acrophobia.	哈利：不了，不用了。我有懼高症。
Jacob: Right. And I have hydrophobia. C'mon. You're fine on the suspension bridge, aren't you?	雅各：我還有懼水症呢，少來，你走吊橋就不怕，不是嗎？
Harry: That's two very different things, okay? It's like being able to going into a small warehouse doesn't mean you don't have claustrophobia.	哈利：這根本是兩回事好嗎？就像你就算能走進小倉庫也不代表你沒有幽閉恐懼症。
Jacob: Fine. But what about xenophobia? Is one person going to avoid foreigners the whole lifetime? That's absurd!	雅各：好吧。那外國人恐懼症呢？一生都要避開外國人嗎？太荒謬了！
Harry: If it's possible, why not? Think about a person having nyctophobia. He couldn't escape nighttime!	哈利：如果可以的話，為什麼不行？像有黑暗恐懼症的人，他就避不掉夜晚！
Jacob: You're helpless!	雅各：你很沒用！

 單字解析零距離

1 **acro** 頂端；高處 ＋ **phobia** 恐懼

acrophobia [ˈækrəˈfobɪə] 名 懼高症

延伸片語 **to be troubled by acrophobia** 有懼高症的困擾

▶ My little brother is troubled by acrophobia, and it keeps him from going on to the suspension bridge all the time.
我弟弟受懼高症所苦，一直以來都讓他無法克服走吊橋的障礙。

Ch 2

Part 1

Part 2

Part 3

Part 4

表示情緒、認知、抽象事物

❷ hydro 水 **＋ phobia** 恐懼

hydrophobia [ˌhaɪdrəˋfobɪə] 名 恐水症

延伸片語 **to suffer from hydrophobia** 深受恐水症之苦

▶ If you suffer from hydrophobia, scuba diving may not be a suitable option for you.
如果你患有懼水症，潛水可能對你不是一個好選擇。

· ·

❸ claustro 關閉；幽閉 **＋ phobia** 恐懼

claustrophobia [ˌklɔstrəˋfobɪə] 名 幽閉恐懼症

延伸片語 **to give someone claustrophobia** 使某人幽閉恐懼症發作

▶ The dark and little room at the end of the hall way had started to give me claustrophobia and I just wanted to run away.
在走廊盡頭的暗處以及小房間已經開始讓我幽閉恐懼症發作，我只想逃離這裡。

· ·

❹ xeno 外來 **＋ phobia** 恐懼

xenophobia [ˌzɛnəˋfobɪə] 名 恐外症；對外國人（或外國習俗、宗教等）的憎惡（或恐懼）

延伸片語 **the phenomenon of xenophobia** 恐外症的症狀

▶ Generally, our generation did not witness the beginning of the phenomenon of xenophobia.
一般來說，我們這一代沒有參與到排外現象的起源。

· ·

❺ nycto 夜；暗 **＋ phobia** 恐懼

nyctophobia [ˌnɪktəˋfobɪə] 名 （精神分析）黑夜恐懼症

延伸片語 **to be racked with nyctophobia** 深受黑夜恐懼症折磨

▶ My mom, turning 40, is now oftentimes racked with nyctophobia and has a hard time falling asleep.
我媽媽快40歲，現在經常受黑夜恐懼症困擾且很難入眠。

💡 延伸補充 **自然學**

☆ **arachnophobia**	蜘蛛 + 恐懼	名 蜘蛛恐懼症
☆ **monophobia**	單一；孤獨 + 恐懼	名 孤獨恐懼症
☆ **germophobia**	細菌；發芽 + 恐懼	名 細菌恐懼症；潔癖

根 the(o) 神

情境對話試水溫

Charlie: I've always wanted to go to the Pantheon. I heard it's magnificent.	查理：我一直想要去萬神殿看看，聽說很壯觀。
Thomas: I thought you're an atheist?	湯瑪士：我以為你是無神論者？
Charlie: Well, believing in atheism doesn't mean you can't appreciate mythological figures, right?	查理：嗯，相信無神論並不代表你不能欣賞神話人物呀，對吧？
Thomas: That's true.	湯瑪士：說的也是。
Charlie: You? I heard that you're now studying some sort of ... theology, right?	查理：你呢？聽說你正在研究某種……神學？是嗎？
Thomas: Yes. In fact, I'll going to become a theologist after I graduate.	湯瑪士：對，實際上，我畢業後會當神學家。
Charlie: Where are you going to work though?	查理：那你會在哪裡工作？
Thomas: Don't worry. My advisor has already procured a position in a college for me. The pay is rather high.	湯瑪士：別擔心。我的導師已經在大學裡幫我找到一個職位，薪水還很高！
Charlie: Good for you!	查理：恭喜你！

單字解析零距離

❶ pan 全部；泛 **＋ theo** 神 **＋ n**

Pantheon [ˈpænθɪən] **名** 萬神廟；諸神殿；偉人祠堂；眾神之廟

延伸片語 to visit the Pantheon 參觀萬神廟

▶ Our family decided to visit the Pantheon this summer vacation.
我家人決定這個暑假要去參訪萬神殿。

Ch 2

Part 1

Part 2

Part 3

Part 4

表示情緒、認知、抽象事物

❷ a 沒有 **+ the** 神 **+ ist** 名詞字尾，表示人

atheist [ˋeθɪɪst] 名 無神論者

延伸片語 **to be a fully-committed atheist** 成為一位十分虔誠的無神論者

▶ After he lost all his families in a car accident, he became a fully-committed atheist.
在車禍中痛失了所有家人後，他就成了完全的無神論者。

- -

❸ a 沒有 **+ the** 神 **+ ism** 名詞字尾，表示主義或行為

atheism [ˋeθɪˏmzəm] 名 無神論

延伸片語 **to embrace atheism** 包容無神論

▶ In this era, there's nothing wrong to embrace atheism, but in the old times, you may get accused and exiled because of it.
在這時代，信奉無神論一點都不奇怪，但在過去，你可能會被指責甚至流放。

- -

❹ theo 神 **+ logy** 名詞字尾，表示學科、學術

theology [θɪˋɑlədʒɪ] 名 神學；宗教理論；宗教體系

延伸片語 **to study theology** 研讀神學

▶ My brother told me that he has decided to study theology and contribute to mankind.
我哥哥告訴我他決定要研究神學並為人類奉獻。

- -

❺ theo 神 **+ log(y)** 名詞字尾，表示學科、學術 **+ ist** 名詞字尾，表示人

theologist [θɪˋɑlədʒɪst] 名 神學家；神學研究者

延伸片語 **to serve as a theologist** 擔任神學家

▶ Many graduates from that Christian Seminary serve as theologists in churches all around Taiwan.
那間基督教神學院中有很多畢業生都在台灣各地的教堂擔任神學家。

💡 延伸補充**自然學**

☆ **monotheism**	單一 + 神 + 主義或行為	名 一神論；一神教
☆ **polytheism**	多 + 神 + 主義或行為	名 多神教；多神論
☆ **theocracy**	神 + 統治；支配	名 神權政治；僧侶政治；神權國家

根 therm 熱

情境對話試水溫

Connor: Do you know that we're going on an expedition this summer?

康納：你知道我們這個夏天要去探險嗎？

Oscar: Yes, I know. It's a big one. We're going to measure...the thermal...

奧斯卡：我知道，是個大活動。我們要去測量……熱……

Connor: The thermal expansion.

康納：熱膨脹。

Oscar: Yes. You're so smart. How can I live without you?

奧斯卡：對！你好聰明，沒有你我該麼辦？

Connor: That's also why I need to remind you to prepare the thermos, the thermometer, and thermostat for this activity. It could be very dangerous. We're going to climbing up and down with lots of gears.

康納：所以我才要提醒你活動要準備保溫瓶、溫度計跟恆溫器。活動會很危險，要背很多裝備爬上爬下。

Oscar: I know. Thanks. I'm aware that it could get really cold at night. Some even died of hypothermia.

奧斯卡：我知道，謝謝。我知道晚上會變很冷，有些人甚至死於低溫。

Connor: A careless person like you needs to extra careful, okay?

康納：像你這樣粗心的人需要更小心好嗎？

Oscar: I know!

奧斯卡：我知道！

單字解析零距離

❶ **therm** 熱 ＋ **al** 形容詞字尾，有……性質的

thermal [ˈθɝml] 形 熱的；熱量的；溫泉的

延伸片語 to visit the thermal valley 參觀地熱谷

Ch 2

Part 1

Part 2

Part 3

Part 4

表示情緒、認知、抽象事物

▶ Many tourists went to Beitou to visit the thermal valley.
很多遊客都去北投參觀地熱谷。

❷ therm 熱 **＋ os** 名詞字尾

thermos [ˈθɝməs] 名 熱水瓶；保溫瓶

延伸片語 **to carry a thermos around** 隨手攜帶保溫瓶

▶ I always carry a thermos around in case I need to drink water.
我總是隨身攜帶保溫瓶確保我在需要時隨時有水喝。

❸ thermo 熱 **＋ meter** 名詞字尾，表示測量

thermometer [θɚˈmɑmətɚ] 名 溫度計

延伸片語 **to adjust a thermometer** 調整溫度計

▶ Adjusting a thermometer is necessary for measurement precision. 調整溫度計對於測量的準確度來說是必要的。

❹ thermo 熱 **＋ stat** 名詞字尾，表示直立

thermostat [ˈθɝməˌstæt] 名 自動調溫器；恆溫器

延伸片語 **to employ a thermostat** 使用自動調溫器

▶ Many inventors now employ a thermostat that can detect even the slightest changes in temperature to ensure the stability and quality of a produce. 很多發明家現在都使用恆溫計，它能夠偵測到最細微的溫度變化，確保產品的穩定性及品質。

❺ hypo 在……下方；低於 **＋ therm** 熱 **＋ ia** 名詞字尾，表示疾病

hypothermia [ˌhaɪpəˈθɝmɪə] 名 低體溫症

延伸片語 **to die from hypodermia** 死於低體溫症

▶ Many mountain climbers died from hypothermia not because they didn't protect themselves enough, but because the weather is way too unpredictable. 很多登山客都死於失溫並非因為防護措施不夠，而是因為天氣實在是太難預測。

延伸補充 自然學

☆ **electrothermal**	與電相關的＋熱＋形容詞字尾	形 電熱的
☆ **geothermal**	地＋熱＋形容詞字尾	形 地熱的
☆ **isothermal**	同等＋熱＋形容詞字尾，有……性質的	形 等溫的

尾 ache 疼痛

William:	I'm having a serious headache for almost a week now.
Ethan:	Are you okay?
William:	And this headache comes with a severe backache. I feel like I can't either walk or sit.
Ethan:	That sounds terrible. But at least you didn't have a stomachache. Then you wouldn't be able to sleep as well.
William:	As a matter of fact, I do also have a mild stomachache, and toothache. I can't eat!
Ethan:	Guess what. I think you're just having a heartache from the breakup. YOU ARE FINE.
William:	How could you say that? Take me to the hospital!

威廉：我已經嚴重頭痛幾乎一個星期了。

伊森：你還好嗎？

威廉：我的頭痛還伴隨嚴重的背痛。我覺得我沒辦法站或坐。

伊森：聽起來很糟。但是至少你沒有胃痛。不然你甚至會睡不好。

威廉：事實上，我的確為有點痛，還有牙痛。我根本不能吃！

伊森：我覺得你只是分手後心痛而已，你什麼事都沒有。

威廉：你怎麼這樣說話？帶我去醫院！

單字解析零距離

❶ head 頭 **＋ ache** 疼痛

headache [ˋhɛd͵ek] 名 頭痛

延伸片語 **to suffer from chronic headaches** 深受慢性頭痛之苦

▶ My mom suffers from chronic headaches and needs prescriptions to ease her pain.
我媽媽受慢性頭痛所苦，且需要處方來減緩疼痛。

表示情緒、認知、抽象事物

②　back 背＋**ache** 疼痛

backache [ˈbækˌek] 名 背痛

延伸片語 **to diagnose the cause of backache** 診斷背痛的起因

▶ The doctor said that he needed to diagnose the cause of backache my father has been suffering.
醫生說他需要診斷我父親背痛的原因。

• •

③　stomach 胃＋**ache** 疼痛

stomachache [ˈstʌməkˌek] 名 胃痛；腹痛

延伸片語 **to get rid of stomachache** 擺脫胃痛

▶ Our teacher taught us some tips to get rid of stomachache.
我們老師教我們幾個小妙招來擺脫胃痛。

• •

④　tooth 牙齒＋**ache** 疼痛

toothache [ˈtuθˌek] 名 牙痛

延伸片語 **to kill a toothache** 消除牙痛

▶ This video shows you how to kill a toothache with scientifically-proven methods.
這影片教你如何用科學證實的方法來終止胃痛。

• •

⑤　heart 心＋**ache** 疼痛

heartache [ˈhɑrtˌek] 名 痛心；悲痛

延伸片語 **to cure a heartache** 治癒心痛

▶ Do you know that sometimes, it is impossible to cure a heartache? 你知道有時候，要治療心痛是不可能的嗎？

延伸補充 自然學

與 ache 近義的字首：agon

☆ **agony**　　疼痛＋名詞字尾　　　　　　　名 極度痛苦；苦惱

與 ache 近義的字首：alg（多為醫學用法）

☆ **arthralgia**　關節＋疼痛＋名詞字尾，表示疾病　名 關節痛

chapter3

根 **spect** 看

情境對話試水溫 🎧 *Track 065*

Molly: I love the way Ms. Liu guided us to make use of conspectus methodology in writing collection development.	莫莉：我很喜歡劉老師引導我們利用大綱方法論來寫館藏發展的做法。
Chelsea: I once attend a speech given by her, and it drew thousands of spectators. I respect her so much because she makes efforts to not only academic research but environmental protection.	雀兒喜：我之前參加過她的演講，吸引了超多觀眾。我非常尊敬她，因為她不只在學術研究上著力，也致力於環境保護。
Molly: My professor is inviting her to give a speech to us at the end of this semester. I'm so excited about the prospect of it! I heard that Ms. Liu's book will publish this summer, and her team is inspecting the contents for errors and typos.	莫莉：我教授邀請她學期末來跟我們演講，我超級期待！我聽說劉老師的新書這個夏天要發行了，她的團隊正在檢察內容的錯誤與誤植。
Chelsea: Lots of things to do this summer. It's quite an amazing journey in retrospect.	雀兒喜：這個夏天好多事情哦！回想起來真的是趟驚喜的旅程。
Molly: True.	莫莉：真的！

 單字解析零距離

❶ con 一同 **＋ spect** 看 **＋ us** 物品

conspectus [kən`spɛktəs] 名 要領

延伸片語 conspectus methodology 大綱方法論

▶ The conspectus methodology plays an important role in

Ch 3

Part 1

表示五官動作

Part 2

Part 3

Part 4

collection development and collection evaluation.
大綱方法論在館藏發展及館藏評鑑中佔有重要地位。

② in 內、裡 ＋ spect 看

inspect [ɪn`spɛkt] 動 視察

延伸片語 inspect...for... 為……進行審查

▶ The doctor inspected the patient carefully for lesions.
醫生為尋找病灶仔細檢查病人。

③ pro 往前 ＋ spect 看

prospect [`prɑspɛkt] 名 前景

延伸片語 prospect of... 對……的期盼

▶ The prospect of giving a public speech makes me nervous.
一想到要上台演說我就緊張。

④ re 再 ＋ spect 看

respect [rɪ`spɛkt] 動 尊敬

延伸片語 in respect of 關於

▶ The job is good in respect of its salary. 這份工作的薪水很好。

⑤ retro 往後 ＋ spect 看

retrospect [`rɛtrəˌspɛkt] 名 回溯

延伸片語 in retrospect 回顧；追溯往事

▶ Their marriage life seems pretty unhappy in retrospect.
他們的婚姻生活回想起來似乎很不幸福。

⑥ spect 看 ＋ ator 人

spectator [spɛk`tetɚ] 名 目擊者

延伸片語 spectator sport 群眾愛看的運動

▶ Baseball is a spectator sport in Taiwan.
棒球在台灣是一個群眾愛看的運動。

延伸補充 自然學

| ☆ despise | 往下看 | 動 瞧不起 |
| ☆ despicable | 讓人看不起的 | 形 低劣的 |

根 vis, vid 看

💬 情境對話試水溫

Sabrina: Do you believe that visual content is more impactful than texts?

莎賓娜：你覺不覺得看視覺元素的內容會比看文字更具影響力？

Tanya: Actually, I think reading texts can help the mind create visions that are just as powerful.

坦雅：其實，我覺得單看文字讓腦海裡創造出來的畫面更有力量。

Sabrina: But visible images, for example, videos, are more direct.

莎賓娜：但像是影片這類的視覺媒體比較能直接傳達內容。

Tanya: For me, the magic of texts lies in its flexibility. By revising paragraphs or simply by substituting one word with another, you create a whole new scenario that is not visible to the eyes but the mind.

坦雅：對我來說，文字的魅力在於其靈活度，透過段落修改或是簡單的替換單字，就可以產生一個眼睛看不見的但心看的見的場景。

⚡ 單字解析零距離

❶ vis 看 **+ ual** 形容詞字尾

visual [ˋvɪʒuəl] 形 視覺的

延伸片語 **visual art** 視覺藝術

▶ The National Palace Museum is having a special exhibition of visual arts. 國立故宮博物館正在辦一場視覺藝術的特展。

• •

❷ vis 看 **+ ion** 名詞字尾

vision [ˋvɪʒən] 名 視覺；視力；所見的人事物

Ch 3

Part 1

Part 2

Part 3

Part 4

表示五官動作

延伸片語 **have visions of** 幻想，憧憬

▶ When I watch Korean drama, I always have visions of me getting married to those attractive and wealthy entrepreneurs.
我在看韓劇時，總是會幻想嫁給那些帥氣又有錢的企業家結婚。

- -

❸ vid 看 **+ eo**

video [ˈvɪdɪo] 名 影像

延伸片語 **video camera** 攝影機

▶ Hidden video cameras that are set up in public toilets are causing wide-spread panic in the Korean society.
那些安裝在公廁裡的針孔攝影機正引起韓國社會大眾的恐慌。

- -

❹ re 再度 **+ vise** 看

revise [rɪˈvaɪz] 動 修改

延伸片語 **revise the law** 修法

▶ The legislators have vowed to revise the law in favor of those disadvantaged. 這些立法委員立誓要修法支持弱勢族群。

- -

❺ vis 看 **+ ible** 形容詞字尾，表示可能、可以的

visible [ˈvɪzəbl] 形 可看見的

延伸片語 **visible to** 可看見的

▶ These tiny insects that are hardly visible to the naked eye have sparked ecological disaster.
這些小到肉眼幾乎看不見的昆蟲引起了生態災害。

延伸補充 自然學

☆ **provident**	時間與空間上較前 + 看 + 形容詞字尾	形 有先見之明的；深謀遠慮的；節儉的
☆ **evident**	向外 + 看 + 形容詞字尾	形 明顯的；明白的

首 audi, audit 聽

情境對話 試水溫

Frank: Guess what? The company has reserved an entire music hall in the National Auditorium for the finance department to enjoy an orchestra concert tonight.

法蘭克：嘿！這間公司竟然為了財務部門包下國家體育館的整個音樂廳讓大家可以享受今晚的管絃音樂會。

Adam: Only the finance department? I am assuming all the auditors will be going then. I heard that Nancy is quite an expert when it comes to the audio equipment. Her family runs a live sound product business.

亞當：只為了財務部？我以為所有審計員都可以參加。講到音效設備，聽說南西是專家，他家在開音響公司。

Frank: Then she will definitely hold a high standard for the sound quality tonight.

法蘭克：那今晚的音樂會她絕對會用高標準檢視。

Adam: You bet, though I personally couldn't care less about the audio effect as long as it's audible. At the end of the day, it's the FREE concert that matters.

亞當：當然，雖然我自己對音效要求不高，只要聽得見就可以。重點是，今天最後就是免費的音樂會了。

Frank: True. Forget about work and just enjoy the show with the rest of the audience. Have a good night!

法蘭克：是阿，拋開工作只要專心跟觀眾一起享受音樂就好。希望一切順利！

單字解析 零距離

❶ audit 聽 ＋ **orium** 名詞字尾，表示專業場所

auditorium [ˌɔdə`torɪəm] **名** 聽眾席；觀眾席；會堂

Ch 3
Part 1
表示五官動作
Part 2
Part 3
Part 4

延伸片語 an auditorium with a seating capacity of 可容納⋯⋯人的劇院／音樂廳

▶ With a seating capacity of 3 million people, The Redemption Camp is the world's biggest church auditorium.
救主堂是全世界最大的教堂，可容納三百萬人。

❷ **audit** 聽 + **or** 名詞字尾，表示人

auditor [ˋɔdɪtɚ] 名 查帳員，稽核員，審計員

延伸片語 auditor general 審計長

▶ The auditor general of our country was sentenced to 10 years in prison. 我國的審計長判入監服刑10年。

❸ **audi** 聽 + **o**

audio [ˋɔdɪo] 形 聽覺的，聲音的

延伸片語 audio system 音響設備

▶ This car is outfitted with a state-of-the-art audio system.
這台車配備最新的音響設備。

❹ **audi** 聽 + **(i)ble** 形容詞字尾，表示可能、可以的

audible [ˋɔdəbl] 形 可聽見的，聽得見的

延伸片語 make an audible sound 發出聽的到的聲音

▶ She hinted at my open fly by making an audible sound and pointing at my crotch.
她發出細微的聲音，指著我的褲襠來暗示我拉鍊沒拉。

❺ **audi** 聽 + **ence** 名詞字尾

audience [ˋɔdɪəns] 名 聽眾，觀眾

延伸片語 a large / small audience 很多／很少觀眾

▶ I get butterflies in my stomach when giving a speech in front of a large audience. 當我在很多觀眾面前演講的時候，我非常緊張。

延伸補充 自然學

| ☆ **inaudible** | 否；無 + 聽 + 形容詞字尾，表示可能、可以的 | 形 聽不見的；無法聽懂的；不可聞的 |
| ☆ **audibility** | 聽 + 名詞字尾，表示可⋯⋯性 | 名【物】可聞度；（聲音的）清晰度 |

根 ton(e) 聲音

Track 068

情境對話試水溫

Anderson: I'm so tired of my monotonous life routine.

安德森：我對於一成不變的生活真心感到厭煩！

Bill: What about joining some clubs, like chorus?

比爾：要不要加入一些社團？像是合唱團之類的？

Anderson: You don't know I'm poor at singing?? Singing and intoning with musical intonation are only dreams for me. I can only sing atonal music in my life.

安德森：你不知道我超不會唱歌嗎？吟唱悅耳的音調對我來說就是夢一場。我只能唱沒有調性的音樂。

Bill: That's ridiculous!

比爾：你很誇張欸！

Anderson: Any tonal music will end in disaster because of me.

安德森：任何有音調的音樂在我這裡就會變成災難。

單字解析零距離

❶ **a** 沒、無 ＋ **ton** 聲音 ＋ **al** 形容詞字尾

atonal [eˋtonl] 形 （音）不成調性的

延伸片語 **atonal music** 無調性音樂

▶ Atonal music is hardly pleasant to the ear because it lacks of melody.
無調性音樂因缺乏旋律而不悅耳。

❷ **in** 入內 ＋ **ton** 聲音 ＋ **ation** 名詞字尾

intonation [ˌɪntoˋneʃən] 名 聲調

延伸片語 **musical intonation** 悅耳的語調

Ch 3

Part 1

Part 2

Part 3

Part 4

表示五官動作

▶ The children recite the poems with musical intonation.
孩童們以悅耳的語調朗誦詩歌。

・・・・・・・・・・・・・・・・・・・・・・・・・・・・・・・・・・・

❸ in 入內 ＋ **tone** 聲音

intone [ɪnˈton] 動 詠唱
延伸片語 **intone the anthem** 吟詠讚美詩

▶ Everyone was overwhelmed by the beautiful voice intoning the anthems.
所有人都被吟詠讚美詩的美麗歌聲感動得不得了。

・・・・・・・・・・・・・・・・・・・・・・・・・・・・・・・・・・・

❹ ton 聲音 ＋ **al** 形容詞字尾

tonal [ˈtonl] 形 音調的
延伸片語 **a tonal language** 有音調的語言

▶ A tonal language such as Chinese is difficult for a foreigner to learn.
像中文這樣有音調的語言，對外國人來說很難學。

・・・・・・・・・・・・・・・・・・・・・・・・・・・・・・・・・・・

❺ mono 單一 ＋ **ton** 聲音 ＋ **ous** 形容詞字尾

monotonous [məˈnɑtənəs] 形 單調的、沒變化的
延伸片語 **monotonous diet** 單調的飲食

▶ He is sick of the monotonous diet in the desert.
他厭倦了沙漠中的單調飲食。

延伸補充 自然學

☆ **baritone**	重的 ＋ 聲音	名 男中音
☆ **overtone**	超過範圍的 ＋ 聲音	名 泛音
☆ **semitone**	半的 ＋ 聲音	名 （音樂）半音程
☆ **undertone**	底下的 ＋ 聲音	名 潛在的含義

根 **son** 聲音

 情境對話試水溫

🎧 *Track 069*

Emma:	I thought it was a disaster when I first heard Eddie's playing Beethoven moonlight sonata.
Betty:	Haha! Your view was consonant as mine. Especially when he played the sonata in a hall, the hall was resonated with dissonant chord and noise. Just can't believe he's holding his music concert next month. He has made a huge progress.
Emma:	Chris will be the special guest in the concert. He will sing with Eddie. He has a deep sonorous voice.
Betty:	I bumped into Eddie's cousins this morning, and I invited them to the concert. They answered okay in unison in one second.
Emma:	Just can't wait!

艾瑪：我第一次聽艾迪演奏貝多芬月光奏鳴曲時，我認為那是一場災難。

貝蒂：哈哈！你的想法跟我一樣，尤其當他是在禮堂裡演奏，整個禮堂都充滿了不和諧的和弦跟噪音，簡直無法相信他下個月要舉辦自己的音樂會了！他真的進步好多。

艾瑪：克里斯會擔任他音樂會的特別來賓，他們會一起合唱，他有很渾厚響亮的嗓音。

貝蒂：我今早恰巧碰見艾迪的表弟們，我邀請他們去音樂會，他們一秒齊聲答應。

艾瑪：等不及啦！

單字解析零距離

❶ con 共同 ＋ **son** 聲音 ＋ **ant** 形容詞字尾

consonant ['kɑnsənənt] 形 一致的

延伸片語 **voiceless consonant** 無聲子音

▶ "p" is a voiceless consonant while "b" is a voiced consonant.
「p」是無聲子音，而「b」是有聲子音。

Ch 3

Part 1

表示五官動作

Part 2

Part 3

Part 4

② **dis** 不、否 ＋ **son** 聲音 ＋ **ant** 形容詞字尾

dissonant [ˈdɪsənənt] 形 不一致的

延伸片語 **dissonant chord** 不和諧的和弦

▶ The dissonant chords that he's playing sound really uncomfortable. 他彈出的不和諧和弦聽起來真不舒服。

. . . .

③ **re** 回、返 ＋ **son** 聲音 ＋ **ate** 使

resonate [ˈrɛzəˌnet] 動 （使）回響

延伸片語 **resonate with something** 充滿

▶ The whole church was resonated with the beautiful sound of the choir's singing. 整個教堂充滿了唱詩班的美麗歌聲。

. . . .

④ **son** 聲音 ＋ **ata** 曲子

sonata [səˈnɑtə] 名 奏鳴曲

延伸片語 **piano sonata** 鋼琴奏鳴曲

▶ Jennifer played a piano sonata to entertain the guests after dinner. 珍妮佛在晚餐後彈了一曲鋼琴奏鳴曲以饗賓客。

. . . .

⑤ **son** 聲音 ＋ **orous** 形容詞字尾

sonorous [səˈnorəs] 形 （聲音）響亮的

延伸片語 **sonorous voice** 聲音響亮

▶ She has a deep and sonorous voice. 她的聲音渾厚響亮。

. . . .

⑥ **uni** 統一 ＋ **son** 聲音

unison [ˈjunəsn] 名 齊奏

延伸片語 **in unison** 一致行動

▶ It was the first time that the two organizations worked in unison. 那是第一次這兩個組織行動一致。

延伸補充 **自然學**

☆ **super**sonic   超越 ＋ 聲音 ＋ 形容詞尾   形 超音速的

153

根claim 喊叫、聲音

情境對話試水溫

Sofy: Do you know the world-acclaimed art work, the twelve Chinese Zodiac statues?

蘇菲：你知道飽受國際讚譽的藝術品，十二生肖的雕像嗎？

Patty: Yes, they were originally on display in Yuanmingyuan until 1860 when they were snatched away by the foreign invaders.

佩蒂：知道，最初都在圓明園展示，直到西元1860年被一群外國竊賊偷走。

Sofy: I was watching a documentary about the statues and can't help but exclaimed with surprise at how finely those statues were made.

蘇菲：我之前在看這部紀錄片，才很訝異，覺得這些雕像做工非常精細。

Patty: The Chinese government should really take a strong stance and reclaim what were theirs.

佩蒂：中國政府真的應該要展現強硬的立場，奪回這些資產。

Sofy: I heard that some collectors have showed great sense of justice and proclaimed that they will return the statues to China unconditionally.

蘇菲：我聽說有些收藏家還是有正義感的，並聲稱會無條件將手中雕像還給中國。

Patty: Ultimately, the Chinese government has the claim to those artworks.

佩蒂：但最後中國政府仍有權利處理這些雕像。

單字解析零距離

❶ ac 朝向 ＋ **claim** 喊叫

acclaim [ə'klem] 勔 稱讚

Ch 3

Part 1

表示五官動作

Part 2

Part 3

Part 4

延伸片語 **be acclaimed for** 因……備受讚譽

▶ The director is acclaimed for this poetic imagery in his latest film. 這位導演因在其新作中的詩意意象而備受讚譽。

- -

❷ **ex** 向外 + **claim** 喊叫

exclaim [ɪksˋklem] 動 驚叫

延伸片語 **exclaim with** （帶……的情緒）驚叫

▶ I exclaimed with excitement when my boyfriend proposed to me. 男友向我求婚時我興奮地驚叫。

- -

❸ **re** 再 + **claim** 喊叫、聲音

reclaim [rɪˋklem] 動 收回

延伸片語 **reclaim the throne** 奪回王位

▶ The ousted prince has pledged to reclaim the throne and restore the country to its former glory.
這位被驅逐的王子承諾將奪回王位並恢復昔日國家輝煌。

- -

❹ **pro** 時間與空間上較前 + **claim** 喊叫

roclaim [prəˋklem] 動 聲明

延伸片語 **proclaim that** 宣佈；宣佈；聲明

▶ He proclaimed in his speech that the company will go public in due course. 他在演講中聲明，這家公司將在適當的時間點上市。

- -

❺ **claim** 喊叫、聲音

claim [klem] 動 （根據權利）要求；認領；索取；自稱；聲稱 名 權利

延伸片語 **have claim on...** （對某事物的）權利；所有權

▶ A wife is not her husband's property; in others words, the husband has no claim on her. 婚姻關係中，妻子並非其丈夫資產；也就是說，這位丈夫並不擁有對他妻子的所有權。

💡 延伸補充 **自然學**

claim的變化型：clam

✫ **clamor**　　喊叫的狀態　　　　　　　名 喧鬧

根 ed, vo(u)r 吃

情境對話試水溫

🎧 *Track 071*

Sandy: Did you see that plate of vegetable on the table? I've never seen that kind before... I wonder if they are edible.	珊蒂：你有看到桌上那盤蔬菜嗎？我從沒見過這種菜，不知道能不能吃。
Mandy: I think they are. There were two plates of them and I saw Hank devour one of them just 10 minutes ago.	曼蒂：應該可以，原本有兩盤，我看到漢克十分鐘前狼吞虎嚥地吃掉了其中一盤。
Sandy: That can't really prove anything. You know what a voracious eater Hank can be. He probably paid little attention to what was going down his throat.	珊蒂：這算什麼。你很清楚漢克多愛吃。也許他根本不知道自己吞下什麼東西。
Mandy: I am just happy that he's not carnivorous. With that kind of appetite, he could make half of the planet's animal go extinct.	曼蒂：好險他不是吃肉的，不然像他這樣的食量，會讓這星球上一半的動物都絕種。
Sandy: True. Sometimes it seems like nothing is inedible to him.	珊蒂：真的，有時候我都覺得沒有什麼是他不能吃的。

單字解析零距離

❶ ed 吃＋ **ible** 形容詞字尾，表示可……的

edible [ˈɛdʒəbl] 形 可食用的

延伸片語 **edible plant** 可食性植物

Ch 3

Part 1

表示五官動作

Part 2

Part 3

Part 4

▶ When I go hiking with my Dad, he'd often show me where the edible plants are.
我跟我爸去健行的時候，他常告訴我那些是可食性植物。

② **de** 除去＋**vour** 吃

devour [dɪˋvaʊr] 動 狼吞虎嚥地吃

延伸片語 **devour greedily** 貪婪地吃

▶ As soon as the bug got trapped in the web, the spider devoured it greedily.
一旦蟲子被困在網子上，蜘蛛就會立刻狼吞虎嚥地吃了牠。

③ **vor** 吃＋**acious** 形容詞字尾，表示有……性質的

voracious [voˋreʃəs] 形 狼吞虎嚥的

延伸片語 **voracious appetite** 貪吃；食量大

▶ In order to lose weight, one must first learn to suppress his/her voracious appetite.
為了減肥，他／她首先必須要學會克制自己的大食量。

④ **carni** 肉＋**vor** 吃＋**ous** 形容詞字尾，表示充滿的

carnivorous [karˋnɪvərəs] 形 肉食的

延伸片語 **carnivorous animal** 肉食動物

▶ A carnivorous animal is one that eats the flesh of other animals.
肉食性動物指的是會吃其他動物肉的食肉動物。

⑤ **in** 表否定＋**ed** 吃＋**ible** 形容詞字尾，表示可……的

inedible [ɪnˋɛdəbl] 形 無法食用的

延伸片語 **inedible mushroom** 不能吃的蘑菇

▶ Inedible mushrooms are mostly poisonous, with some being fatal.
不能吃的蘑菇通常都有毒，甚至有些會致命。

延伸補充 自然學 學

☆ **carnivore** 肉＋吃 　　　　　 名 食肉動物
☆ **omnivorous** 全部；泛＋吃＋形容詞字尾， 形 雜食的；什麼都讀的
　　　　　　　　 表示充滿的

根 spir(e) 呼吸

💬 情境對話試水溫

🎧 *Track 072*

Naomi:	My grandma finally had senior checkup, including bone marrow aspirated. She had been feeling ill for days, but unwilling to see a doctor.	娜奧美：我的祖母終於做了老年健檢，包含了骨隨穿刺。她已經身體不舒服好多天了，但一直不願意去看醫生。
Kyle:	Why was she reluctant to have health checkup?	凱爾：為什麼她不願意做健康檢查？
Naomi:	She had white coat hypertension – getting extremely anxious, nervous, and hands perspiring whenever she sees a doctor.	娜奧美：她有白袍症，每次看醫生會極度焦慮、緊張，而且手冒汗。
Kyle:	Did you check her health checkup report with the doctor?	凱爾：你跟醫生看過檢查報告了嗎？
Naomi:	Yes, we did. It's leukemia... My grandma was clam when she heard this. She aspired to fully recover from the illness for accompanying her little grandson, Den, to grow up. We all had a big respire of relief when hearing her saying.	娜奧美：有，是白血症……祖母聽到的時候很冷靜，她想要痊癒，因為要陪伴她的小孫子，班班一起長大。我們聽到以後都鬆了一口氣。
Kyle:	You should inspire her to stay positive and build cooperative doctor/patient relationship. Let me know if you need any assistance. I'm with you and your grandma in spirit.	凱爾：你們應該鼓舞他積極面對而且建立好醫生病人的合作關係，有任何需要幫忙的務必讓我知道，我與你以及祖母精神同在！

Ch 3

Part 1

表示五官動作

Part 2

Part 3

Part 4

單字解析零距離

1 **a** 向、朝 ＋ **spir** 呼吸 ＋ **ate** 使……成為

aspirate [ˈæspəˌret] **動** 吐氣

延伸片語 **bone marrow aspirate** 骨髓穿刺

▶ The doctor determined to have the patient's bone marrow aspirated in order to make correct diagnosis.
為了做正確的診斷，醫生決定為病人做骨髓穿刺。

- -

2 **a** 向、朝 ＋ **spire** 呼吸

aspire [əˈspaɪr] **動** 嚮往

延伸片語 **aspire to** 渴望

▶ When you're young, you aspire to wealth; when you're old, you aspire to health. 年輕時渴望財富；年老時渴望健康。

- -

3 **spir** 呼吸 ＋ **it** 走動

spirit [ˈspirit] **名** 靈魂

延伸片語 **spirit up** 鼓舞

▶ We need to keep our spirits up to believe we could win out!
我們要保持高昂的心情相信我們會勝出！

- -

4 **in** 往內 ＋ **spire** 呼吸

inspire [ɪnˈspaɪr] **動** 激發靈感

延伸片語 **inspire ... in someone** 使人產生某種感覺

▶ The encouraging letter from his father inspired confidence in John. 父親所寫的鼓勵信件激起了約翰的信心。

- -

5 **per** 全部 ＋ **spire** 呼吸

perspire [pəˈspaɪr] **動** 出汗

延伸片語 **hand perspire** 手出汗

▶ That his hands perspire bothers him. 手會出汗這件事讓他很困擾。

- -

6 **re** 再 ＋ **spire** 呼吸

respire [rɪˈspaɪr] **動** 呼吸

延伸片語 **a respire of relief** 鬆一口氣

▶ Peter had a big respire of relief when he passed the exam.
彼得通過考試時，大大的鬆了一口氣。

💬 情境對話**試水溫**

🎧 *Track 073*

Marvin: Have you heard that the jury had reached a verdict of guilty?	馬文：你有聽說陪審團已判決有罪了嗎？
Alice: Which case? The Anderson case?	艾莉絲：哪個案子？安德森案？
Marvin: Yes, but I think the defendant's current testimony contradicted greatly with his previous one.	馬文：對，但我覺得前後證詞不一。
Alice: Then we can predict that the judgment may be overruled?	艾莉絲：所以我們可以預測這案子會被駁回嗎？
Marvin: I'm not sure. The man had been indicted with similar charges before. I guess the decision is final.	馬文：我不確定。這個人之前有被起訴過類似的案，我想結果應該不會變。
Alice: Maybe the jury had their own concerns. I mean, we were not present in the court session.	艾莉絲：也許陪審團有他們的考量。我是說，我們又不在場。
Marvin: I know. If my doctor dictated that I could be discharged from hospital then, I would know more details!	馬文：我知道。如果我的醫生當時口頭決定讓我出院的話，我就能知道更多細節了。
Alice: C'mon. Rest now, will you?	艾莉絲：拜託。你先好好休息，好嗎？

⚡ 單字解析**零距離**

❶ **ver** 真實 ＋ **dict** 說、言

verdict ['vɜdɪkt] 動 定論

延伸片語 **pass one's verdict upon** 對……下判斷

表示說話、語言

▶ I don't think it's right to pass your verdict upon people by appearance. 我認為你以貌取人是不對的。

❷ contra 相反 **＋ dict** 說、言

contradict [ˌkɑntrəˈdɪkt] 動 抵觸

延伸片語 contradict oneself 自相矛盾

▶ If it contradicts itself, then it is unbelievable.
如果自相矛盾，那它就是不可信了。

❸ pre 先、前 **＋ dict** 說、言

predict [prɪˈdɪkt] 動 預言

延伸片語 predict the weather 預測天氣

▶ Can you predict the weather through the clouds?
你能通過雲來預測天氣嗎？

❹ in 往內 **＋ dict** 說、言

indict [ɪnˈdaɪt] 動 控告

延伸片語 indict a person for murder 以殺人罪起訴某人

▶ He might indict that young man for murder.
他可能會以殺人罪起訴那個年輕人。

❺ dict 說、言 **＋ ate** 動詞字尾，使……變成

dictate [ˈdɪktet] 動 口述

延伸片語 dictate to one's secretary 向秘書口述要事

▶ The general manager is dictating to his secretary now.
總經理正在向他的秘書口述要事。

延伸補充 自然學

dict的變化型：dic

☆ **valediction**   再見的話語   名 告別演說

☆ **dictator**   口頭傳授命令的人   名 獨裁者

☆ **benediction**   好的 ＋ 語言   名 祝福

☆ **abdicate**   使之離開的命令   動 退位

根 lingu 語言、舌頭

Mandy:	How's your second-language learning going?	曼蒂：你的第二外語學得怎樣？
Nick:	Pretty smoothly. I think I've made great progress toward my dream of becoming a well-known linguist!	尼克：還蠻順利的。我覺得我又離夢想更近一步了，就是要當一個有名的語言學家。
Mandy:	But I heard that you failed linguistics last term...	曼蒂：但我聽說你上學期語言學被當了⋯⋯
Nick:	Well, that was an accident. You know how talented I am.	尼克：好吧，那是意外。你知道我是很有才華的。
Mandy:	I surely do, but one's linguistic ability may drop if efforts are not made.	曼蒂：我當然知道，但如果沒有持續努力，每個人的語言能力可能都會退步。
Nick:	You're just jealous that I'm multilingual.	尼克：你只是忌妒我會很多語言吧。
Mandy:	Listen to yourself...I'm not lending you my notes anymore.	曼蒂：我聽不下去了⋯⋯我不要借你筆記了。
Nick:	C'mon! I'm just joking with you! I'm only bilingual!	尼克：拜託！我跟你鬧著玩的！我只會說雙語！
Mandy:	Get over yourself!	曼蒂：省省吧！

單字解析零距離

1 lingu 語言 ＋ **ist** 名詞字尾，表示人

Ch 3

Part 1

Part 2

Part 3

Part 4

表示說話、語言

linguist [ˈlɪŋgwɪst] 名 語言學者

延伸片語 a linguist 一位語言學者

▶ I want to be a linguist in the future. 我將來想成為一位語言學者。

- -

② **lingu** 語言 ＋ **ist** 人 ＋ **ics** 名詞字尾，表示學說、知識

linguistics [lɪŋˈgwɪstɪks] 名 語言學

延伸片語 the study of linguistics 語言學研究

▶ My brother decided to pursue the study of linguistics after he discovered the beauty of language.
我哥哥自從發現語言的美之後，便決定要繼續語言學的研究。

- -

③ **multi** 多 ＋ **lingu** 語言 ＋ **al** 形容詞字尾

multilingual [ˈmʌltɪˈlɪŋgwəl] 形 使用多種語言的

延伸片語 to use a multilingual platform 使用多種語言的平台

▶ Due to the great number of international students in our class, we have to use a multilingual platform to finish our final exam.
我們必須使用一個多語言的平台來完成期末考試，因為我們班上有很多交換學生。

- -

④ **lingu** 語言 ＋ **ist** 名詞字尾，表示人 ＋ **ic** 形容詞字尾

linguistic [lɪŋˈgwɪstɪk] 形 語言學的

延伸片語 linguistic form 語言型態

▶ Bob was studying linguistic form last night.
包柏昨晚在研讀語言型態。

- -

⑤ **bi** 雙 ＋ **lingu** 語言 ＋ **al** 形容詞字尾

bilingual [baɪˈlɪŋgwəl] 形 雙語的

延伸片語 bilingual education 雙語教育

▶ Julia decided to send her daughter to the bilingual education school. 茱莉亞決定將他女兒送去雙語教育學校。

延伸補充 自然學

☆ **trilingual** 三＋形容詞字尾，語言的 形 三種語言的

☆ **monolingual** 單一 ＋ 語言 ＋ 形容詞字尾，……的 形 單語的；僅懂一種語言的

根  liter 字母

情境對話 試水溫

Nancy: How do you enjoy our literature class?	南西：你文學課上的如何？
Ellie: Pretty good. But I'm having a hard time understanding some of the poems mentioned in today's class.	艾利：蠻好的。但我不太理解今天上的詩。
Nancy: You mean the metaphors, alliterations, and all those stuff?	南西：你是說隱喻、押頭韻這些東西嗎？
Ellie: Yep. I can't quite grasp the core of the meanings.	艾利：對。我不太能抓到這些重點。
Nancy: Well, you can't approach poetry literally. You have to obliterate prejudice and judgment, and immerse yourself into the situation the author created.	南西：恩，你不能單從字面上來看。你必須要先抹除掉偏見跟評斷，讓自己沉浸在作者創造的情境中。
Ellie: What does that even mean?	艾利：什麼意思？
Nancy: It means that in order to really enter the literary world, you have to get rid of presumptions, and think about why this word is used instead of the other.	南西：也就是說為了要讓你真的進入到文學的世界，你必須要拋開所有假設，思考作者使用每個詞的理由。
Ellie: I'm dropping out of this class.	艾利：我要棄修了。

 單字解析 零距離

❶ liter 字母 **+ ature** 名詞字尾

literature [ˈlɪtərətʃɚ] 名 文學；文學作品

Ch 3
Part 1
Part 2
Part 3
Part 4

表示說話、語言

延伸片語 modern literature 現代文學
▶ He's very keen about modern literature.
他很熱衷於現代文學。

❷ **al** 朝向 **+ liter** 字母 **+ ation** 名詞字尾，表示行動

alliteration [əˌlɪtə`reʃən] 名【語】頭韻（法）
延伸片語 the use of alliteration 頭韻的使用
▶ The brilliance of this poem lies in the use of alliteration and imageries. 這首詩的亮點在於它頭韻的使用及意象。

❸ **liter** 字母 **+ ary** 形容詞字尾 **+ ly** 副詞字尾

literally [`lɪtərəlɪ] 副 逐字地；照字面地；正確地；實在地
延伸片語 to be literally over the moon 欣喜若狂
▶ Our whole family were literally over the moon when we knew we won the lottery! 當得知我們中了樂透時，全家人都欣喜若狂。

❹ **ob** 反 **+ liter** 字母 **+ ate** 動詞字尾使……成為

obliterate [ə`blɪtəˌret] 動 消滅；忘掉；忘卻
延伸片語 to obliterate memories 忘卻回憶
▶ Many people wish to obliterate memories, especially the painful ones. 許多人都希望能夠抹除記憶，特別是那些受過傷害的人。

❺ **liter** 字母 **+ ary** 形容詞字尾，……領域的

literary [`lɪtəˌrɛrɪ] 形 文學的
延伸片語 literary film 文藝片
▶ Jack says actually he doesn't like to see literary film with his girlfriend. 傑克說其實他不喜歡陪他女朋友一起看文藝片。

延伸補充 自然學

☆ **literate**	字母 + 形容詞字尾，有……性 形 有讀寫能力的質的
☆ **illiterate**	否定 + 字母 + 形容詞字尾，有……性質的 形 文盲的；未受教育的；知識淺陋的
☆ **literacy**	字母 + 名詞字尾，表示性質 名 識字；讀寫能力；知識

根 loqu, log, logue 說

情境對話試水溫

Peggy: Are you excited about the play we're going to see?

佩姬：你對我們待會要看的劇，有很興奮嗎？

Allen: Of course! I've wanted to watch that famous soliloquy for a long time!

艾倫：當然！我一直都想要看那段有名的獨白！

Peggy: And the prologue! It's said that the art director made several adjustment to the previous one, and we are about to see a theatre design that makes good use of technology.

佩姬：還有序幕！聽說藝術總監調整了很多地方，我們將會看到一場充滿科技感的劇院設計。

Allen: That would certainly enhance the brilliance of the dialogue as well. The lines are known for natural images.

艾倫：那一定也會為這些對白增添很多亮點。這些台詞都是以自然圖像聞名的。

Peggy: We do can expect that. I wonder how the eulogy made by the King is going to be presented. Imaging the transition of the damp and dark forest to the moor!

佩姬：精彩可期。我很好奇國王的頌辭會怎麼被詮釋。還有從潮濕又黑暗的森林到停泊中間的轉換。

Allen: Wait, I think we should look that the catalogue here... What? We got the time wrong!

艾倫：等等，我覺得我們應該要看一下表演目錄。什麼？我們弄錯時間了啦！

單字解析零距離

❶ soli 單一的 **＋ loqu** 說 **＋ y** 名詞字尾

soliloquy [sə`lɪləkwɪ] 名 自言自語

延伸片語 **soliloquy of spirit** 心靈的獨白

表示說話、語言

▶ Hamlet's soliloquy of spirit is my favorite part of this book.
哈姆雷特心靈獨白那一段是這本書中我最愛的部分。

---

❷ pro 時間或空間上較前的 **＋ logue** 說、言

prologue [ˋproˌlɔg] 名 序言

延伸片語 to be the prologue to... ……的序言

▶ The sorrow of bereavement was the prologue to this play.
喪親之痛是這部劇的序幕。

---

❸ dia 穿越；跨越 **＋ logue** 說、言

dialogue [ˋdaɪəˌlɔg] 名 對話；交談；（戲劇、小說等中的）對話；對白

延伸片語 the dialogue between A and B　A與B之間的對話

▶ We saw the live broadcast of the final dialogue between the government officials and the host of the march.
我們昨晚看了政府官方與示威主導人之間最後對談的直播。

---

❹ eu 美好的 **＋ log** 說、言 **＋ y** 名詞字尾

eulogy [ˋjulədʒɪ] 名 頌辭

延伸片語 God's eulogy　神的讚頌

▶ There is a book full of God's eulogy in this museum.
這間博物館裡有一本書滿載神的讚頌。

---

❺ cata 下方 **＋ logue** 說、言

catalogue [ˋkætəlɔg] 名 （圖書，商品等的）目錄；目錄冊

延伸片語 to design a catalogue　設計型錄

▶ If you want to open a restaurant, the first thing you need to do is to design a catalogue.
如果你想要開餐廳，首先你需要先設計菜單目錄。

💡 延伸補充 自然學

☆ **analogy**　　　　相同＋說、言＋名詞字尾　　名 相似、類似
☆ **monologue**　　　單一＋說、言　　　　　　名 獨白
loqu的變化型：locu
☆ **circumlocution**　圓＋說、言＋名詞字尾　　名 說話婉轉

根 mot 動

情境對話試水溫

🎧 *Track 077*

Lily: I think Peter let his emotions control him again. His motive of bringing up this proposal is absurd.

莉莉：我覺得彼得又得又被他的情緒控制了。他提出這項案子的動機很荒謬。

Benson: What can I say? He always makes a commotion about nothing.

班森：我能説什麼？他總是可以把沒有的事搞出一場風波。

Lily: I wish he could stop being such a troublemaker. Everytime he walks past me, I pay attention to his every motion. I'm afraid that he's going to critize me again.

莉莉：我希望他可以停止當一個麻煩製造者。每次他經過我，我都會注意他的所有動作。我就怕他又要開始批評我。

Benson: Last time, I was rearragning my locomotive models, and he said "Why spent money on this?" And started bragging about how he managed his earnings.

班森：上次，我在整理我的火車頭模型，然後他説「幹嘛花錢在這東西上？」然後就開始自吹自擂自己是怎麼理財。

Lily: I seriously can't stand him. I need to vote against the proposal.

莉莉：我真的無法忍受他。這個案子我要投反對票。

單字解析零距離

① e 外 + mot 動 + tion 名詞字尾

emotion [ɪ'moʃən] 名 情緒

延伸片語 with emotion 感慨地、富情感地

Ch 3

Part 1

Part 2

Part 3

Part 4

表示四肢動作

▶ The graduate representative delivered a speech of thanks with emotion. 畢業生代表感慨地致感謝詞。

● ●

❷ mot 動 **+ ive** 有～的傾向

motive [`motɪv] 名 動機

延伸片語 motive power 原動力

▶ Water and wind can both be used as motive powers to drive machinery.
水及風都能被用來作為驅動機器的原動力。

● ●

❸ com 共同 **+ mot** 動 **+ tion** 名詞字尾

commotion [kə`moʃən] 名 騷動

延伸片語 make a commotion about nothing 無理取鬧

▶ Jason's wife is making a commotion about nothing again.
傑森的老婆又在無理取鬧了。

● ●

❹ mot 動 **+ ion** 名詞字尾

motion [`moʃən] 名 動作

延伸片語 of one's own motion 出於自願

▶ The little boy donated all his savings of his own motion.
小男孩出於自願地捐出了他所有的積蓄。

● ●

❺ loco 地方、地點 **+ mot** 動 **+ ive** 有～的傾向

locomotive [ˌlokə`motɪv] 名 火車頭

延伸片語 steam locomotive 蒸氣火車頭

▶ The Museum of Transport is having an exhibition of steam locomotives.
交通博物館正推出蒸氣火車頭展覽。

💡 延伸補充 自然學

mot 的變化型：mote

☆ **demote**	往下移動	動 降級
☆ **promote**	向上移動	動 提升；宣傳
☆ **remote**	返、再 + 移動	形 遠的

根 scrib 寫

💬 情境對話試水溫

🎧 *Track 078*

Melissa: Holly just got the admission notice delivered by the best university of her city. She ascribed all of this to her incredibly hard work. She described her senior life as sheer hell. She arranged a tight study schedule and strictly forced herself to follow it for circumscribing any slackness. No social life, no party, no leisure time.

瑪莉莎：荷莉收到城裡最好大學的錄取通知了！她把這些歸因於極努力的付出。她形容她的高三生活就是一個全然的地獄。她安排了超級滿的讀書行程，逼著自己依據時程讀書，杜絕任何怠惰。沒有社交生活、沒有派對、沒有休閒時間。

Phoebe: Actually…I don't really subscribe to this way of studying. Though entering a dream university is crucial, she should also enjoy her life as a senior high school student.

菲比：事實上……我並不同意她這種讀書方法，雖然進入好大學十分重要，但她也應該享受她的高中生活。

Melissa: Her parents said so, but no one can prescribe to her what to do.

瑪莉莎：他父母也這樣說，但沒人能指使她做任何事。

Phoebe: The saying: "Eat, Drink, Drunk for tomorrow we die." is always inscribed in my mind.

菲比：「在死之前吃吧！喝吧！醉吧！」這句一直刻在我心裡。

Melissa: Ummm…and maybe that's why you failed in your final exam.

瑪莉莎：痾……這大概也是為什麼你期末考不及格吧。

⚡ 單字解析零距離

❶ a 朝向 **+ scribe** 寫

ascribe [əˋskraɪb] 動 將……歸因於

延伸片語 **ascribe something to** 將某事歸因於……

Ch 3

Part 1

Part 2

Part 3

表示四肢動作

Part 4

▶ Most scientists ascribe the climate change to global warming.
大部分科學家將氣候變遷歸因於地球暖化。

② **circum** 周圍 ＋ **scribe** 寫

circumscribe [ˈsɝkəmˌskraɪb] 勔 限制

延伸片語 circumscribe a circle 外切圓

▶ The teacher is demonstrating how to circumscribe a circle.
老師正在示範如何做一個外切圓。

③ **de** 加強 ＋ **scribe** 寫

describe [dɪˈskraɪb] 勔 描述　　延伸片語 describe... as... 將……稱為……

▶ The man described his wife as a battleaxe.
那個男人把他的老婆形容為悍婦。

④ **in** 裡面 ＋ **scribe** 寫

inscribe [ɪnˈskraɪb] 勔 題寫；刻；牢記

延伸片語 inscribe... to/ for... 將……題獻給某人

▶ The author inscribed his new book to his parents.
作家將他的新書題獻給他的雙親。

⑤ **pre** 先、前 ＋ **scribe** 寫

prescribe [prɪˈskraɪb] 勔 （開）處方　延伸片語 prescribe for 為某人開藥方

▶ The doctor cannot prescribe for you until he knows what your problem is. 醫生要知道你的問題所在才能幫你開藥方。

⑥ **sub** 在……底下 ＋ **scribe** 寫

subscribe [səbˈskraɪb] 勔 訂閱　　　　延伸片語 subscribe to 同意；支持

▶ I don't subscribe to your point of view. 我不同意你的看法。

延伸補充 自然學

與 scrib 近義的字尾：-script

☆ **postscript**　　後來才寫上的　　　名 附錄

☆ **manuscript**　　親手寫的東西　　　名 原稿

尾 graph 紀錄、書寫

情境對話 試水溫

Annie: I went to the dance room the other day to meet Alice and she was choreographing for a new performance. Her moves totally dazzled me! I wish I had a camera to take a photograph of her at the moment.

安妮：我前幾天在舞蹈室看見愛麗絲，她正在為新表演編舞。她的動作完全吸引到我！如果當時手上有一台相機可以把那一刻拍照下來就好了。

Peter: I know! She's absolutely amazing. One time I was watching her practicing and then realized art can come in so many different forms. It can be static like a lithograph or mobile like dancing.

彼得：我懂！她真的很棒。有一次我在看她練習，我才了解藝術原來可以用這麼多種面向呈現。靜態的像是石板畫，動態的就以舞蹈為例。

Annie: Indeed, I once read a monograph written by a highly respected art professor. In that was a paragraph that described the versatility of art and I cannot agree with it more.

安妮：沒錯，我曾經讀過一位名望很高的教授的著作，其中一段就在描述藝術的多樣性，我非常同意。

單字解析 零距離

❶ **chor** 唱、跳 + **eo** + **graph** 紀錄、書寫

choreograph [ˈkɔrɪəˌɡræf] 動 為……編舞

延伸片語 choreograph a dance 編舞

▶ Betty is in charge with choreographing a new jazz dance for her clients.
貝蒂負責幫她的客戶編一段新爵士的舞蹈。

Ch 3

Part 1

Part 2

Part 3

Part 4

表示四肢動作

❷ photo 光 **+ graph** 紀錄、書寫

photograph [ˈfotəˌgræf] 名 照片

延伸片語 **take a photograph** 拍照

▶ Paris is such a beautiful place that most tourists would take millions of photographs before leaving the city.
巴黎是個美到大多數觀光客在離開前都會拍幾百萬張照片的地方。

• •

❸ litho 石質的 **+ graph** 紀錄、書寫

lithograph [ˈlɪθəˌgræf] 名 平版印刷

延伸片語 **make a lithograp** 做平版印刷畫

▶ There are classes in town that teach people how to make a lithograph in two hours.
城裡有開一些課，教大家如何在兩小時內創作出一幅平版印刷畫。

• •

❹ mono 單一 **+ graph** 紀錄、書寫

monograph [ˈmɑnəˌgræf] 名 專題論文；專題著作

延伸片語 **a monograph on** 關於……的專著

▶ Dr. Lee dedicated all his life to writing a monograph on the poems of Shakespeare.
李博士的一生都致力於寫關於莎士比亞詩作的專題。

• •

❺ para 旁邊；並列 **+ graph** 紀錄、書寫

paragraph [ˈpærəˌgræf] 名 （文章的）段；節

延伸片語 **concluding paragraph** 結尾段落

▶ A well-structured article usually involves a powerful concluding paragraph that reiterates the central argument.
通常一篇結構完整的文章包含一段有力的結尾段落，以重申主要論點。

延伸補充 自然學

與 graph 近義的字根：gram

✡ **telegram**　　　距離遙遠；在遠處 + 紀錄、書寫　　名 電報

✡ **cardiogram**　　心 + 紀錄、書寫　　名 心電圖

根 ject 投擲、丟

情境對話試水溫

Sam: Did you see how dejected Adam is? I wonder what happened to him.

山姆：你有看見亞當多沮喪嗎？不曉得發生什麼事。

Suzy: You know the multibillion project he's been working on since a year ago? He was removed from it this morning and will be returning to his original post starting next week.

蘇西：你知道他去年開始持續在做一個高達數十億美金的專案嗎？他今天早上從專案中被除名，下禮拜開始回去接他原本的案子。

Sam: How does that happen? Only a month ago he told me he's probably getting a promotion soon.

山姆：怎麼會發生這種事？上個月才聽他説他可能會升職。

Suzy: Well...rumor has it that he presented a terrible proposal last week. Apparently the clients think most of his research was unfounded and that his recommendations are mainly based on conjecture.

蘇西：嗯……聽説他上星期提了一個很爛的提案。很明顯這客戶覺得他大部分的研究沒有根據，而給的提議都只是猜測。

Sam: That must have been really embarrassing for him.

山姆：他一定覺得很尷尬。

Suzy: Indeed it was. Some colleagues who were present told me the clients kept interjecting with harsh comments and questions throughout his speech and in the end rejecting every single idea Adam had proposed.

蘇西：絕對是，有些在場的同事也説客戶在提案中一直插嘴，用很嚴厲的評論來刁難、質疑他，最後還拒絕了亞當提出的每個想法。

Ch 3

Part 1

Part 2

Part 3

表示四肢動作

Part 4

 單字解析零距離

1 **de** 向下 ＋ **ject** 投擲、丟

dejected [dɪ'dʒɛkt] 形 沮喪

延伸片語 **in a dejected tone** 用沮喪的語氣講

▶ "My dad is admitted into the hospital," he said in a dejected tone. 他用沮喪的語氣講：「我爸爸住院了。」

· ·

2 **pro** 時間與空間上較前的 ＋ **ject** 投擲、丟

project [prə'dʒɛkt] 名 計畫

延伸片語 **abandon the project** 放棄計畫

▶ They couldn't find enough sponsors and had to abandon the project. 他們因找不到足夠的贊助商而必須放棄這計畫。

· ·

3 **con** 一起；共同 ＋ **ject** 投擲、丟 ＋ **ure** 名詞字尾

conjecture [kən'dʒɛktʃɚ] 動 猜測

延伸片語 **make conjectures on** 對⋯⋯做猜測

▶ I loatch making conjectures on other people's intentions. 我厭惡對他人的意圖做臆測。

· ·

4 **inter** 中間 ＋ **ject** 投擲、丟

interject [ˌɪntɚ'dʒɛkt] 動 插話

延伸片語 **interject in a conversation** 在談話中插話

▶ It is considered extremely inappropriate to interject in a conversation. 在對談中插話被視為是一個非常不恰當的事情。

· ·

5 **re** 反對 ＋ **ject** 投擲、丟

reject [rɪ'dʒɛkt] 動 拒絕；抵制；去除；丟棄

延伸片語 **reject suggestion** 拒絕建議

▶ The city mayor rejected suggestion that he should run for president. 市長拒絕了競選總統的提議。

延伸補充自然學

☆ **inject** 往內 ＋ 投擲、丟 動 注射

 根 cept 拿取

情境對話試水溫

Track 081

Sophia: I heard all the students in Frankie's class, except him, got accepted into NTU.

蘇菲亞：我聽説法蘭克班上，除了他自己之外，全都錄取台大了？

Jackson: I am not even surprised. They've all been straight-A students since elementary school.

傑克森：我沒有很意外，他們從國小開始就全都是學霸。

Sophia: But I can't help but feel sorry for Frankie. He's a very versatile student who has achievements in many different areas, including music, sports, just to name a few.

蘇菲亞：但我對法蘭克覺得很遺憾，他在很多領域都很有很好的成績，像是音樂、體育等等。

Jackson: True, the university admission committee should embrace the new concept that grades do not define an individual.

傑克森：是呀，入學委員會應該要嘗試接受「成績不代表一切」的新概念。

Sophia: Characters are more important. There have been cases of honor students getting involved in both petty offenses like deception and serious crimes like murder.

蘇菲亞：人格特質重要多了，有很多資優生也會涉嫌一些像是詐欺的輕罪甚至是謀殺之類的重刑。

Jackson: Sadly, people tend to believe they are innocent and make exceptions for them only because they excel academically.

傑克森：可悲的是，民眾總會因為他們功課很好就相信他們無罪甚至認為這只是例外。

單字解析零距離

1 ac 朝向 ＋ cept 拿取

Ch 3

Part 1

Part 2

Part 3

表示四肢動作

Part 4

accept [ək`sɛpt] 動 接受、同意

延伸片語 **accept the offer** 接受提議、工作邀約

▶ I accepted the offer from Louis Vuitton and will heat to Paris to work in the headquarters. 我接受了LV的約聘，將出發去巴黎總部上班。

- -

② **ex** 向外 ＋ **cept** 拿取

except [ɪk`sɛpt] 介 除……外

延伸片語 **except the fact that** 除了……之外

▶ He has always been a caring husband, except the fact that he will go nuts when drunk. 他是個體貼的丈夫，除了會發酒瘋之外。

- -

③ **con** 共同 ＋ **cept** 拿取

concept [`kɑnsɛpt] 名 概念；觀念；思想

延伸片語 **the concept of** ～的觀念

▶ The concept of feminism has become widely accepted now. 女性主義的觀念現在已被廣泛地接受。

- -

④ **de** 向下 ＋ **cept** 拿取 ＋ **ion** 名詞字尾

deception [dɪ`sɛpʃən] 名 欺騙；欺詐

延伸片語 **practice deception on** 欺騙某人

▶ Some immoral insurance sales agent would practice deception on the elderly and cheat them into buying plans they don't need.
有些沒道德的保險業務會欺騙老人，騙他們買下他們不需要的方案。

- -

⑤ **ex** 向外 ＋ **cept** 拿取 ＋ **ion** 名詞字尾

exception [ɪk`sɛpʃən] 名 例外；例外的人（或事物）

延伸片語 **make exception for** 替……做例外

▶ My professor made an exception for me to take oral exams only. 我的教授准許我例外只參加口試。

延伸補充 自然學

cept的變化型： ceive

| ✩ **receive** | 再度＋拿取 | 動 收到 |
| ✩ **deceive** | 向下＋拿取 | 動 欺騙 |

根 **tort** 扭曲

🗨 情境對話試水溫

🎧 *Track 082*

Alex:	Why do you always distort my words? It's such a torture to talk to you.	艾歷克斯：為什麼你總是要曲解我的話？跟你說話真是種折磨。
Mandy:	Seriously? You spit out those harmful words first!	蔓蒂：你認真的嗎？是你先口出惡言的！
Alex:	That's because you kept retorting and arguing with me.	艾歷克斯：那是因為你一直反駁還和我爭論。
Mandy:	You're unbelievable. You should go look into the mirror and see how your face is contorted with pretentiousness!	蔓蒂：真是不可置信。你應該去照照鏡子，看看你的臉是如何因自負扭曲！
Alex:	Are you serious? Your explanations are certainly more tortuous.	艾歷克斯：你是認真的嗎？你的解釋還真是比較婉轉！

 單字解析零距離

❶ **dis** 離開 ✛ **tort** 扭曲

distort [dɪsˈtɔrt] 動 扭曲

延伸片語 distort the facts 歪曲事實

▶ What he said to you totally distorted the facts.
他對你說的話完全不是事實。

Ch 3

Part 1

Part 2

Part 3

Part 4

表示四肢動作

② **tort** 扭曲 + **ure** 行為

torture [ˈtɔrtʃɚ] 動 折磨

延伸片語 **under torture** 受到酷刑、折磨

▶ Frank confessed to false charges under torture.
法蘭克被屈打成招。

- -

③ **re** 再 + **tort** 扭曲

retort [rɪˈtɔrt] 動 反駁

延伸片語 **retort pouch** 真空殺菌調理包；蒸煮袋

▶ The food company makes a fortune by selling their products in retort pouches.
該食品公司以調理包販售他們的產品而發了大財。

- -

④ **con** 一起 + **tort** 扭曲

contort [kənˈtɔrt] 動 扭曲

延伸片語 **to be contorted with fury** 因暴怒而扭曲

▶ The man's face was contorted with fury when he found his son stealing his money.
發現兒子偷錢讓男人的臉因暴怒而扭曲。

- -

⑤ **tort** 扭曲 + **uous** 形容詞字尾

tortuous [ˈtɔrtʃuəs] 形 繞圈子的

延伸片語 **tortuous colon** 曲折的結腸

▶ The doctor uses a colonoscopy to inspect the patient's tortuous colon.
醫生用結腸鏡檢視病人彎彎曲曲的結腸。

💡 延伸補充**自然學**

| ☆ **extort** | 向外 + 扭曲 | 動 敲詐 |
| ☆ **extortioner** | 向外 + 扭曲 + 人 | 名 敲詐的人 |

根 port 拿、帶

Bob:	Did you know that Harry's father is the CEO of the country's biggest trading company?	鮑伯：你知道哈利的爸爸是我們國家最大貿易公司的老闆嗎？
Barbara:	You mean the one that is in charge of importing and exporting 80% of our country's farm goods?	芭芭拉：你是說那間負責我國8成農產品進出口的貿易公司嗎？
Bob:	Exactly. With that much family fortune, Harry could have the whole world at his fingertip.	鮑伯：沒錯。家裡這麼有錢，哈利根本就已經擁有全世界。
Barbara:	Um....I wonder if Harry can help me transport something from abroad..	芭芭拉：恩……不曉得哈利能不能幫我從國外運送一些東西回來。
Bob:	His family runs a serious business, not some illegal trafficking. All the details of their cargo must be reported and registered into the government database. If anything suspicious comes up in the shipment, the whole family could get deported from the country!	鮑伯：他家是正當經營，不是做非法販運的。所有進出口的貨物細節都必須上呈，還要登錄進政府的資料庫。過程中有任何可疑的地方，全家都會被驅逐出境！
Barbara:	Calm down, dude. I was just joking.	芭芭拉：冷靜點，老兄，我開玩笑的。

單字解析零距離

❶ **im** 向內 ＋ **port** 拿、帶

　　import [ˈɪmport] 勔 進口；輸入；引進

Ch 3

Part 1

Part 2

Part 3

表示四肢動作

Part 4

延伸片語 import from 從……進口

▶ All goods imported from the Nuclear-affected areas must be demolished.
從所有受核能影響地區進口的貨物，都必須被銷毀。

- -

② **ex** 向外 **＋ port** 拿、帶

export [ɪksˋport] 動 輸出，出品　　延伸片語 **export trade** 出口貿易

▶ The export trade of the country has decrease exponentially after the civil war. 內戰之後，該國家的出口貿易指數呈倍數下滑。

- -

③ **trans** 穿越 **＋ port** 拿、帶

transport [ˋtræns͵port] 動 運送；運輸；搬運
延伸片語 **transport goods** 運送貨物

▶ According to the report, the truck that caused the severe accident was on its way to tranport goods to the capital.
根據報導，造成此嚴重車禍的貨車正在到首都運送貨物的途中。

- -

④ **re** 往回 **＋ port** 拿、帶

report [rɪˋport] 動 報告；報導　　延伸片語 **report to** 向……匯報

▶ Report to me on the daily basis so that i can be in control of all the details in this project.
請每日向我匯報，以便我掌控此專案的所有細節。

- -

⑤ **de** 遠離 **＋ port** 拿、帶

deport [dɪˋport] 動 驅逐出境　　延伸片語 **deport refugess** 遣返難民

▶ The government refused to provide asylums and are determined to deport refugess. 政府拒絕提供庇護並堅決遣返難民。

⚡ 延伸補充 自然學

☆ **porter**　　拿、帶＋名詞字尾，表示人　　名 （車站，機場等的）搬運工人

☆ **portable**　　拿、帶＋形容詞字尾　　名 便於攜帶的；手提式的；輕便的

根 tract 拉

💬 情境對話試水溫

Robert: The director of HDC Co. Ltd. retracted his statement and refused to contract with us. Kevin tried to convince him but to no avail. The bad news obviously distracted him from the morning meeting. He was not all there.

羅柏：HDC的經理撤回之前的聲明，拒絕和我們簽約。凱文嘗試要說服他但徒勞無功。這壞消息顯然讓他在晨會上分心了，他整個人心不在焉。

Paul: Too bad! We've been working on this project for a while! How come?

保羅：真糟！我們已經在這個專案上努力很久了耶！怎麼會？

Robert: Nobody knows. Kevin's trying to extract information from staff involved.

羅柏：沒人知道為什麼。凱文設法從涉及的人員裡得到資訊。

Paul: Maybe there's another company offering better trade terms for HDC, which attracted them eventually. Therefore, canceling the agreement subtract nothing from them.

保羅：也許是其他公司提供了更好的交易條件，最終吸引了HDC，因此取消跟我們的協議對他們而言也不會造成任何減損。

⚡ 單字解析零距離

① **at** 向 ＋ **tract** 拉

attract [əˋtrækt] 動 吸引

延伸片語 opposites attract 異性相吸

▶ The reason Nathan are with his kooky friends is that opposites attract. 奈森會跟他那些怪朋友在一起乃是出於異性相吸。

Ch 3

Part 1

Part 2

Part 3

Part 4

表示四肢動作

2 **con** 共同＋**tract** 拉

contract [`kɑntrækt] 名 合約

延伸片語 **contract... out** 訂約把……承包出去

▶ In order to meet the deadline, they had to contract the painting work out. 為了趕上交差日期，他們必須把油漆工程承包出去。

- -

3 **dis** 分開＋**tract** 拉

distract [dɪ`strækt] 動 使……分心

延伸片語 **distract... from...** 使從……分心

▶ The noise from the street distracted the boy from his book. 街上的吵鬧聲使男孩無法專心看書。

- -

4 **ex** 往外＋**tract** 拉

extract [ɪk`strækt] 動 提煉

延伸片語 **extract from** 提煉；摘選

▶ The story that he told you was extracted from this book. 他所告訴你的故事是從這本書摘選出來的。

- -

5 **re** 回、返＋**tract** 拉

retract [rɪ`trækt] 動 撤銷

延伸片語 **retract a promise** 食言

▶ It is unwise to believe a man who tends to retract his promises. 相信一個老是食言的人是很愚蠢的。

- -

6 **sub** 在……下面＋**tract** 拉

subtract [səb`trækt] 動 刪減

延伸片語 **subtract from** 從……減去

▶ Subtract seven from twelve and you get five. 十二減七等於五。

延伸補充 自然學

⭐ **tractable**　　　　能夠被拉動的　　　　形 溫馴的

根 turb 攪動

Paige: Candy dropped out of school last week. | 佩姬：坎蒂上星期退學了。

Melissa: I don't want to be mean, but it's such a relief to hear that. Some of her quirky behaviors are really perturbing the class. She looks very disturbed sometimes. | 梅麗莎：我不想當苛薄的人，但這消息讓我鬆了一口氣。她有些奇怪的行為真的讓班上很不安寧，她有時看起來很不正常。

Paige: Last month we were having science class, and then out of nowhere she appeared with a bottle of turbid-looking liquid in her hand and started splashing it onto us. | 佩姬：上個月我們在上自然課的時候，她不知從哪裡冒出來，手上還拿著一瓶混濁的液體，開始潑在我們身上。

Melissa: I remember that. But come to of think it, Terry is quite a weirdo, too. While Candy was causing such a big turbulence, he remained seated and looked undisturbed the whole time! | 梅麗莎：我記得，但講到這個，泰瑞也是個怪人，坎蒂在引起大家恐慌的時候，他都很淡定坐著，一副不為所動的樣子！

Paige: They could be really good friends if Candy didn't drop out. | 佩姬：如果坎蒂沒有輟學的話，他們真的可以當好朋友。

單字解析零距離

❶ dis 分開 **＋ turb** 攪動

disturb [dɪs`tɜb] 動 妨礙；打擾；擾亂；搞亂

Ch 3

Part 1

Part 2

Part 3

Part 4

表示四肢動作

延伸片語 **disturb sb.** 打擾（人）

▶ Ms. Chen is meditating so I would suggest you not to disturb her at this moment.
陳小姐正在冥想，我建議你這時候不要打擾她。

- -

② **turb** 攪動 **+ id** 形容詞字尾，表示……狀態的

turbid [ˈtɜbɪd] 形 混亂的；渾濁的；汙濁的

延伸片語 **go turbid** 變混濁

▶ Decades of pollution have caused the river to go turbid.
數十年來的汙染，導致這條河流變得混濁。

- -

③ **per** 橫過 **+ turb** 攪動

perturb [pɚˈtɜb] 動 使……心煩

延伸片語 **perturb sb.** 使（人）煩惱、擔心

▶ News about the serial killer who has escaped from prison a few days ago is perturbing the neighborhood.
關於那連環殺手前幾天越獄的新聞，使這社區人心惶惶。

- -

④
turb 攪動 **+ ulence** 名詞字尾

turbulence [ˈtɜbjələns] 名 騷動

延伸片語 **political turbulence** 政治動亂

▶ The political turbulence has severely undermined the country's economic growth. 這場政治動亂已經嚴重損害到這國家的經濟成長。

- -

⑤ **un** 否；無 **+ dis** 分開 **+ turb** 攪動 **+ ed** 形容詞字尾

undisturbed [ˌʌndɪˈstɜbd] 形 未受干擾的；未被碰過的

延伸片語 **undisturbed sleep** 安靜的睡眠

▶ Ten hours of undisturbed sleep fully energized him.
十小時寧靜的睡眠已讓他活力充沛。

 延伸補充 自然學

turb的變化形：tumb

☆ **tumble**　　　　被攪動的　　　　名/動 跌倒；摔倒

 根 **cise** 切、割

💬 情境對話試水溫　　　　　🎧 *Track 086*

Betty: Do you know that in some African countries they circumcise teenage girls to keep their virginity?

貝蒂：你知道嗎？在一些非洲國家，他們對青少女執行割禮來保護她們的貞操。

Jessica: That sounds absolutely brutal. I understand that some cultures have their own traditional rituals; for example, some aborigines incise words and patterns onto the body as a concise message to their ancestors. However, no religious or cultural beliefs could justify removing parts from a girls' body without her consent.

潔西卡：聽起來超殘忍，我可以理解有些文化有自己的傳統儀式；例如，有些原住民會在身上刻一些圖騰或文字當作傳遞給他們祖先的一些簡短訊息。但是，沒有任何宗教或文化信仰能夠去證實說未經其同意就奪走一名女孩身上的一部分是合理的事情。

Betty: I guess it's hard for these people to draw the line between precise and imprecise behaviors when it comes to tradition.

貝蒂：提到傳統，我猜這些人很難判斷這些行為是精確的還是不精確的。

⚡ 單字解析零距離

❶ **circum** 周圍 ＋ **cise** 切、割

circumcise [ˋsɝkəmˌsaɪz] 動 割包皮

延伸片語 **get circumcised** 行割禮

▶ The girl got circumcised when she was a baby and has since suffered from serious gynecological problems.
在這女孩還是個嬰兒時，她就被施行割禮，從那時起便一直有嚴重的婦科疾病。

Ch 3

Part 1

Part 2

Part 3

Part 4

表示四肢動作

❷ in 向內 **＋ cise** 切、割

incise [ɪnˋsaɪz] 動 切開；刻；雕

延伸片語 **incise into** 在⋯⋯上面雕刻

▶ The design, which was incised into clay, was considered one of the best art work of the century.
這個黏土上的雕刻設計，被認為是本世紀最棒的藝術作品。

- -

❸ con 共同 **＋ cise** 切、割

concise [kənˋsaɪs] 形 簡明的、簡潔的

延伸片語 **concise arguments** 簡潔的論點

▶ Treat every proposal as an elevator pitch and make your arguments as concise and possible.
簡短地做每個提案，讓你的論點盡可能越簡潔越好。

- -

❹ pre 之前 **＋ cise** 切、割

precise [prɪˋsaɪs] 形 精確的；確切的；明確的；清晰的

延伸片語 **at the precise moment** 就在那一瞬間

▶ She raised her hand and at the precise moment gave his husband a loud slap.
她舉起手，就在那一瞬間，給了她老公一大巴掌。

- -

❺ im 否；無 **＋ pre** 之前 **＋ cise** 切、割

imprecise [ˌɪmprɪˋsaɪs] 形 不嚴密的；不精確的；不正確的

延伸片語 **imprecise term** 錯誤用語

▶ Imprecise terms have normally been circulating for such a long time that it would be difficult for people to quit using them.
通常錯誤用語都會被沿用很長一段時間，大家一時也很難去修正。

延伸補充自然學

cise的變化形：cide

☆ **decide** 　　　向下＋切、割　　　動 決定

☆ **suicide** 　　　自己＋切、割　　　名 自殺行為

 根 **vert** 轉

情境對話試水溫

Claudia: Did you see the news today? The government of was subverted by the rebel army and the president fled from the palace.

克勞蒂亞：你看到今天新聞了嗎？叛軍推翻了政府，總統也逃離了總統府。

Peter: All I can say is that he deserved it. His incompetence has resulted in economic recession and civil disorder, but he's been trying to divert the attention away from the real problems and instead blame the opposition party for inciting riot. He's the main reason why people are being converted into activists.

彼得：我只能說他活該。他的無能導致經濟衰退和內亂，但他不正視真正的問題一直轉移焦點，反而來指責在野黨煽動騷亂。他才是民眾轉變成激進分子的主因。

Claudia: He appeared guilty and averted all eye contact in front of the camera today. Hopefully he actually realizes his own mistake.

克勞蒂亞：他今天看起來很愧疚，眼神還避開鏡頭。希望他能真正知道自己犯的錯誤。

Peter: I hope that our country would revert to its previous peaceful state after all this chaos.

彼得：我希望這混亂結束後，我們國家可以恢復以前的和平狀態。

 單字解析零距離

1 **sub** 在下面 **＋ vert** 轉

subvert [səb'vɜt] 動 推翻；破壞

延伸片語 subvert the dynasty 推翻……朝代

Ch 3

Part 1

Part 2

Part 3

Part 4

表示四肢動作

▶ Serious political corruption is the main reason why the Ming dynasty was subverted. 嚴重的政治腐敗是明朝滅亡的主因。

② di 分開 ＋ **vert** 轉

divert [daɪˋvɜt] 動 轉向、改變信仰

延伸片語 **divert attention from...** 從哪裡……轉移注意力

▶ I have to divert my attention from the domestic affairs and focus on my job at hand.
我必須要將注意力從家務事的部分轉移到我手邊的工作。

③ con 一併 ＋ **vert** 轉

convert [kənˋvɜt] 動 轉變

延伸片語 **convert to** 皈依

▶ He converted to Christianity when he was very little.
她很小的時候就轉為信奉基督教。

④ re 再度 ＋ **vert** 轉

revert [rɪˋvɜt] 動 回復

延伸片語 **revert to** 回到……狀態／主題

▶ The conversation went astray and the chairman had to interrupt so the committee would revert to the previous subject.
對話已經離題，主席必須要打斷對話才能讓這場委員會回到先前的主題。

⑤ a 遠離 ＋ **vert** 轉

avert [əˋvɜt] 動 避開

延伸片語 **avert gaze** 避開目光注視

▶ Reluctant to show his vulnerability, Frank averted his wife's intense gaze. 法蘭克不願表現出脆弱的一面，只是避開他太太的注視。

延伸補充 自然學

vert 的變化形：verse

☆ **averse**	遠離 ＋ 轉	形 不同意的；反感的
☆ **diverse**	分開 ＋ 轉	形 多變化的；多樣的
☆ **reverse**	反 ＋ 轉	形 倒轉的

情境對話試水溫

🎧 *Track 088*

Manager: Lee, make sure you keep maintaining good relations with Dill so that we can still obtain more projects for BU5 this year.

經理：李，設法確保今年我們能跟迪爾保持良好關係才能為第五事業群拿到更多的案子。

Lee: Yes, sir. I will retain on frequenting to their office and ensure they can be impressed by our initiatives and quotations.

李：是的，經理。我會保持常常拜訪他們的辦公室，並確保迪爾對我們的積極和報價滿意。

Manager: Thanks. But, please also remember to contain the quotations of regulatory and sustaining parts. We need to attain the sales goal this year because the head thinks highly of us bringing in good profits for the company.

經理：謝了。但也請記住報價須包含認證單位及維持產品後續上市的費用。因為上頭很看好我們今年能為公司帶來更好的獲利，所以我們必須達到今年的業績目標。

Lee: Copy that.

李：收到！

單字解析零距離

1 **main** 手部 ＋ **tain** 握

maintain [mənˈten] 🔲 維持

延伸片語 maintain good relations with... 與……保持良好關係

▶ It is important to maintain good relations with your neighbors.
與鄰居保持良好關係是很重要的。

2 **ob** 加強語氣 ＋ **tain** 握

obtain [əbˈten] 🔲 獲取

Ch 3

Part 1

Part 2

Part 3

Part 4

表示四肢動作

延伸片語 **no longer obtain** 不復存在

▶ Customs such as burying people alive with the dead no longer obtain in modern society.
像活人陪葬那樣的習俗在現代社會中已不復存在。

- -

③ re 返、回 ＋ **tain** 握

retain [rɪˈten] 動 保持

延伸片語 **retain a memory of...** 保有……的記憶

▶ We still retain a clear memory of our childhood.
我們仍對童年時光有著清晰的記憶。

- -

④ con 共同 ＋ **tain** 握

contain [kənˈten] 動 包含

延伸片語 **self-contained** 獨立的；自給的

▶ It is a small but self-contained country.
它是個面積小卻能自給自足的國家。

- -

⑤ sus 底下 ＋ **tain** 握

sustain [səˈsten] 動 承擔；維持；承受

延伸片語 **be sustained by facts** 有事實證明

▶ That the man has reformed himself is sustained by facts.
事實證明那個人已經改過自新了。

- -

⑥ at 加強 ＋ **tain** 握

attain [əˈten] 動 達成；獲得

延伸片語 **attain to** 到達；達到

▶ It's hard to believe that our little girl has attained to marriageable age. 真難相信我們的小女孩已經到達適婚年齡了。

延伸補充 自然學

tain 的變化型：ten

✡ **tenable** 握＋能夠的 形 可維持的

✡ **tenacious** 有握住的性質的 形 緊握不放的

根 tend 伸

💬 情境對話試水溫

Tess: My son attended a volunteering program last month, and he just came back last night. He spent more than two hours sharing his experiences. He was responsible for ten kindergarten kids, who gave him a cordial welcome by extending their hands in greeting when they first met. The enthusiasm impressed him a lot.

黛絲：我兒子上個月參加了一個志工計畫，昨晚才回來。他花了兩個多小時告訴我們他的體驗。他負責十位幼稚園孩子，而這些孩子在他們第一次見面的時候就給了他熱烈地歡迎，他們伸出手表示歡迎。這樣的熱情讓他印象很深刻。

Carol: There is a tendency for young people to take part in volunteering programs now, especially international ones. My son intends to join one in Tanzania next August.

凱蘿：志工計畫現在在年輕人中正是一個趨勢，尤其是國際志工。我兒子明年八月也打算參加坦尚尼亞的志工計畫。

Tess: That would be great! My son is so thankful for what he has now. He now knows there are refugees contending with health issues; some refugees' stomachs distend because they've been starving for too long, and some are diagnozed with AIDS when they were born. After witnessing all these, there's nothing for him to complain about his life anymore.

黛絲：太棒了！我兒子現在很感恩擁有的一切。當他知道有些難民需要面對健康問題，有些因為長期挨餓而腹部腫脹，有些一出生就被診斷出患有愛滋病，目睹以上這些情況，他對現在的生活也沒甚麼好抱怨的了。

⚡ 單字解析零距離

1 at 向、朝 + tend 伸

attend [ə`tɛnd] 動 參加　　　　　延伸片語 attend on 照料

表示四肢動作

▶ I have to attend on my sick brother everyday.
我每天都必須照顧生病的弟弟。

∙∙

❷ **con** 共同 ＋ **tend** 伸

contend [kən`tɛnd] 動 競爭　　　延伸片語 contend with　對付、處理

▶ The customer center has to contend with complaints from their customers. 顧客服務中心必須處理顧客的抱怨和投訴。

∙∙

❸ **dis** 分散 ＋ **tend** 伸

distend [dɪ`stɛnd] 動 膨脹　　　延伸片語 distended tummy　腹部腫脹

▶ The child with a distended tummy is seriously undernourished.
那個腹部腫脹的小孩有嚴重的營養不良。

∙∙

❹ **ex** 往外 ＋ **tend** 伸

extend [ɪk`stɛnd] 動 擴張

延伸片語 extend one's hand in greeting　伸出手表示歡迎

▶ The man extended his hands in greeting when he welcomed his guests. 男子迎接賓客時，伸出手表示歡迎。

∙∙

❺ **in** 向內 ＋ **tend** 伸

intend [ɪn`tɛnd] 動 想要

延伸片語 intend... for...　打算讓……做某用途

▶ George intended his son for a lawyer. 喬治打算讓他兒子當律師。

∙∙

❻ **tend** 伸 ＋ **ency** 名詞字尾

tendency [`tɛndənsɪ] 名 趨勢

延伸片語 a tendency towards something　偏好……；有……的傾向

▶ It is obvious that Jack has a tendency towards communism.
傑克顯然有共產主義的傾向。

> **延伸補充 自然學**

tend 的變化型：tent

✫ **contention**　　一起伸張　　　　名 爭辯

✫ **attentive**　　　向某方向伸的　　　形 注意力集中的

根 fact 製作、做

🎧 *Track 090*

情境對話試水溫

Tina: Jake told me today that his dad runs a factory that manufactures wooden products.

蒂娜：傑克今天跟我說他爸爸在經營一家生產木製品的工廠。

Gina: Also, his dad is a very generous benefactor for the association of ex-criminals. He even visits the prison once a month to give lessons on making artifacts using wood.

吉娜：還有，他爸爸還是對更生人協會非常慷慨的大善人，甚至每個月都會去監獄教大家用木頭製作藝術品。

Tina: The prisoners may be evil malefactors to the public; but for him, they are normal people that deserve equal respect and rights.

蒂娜：也許這些罪犯在大眾眼中是壞人，但對他來說，他們也是值得公平地受到尊重及享有權利的普通人。

單字解析零距離

❶ **fact** 製作、做 **＋ ory** 名詞字尾，表示地方

factory [ˈfæktərɪ] 名 工廠

延伸片語 **textile factory** 紡織廠

▶ Laborers in the textile factory are often subject to long working hours and inadequate pay.
紡織廠的員工經常受制於工時長薪水又低。

Ch 3

Part 1

Part 2

Part 3

表示四肢動作

Part 4

② **manu** 手 + **fact** 製作、做 + **ure** 動詞字尾

manufacture [ˌmænjəˈfæktʃə] 勔 製造

延伸片語 **manufacture car parts** 生產汽車零件

▶ My dad's company specializes in manufacturing car parts.
我爸爸的公司專門生產汽車零件。

- -

③ **bene** 好 + **fact** 製作、做 + **or** 名詞字尾，表示物品

benefactor [ˈbɛnəˌfæktə] 名 捐助人；恩人

延伸片語 **generous benefactor** 慷慨大方地贊助

▶ He is not only a well-respected business tycoon but also a generous benefactor who donates millions of dollars to multiple charities every month.
他不僅是一位備受尊崇的商業巨擘，更是一位慷慨大方的贊助人，每個月捐贈上百萬美元給不同的慈善單位。

- -

④ **arti** 藝術；技術 + **fact** 製作、做

artifact [ˈɑrtɪˌfækt] 名 工藝品；手工藝品；加工品

延伸片語 **prehistoric artifacts** 史前文物

▶ The excavation of prehistoric artifacts requires great deal of patience and diligence.
挖掘史前文物需要很大的耐心跟勤奮。

- -

⑤ **male** 惡 + **fact** 製作、做 + **or** 名詞字尾

malefactor [ˈmæləˌfæktə] 名 壞人

延伸片語 **be treated like a malefactor** 被當成罪犯看待

▶ Being a child borne by the mistress, Frank is treated like a malefactor by hostess of the family.
法蘭克生為私生子，在家中總被女主人當成罪犯看待。

延伸補充 自然學

fact 的變化形：fect

| ☆ **perfect** | 貫穿 + 製作 | 形 完美的 |
| ☆ **infect** | 往內 + 製作 | 動 感染 |

根 gest 搬運、攜帶

💬 情境對話試水溫

Owen: One of my students gestured to me in class today and signified that he needs to use the toilet. He's been doing that several times in the past month. I think he might have some digestive problems.

歐文：我有一個學生今天在課堂上比手勢示意他要上廁所，這個月已經很多次。我覺得他可能有一些消化問題。

Tanya: I suffer from the opposite condition! I've been constipated for months. It feels like all the food I consume are congested in the stomach and never going down.

坦雅：我正好相反！我已經便秘好幾個月了。感覺就像我吃的所有食物都在塞在胃裡出不來。

Owen: I suggest both of you go see a doctor and watch very carefully what food you are ingesting.

歐文：我建議你們兩個去看醫生，且要特別注意你們日常飲食。

⚡ 單字解析零距離

① gest 搬運、攜帶 **＋ ure** 名詞字尾

gesture [ˈdʒɛstʃɚ] 名 姿勢；手勢

延伸片語 make a gesture of 做……的動作

▶ The man made a gesture of refusal with his head when the police requested for his driver's license.
當警察要求這男子出示他的駕照，他搖頭拒絕了。

Ch 3

Part 1

Part 2

Part 3

表示四肢動作

Part 4

2 **di** 分離 ＋ **gest** 搬運、攜帶 ＋ **ive** 形容詞字尾

digestive [də`dʒɛstɪv] 形 消化的；助消化的

延伸片語 **digestive organs** 消化器官

▶ As we get old, the digestive organs begin to retrograde, hence the smaller appetite.
隨著我們年紀越大，消化器官開始退化，因此食量也會變小。

- -

3 **con** 一同 ＋ **gest** 搬運 、攜帶

congest [kən`dʒɛst] 動 使擁擠

延伸片語 **congested traffic** 交通堵塞

▶ The congested traffic on the highway obstructed the rescue operation.
高速公路上交通堵塞，妨礙了救援行動。

- -

4 **sug** 向上 ＋ **gest** 搬運、攜帶

suggest [sə`dʒɛst] 動 建議

延伸片語 **suggest that** 建議

▶ The supervisor shook her head with disapproval and suggested that we rewrite the proposal.
主管搖搖頭表示不滿意並建議我們重寫提案。

- -

5 **in** 向內 ＋ **gest** 搬運、攜帶

ingest [ɪn`dʒɛst] 動 吸收；嚥下；攝取

延伸片語 **ingest calories** 攝取卡路里

▶ When going on a diet, people tend to be wary about how much calories they are ingesting.
在減肥的時候，大家往往對自己攝取的卡路里很謹慎。

延伸補充 自然學

✿ **decongest** 　　　　除去 + 擁擠的現象 　　　動 消除擁擠

根 pos(e) 放置

Track 092

情境對話 試水溫

Ella: Tony is going to propose to Emily with a song written by a well-known composer. It's customized song that depicts their relationship.

Rio: I know. The plan is cool, but it's exposed now, and Emily is quite upset Tony told everybody about his plan. Moreover, Emily's parents are opposed to their marriage because he's not the second generation of the rich. They even asked Tony to put a huge amount of money in Emily's deposit account.

Ella: Too bad. It's really difficult for them to get married.

艾拉：湯尼將要以一首由知名作曲家所做的歌跟艾蜜莉求婚了。那是一首專門為他們交往時光所寫的歌呢。

里奧：我知道啊，這計畫很酷，但曝光了。艾蜜莉還蠻生氣湯尼到處跟別人說他的計畫。而且因為湯尼不是富二代，所以艾蜜莉的爸媽反對這門親事。他們甚至要求湯尼存入一筆鉅款到艾蜜莉的存款帳戶裡。

艾拉：太糟了，他們要結婚根本是一波三折。

單字解析 零距離

❶ pro 往前 **+ pose** 放置

propose [prə`poz] **動** 提議；求婚

延伸片語 propose a toast 提議為……乾杯

▶ He proposed a toast to the prize winner.
他提議為得獎者乾杯。

表示四肢動作

2 com 一起 ＋ pos 放置 ＋ er 人

composer [kəm`pozɚ] 名 作曲家

延伸片語 music composer 音樂作曲家

▶ Beethoven is one of the most remarkable music composers in history.
貝多芬是史上最卓越的音樂作曲家之一。

3 ex 向外 ＋ pose 放置

expose [ɪk`spoz] 動 暴露

延伸片語 expose...to... 使……接觸……

▶ We should avoid exposing ourselves to second-hand smoke.
我們應該避免吸入二手煙。

4 op 相反 ＋ pose 放置

oppose [ə`poz] 動 反對

延伸片語 be opposed to 反對……

▶ The villagers are opposed to a new nuclear power plant in the village.
村民反對在村裡興建新的核電廠。

5 de 往下 ＋ pos 放置 ＋ it 走動

deposit [dɪ`pɑzɪt] 名 押金

延伸片語 safe deposit 保險箱

▶ The woman keeps all her jewelry in the safe deposit.
婦人將她所有的首飾都放在保險箱裡。

延伸補充 自然學

☆ **depose**	往下放	動 罷黜
☆ **reposit**	放回去	動 使……恢復
☆ **interpose**	放在……之間	動 打岔、插話
☆ **transpose**	換放的位置	動 換位置

根 lev, liev 舉、輕

Bobby: Did you know the elevator in our office building free fell last Monday with the general manager and several other colleagues inside?	鮑比：你知道我們公司大樓的電梯上週一掉下來嗎？當時裡面還有總經理和其他幾位同事。
Ruth: What?!	露絲：什麼？！
Bobby: Don't panic. You will be relieved to hear that no one was hurt.	鮑比：別驚慌，聽到沒有人受傷你就會鬆一口氣了。
Ruth: But still, it sounds very scary.	露絲：但是聽起來還是非常可怕。
Bobby: Exactly, going down at that rapid speed, everyone inside the elevator must have been levitating in mid-air.	鮑比：沒錯，高速掉落，電梯裡每個人一定都飄起來了。
Ruth: It frightens me just to imagine it. My dad always educates me that when such thing happens, I should grab onto the hand rail and slightly bend the knees to alleviate the impact of the crash when it lands. I wonder if that actually helps.	露絲：光是想像就讓我害怕，我爸爸總告訴我，當這種事情發生時，我應該抓住扶手並稍微彎曲膝蓋，以減緩墜落時撞擊的影響，不知道到底有沒有用。
Bobby: I am thinking about joining the International Balloon festival in Taitung this year.	鮑比：我正考慮參加今年台東的國際氣球節。
Ruth: Is that question even relevant to our discussion right now?!	露絲：這個問題跟我們正在討論的有關嗎？！

表示四肢動作

單字解析零距離

① re 再度＋**lieve** 輕

relieve [rɪˈliv] **動** 緩和，減輕；解除

延伸片語 **relieve stress** 舒緩／紓解壓力

▶ Mediation is said to be helpful to relieve the stress.
據說暝想對紓解壓力很有幫助。

. . . .

② e 往外＋**lev** 舉＋**at(e)** 進行一項行為＋**or** 名詞字尾

elevator [ˈɛləˌvetə] **名** 電梯；升降機；起重機

延伸片語 **ride the elevator** 搭電梯

▶ Speak sparingly to avoid disturb others when riding the elevator.
搭乘電梯時，請盡量避免說話而打擾他人。

. . . .

③ lev 舉＋**i**＋**ate** 動詞字尾，表示使行動

levitate [ˈlɛvəˌtet] **動** 升空，飄浮

延伸片語 **levitate from the ground** 漂浮到空中

▶ All the audience was dumbfounded when the magician levitated from the ground.
當魔術師漂浮到空中時，所有觀眾都傻住了。

. . . .

④ al 向、朝＋**lev** 輕＋**iate** 進行一項行為

alleviate [əˈlivɪˌet] **動** 減輕

延伸片語 **alleviate bad mood** 緩解壞心情

▶ Fast foods are the best remedies to alleviate bad mood.
吃速食是舒緩壞心情的絕佳方法。

. . . .

⑤ re 再度＋**lev** 舉＋**ant** 形容詞字尾

relevant [ˈrɛləvənt] **形** 有關的；切題的；恰當的

延伸片語 **relevant to** 和……有關

▶ The agent of the super star demanded the reporters ask questions relevant to the topic.
這位巨星的經紀人要求記者問與該主題相關的問題。

根 scend 攀爬、上升

情境對話試水溫

🎧 *Track 094*

Alex: Did you know that Bob Miller, the showbiz super star, is the descendant of the business tycoon, Frank Miller?

亞歷克斯：你知道演藝界超級巨星鮑勃米勒是商業大亨弗蘭克米勒的後代嗎？

Ruby: You mean Miller as in the Miller Enterprise? The company that was founded in 1949 and quickly transcended all its competitors and ascended to be the top conglomerate in the world and remained its status even til now?

魯比：你是説米勒企業的那個米勒？那家1949年成立，快速超越所有競爭對手，成為世界頂尖的企業集團，到現在仍保持其地位的米勒企業？

Alex: Yes, THAT Miller.

亞歷克斯：沒錯，那家米勒。

Ruby: Wow. With that kind of family glory and fame, you'd expect Bob Miller to be the most condescending and arrogant celebrity ever. But instead, he's polite, humble, and sweet to all his fans.

魯比：哇。有這種家庭的光環和名氣，你應該覺得鮑勃米勒會是最高傲和傲慢的明星。但正好相反，他對所有粉絲都很有禮貌，又謙虛又貼心。

Alex: Exactly the reason why the Miller family's reputation has never descended the least bit even after 70 years in the spotlight.

亞歷克斯：正因如此，才讓米勒家的名聲能夠在聚光燈下維持其地位，還能七十年不墜。

單字解析零距離

❶ de 往下 + scend 上升 + ant 名詞字尾，表示人
descendant [dɪˋsɛndənt] 名 後代

Ch 3

Part 1

Part 2

Part 3

表示四肢動作

Part 4

延伸片語 descendant of ……的後裔

▶ As the descendant of one of the century's most celebrated musician, Annie is expected to be born with innate music talents.
作為本世紀最出名音樂家的後代，安妮被冀望有著極高的音樂天賦。

② **trans** 穿越 ＋ **scend** 攀爬

transcend [træn'sɛnd] 動 超越

延伸片語 transcend time and space 超越時間跟空間

▶ Hatred is only temporary while love can easily transcend time and space. 仇恨只是暫時的，而愛才能夠輕易地超越時空。

③ **a** 朝向 ＋ **scend** 攀爬、上升

ascend [ə'sɛnd] 動 攀升；登上

延伸片語 ascend the throne 當上國王／女王

▶ The whole nation witnessed with excitement as the prince finally ascends the throne.
當王子登上王位時，全國百姓都見證了這興奮的時刻。

④ **con** 全 ＋ **de** 向下 ＋ **scend** 攀爬 ＋ **ing** 形容詞字尾

condescending [ˌkɑndɪ'sɛndɪŋ] 形 高傲的

延伸片語 condescending tone/attitude 高人一等的語氣／態度

▶ The supervisor divides the work among employees with a condescending attitude.
主管用一種高人一等的態度在分配工作給員工。

⑤ **de** 向下 ＋ **scend** 攀爬

descend [dɪ'sɛnd] 動 下降

延伸片語 the night descends 夜幕落下

▶ As the night descends, the nocturnal animals leave their lairs to begin the day.
隨著夜幕降臨，夜行性動物離開洞穴開始一天的活動。

根 **flect** 彎曲

🎧 *Track 095*

Hans: How did you spend your weekend?

漢斯：你週末怎麼過？

Ursula: I went to a Catholic church with my mother-in-law and she showed me how they worship. Everyone was genuflecting on one knee as a pledge of service.

烏蘇拉：我跟婆婆去了天主教堂，她向我示範如何禱告，每個人都單膝跪地表示誠意。

Hans: I am more of an atheist so I find it hard to understand those religious rituals.

漢斯：我其實是一個無神論者，所以我很難理解這些宗教儀式。

Ursula: Then you should definitely come next time. Just one visit and they have completely converted me into a believer.

烏蘇拉：那你下次應該一起來，我才去一次他們就完全把我變成信徒。

Hans: How's that so?

漢斯：怎麼說？

Ursula: The inflection in the priest's voice are so soothing that I can feel all my worries fly away, but the message in his preach are so powerful to an extent that it can make bullets deflect.

烏蘇拉：牧師的語調非常鎮靜，我可以感受到所有煩惱瞬間消失，但他的講道所傳遞的訊息非常強大，大到感覺能讓子彈轉彎。

Hans: Wow. They have totally got into your head.

漢斯：哇，你完全被他們洗腦了。

Ursula: Don't be so mean and sarcastic. Just start with reading the bible. All gods' wisdom is reflected in the book.

烏蘇拉：別那麼刻薄又諷刺，趕快開始讀聖經，眾神的智慧都反映在書中。

Hans: I will consider your unreflective remark as a temporary mental lapse and that this conversation never happened.

漢斯：我就當作你這些未經反思的話只是暫時精神錯亂，而我們從來沒聊過這些。

Ch 3

Part 1

Part 2

Part 3

表示四肢動作

Part 4

單字解析零距離

1 **genu** 膝蓋 + **flect** 彎曲

genuflect [ˈdʒɛnjuˌflɛkt] 動 屈膝；跪（尤指為了膜拜）

延伸片語 genuflect before the altar 在祭壇前跪拜

▶ She genuflected before the altar and with all sincerity swore to serve the God. 她在祭壇前跪拜，虔誠地發誓要為神所用。

- -

2 **in** 往內 + **flect** 彎曲 + **ion** 名詞字尾

inflection [ɪnˈflɛkʃən] 名 變音；轉調；彎曲；曲折變化

延伸片語 the mastery of inflection 對語調抑揚頓挫的精通

▶ The mastery of inflection is particularly important when giving a speech. 在演講時，對於音調的掌握是很重要的。

- -

3 **de** 去除 + **flect** 彎曲

deflect [dɪˈflɛkt] 動 使……偏斜

延伸片語 deflect the attention away from 從……轉移走注意力

▶ Wear clothes with low-key color when you attend a wedding in order not to deflect the attention away from the bride.
參加婚禮時穿著低調色的服裝，是為了不要搶走新娘的風采。

- -

4 **re** 返 + **flect** 彎曲

reflect [rɪˈflɛkt] 動 反射；照出；映出；反映

延伸片語 reflect in 反映在……

▶ His complete lack of sympathy is well reflected in his reaction to this tragic event.
從這悲劇事件可以完整地看出他這個人完全沒有同情心。

- -

5 **un** 否；無 + **re** 返 + **flect** 彎曲 + **ive** 形容詞字尾

unreflective [ˌʌnrɪˈflɛktɪv] 形 粗心大意的

延伸片語 unreflective action 未經深思熟慮的行動

▶ Your hasty and unreflective action has seriously undermined our operation.
你急躁又粗心的行為嚴重地影響了我們的營運。

 情境對話試水溫

🎧 *Track 096*

Cynthia: I saw on the news that the residents of the eastern neighborhood are demonstrating before the city government today.

辛西婭：我在新聞中看到東區的居民今天在市政府前示威。

Peter: Why? What happened?

彼得：為什麼？發生什麼事？

Cynthia: That part of the city is subsiding due to inappropriate land development. Apparently the government has been taking bribes from companies and issuing licenses to projects that have never passed the environmental assessment.

辛西婭：不當的土地開發，這城市的其中一區正在下陷。很明顯地，政府一直在收賄，並發放許可證給未通過環境評估的公司。

Peter: Shouldn't the authority provide some kind of subsidy to the residents?

彼得：當局難道不該提供一些津貼給居民嗎？

Cynthia: They did. But the amount was dismally small and the government speaker was caught on camera saying something like 'Those people should stop being obsessed with lands".

辛西婭：有呀，但非常少，而且政府發言人還被拍到說：「民眾不該執著於那些土地。」

Peter: How could she say that? The residents not only legally possess those lands but also have emotional attachment to the houses. They have every right to be angry with the government.

彼得：她怎麼講這種話？居民不只合法擁有這些土地，還對這些房子有感情，他們完全有權利對政府發脾氣。

Ch 3

Part 1

Part 2

Part 3

Part 4

表示四肢動作

單字解析零距離

1 re 返回 ＋ sid 坐 ＋ ent 名詞字尾

resident [ˈrɛzədənt] 名 居民；定居者

延伸片語 resident of/ in 哪裡……的居民

▶ She immigrated from Taiwan in 1890 and is currently a resident in Sydney. 她1890年從台灣移民，目前住在雪梨。

. . . .

2 sub 在下面 ＋ side 坐

subside [səbˈsaɪd] 動 退落；消退；消失

延伸片語 subside rapidly 快速消退

▶ The water subsides rapidly after the plug was removed. 把塞子移除後，水很迅速地就消退了。

. . . .

3 sub 在下面 ＋ sid 坐 ＋ y 名詞字尾

subsidy [ˈsʌbsədɪ] 名 津貼；補貼；補助金

延伸片語 provide subsidy 提供補助

▶ The government provides subsidy for companies that recruit foreign workers. 政府有提供補助給雇用外籍勞工的公司。

. . . .

4 ob 朝向 ＋ sess 坐

obsess [əbˈsɛs] 動 迷住；使著迷；纏住

延伸片語 be obsessed with/over 為……著迷

▶ You should stop being obsessed with other's opinions and start thinking independently. 你該停止執著於別人的意見，而開始獨立思考。

. . . .

5 pos 能夠 ＋ sess 坐

possess [pəˈzɛs] 動 擁有，持有

延伸片語 possess ... qualities 有……的特質／特性

▶ The herb possesses healing qualities and is often used in doctor prescriptions. 這草藥具有治療功效，經常出現在醫師的處方籤。

根 act 行動

Emily: Do you know the leading actor in that action movie is going to Taiwan for the movie premiere? I'm literally on cloud nine!	艾蜜莉：你知道那部動作片的主要演員將要到台灣舉辦電影首映會嗎？我真的樂翻了！
Gigi: Compose yourself! Don't react overly. Have you got the tickets to the premiere?	吉吉：冷靜一點！別反應過度了。你拿到首映會的門票了嗎？
Emily: Definitely! Do you know there will be one lucky audience who can have the opportunity to interact with him? I want to be the one!	艾蜜莉：當然啊！你知道將會有一位幸運的觀眾可以與他互動嗎？我想當那個人！
Gigi: In actual fact, I heard that there will be more than one audience able to get close to him. But we will only know the exact number when we are there.	吉吉：事實上，我聽說不只一位的觀眾可以與他接觸，但需要等我們到那時才會知道準確的人數。
Emily: Really? Keep our fingers crossed!	艾蜜莉：真的嗎？讓我們祈求好運！

 單字解析零距離

❶ act 行動 ＋ or 人

actor [ˋæktɚ] 名 演員

延伸片語 **leading actor** 男主角

▶ Tom is the leading actor of this lousy movie.
湯姆是這部爛片的男主角。

Ch 3

Part 1

Part 2

Part 3

Part 4

表示四肢動作

② **act** 行動 ＋ **ion** 表示行為

action [ˈækʃən] 名 動作

延伸片語 **action movie** 動作片

▶ It seems so easy to hack a computer in action movies.
動作片裡演得好像很容易駭侵進別人的電腦。

· ·

③ **re** 再次 ＋ **act** 行動

react [rɪˈækt] 動 做出反應

延伸片語 **react on** 影響

▶ The rise in oil price has reacted on the price of food.
油價的上漲已經影響了食物價格。

· ·

④ **inter** 互相 ＋ **act** 行動

interact [ˌɪntəˈrækt] 動 互動

延伸片語 **interact with** 與……相互作用

▶ All things are interrelated and interacted with each other.
一切事物都是相互聯繫又相互作用的。

· ·

⑤ **act** 行動 ＋ **ual** 屬於……的

actual [ˈæktʃʊəl] 形 實際上的

延伸片語 **in actual fact** 事實上

▶ Sarah looks younger than his husband, but in actual fact she is older.
莎拉看起來比他丈夫年輕，可是實際上她大很多。

· ·

⑥ **ex** 向外、之前的 ＋ **act** 行動

exact [ɪgˈzækt] 形 精確的

延伸片語 **exact time** 準確時間

▶ Could you tell me the exact time now?
請你告訴我現在準確的時間好嗎？

 根 **ambul** 走動、行走

情境對話試水溫

🎧 *Track 098*

Cindy: How's work in the hospital?	辛蒂：最近醫院工作怎麼樣？
Candice: As stressful as always. Some are bed-ridden, some are ambulant, but both kinds require huge amount of attention.	坎蒂絲：老樣子，壓力很大。有些臥床不起，有些還能走動，但這兩種都很需要人力照顧。
Cindy: Really? I thought those who can ambulate are more capable of caring for themselves.	辛蒂：是嗎？我以為那些可以走動的人比較有能力照顧自己。
Candice: We need to keep ourselves on high alert 24/7. Some nurses are so tired that they started to develop mental illness like insomnia. The other day we even got a nurse somnambulating in the hallway during her shift.	坎蒂絲：我們都要 24 小時保持高度警覺。有些護理師太累了，就開始出現像是失眠等精神問題。前幾天，我們甚至有個護理師值班時間在走廊上夢遊。
Cindy: You should take some time off work and travel abroad.	辛蒂：你應該抽空休個假或出國旅行。
Candice: Or just take a break and perambulating in a nearby park will do.	坎蒂絲：其實只要稍微休息一下，或在附近的公園晃晃就好了。
Cindy: That's how tired you are, huh? Come on! Imagine yourself circumambulating Champ de Mars while admiring the beauty of Eiffel tower.	辛蒂：可見你有多累，是吧？來吧！想像一下，你欣賞艾菲爾鐵塔美景的同時繞著戰神廣場打轉的場景。
Candice: That does sound tempting.	坎蒂絲：聽起來好誘人。

Ch 3

Part 1

Part 2

Part 3

Part 4

表示四肢動作

單字解析零距離

❶ ambul 行走、行動 **+ ant** 名詞字尾，表示做某事的人

ambulant [ˋæmbjələnt] 形 【醫】（病人）可走動的；（治療時）病人不需臥床的

延伸片語 **ambulant patient** 可行走的病人

▶ The hospital is renovating its facilities to better care for the ambulant patients.
這家醫院正在修繕院內設備，讓病患能享有更好的醫療照護。

❷ ambul 行走、行動 **+ ate** 動詞字尾

ambulate [ˋæmbjəˌlet] 動 移動、步行

延伸片語 **ambulate in** 在……走動

▶ Only one day after regaining consciousness, she has started ambulating in the room. 在恢復意識的隔天，她已開始在房間裡走動。

❸ somn 睡眠 **+ ambul** 行走、行動 **+ ate** 動詞字尾

somnambulate [sɑmˋnæmbjəˌlet] 動 夢遊

▶ He somnambulates — he walk in his sleep and climb back to bed without remembering anything.
他夢遊了——在睡夢中踱步，然後爬回床上，完全不記得任何過程。

❹ per 貫穿 **+ ambul** 行走、行動 **+ ate** 動詞字尾

perambulate [pəˋæmbjəˌlet] 動 走過；在……散步；巡行於；勘查

延伸片語 **perambulate up and down** 在……到處漫步、徜徉

▶ Betty's dad was fired a month ago, but he wouldn't face the reality and still dresses himself in suit and tie, perambulating up and down the plaza before the company. 貝蒂的爸爸上個月被解雇，但他不願面對現實，仍穿西裝打領帶，在公司前的廣場閒晃。

❺ circum 周圍 **+ ambul** 行走、行動 **+ ate** 動詞字尾

circumambulate [ˌsɝkəmˋæmbjəˌlet] 動 巡行

延伸片語 **circumambulate the wall** 繞著牆走

▶ She circumambulated the wall while murmuring to herself.
她繞著牆走，一邊自言自語。

Unit 99 根 cede, ceed 行走、移動、屈服

🎧 *Track 099*

💬 情境對話試水溫

Frank: Great job on your proposal, Yuna! Your performance has greatly exceeded my expectation.	法蘭克：你的建議很棒，尤娜！你的表現大大超出了我的預期。
Yuna: Thank you, sir!	尤娜：謝謝你，長官！
Frank: The research you did was so thorough and clear that I can imagine all the hard work preceding this proposal.	法蘭克：你做的研究非常徹底又清楚，我可以想像這個準備提案先前的所有辛苦。
Yuna: I will proceed with the same diligence towards job and will not let you down.	尤娜：我會繼續努力工作，不讓你失望的。
Frank: Keep up with the good work. In order to succeed as a project manager, you need to dedicate 100% of yourself into this job. Just take a look at my receding hairline and you will understand.	法蘭克：繼續做好工作吧，要成功成為專案經理，您必須將100％的精力投入到這項專案中，你看我逐漸退後的髮際線你就會明白的。

單字解析零距離

❶ ex 向外 **+ cede** 移動

exceed [ɪk`sid] **動** 超過；勝過

延伸片語 **exceed (number)** 超過……數字

▶ The wind velocity exceeds 20km and the weather bureau has declared a state of emergency.
這風速高過20公里，氣象局已經發布警報。

Ch 3

Part 1

Part 2

Part 3

表示四肢動作

Part 4

❷ pre <u>前、在前</u> **＋ cede** <u>移動</u>

precede [prɪˋsid] **動**（順序、位置或時間上）處在……之前

延伸片語 **be preceded by** 前面有……

▶ The afternoon session will be preceded by a luncheon to which all keynote speakers are invited.
下午會議開始之前還有場午餐研討會，所有專題講師均受邀參加。

- -

❸ pro <u>時間或空間上較前的</u> **＋ cede** <u>移動</u>

proceed [prəˋsid] **動** 繼續進行；繼續做；開始；著手

延伸片語 **proceed with caution** 謹慎行事

▶ The police are advised to proceed with caution in order not to enrage the abductor.
這警察被要求謹慎行事，以免激怒綁匪。

- -

❹ suc <u>向下</u> **＋ cede** <u>移動、屈服</u>

succeed [səkˋsid] **動** 成功；獲得成效

延伸片語 **succeed in** 在……成功

▶ He didn't succeed in getting the promotion.
他並沒有升遷成功。

- -

❺ re <u>往回</u> **＋ cede** <u>移動、屈服</u>

recede [rɪˋsid] **動** 收回、撤回

延伸片語 **recede into the distance** 從遠方淡出

▶ As the car moves forward, I watched my mom receding into the distance.
隨著車往前開，我看著我媽媽從遠方淡出。

延伸補充自然學

☆ **intercede**　　　向內＋屈服　　　　**動** 仲裁；說項；求情

Unit 100 根 cur(r) 跑

💬 情境對話試水溫

Dennis: Where's the destination of our next school excursion?

丹尼斯：我們下次戶外教學是去哪裡？

Ethan: I heard that the student association had a closed-door meeting last Friday and decided on Tibet.

伊桑：聽説學生會上週五開會，決定去西藏。

Dennis: Tibet? Really? Wasn't there supposed to be a poll? It's not the first time this has occurred. There have been several instances where such black-room deals were made ever since the new chairman was elected.

丹尼斯：西藏？真的嗎？不是應該要投票嗎？這不是第一次發生了。自從新的主席當選以來，已經有很多次黑箱作業。

Ethan: Come to think of it.... the current student association has indeed failed at representing our voices.

伊桑：你想想……目前的學生會確實沒有人替我們發聲。

Dennis: If events like this keep recurring, I am sure they will incur unnecessary protest and anger from all students.

丹尼斯：如果這樣的事件繼續發生，我相信他們會引發所有學生不必要的抗議和怨氣。

⚡ 單字解析零距離

❶ **ex** 向外 **+ cur** 跑 **+ sion** 名詞字尾，表示行為

excursion [ɪkˋskɝʒən] 名 遠足；短途旅行

延伸片語 excursion to 去……遠足、短程旅行

▶ After an excursion to Europe, he's relieved of all pressure from work.
結束了短暫的歐洲行，他釋放了工作上所有的壓力。

Ch 3

Part 1

Part 2

Part 3

表示四肢動作

Part 4

❷ oc 向 ＋ **cur** 跑

occur [əˋkɝ] 動 發生；出現；存在

延伸片語 **occur to** 想到

▶ Has it ever occurred to you I am a person with feelings too?
你有沒有想過我也是個有情感的人？

- -

❸ curr 跑 ＋ **ent** 形容詞字尾，表示……狀態的

current [ˋkɝənt] 形 目前的；現時的，當前的；現行的；通用的

延伸片語 **under the current circumstances** 在目前的情況下

▶ No one will be allowed to leave this room without my consent under the current circumstances.
以目前情況來看，沒有人能夠不經我允許就離開這房間。

- -

❹ re 再次 ＋ **cur** 跑

recur [rɪˋkɝ] 動 再發生；復發；（往事等）再現；重新憶起

延伸片語 **recur periodically** 週期性復發

▶ This disease is incurable and will recur periodically, so we suggest that you make regular visit to the hospital.
這種病無法根治，且會定期復發，所以我們建議你定期去醫院就診。

- -

❺ in 向內 ＋ **cur** 跑

incur [ɪnˋkɝ] 動 帶來；招致

延伸片語 **incur costs** 導致費用

▶ The company will be responsible for all the costs incurred by this accident.
這家公司會針對此意外所產生的所有費用負起全責。

延伸補充 自然學

cur的變化型：curs

☆ **cursory**　　跑＋形容詞字尾　　　　　　　 形 匆忙的；粗略的

☆ **precursor**　前的＋跑＋名詞字尾，表示人　名 前導；先驅；前輩

根 vene(t) 來

情境對話 試水溫

Ottis: Did you hear that one of the buyers secretly intervened in the bidding process in his own favor?

奧蒂斯：你有沒有聽説其中一位買家為了自己的利益而秘密介入競標過程？

Ryan: That's clearly contravening the terms and conditions!

萊恩：這完全違反規則！

Ottis: Exactly. I think the council is convening a meeting today to discuss it.

奧蒂斯：沒錯。我認為理事會今天會召開會議討論這個問題。

Ryan: I hope they could come up with some practical solutions to prevent similar events from happening again.

萊恩：希望他們能夠提出一些實際可行的解決方案來防止類似事件再發生。

Ottis: I still can't believe that the buyer would risk the reputation of his own company and venture into doing such a thing.

奧蒂斯：我還是無法相信買家會拿自己公司的聲譽冒險做這樣的事情。

Ryan: Do you know the venue of the meeting today? I'd like to sit in and hear all the details regarding this matter.

萊恩：你知道今天會議的地點嗎？我想坐下來聽聽有關此案的所有細節。

單字解析 零距離

❶ inter 在……中間 ＋ **vene** 來

intervene [ˌɪntɚˋvin] 動 介入、干預

延伸片語 intervene in 干涉……

Ch 3

Part 1

Part 2

Part 3

Part 4

表示四肢動作

▶ Asians tend to shy away from intervening in their neighbor's domestic affairs. 亞洲人通常會避開鄰居的家務事。

② **contra** 反 ＋ **vene** 來

contravene [ˌkɑntrəˈvin] 動 違反（法律、規定）

延伸片語 contravene the law 違反法律

▶ Any citizens whose behavior contravenes the law should be punished accordingly. 任何違反法律行為的公民都應受到相對的懲罰。

③ **con** 一併 ＋ **vene** 來

convene [kənˈvin] 動 集會；聚集

延伸片語 convene a meeting/ conference 召開會議

▶ The board convened an urgent meeting to replace the CEO. 董事會召開緊急會議要撤換總裁。

④ **pre** 前面 ＋ **vent** 來

prevent [prɪˈvɛnt] 動 防止；預防；阻止；制止

延伸片語 prevent... from... 避免……再次發生

▶ A legally binding contract should be signed in order to prevent business fraud from happening.
應該要簽一份合法具約束力的合約，避免商業詐欺等事件再次發生。

⑤ **ven** 來 ＋ **ue** 名詞字尾

venue [ˈvɛnju] 名（事件、行動等的）發生地；集合地

延伸片語 choice of venue 地點的選擇

▶ The choice of venue decides whether the party will be successful or not. 場地的選擇決定了此政黨是否會成功。

延伸補充 自然學

☆ **event**	前＋來	名 事件
☆ **advent**	朝向＋來	名 出現；到來；基督降臨；降臨節

情境對話試水溫

🎧 *Track 102*

Volunteer: This refugee camp consists of at least 100 refugees who came from the chaos of the war in Syria and Iraq as well as 15 volunteers from UN to assist those people for daily necessities and support.

志工：這個難民營是由至少一百位從敘利亞及伊拉克戰亂逃出的難民及十五位來自聯合國的義工為了幫助他們的生活起居而組成的。

Correspondent: It's very sad for me to see them being unable to subsist on their own because their home was destroyed. I know they also wanted to resist the totalitarians, but all they can do was so scarce that they couldn't fight back.

通訊記者：看著他們因為家園被摧毀而不能自力更生，我感到很傷心。我知道他們也想反抗這些極權分子，但他們能做的是這麼地微薄，微薄到無法反擊。

Volunteer: Even though they couldn't do much but stay alive bravely, they should also persist in their efforts to rebuild their home. I believe if the rest of the world draw together, the ISIS can be eliminated soon.

志工：即使他們能做的不多，但現在唯一能做的就是勇敢地活下去。他們也應該堅持下去，重建他們的家園。我相信如果全世界能團結在一起，將能很快地殲滅伊斯蘭國。

 單字解析零距離

① con 共同 **+ sist** 站立

consist [kənˈsɪst] 動 由……組合而成

延伸片語 consist with 一致、符合
▶ The evidence consists with his confession.
　證據與他的供詞相符。

- -

② as 向、朝 ＋ sist 站立

assist [əˋsɪst] 動 幫忙

延伸片語 assist at 到場、出席
▶ Please assist at the ceremony on time.
　請準時出席典禮。

- -

③ sub 下 ＋ sist 站立

subsist [səbˋsɪst] 動 生存

延伸片語 subsist on 靠……活下去
▶ It is a disaster that the survivors from the shipwreck had to subsist on the dead bodies of their companions.
　船難的倖存者必須吃同伴的屍體才能生存下去，真是人間慘劇。

- -

④ re 加強 ＋ sist 抵擋

resist [rɪˋzɪst] 動 反抗

延伸片語 resist disease 抵抗疾病
▶ Strengthen your immunity in order to resist diseases.
　增強你的免疫力以抵抗疾病。

- -

⑤ per 貫穿 ＋ sist 抵擋

persist [pɚˋsɪst] 動 堅持

延伸片語 persist in 堅持
▶ Strengthen your immunity in order to resist diseases.
　增強你的免疫力以抵抗疾病。

延伸補充 自然學

☆	desist	解除站立的狀態	動 停止
☆	assistant	站在旁邊的人	名 助手
☆	persistent	能夠始終站立著的	形 持久的

首 a　朝向、動作的進行、不、加強語氣

情境對話試水溫

Andy: Hey, Dave. What's up? Why do you look so bothered?

安迪：嘿，戴夫！發生什麼事了？你為什麼看起來這麼懊惱？

Dave: Man, I'm screwed. It all arose from the financial crisis I am encountering now. My avocation of a French restaurant is on the edge of bankruptcy. I have fancied this could work and lead my family to a better life. However, it all changed when my partner made off with loads of money.

戴夫：老兄，我真的完蛋了。這全是我目前面臨的財務危機而引起的。我開的副業法式餐廳即將面臨破產了，我曾經想著它能夠成功，能帶給我家人更好的生活。然而，一切都變了，因為我的合夥人捲款潛逃了。

Andy: Oh, that's terrible. How did your wife react over this now?

安迪：哦，真是太糟了！那你老婆是如何看待這件事的？

Dave: Don't even mention her. Wherever I am awake, I can hear my wife complaining aloud on the phone for not giving her the life I once promised and even claiming she's leaving me.

戴夫：別提了！只要我醒著，我就會聽到我老婆在電話裡大聲抱怨我答應給她的生活卻沒做到，而且還嚷嚷著要離開我。

Andy: Well, man. I'm really sorry about that. You should try to turn to the bank for debt agreement first. Let me know if there's anything I can help. Take care.

安迪：嗯，老兄，我真的對此感到很抱歉。你應該先試著尋求銀行的貸款協商。如果有需要我幫忙的地方，再跟我說吧！保重！

Ch 3

Part 1

Part 2

Part 3

Part 4

表示行為、動作

 單字解析零距離

1 a 朝向 ＋ **rise** 升起

arise [ə`raɪz] 動 升起

延伸片語 **arise from...** 由……引起

▶ His illness arose from excessive work. 他的病是工作過度所引起的。

- -

2 a 遠離 ＋ **vocation** 職業

avocation [ˌævəˈkeʃən] 名 副業

延伸片語 **life-long avocation** 終生的業餘愛好

▶ Jimmy regards photography as his life-long avocation.
吉米將攝影視為他終生的業餘愛好。

- -

3 a 加強語氣 ＋ **wake** 醒著

awake [əˈwek] 形 醒著的

延伸片語 **wide awake** 完全清醒的；警覺的

▶ The security guard should be wide awake against any questionable visitors. 警衛應該對任何可疑的訪客保持警覺。

- -

4 a 加強語氣 ＋ **loud** 大聲

aloud [əˈlaʊd] 副 大聲地

延伸片語 **think aloud** 自言自語；邊想邊說

▶ The man is not talking to you. He is just thinking aloud.
那男人不是在跟你講話。他只是在自言自語。

延伸補充自然學

☆	**accompany**	朝某方向 ＋ 陪伴	動 伴隨
☆	**adjoin**	朝某方向 ＋ 加入	動 貼近
☆	**adapt**	將能力朝某方向 ＋ 發揮	動 適應
☆	**ascend**	朝 ＋ 上爬	動 攀爬

首 re- 反向、再次、強調

Kevin: It's great to have a classmate reunion. Been a long time.

凱文：能夠辦個同學的團聚真好。過了好久了。

Richard: Yeah. I still sometimes recall the memories when we two were working on that research project.

理查：真的。我偶爾仍然會回憶起我們兩個為那個研究案子工作的時候。

Kevin: We put so much effort in that one! And remember when we tried to replace a paragraph, and the professor blew off? I still think mine was better.

凱文：我們付出了超多心力！而且還記得我們試著要替換掉一個段落，然後教授非常生氣嗎？我還是覺得我的比較好。

Richard: The professor was just afraid that people might consider you more capable than him. His reaction was truly over, though.

理查：教授就是怕別人會覺得你比他有能力。但他的反應真的太超過就是了。

Kevin: Glad we graduated!

凱文：真高興我們畢業了！

 單字解析零距離

1 re 再次 + union 組織

reunion [ri`junjən] 名 團聚

延伸片語 **a monthly reunion** 每月的聚會

▶ Our class has a monthly reunion, and we enjoy ourselves everytime.
我們班每個月都會有聚會，而且我們每次都玩得很開心。

Ch 3

Part 1

Part 2

Part 3

Part 4

表示行為、動作

② re 再次 + call 呼叫

recall [rɪˋkɔl] 動 回憶、回想；召回

延伸片語 **to recall...** 回憶起～

▶ I can still recall our first holding hands together.
我仍然可以回憶起我們第一次牽手的時候。

③ re 表強調 + search 尋找

research [rɪˋsɝtʃ] 動／名 研究

延伸片語 **the research of** ～的研究

▶ I wan to focus on the research of Romanticism in the following year.
我想要在接下來這一年專注在浪漫主義的研究。

④ re 再次 + place 放置

replace [rɪˋples] 動 取代

延伸片語 **to replace A with B** 用 B 取代 A

▶ My mom asked me to replace the dirty tablecloth with a new one.
我媽要求我把舊的桌巾換成新的。

⑤ re 返回 + act 動作 + tion 名詞字尾

reaction [rɪˋækʃən] 名 反應

延伸片語 **reaction to...** 對～的回應

▶ My father's reaction to my plan was not what I had expected.
我爸爸對我的計畫的回應並不是我所預期的。

延伸補充 自然學

☆ **recede**	退回 + 後退	動	倒退、收回
☆ **reverse**	再次 + 反轉	動	倒轉、翻轉

首 CO 共同

Julie: Hey, Ben! There's a beach cleanup held by NTOU cooperating with SOW in Yilan next weekend. It's such a coincidence that I have been taking an eye on the environmental protection recently, for I saw a picture in which there's a straw stuck in the turtle's nose. Hence, I want to join it.

茱莉：嘿，班！下週末在宜蘭有個國立台灣海洋大學與荒野保護協會合辦的淨灘活動。最近我剛好因為看到一張烏龜鼻子裡有吸管的照片，所以開始留意環境保護議題。我想參加這個活動！

Ben: Sounds good! We should indeed take our environment seriously, and do our best to ensure the coexistence between human beings and animals. But, aren't only students allowed to join this activity?

班：聽起來不錯！我們真的應該重視我們的環境，並盡力確保人類與動物的共存。但這個活動不是僅限於學生參加嗎？

Julie: No, not at all. So we can join them, and ask some of our coworkers to participate in this meaningful event as well.

茱莉：不，我們可以參加！而且我們也可以邀請一些同事參與這項有意義的活動。

Ben: You can say that again! It's so critical to restore the pollution-free habitats where the animals can cohabit with us and be free from getting hurt by those trash.

班：你說得沒錯！恢復無汙染的棲息地讓動物們可以與我們同住，以及不被垃圾所傷害是非常重要的。

Julie: I can't agree with you any more. Let's sign up for this!

茱莉：我非常同意，那我們來報名吧！

 單字解析零距離

1 co 共同 ＋ **operate** 運作

表示行為、動作

cooperate [koˋɑpəˌret] 勔 互助合作

延伸片語 **cooperate in/on...** 在……上配合

▶ In order to get the job done, we need to cooperate in the investigation. 為了完成這項工作，我們必須一起做這項調查研究。

❷ co 共同 **+ incidence** 影響

coincidence [koˋɪnsɪdəns] 名 巧合

延伸片語 **pure coincidence** 純屬巧合

▶ It is pure coincidence that we both named our first baby "Julia". 我們把第一個孩子都取名為「茱莉亞」乃純屬巧合。

❸ co 共同 **+ existence** 存在

coexistence [ˋkoɪgˋzɪstəns] 名 並存

延伸片語 **peaceful coexistence** 和平共存

▶ The peaceful coexistence between the two countries is unreachable. 兩國之間的和平共存是遙不可及的。

❹ co 共同 **+ worker** 工作的人

coworker [ˋkoˌwɜkɚ] 名 同事

延伸片語 **coworker conflict** 同事間的衝突

▶ Danny doesn't know how to deal with coworker conflicts in his office. 丹尼不知道如何處理公司裡同事間的衝突。

❺ co 共同 **+ habit** 居住

cohabit [koˋhæbɪt] 勔 同住

延伸片語 **cohabit with someone** 與某人同居

▶ Judy and Andy had cohabited with each other for ten years before they got married. 茱蒂和安迪在結婚前同居了十年。

延伸補充自然學

☆ **collocate**	共同 + 放置	勔 排列組合
☆ **correspond**	相同的 + 回答	勔 符合
☆ **combine**	共同 + 在一起	勔 聯合、組合

Part4
Unit 106 首 syn,sym
和、一起、相同

情境對話 試水溫

🎧 *Track 106*

David: Do you know how to syncrhonize these two machines? If they don't work simultaneously, I won't be able to detect this synthetic drug.	大衛：你知道要如何同步這兩台機器嗎？如果它們無法同時運作，我就不能測試這個綜合性的藥物了。
Lana: I'm sorry. This is beyond my scope.	拉娜：很抱歉。這超出我領域了。
David: Well, I'm going to get harshly blamed tomorrow.	大衛：好吧，我明天準備被痛罵一頓。
Lana: Let me express my sympathy…	拉娜：讓我表示我的同情……
David: Do you know sometimes sympathy is the synonym for the word, ridicule?	大衛：你知道有時候同情和嘲諷是同義詞嗎？
Lana: I'm sure you're strong enough to deal with everything, okay? C'mon. Let's relax and go for the symphony perforamnce we've been talking about for months.	拉娜：我相信你足夠堅強面對所有事的。好啦，我們來放鬆然後去看那場我們講了好幾個月的交響樂表演吧。
David: Good idea.	大衛：好主意。

單字解析 零距離

1 **syn** 一起 ＋ **chron** 時間 ＋ **ize** 動詞字尾

synchronize ['sɪŋkrənaɪz] 動 使同時發生、同步

延伸片語 to synchronize A with B 讓 A 和 B 同步

226

Ch 3

Part 1

Part 2

Part 3

Part 4

表示行為、動作

▶ The lab manager asked us to synchronize the new machine with the old one.
實驗室管理員要我們把新的機器和舊的同步。

❷ **syn** 同一的 ＋ **thet** 位置 ＋ **ic** 形容詞字尾

synthetic [sɪnˈθɛtɪk] 形 合成的

延伸片語 synthetic fibres 人造纖維

▶ Our company mostly produces clothing made from synthetic fibres.
我們公司主要生產由人造纖維製成的衣服。

❸ **sym** 共同 ＋ **pathy** 感覺

sympathy [ˈsɪmpəθɪ] 名 同情

延伸片語 have sympathy for 對～的同情

▶ I always have great sympathy for homeless children.
我總是對無家可歸的孩子充滿同情。

❹ **syn** 共同 ＋ **onym** 名字

synonym [ˈsɪnəˌnɪm] 名 同義詞

延伸片語 to be a synonym for 對～是同義詞

▶ "Beauty" is sometimes considered to be a synonym for "prettiness."
beauty 有時候會被視為是 prettiness 的同義詞。

❺ **sym** 一起 ＋ **phony** 聲音

symphony [ˈsɪmfənɪ] 名 交響樂；和諧

延伸片語 symphony orchestra 交響樂團

▶ My sister finally achieved her dream of playing in a symphony orchestra.
我姊姊終於達成了在交響樂團中演奏的夢想了。

延伸補充 自然學

☆ **symmetry**	共同 + 測量	動 對稱
☆ **synopsis**	一起 + 看	名 概要

227

根 junct 連接

情境對話 試水溫

Mandy: Did you know that the court has issued an injunction ordering that Blueprint corp. should stop raising funds for its new product?

曼蒂：你知道法院已經對藍圖公司發布強制令，不准它再為新產品籌集資金嗎？

Dorothy: What is Blueprint?

桃樂絲：哪間藍圖公司？

Mandy: It's a subsidiary company adjunct to the international enterprise Redsea. Thanks to the recent financial scandal, their name is on the news headline everyday.

曼蒂：是紅海國際企業的子公司，多虧他們最近的財務醜聞，這公司天天都上新聞。

Dorothy: Oh! THAT Blueprint. It is indeed a very critical juncture for them. The recent conjuncture of events has made the public lose total faith in the company.

桃樂絲：哦！那間藍圖，對他們來說，這真的是危機情況。最近一連串的事件使大眾已經對這公司完全失去信心。

Mandy: The investors should work in conjunction with the government and provide any concrete evidences that could put those responsible behind bars.

曼蒂：投資者應該與政府合作，並提供具體的證據，把那些主使者關進監獄。

單字解析 零距離

❶ **in** 否 + **junct** 連接 + **ion** 名詞字尾

injunction [ɪnˈdʒʌŋkʃən] 名 命令；指令；訓諭

延伸片語 issue an injunction 頒布臨時禁止令

Ch 3

Part 1

Part 2

Part 3

Part 4

表示行為、動作

▶ The court issued an injunction prohibiting the use of certain drugs by professional athletes.
法院頒布禁止令，禁止專業運動員攝取特定藥物。

② **ad** 向、朝 ＋ **junct** 連接

adjunct [ˈædʒʌŋkt] 形 附屬的；兼職的；副的

延伸片語 adjunct professor 兼任教授；客座教授

▶ Despite an unremarkable educational background, he was hired as an adjunct professor due to his hands-on experience in the field. 儘管學歷不好，但憑著在產業實戰經驗，他仍被聘用為客座教授。

③ **junct** 連接 ＋ **ure** 名詞字尾

juncture [ˈdʒʌŋktʃɚ] 名 重要關頭、危機時刻；接合處；連接點

延伸片語 at this juncture 在這個關頭

▶ At this juncture, we had no option but to give up.
在這個關鍵時刻，我們沒有選擇，只能放棄。

④ **con** 共同 ＋ **junct** 連接 ＋ **ure** 名詞字尾

conjuncture [kənˈdʒʌŋktʃɚ] 名 事情或情況共同發生；（緊要）關頭

延伸片語 the conjuncture of events 一連串的事件在這個關頭

▶ The unfortunate conjuncture of events has completely destroyed his confidence.
一連串不幸的事件在這個關頭已經完全摧毀了他的信心。

⑤ **con** 共同 ＋ **junct** 連接 ＋ **ion** 名詞字尾

conjunction [kənˈdʒʌŋkʃən] 名 結合；關聯；連接

延伸片語 in conjunction with 聯合；結合

▶ Take this medicine in conjunction with other supplement to maximize its effects. 將這顆藥跟其他補品一起吃以發揮其最大功效。

⚡ 延伸補充 **自然學**

junct的變化型：joint、join

☆ **adjoin** 朝、向 ＋ 連結　　　　　　動 貼近；毗連

☆ **disjointed** 分離 ＋ 連結 ＋ 形容詞字尾 形 脫臼的；無關聯的；無條理的

根 her(e) 黏著

情境對話 試水溫

Teacher: Adhere to the rules I listed in this book and you will be able to write coherent and well-structured essays.

老師：按照我這本書中列的規則，你就可以寫出條理清楚且結構良好的論文。

Student: From my perspective, adherence to fixed rules will greatly limit student's imagination and all our work will turn out similar.

學生：我覺得，遵守固定規則會完全侷限學生的想像力，我們所有呈現的作品都會很相似。

Teacher: Some students are born writers. The ability to combine written words in a meaningful way inheres within their blood. However, other students need help to reach such level, and this book will be their best savior.

老師：有些學生是天生的作家，血中本質上就流著能夠賦予文字意義的能力。但其他學生需要幫助才能達到這樣的水準，這本書就會他們最好的選擇。

Student: I believe all human beings have inherent ability to write. They just need to be inspired and learn how to set their creativity loose.

學生：我相信所有人都有內在的寫作能力，只需要被啟發並學習如何發揮創造力。

單字解析 零距離

❶ ad 向、朝著 **＋ here** 黏著

adhere [əd'hɪr] **動** 堅持、緊黏

延伸片語 adhere to 遵守；堅守

▶ She's a person with great self-discipline and adheres to her own principles with no exceptions.
她是一個非常自制並堅守原則的人。

表示行為、動作

② **co** 共同 **+** **her** 黏著 **+** **ent** 形容詞字尾

coherent [ko`hɪrənt] 形 一致的；協調的

延伸片語 an coherent argument 條理分明的論述

▶ As a great orator, he is able to make coherent arguments.
身為一個偉大的演說家，他能夠做出條理分明的論述。

- -

③ **ad** 向、朝著 **+** **her** 黏著 **+** **ence** 名詞字尾

adherence [əd`hɪrəns] 名 堅持；嚴守；固執；依附；信奉；忠誠

延伸片語 adherence to 遵守；堅守

▶ Their unwavering adherence to family value is what keep them together through all the tragedies..
使這家人順利渡過所有困境的原因是他們對於家庭核心價值的堅持。

- -

④ **in** 裡、內 **+** **here** 黏著

inhere [ɪn`hɪr] 動 生來即存在的；本質上即是的

延伸片語 inhere in 固有

▶ The hungry for success inheres in all human beings.
所有人心中皆固有對於成功的渴望。

- -

⑤ **in** 裡、內 **+** **her** 黏著 **+** **ent** 形容詞字尾

inherent [ɪn`hɪrənt] 形 內在的；固有的；與生俱來的

延伸片語 inherent in 固有

▶ An inherent flaw in the system predicts the plan's early failure.
系統中固有的瑕疵，早就注定了這個計畫的失敗。

延伸補充 自然學

her(e) 的變化型：hes

☆ **adhesive** 朝、向 + 黏著 + 形容詞字尾 形 黏的；黏著的；有黏性的

☆ **cohesion** 共同、一起 + 黏著 名 結合；凝聚；團結力；附著

根 struct 建造

情境對話 試水溫

William: What's happening over there? Did you see that large crowd of people sitting on the street?

威廉：那邊發生什麼事？你有看到一堆人坐在街上嗎？

Sabrina: The residents are going on a hungry strike, an attempt to obstruct the process of the urban renewal.

薩布麗娜：居民正在絕食抗議，想要阻礙都更的進度。

William: I find it hard to resonate with their feelings. Their houses are old and dangerous and should be torn down by the government to make spaces for constructing infrastructures that benefit all citizens.

威廉：老實說我很難理解他們，他們的房子又老又危險，應該讓政府拆除，才有空間能建造有利於所有公民的基礎建設。

Sabrina: It's harsh and cruel for you to say that. The houses are not just cement structures to them. They represent all the memories of living with the family in this city. The disappearance of the houses will simultaneously destruct their connection to this land.

薩布麗娜：你這樣很殘忍，房子不僅僅是水泥建築物而已，它們還代表了跟家人生活在這城市的所有回憶，房子消失同時會毀了他們與這片土地的連結。

單字解析 零距離

1 ob 反 **+ struct** 建造

obstruct [əbˋstrʌkt] 動 阻塞；堵塞；妨礙；阻擾；阻止

延伸片語 obstruct justice 妨害司法公正

▶ He abused his authority and obstructed justice.
他濫用職權，妨害司法公正。

Ch 3

Part 1

Part 2

Part 3

Part 4

表示行為、動作

❷ con 一同 **+ struct** 建造

construct [kənˋstrʌkt] 動 建造；構成

延伸片語 construct a building 建造大樓

▶ It takes years, sometimes even decades, to construct a building.
要建造一棟大樓得花上好幾年，甚至數十年。

- -

❸ infra 下面 **+ struct** 建造 **+ ure** 名詞字尾

infrastruct**ure** [ˋɪnfrəˏstrʌktʃɚ] 名 公共建設（如鐵路、公路、下水道等）；基礎建設

延伸片語 infrastructure system 基礎設施系統

▶ A sustainable infrastructure system should be in place to ensure convenience for the citizens.
一個永續的基礎設施系統應該要配合民眾的便利性。

- -

❹ struct 建造 **+ ure** 名詞字尾

structure [ˋstrʌktʃɚ] 名 結構；構造；組織

延伸片語 management structure 管理體系

▶ The CEO hires external business consultant to renovate their old-fashioned management structure.
執行長聘請了外部商業顧問來重整他們過時的管理系統。

- -

❺ de 去除 **+ struct** 建造

destruct [dɪˋstrʌkt] 形 破壞的

延伸片語 self destruct 自我毀滅

▶ All the rockets are equipped with self destruct systems.
所有的火箭都設有自我推毀系統。

Unit 110 根 **gen** 起源、產生

🗨 情境對話試水溫

Gina: I can't believe how polluted our planet has become.

吉娜：真不敢相信我們地球到底被汙染成什麼地步。

Warren: Indeed! Very few people are being considerate about what kind of environment we want to leave to the next generations.

沃倫：的確！似乎沒人考慮到我們要留給下一代的環境。

Gina: I believe all modern diseases must be our karma. With all the artificial foods, plants, and animals we created, God knows how many kinds of unthinkable virus and bacteria we have brought to this world. Carcinogens are certainly a lot less back in the genesis of the cosmos, if not non-existent.

吉娜：我認為所有現代疾病都是我們的報應。就我們所創造的所有加工食品、植物和動物，誰知道我們為這世界帶來了多少你無法想像的病毒和細菌。和宇宙之初比起來，要是有，現在所存在的致癌物質肯定要少得多。

Gina: Also, humans are not treating each other any better than before. I remember how friendly and congenial people used to be, even with strangers.

吉娜：況且，人類也沒有對彼此比較好，我記得人類曾經有多善良、好相處，即使對陌生人也是如此。

Warren: And all the social problems such as gender and race discrimination are not solved either.

沃倫：還有性別和種族歧視等所有社會問題也還沒有解決。

⚡ 單字解析零距離

❶ **gene** 起源；產生 ＋ **ration** 名詞字尾

Ch 3

Part 1

Part 2

Part 3

Part 4

表示行為、動作

generation [ˌdʒɛnəˈreʃən] 名 世代；一代

延伸片語 **generations to come** 接下來的世代

▶ I hope the world will remain in peace in the generations to come. 我希望在接下來的世代都能保持和平。

・・・

❷ carc 癌症 ＋ **ino** ＋ **gen** 起源

carcinogens [karˈsɪnədʒən] 名【醫】致癌物質

延伸片語 **known carcinogens** 已知的致癌物

▶ The book contains detailed explanation of all known carcinogens. 這本書包含了所有已知致癌物詳細的介紹。

・・

❸ gene 起源 ＋ **sis** 名詞字尾

genesis [ˈdʒɛnəsɪs] 名【文】起源；發生；創始

延伸片語 **genesis of...** ～的起源

▶ The genesis of the existing universes no longer remains a mystery. 宇宙的起源不再只是個神秘的傳說。

・・

❹ con 一起 ＋ **gen** 產生 ＋ **ial** 形容詞字尾

congenial [kənˈdʒinjəl] 形 友善的；協調的；一致的；意氣相投的；性格相同的

延伸片語 **congenial personality** 友善的個性

▶ She has a congenial personality so people are naturally attracted to her. 她個性很友善，所以大家都很自然地被她吸引。

・・

❺ gen 產生 ＋ **der** 名詞字尾

gender [ˈdʒɛndɚ] 名 性別

延伸片語 **gender discrimination** 性別歧視

▶ The politician has vowed to exterminate all gender discriminations. 這名政治人物鄭重宣示要消除所有性別歧視。

💡 延伸補充 **自然學**

gen的變化型：gene、gener

☆ **degenerate** 反轉 ＋ 產生 ＋ 動詞／形容詞名詞／字尾　　動／形 衰退（的）；墮落（的）

Unit 111 根 cert 相信、確信

情境對話試水溫

Eugune: How can you be certain this guy is our most ideal candidate for this position?

尤金：你怎麼確定這個人是這職缺最理想的選擇？

Evan: He has multiple certifications that prove his proficiency in this field.

伊凡：他有多項證書，就足以證明他對這領域的熟悉度。

Eugune: If your certitude of his ability is based merely on papers, I highly doubt its credibility. Aren't there better ways to ascertain that he's the guy we are looking for?

尤金：如果你只靠書面來評斷他的能力，我並沒有很看好。難道沒有更好的方法來確定他就是最佳人選嗎？

Evan: One way to certify that is you talk to him personally.

伊凡：不然你可以親自跟他對談來證實。

單字解析零距離

❶ cert 確信 **＋ ain** 形容詞字尾，表示屬於

certain [ˈsɝtən] 形 確鑿的；無疑的；可靠的；確信的
延伸片語 feel certain that 對……感到確定

▶ I feel certain that David's having a crush on you.
我非常確定大衛喜歡你。

❷ cert(i) 相信、確信 **＋ fic ＋ ation** 名詞字尾

certification [ˌsɝtɪfəˈkeʃən] 名 證明；檢定；保證
延伸片語 earn certification 獲得……證照

Ch 3

Part 1

Part 2

Part 3

Part 4

表示行為、動作

▶ He earned certification to perform a highly intricate kind of brain surgery.
他獲得高複雜度腦部手術的證照。

- -

❸ cert(i) 確信 ＋ **tude** 名詞字尾

certitude [ˈsɝtətjud] 名 確實；確信

延伸片語 **degree of certitude** 確信的程度

▶ My degree of certitude regarding the outcome of this matter is based on my knowledge about the individuals in charge of it.
我確信這件事的程度是基於我對於負責團隊的了解。

- -

❹ as 朝向 ＋ **cert** 確信 ＋ **ain** 動詞字尾，表示屬於

ascertain [ˌæsɚˈten] 動 查明；弄清

延伸片語 **ascertain the cause of** 查明……的成因

▶ The police are trying to ascertain the cause of the explosion by interviewing the witnesses.
警察正試著透過訪問目擊者還查明爆炸的原因。

- -

❺ cert 確信 ＋ **ify** 動詞字尾，使……成為

certify [ˈsɝtəˌfaɪ] 動 證明；保證

延伸片語 **certify that** 證明；證實

▶ To certify that she's not pregnant, she clenched fists and hit her own belly very hard.
為了證明她沒有懷孕，她握起拳頭大力揍自己的肚子。

延伸補充 自然學

cert 的變化型：cred

☆ **credence** 相信、確信 ＋ 名詞字尾 　　　　 名 相信；信用；供桌

☆ **credible** 相信、確信 ＋ 形容詞字尾，表示 形 可信的；可靠的 可能、可以的

☆ **credulous** 相信、確信 ＋ 形容詞字尾，表示 形 輕信的，易受騙的 充滿的

根 lect 收集、選擇

情境對話試水溫

Robin: Ted, which party do you support for 2020 election?

羅賓：泰德，2020選舉你要支持哪個政黨呢？

Ted: I'm still waiting and seeing who will be the president candidate. After all, every person they want to nominate is an intellect, so it all depends on how they select based on their strategies.

泰德：我還在觀望哪位總統候選人會出現。畢竟每位他們想提名的人都是精英，所以就取決於他們怎麼照策略選出適合人選。

Robin: Me too. I'm awaiting they finish collecting survey data and see who's up and coming. Every candidate has their merits and drawbacks, so I eagerly want to know who will be the president elect and how he/she will lead Taiwan.

羅賓：我也是。我仍在等待他們收集完民調，看看哪位會嶄露頭角。每位候選人都有他們的優缺點，所以我迫不及待想知道誰是總統當選人，以及如何帶領台灣。

Ted: Soon we'll know. Just keep patient and objective.

泰德：我們很快就會知道，現在就耐住性子、保持客觀。

單字解析零距離

❶ e 外 ＋ lect 選擇 ＋ ion 性質

election [ɪˈlɛkʃən] 名 選舉

延伸片語 Federal Election Commission 聯邦選舉委員會

▶ Recently there are a lot of scandals about Federal Election Commission.
最近有相當多關於聯邦選舉委員會的醜聞。

Ch 3

Part 1
Part 2
Part 3
Part 4

表示行為、動作

② intel 裡、內 ＋ lect 收集

intellect [`ɪntl̩ˌɛkt]` 名 知識份子、才華出眾之人

延伸片語 **intellect ball** 扭轉魔球（一種玩具）

▶ Little Sam asked an intellect ball for his birthday present.
小山姆要求一顆旋轉魔球作為他的生日禮物。

- -

③ se 分 ＋ lect 選擇

select [sə`lɛkt]` 動 挑選、選拔

延伸片語 **select committee** 特別委員會

▶ The government is going to have a select committee to
investigate this murder.
政府將成立特別調查委員會去調查這起謀殺案。

- -

④ col 共同 ＋ lect 收集

collect [kə`lɛkt]` 動 採集、集合

延伸片語 **re-collect** 回憶

▶ I am really mad at my mom for throwing my pictures away. All
of them are childhood re-collected.
我真的很氣我媽媽把我的照片丟掉。那些都是兒時回憶。

- -

⑤ e 外 ＋ lect 選擇

elect [ɪ`lɛkt]` 動 推舉、推選

延伸片語 **president elect** 總統當選人

▶ Who is the president elect this year?
誰是今年的總統當選人？

延伸補充 自然學

lect 的變化型：leg、lig

☆ **eligible** 可被選出的　　　形 合適的
☆ **legion** 聚集的情況　　　名 眾多

根 mit, miss 送

情境對話試水溫 🎧 *Track 113*

Betty: The General of the Army just admitted that the missile launch was a careless mistake.

貝蒂：陸軍將軍剛剛承認導彈是不小心發射出去的。

Urania: A careless mistake? That is a very irresponsible remark.

烏拉尼亞：不小心，這是非常不負責任的說法。

Betty: According to him, a soldier dozed off during watch and accidentally hit the button that transmits launch signals to the missile.

貝蒂：根據他的說法，一名士兵在值勤期間打瞌睡，不小心碰到按鈕，向導彈發射信號。

Urania: He should submit a 5000-word letter of apology to the public. The missile landed in a residential area! Though no one was hurt, the residents were surely terrified when the burnt missile crashed onto ground and emitted clouds of smoke.

烏拉尼亞：他應該繳交一份5000字的道歉信給社會大眾。導彈降落在住宅區！雖然沒有人受傷，但當被燒毀的導彈撞到地面並散發出濃煙時，居民們肯定很害怕。

單字解析零距離

1 **ad** 向、朝 ＋ **mit** 送

admit [əd'mɪt] 動 承認

延伸片語 admit defeat 認輸

▶ My motto is to never admit defeat and always do my best.
我的座右銘是永不認輸，做到最好。

Ch 3

Part 1

Part 2

Part 3

Part 4

表示行為、動作

❷ **miss** 送 ＋ **ile** 物體

missile [ˈmɪsl] 名 飛彈；導彈；投射物；投射武器

延伸片語 missile strike 導彈攻擊

▶ My ears are ringing after the intensive missile strike.
在密集的導彈攻擊後，我出現耳鳴的狀況。

・・・・・・・・・・・・・・・・・・・・・・・・・・・・・・・・・・

❸ **trans** 穿越 ＋ **mit** 送

transmit [trænsˈmɪt] 動 傳送；傳達；傳（光、熱、聲等）；傳動

延伸片語 transmit virus 傳播病毒

▶ Wear face masks when you catch a cold to avoid transmitting virus to others.
感冒時要戴口罩，避免將病毒傳染給他人。

・・・・・・・・・・・・・・・・・・・・・・・・・・・・・・・・・・

❹ **sub** 下方 ＋ **mit** 送

submit [səbˈmɪt] 動 遞交；使服從；使屈服

延伸片語 submit application 提交申請

▶ Make sure to submit the application before the deadline.
確認在截止日之前提交申請。

・・・・・・・・・・・・・・・・・・・・・・・・・・・・・・・・・・

❺ **e** 外 ＋ **mit** 送

emit [ɪˈmɪt] 動 發射；發出

延伸片語 emit odor 發出臭味

▶ Some insects emit odor to fend off enemies.
有些昆蟲會散發出氣味來抵擋敵人。

💡 延伸補充 **自然學**

mit、miss的變化型：mise

| ☆ **surmise** | 上方 ＋ 送 | 動 推測；猜測 |
| ☆ **premise** | 先前 ＋ 送 | 動 提出前提 |

根 duct 引導

情境對話試水溫

🎧 *Track 114*

Rita: What are the headlines for today?	麗塔：今天頭條新聞是什麼？
Vicky: A guy hijacked a mid-night bus and abducted all the passengers.	薇琪：有個人劫持一輛夜間巴士，綁架了所有乘客。
Rita: Seriously, Where are they now?	麗塔：真的嗎？那他們現在在哪裡？
Vicky: Seems like the conductor was somehow able to escape. The police are questioning the conductor to see if they could find out the passengers' whereabouts.	薇琪：好像是車上的售票員找到機會逃脫。警方正在詢問售票員，看看是否能查到乘客的下落。
Rita: Only the conductor escaped? Umm....why do I smell something fishy.	麗塔：只有售票員逃脫了？嗯……事有蹊蹺。
Vicky: Same here. Anyway, looks like the main chief officer responsible for conducting the rescue operation has some extraordinary history in solving cases like this.	薇琪：我也覺得，反正，這次執行救援行動的警察對這類案子很有經驗。
Rita: Has the abductors revealed their intention?	麗塔：歹徒是否透露他們的動機？
Vicky: Apparently they are asking for large ransom. The victim's families are trying hard to negotiate the price and deduct as much as possible.	薇琪：顯然他們要鉅額的贖金。受害者家屬正努力談判價格，盡量降低數目。
Rita: What do we know about the abductors?	麗塔：那我們對歹徒了解多少？

Ch 3

Part 1
Part 2
Part 3
Part 4

表示行為、動作

Vicky: Apparently they've all received high education. One of them was even inducted into the government several years ago.

薇琪：很明顯他們都是高知識分子，其中一個甚至幾年前還被招入進政府工作。

單字解析零距離

1 **ab** 離開 ＋ **duct** 引導

abduct [æbˋdʌkt] 動 誘拐；綁架；劫持

延伸片語 **abduct child** 綁架兒童

▶ This criminal organization abducted child from parks and should be sentenced forever. 這個犯罪組織從公園綁架孩童，他們應被終身監禁。

2 **con** 共同 ＋ **duct** 引導 ＋ **or** 名詞字尾，表示人

conductor [kənˋdʌktɚ] 名 領導者；管理人；響導

延伸片語 **train conductor** 列車長

▶ The train conductor was found drunk on duty and laid off.
這位火車售票員被發現在值勤時間喝醉而被解雇了。

3 **con** 共同 ＋ **duct** 引導

conduct [kənˋdʌkt] 動 引導，帶領；實施；處理

延伸片語 **conduct survey** 進行調查

▶ I conducted a survey to find out how often people have soda drinks. 我進行了一項調查，研究民眾喝蘇打水的頻率。

4 **de** 除去 ＋ **duct** 引導

deduct [dɪˋdʌkt] 動 扣除

延伸片語 **deduct points** 扣分

▶ The student had points deducted from his essay score for plagiarizing other's ideas. 這學生的論文抄襲他人想法，因而被扣分。

5 **in** 入 ＋ **duct** 引導

induct [ɪnˋdʌkt] 動 使正式就任；吸收……為會員；徵召……入伍

延伸片語 **induct into** 正式就任某職

▶ My father was inducted into the Ministry of National Defense in 1993. 我爸爸在1993年正式就任國防部長。

243

根 pend 懸掛、費用

情境對話試水溫

Melvin: My sister was suspended from school for stealing from a jewelry store.

梅爾文：我妹妹在一家珠寶店偷竊而被迫停學。

Nicky: I don't understand. Your family is rich! Why would your sister ever steal?

尼基：我不懂，你家已經很有錢！為什麼你妹妹需要偷東西？

Melvin: Well…my sister is obsessed with shiny stuff and my mom asks her to cut down expenditures on accessories. She wishes my sister could expend her resources on more educational things, but my sister refused.

梅爾文：嗯……她沉迷於那些閃閃發光的東西，我媽要她在配件上省點花費，希望我妹可以將錢花在念書上，但我妹拒絕了。

Melvin: So she stole.

梅爾文：所以她偷東西。

Nicky: Exactly. A very cheap pendant from a nearby store. I guess she was mostly doing it to exasperate my mom.

尼基：沒錯，先偷附近超商裡的便宜吊飾，我猜她是為了激怒我媽。

Nicky: She should be sent to the military school and learn how to be independent.

尼基：她應該被送到軍校，先學習獨立。

單字解析零距離

1 sus 下方 + pend 懸掛

suspend [sə'spɛnd] 動 懸掛；吊；懸浮；使中止

延伸片語 suspend from school 勒令停學

Ch 3

Part 1
Part 2
Part 3
Part 4

表示行為、動作

▶ She was suspended from school for bullying her classmates.
她因為霸凌同學而被迫休學。

❷ **ex** 向外 ＋ **pend** 費用 ＋ **iture** 名詞字尾

expenditure [ɪkˋspɛndɪtʃɚ] 名 消費；支出；用光
延伸片語 expenditure on... ～的開支
▶ Expenditure on private school tuition fees put a lot of pressure on my mom.
私立學校的學費讓我媽媽壓力很大。

❸ **ex** 向外 ＋ **pend** 費用

expend [ɪkˋspɛnd] 動 消費；花費
延伸片語 expend income on 把收入花在
▶ I expend 50% of my income on house rent.
我把收入的一半花在房租上。

❹ **pend** 懸掛 ＋ **ant** 物品

pendant [ˋpɛndənt] 名 下垂物；垂飾；掛件；懸吊裝置；吊燈
延伸片語 diamond pendant 鑽石項鍊
▶ That diamond pendant is my family heirloom.
那條鑽石項鍊是我的傳家寶。

❺ **in** 向內 ＋ **de** 分離 ＋ **pend** 懸掛 ＋ **ent** 形容詞字尾

independent [͵ɪndɪˋpɛndənt] 形 獨立的；自治的；自主
延伸片語 independent organization 獨立組織
▶ We are an non-profit independent organization dedicated to environmental protection .
我們是一個致力於環境保護的非營利獨立組織。

延伸補充 自然學

pend 的變化型：pense

| ☆ **expense** | 向外 ＋ 費用 | 名 費用；價錢 |
| ☆ **dispense** | 分離 ＋ 懸掛 | 動 分配，分發；施給 |

情境對話試水溫

🎧 *Track 116*

Hank: I read a piece of article about the wealth inequality in our city.

漢克：我讀了一篇關於我們城市貧富差距的文章。

Eileen: That certainly is a critical issue. The west side of the city is affluent and enjoys all the resources while the east side lives in slums.

艾琳：這當然是個關鍵問題，城市的西區很富裕，享有所有資源；而東區則生活在貧民窟。

Hank: Did you know that the effluents from local factories are flushed into the reservoirs in the east side?

漢克：你知道當地工廠的污水都沖進東區的水庫嗎？

Eileen: Really? Can't believe those poor people are drinking toxic fluids. They are already poor but now they are even poisoned.

艾琳：真的嗎？真不敢相信那些窮人都在喝有毒液體。他們已經很窮了結果現在甚至還中毒。

Hank: The rich ones should really wield their influence and improve the living quality of their fellow people.

漢克：有錢人應該真正發揮影響力，提高夥伴的生活質量。

單字解析零距離

① **af** 向 ＋ **flu** 流 ＋ **ent** 形容詞字尾，表示……狀態的

affluent [ˈæflʊənt] 形 富裕的；豐富的；富饒的

延伸片語 **affluent neighborhood** 富人區

▶ Grown up in the affluent neighborhood, she was not aware of the real pain and suffering in this world.
她自小在富人區長大，沒有體會過真正的痛苦跟磨難。

Ch 3

Part 1

Part 2

Part 3

Part 4

表示行為、動作

❷ ef 外 **＋ flu** 流 **＋ ent** 形容詞字尾，表示⋯⋯狀態的

effluent [ˈɛflʊənt] 形 流出的 名 廢水

延伸片語 effluent treatment plant 汙水處理工廠

▶ My dad runs an effluent treatment plant and I'd go help him during the summer vacation.
我爸爸經營一間汙水處理工廠，我暑假時都會去幫忙。

· ·

❸ flu 流 **＋ sh** 動詞字尾

flush [flʌʃ] 動 沖水；用水沖洗；使（臉等）漲紅

延伸片語 flush the toilet 沖馬桶

▶ My three-year-old nephew was recently potty-trained but always forgot to flush the toilet.
我三歲的姪子最近會自己去上廁所，但總是忘記沖馬桶。

· ·

❹ flu 流 **＋ id** 形容詞字尾，表示性質

fluid [ˈfluɪd] 形 流動的；流體的 名 流體；流質；液體

延伸片語 body fluid 體液

▶ The doctors are worried that the patient's body fluid could carry viruses.
醫生擔心病人的體液會帶病毒。

· ·

❺ in 內部 **＋ flu** 流 **＋ ence** 名詞字尾

influence [ˈɪnflʊəns] 名 影響

延伸片語 influence on/over 對⋯⋯有影響

▶ My mom is my role model and she's a great influence on me.
我媽媽是我的榜樣，她對我有很深的影響。

⚡ 延伸補充 自然學

flu的變化型：flux

| ☆ **afflux** | 向＋流 | 名 流入；流向；匯入 |
| ☆ **influx** | 向內＋流 | 名 湧進；匯集 |

247

字根 solv(e) 釋放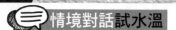

情境對話試水溫

🎧 *Track 117*

Ruby: According to the news, the investigation absolved the politician from the scandal.

露比：新聞説，這調查證明了那位政客跟醜聞無關。

Anita: But it's so obvious that the evident they gathered were all biased.

安妮塔：但是很明顯他們蒐集的證據都有私心。

Ruby: Exactly. So, it's safe to say that this case resolve nothing regarding the changes of the welfare system.

露比：沒錯。所以，我敢説這個案件在福利制度什麼事情都沒有解決。

Anita: It feels like our hopes for a better retirement have dissolved into nothingness. Why is it so hard for the government to simply listen to us?

安妮塔：感覺我們對未來退休計畫的希望已經蕩然無存。為什麼讓政府聽我們説話會這麼難？

Ruby: Because integrity is dissolvable in face of power and money.

露比：因為誠信在權力跟金錢面前是能夠蕩然無存的。

Anita: Well said. How about you running for a legislative seat?

安妮塔：説的好。你想不想去選立委？

Ruby: Why me?

露比：為什麼是我？

Anita: You're a problem solver, and you're genuine!

安妮塔：你是個問題解決者，而且你很真誠！

Ruby: Here's another dark side to become a candidate for legislator. You have to have money first!

露比：當立委的另一個黑暗面就是你必須要先有錢！

單字解析零距離

① **ab** 離開 ＋ **solve** 釋放

Ch 3

Part 1
Part 2
Part 3
Part 4

表示行為、動作

absolve [əbˋsɑlv] 動 寬恕

延伸片語 absolve sb from sth 宣告……無罪；赦免……的罪

▶ Because of the amnesty, all prisoners were absolved from their crimes. 由於特赦，所有犯人都被免除了他們的罪責。

② **re** 再＋**solve** 釋放

resolve [rɪˋzɑlv] 動 解決

延伸片語 resolve on doing... 決心做……

▶ Helen resolved on job-hopping to that computer company for higher salary. 海倫決心為了較高的薪水跳槽到那家電腦公司去。

③ **dis** 除去＋**solve** 釋放

dissolve [dɪˋzɑlv] 動 溶解

延伸片語 dissolve into laughter 忍不住笑起來

▶ The man dissolved into laughter when hearing the joke.
男子聽到那個笑話忍不住笑了起來。

④ **dis** 除去＋**solv** 釋放＋**able** 形容詞字尾，表示能夠……的

dissolvable [dɪˋzɑlvəbl] 形 可溶解的

延伸片語 dissolvable stitches 可分解的手術用縫線

▶ Dissolvable stitches have replaced the traditional ones in modern surgeries. 可分解手術用縫線已在現代手術中取代了傳統縫線。

⑤ **solv** 釋放＋**er** 名詞字尾，表示人

solver [ˋsɑlvɚ] 名 解決者

延伸片語 solver of problem 解決問題者

▶ No one could be the solver of this difficult problem.
沒人能成為解決這個難題的人。

 延伸補充 自然學

與 solv(e) 近義的字根：solu

☆ **soluble** 可以解除的　　　　形 可被溶解的

根 fract, frag
破、打碎

情境對話**試水溫**

🎧 *Track 118*

Liam: The CEO is very fractious. Last time, he agreed to place a big order, but today, he changed his mind, signing us a deal with only a fraction of the previous amount.

連恩：這老闆很難搞。上次，他同意下了一筆大單；結果今天，他就改變心意，跟我們簽約的金額僅是上次協議的一小部分。

Olivia: Well, if a CEO is always predictable, the company will be easily overtaken.

奧莉維亞：嗯，如果一個老闆總是能讓你預測到他的想法，那公司就會很容易被超越。

Liam: However, I heard that in terms of personnel managemetn, he is very strict with rules. A single minor infraction will lead to a lay-off.

連恩：但是，我聽說在人事方面，他也有很多規矩。一次微小的失誤都有可能被他裁員。

Olivaa: That's harsh.

奧莉維亞：太嚴格了吧！

Liam: Last time, a clerk accidentally broke her mug, and she didn't sweep off all the porcelain fragments. The CEO stepped on it. Though unhurt, he scolded the clerk for like half an hour.

連恩：上次有個員工不小心打破她的馬克杯，沒有把碎片掃乾淨結果被老闆踩到。雖然老闆沒受傷，但他罵了這員工將近半小時。

Olivia: Wow, A fragile and careless person like me is certainly below the standard.

奧莉維亞：哇！像我這樣脆弱又粗心的人一定達不到他的標準。

單字解析**零距離**

❶ **fract** 破、打碎 ＋ **ious** 形容詞字尾

Ch 3

Part 1

Part 2

Part 3

Part 4

表示行為、動作

fractious [ˈfrækʃəs] 形 易怒的

延伸片語 **a fractious boy** 一個倔強的男孩

▶ No wonder that he became a factious boy then.
難怪他後來變成個性格倔強的男孩。

- -

❷ **fract** 破、打碎 ＋ **ion** 名詞字尾

fraction [ˈfrækʃən] 名 一小部分

延伸片語 **a fraction of** 一小部分、少許

▶ Tom has done only a fraction of his homework.
湯姆只做了一小部分作業。

- -

❸ **in** 入 ＋ **fract** 破、打碎 ＋ **ion** 名詞字尾

infraction [ɪnˈfrækʃən] 名 違法

延伸片語 **minor infraction** 輕微違法、小孩犯法

▶ I don't think this minor infraction will lead him to death.
我認為這項輕微違法不會導致他死亡。

- -

❹ **frag** 破、打碎 ＋ **ment** 名詞字尾

fragment [ˈfrægmənt] 名 碎片；破片；斷片

延伸片語 **to break into fragments** 破成碎片

▶ The vase fell off from the desk during the earthquake and broke into fragments. 這花瓶在地震時從桌上掉下來，且破成碎片。

- -

❺ **frag** 破、打碎 ＋ **ile** 形容詞字尾，表示能夠的

fragile [ˈfrædʒəl] 形 易碎的；脆的；易損壞的

延伸片語 **to be labeled fragile** 被標示易碎

▶ My luggaged was labeled fragile in case the wine in it went broken. 我的行李被標示易碎，以防裡面的酒破掉。

延伸補充 自然學

☆ **fractional** 一小部分的 形 碎片的

根 rupt 破裂

🎧 *Track 119*

💬 情境對話試水溫

Jean: May and Chip's abrupt breakup was indeed a piece of shocking news. I thought they were made for each other.

珍：梅和奇普突如其來的分手真是一條令人吃驚的消息。

Leo: Not exactly. I heard May found Chip's anger consistently erupted into violence and that he led a corrupt life with excuses of engagement in social activities. May also had a drawback that she was bankrupt of manners, continuously interrupting the conversation between Chip and his parents with clueless interjections.

里歐：不盡然。我聽說梅發現奇普常常發脾氣就會有暴力行為，而且他還以應酬為藉口過著墮落的生活。但梅也有缺點──就是沒禮貌，她總是用白目的話打斷奇普和他父母的談話。

Jean: These really blow my mind. Well, probably they need to learn how to be more mature and get out of the flaws in the relationship for their Mr./Ms. Right.

珍：這些事蹟真是令我大吃一驚。他們也許需要學習如何在感情中更成熟並且改掉惡習才能迎接真命天子／女。

⚡ 單字解析零距離

❶ **ab** 離開 ＋ **rupt** 破

abrupt [əˋbrʌpt] 形 突然的

延伸片語 abrupt manner 唐突的舉止

▶ The man's abrupt manner made her quite uncomfortable.
男子唐突的舉止讓她相當不舒服。

Ch 3

Part 1

Part 2

Part 3

Part 4

表示行為、動作

2 e 向外 + rupt 破

erupt [ɪˈrʌpt] 動 （火山）爆發

延伸片語 **erupt into** 突然發生；爆發

▶ She left her ex-boyfriend as soon as she found his anger consistently erupted into violence.
當她一發現前男友發脾氣總是會有暴力行為，就馬上離開他了。

- -

3 cor 共同 + rupt 破

corrupt [kəˈrʌpt] 形 腐敗的

延伸片語 **a corrupt life** 墮落的生活

▶ Seeing his son leading a corrupt life makes the old father distressed.
看兒子過著墮落的生活讓老父親憂心痛苦。

- -

4 bank 銀行 + rupt 破

bankrupt [ˈbæŋkrʌpt] 動 破產

延伸片語 **be bankrupt of...** 缺乏……

▶ The woman is beautiful but is bankrupt of sympathy.
那個女人漂亮但沒有同情心。

- -

5 inter 在……中間 + rupt 破

interrupt [ˌɪntəˈrʌpt] 動 打岔

延伸片語 **interrupt ... with...** 以……打斷某人或某事

▶ The boy interrupted the two women's conversation with a scream.
男孩以尖叫聲打斷了兩個女人的談話。

延伸補充 自然學

☆ **disrupt**	分開 + 破	動 打亂
☆ **corruption**	一併被破壞	名 墮落、腐敗
☆ **disruptive**	分開 + 破 + 有～傾向	形 具分裂性的

根 **fin** 結束、最終、限制

💬 情境對話試水溫

Gabriel: Did you know that Kuo Hsing-Chun has made it to be the finalist in the weightlifting of Jakarta Palembang 2018 Asian Games?

加百列：你知道郭婞淳已經成為2018雅加達亞運的舉重項目決賽者嗎？

Michael: Really? She is such an impressive athlete that she could beat up the other contestants with finite resource.

麥可：真的嗎？她是一位令人印象深刻的運動選手，運用有限的資源打敗其他的參賽者。

Gabriel: Exactly! She is an outstanding example that proves whoever pulls out all the stops can have infinite potential.

加百列：對啊！她是一位傑出的模範，讓大家知道那些盡全力的人將有無限的潛力。

Michael: Totally! When is the final game then? We should stay tuned to root for her!

麥可：真的！那她最終比賽是什麼時候？我們需要蹲在電視機前面為她加油！

單字解析零距離

1 **fin** 最終 ＋ **al** 形容詞字尾 ＋ **ist** 人

finalist [ˈfaɪnl̩ɪst] 名 參加決賽的人

延伸片語 **finalist works** 入選作品

▶ What do you think of those finalist works?
你如何看待那些入選作品？

表示行為、動作

② **fin** 限制 ＋ **ite** 形容詞字尾

finite [ˈfaɪnaɪt] 形 有限的

延伸片語 **finite resource** 有限資源

▶ Land resource is considered as finite resource.
土地資源是有限的資源。

- -

③ **in** 不 ＋ **fin** 限制 ＋ **ite** 形容詞字尾

infinite [ˈɪnfənɪt] 形 無限的、無邊的

延伸片語 **infinite space** 無限的空間

▶ Does the universe have infinite space?
宇宙擁有無限的空間嗎？

- -

④ **fin** 結束、最終 ＋ **al** 形容詞字尾

final [ˈfaɪnl] 形 最終的

延伸片語 **final aim** 終極的目的

▶ What on earth is his final aim?
他的終極目的到底是什麼？

延伸補充 自然學

☆ **confine**	一起限制	動 限制
☆ **define**	加強限制	動 定義
☆ **refine**	再限制	動 精進

根 clude, close 關閉

Tom:	Adam, I just checked the player list. William is excluded from the starting lineup of the final?	湯姆：艾登，我剛剛看了球員表，威廉被排除在總冠軍賽的先發名單外？
Adam:	He committed flagrant 2 in the semi-final, which involved excessively violent contact to the same player.	艾登：他在決賽時兩次惡意犯規，包含針對同一位球員過度的暴力接觸。
Tom:	However, as the statistic showed, his field goal percentage is quite high. Maybe he will be the key person leading us to win out in the final.	湯姆：但是根據統計顯示，他的投球命中率非常高！也許他能成為讓我們在總冠軍賽勝出的關鍵角色。
Adam:	I talked to William after the game. He admitted he did it on purpose, but refused to disclose the intention.	艾登：我賽後跟威廉談過，他承認他故意犯規，但拒絕透露動機。
Tom:	You planned to seclude him from the team?	湯姆：你打算將他跟球隊隔離嗎？
Adam:	Not really. He's bench player for the final. He must learn to be calm under any situation. Before he makes it, he won't be back to the starting lineup, even if he is veteran.	艾登：不，他在候補球員名單內，他必須學會在任何情況下都保持冷靜。在他做到以前，即便他是資深球員，我也不會讓他回到先發名單。
Tom:	To conclude, you're precluding any possibility of losing championship rings this year, aren't you?	湯姆：總之，你在防止今年輸掉冠軍戒指的任何可能性，對吧？
Adam:	Correct.	艾登：正確。

 單字解析零距離

1 con 共同 ＋ clude 關閉

conclude [kənˋklud] 動 做結論

Ch 3

Part 1

Part 2

Part 3

Part 4

表示行為、動作

延伸片語 **to conclude** 結論是、總之

▶ To conclude, I wish the conference a great success!
總之,預祝大會圓滿成功!

---

❷ **ex** 向外 + **clude** 關閉

exclude [ɪk`sklud] 動 排除

延伸片語 **exclude from** 使……不得進入、把……排除在外、拒絕

▶ He has been excluded from the church. 教堂已經拒絕接納他了。

---

❸ **in** 在……裡面 + **clued** 關閉

include [ɪn`klud] 動 包含

延伸片語 **include among** 包括……在當中、把……算進

▶ She includes herself among the guests. 她把自己算作客人之一。

---

❹ **dis** 相反的 + **close** 關閉

disclose [dɪs`kloz] 動 揭發

延伸片語 **disclose the secret** 揭發秘密

▶ The victim's letter disclosed the secret of murderer's intention.
受害者的信件揭發了兇手的動機。

---

❺ **pre** 之前 + **clude** 關閉

preclude [prɪ`klud] 動 防止

延伸片語 **preclude the possibility of misunderstanding** 防止誤解的可能

▶ Why not preclude the possibility of any misunderstandings?
為什麼不防止任何誤解的可能性呢?

---

❻ **se** 分開 + **clude** 關閉

seclude [sɪ`klud] 動 使……孤立

延伸片語 **seclude oneself from society** 與社會隔絕、過隱居生活

▶ You can't seclude yourself from society. 你不能與社會隔絕啊。

根 **not** 寫、標示

💬 **情境對話**試水溫 🎧 *Track 122*

Ethan: Have you annotated the poem? It's our assignment this week.

伊森：你有沒有註釋這首詩？那是我們這禮拜的功課。

Jacob: Only half way through. I don't quite understand all those connotations. I know this is a notable literary work, but I just can't grasp its meaning.

雅各：只做了一半。我對那些所有的內涵都不太理解。我知道這是一部很有名的文學作品，但我就是無法吸收其中的意義。

Ethan: Take it easy. Maybe you can discuss it with the professor in class.

伊森：放輕鬆點。也許你可以在課堂上跟教授討論？

Jacob: I don't think so. He just sent a notice yesterday, saying that anyone failing to finish the assignment will automatically receive a B.

雅各：我覺得不行。他昨天才剛發公告說沒有完成功課的人會直接拿到 B。

Ethan: Really? How come I didn't know that? I guess I have to notify everyone now.

伊森：真的嗎？我怎麼不知道？我現在應該要通知大家了。

Jacob: Send a group message now!

雅各：現在傳到群組！

⚡ **單字解析**零距離

❶ **an** 添加 ＋ **not** 標示 ＋ **ate** 動詞字尾

annotate [ˈænoˌtet] 🔡 注釋

延伸片語 **annotate on** 為……做詮釋

▶ Jack had to annotate on what his father said in case it got misinterpreted. 傑克必須為父親所說的話作註解，以免被誤解了。

Ch 3
Part 1
Part 2
Part 3
Part 4
表示行為、動作

❷ **con** 共同＋ **not** 標示＋ **ation** 名詞字尾，表示行為、結果

connotation [ˌkɑnəˈteʃən] 名 言外之意

延伸片語 **underlying connotation** 隱含的言外之意

▶ To some people, an underlying connotation of marriage is love's gravestone.
對某些人來說，婚姻隱含著愛情墳墓的言外之意。

❸ **not** 寫、標示＋ **able** 形容詞字尾，表示能夠……的

notable [ˈnotəbl̩] 形 顯著的

延伸片語 **notable difference** 顯著差異

▶ I can't tell any notable difference between the twin brothers.
我無法分辨這兩個雙胞胎兄弟的顯著差異。

❹ **not** 寫、標示＋ **ice** 動詞字尾，表示狀態

notice [ˈnotɪs] 動 注意到 名 注意；通知

延伸片語 **notice of delivery** 提貨通知單

▶ You will receive a notice of delivery as soon as we confirm your remittance.
匯款一經確認，您就會立刻收到提貨通知單。

❺ **not** 寫、標示＋ **ify** 動詞字尾，使……成為

notify [ˈnotəˌfaɪ] 動 通知

延伸片語 **notify someone of something** 將某事通知某人

▶ This letter is to notify you of the expiration of your membership.
這封信件是要通知您，您的會員資格已經期滿了。

延伸補充自然學

☆ **connote**	共同的標記	動 暗示
☆ **notate**	標記號的動作	動 以符號標記
☆ **footnote**	腳＋標記	動 給……作腳註
☆ **endnote**	結尾＋標記	名 尾注

根 test 測試、證據

🎧 *Track 123*

💬 情境對話試水溫

Sophie: The video of that divorce went viral. Have you sen it?

蘇菲：那部離婚的影片一直在洗版，你有看到嗎？

James: Yep. Apparently, the husband and wife detested each other.

詹姆士：有。那對夫妻明顯很討厭彼此。

Sophie: What's interesting is that all their children testified against their father.

蘇菲：有趣的是，他們所有的小孩都跳出為父親作證。

James: And the father protested in court that they made up a conspiracy to intentionally put him into jail! Haha!

詹姆士：這位父親在法庭上抗議說他們規劃了一個陰謀要陷害他入獄。哈哈！

Sophie: It's funny how two people got married at the first place, wishing a fairy tale ending, but ending up all in vain.

蘇菲：有趣的是這兩人雖然在這地方結婚，期望一個童話般的結局，殊不知落得如此下場。

James: It's a contest against human desire, and no one can attest without fail the truth of all the words and promises we make to each other.

詹姆士：這是一場人性慾望的比賽，沒人能夠證實我們當初對彼此所說的話或承諾。

Sophie: How sad. Let's just remain positive!

蘇菲：好難過。我們還是保持樂觀吧！

 單字解析零距離

❶ **de** 去除 ＋ **test** 證據

detest [dɪˋtɛst] 勔 痛恨

Ch 3

Part 1
Part 2
Part 3
Part 4

表示行為、動作

延伸片語 detest doing... 憎恨做某事
▶ Sarah detests babysitting her sister's children.
莎拉討厭幫她姊姊帶小孩。

❷ **test** 證據 ＋ **ify** 動詞字尾

testify ['tɛstə,faɪ] 動 證實
延伸片語 testify to 證明
▶ Jordan's perfect skill testifies to his genius.
喬丹完美的技巧證明了他的天才。

❸ **pro** 往前的 ＋ **test** 測試

protest [prə'tɛst] 名 反抗
延伸片語 protest rally 抗議大會
▶ The workers who got laid off decided to stage a protest rally.
被裁員的工人決定舉行抗議大會。

❹ **con** 一同 ＋ **test** 測試

contest [kən'tɛst] 動／名 競爭
延伸片語 beauty contest 選美比賽
▶ The First Lady used to be the beauty contest winner in 1998.
第一夫人曾是1998年的選美比賽冠軍。

❺ **at** 向、朝 ＋ **test** 試驗

attest [ə'tɛst] 動 證明
延伸片語 attest to 證明
▶ He is the only person to attest to the truth of what he says.
他是唯一能證明他所說的是否正確的人。

延伸補充 自然學

✿ **testament**	具證據的性質	名	證據
✿ **attestor**	提出證明的人，證人	名	證人
✿ **contestable**	一起作證 ＋ 形容詞字尾，表示能夠的	形	可爭辯的

根 sign 記號、標記

情境對話 試水溫

🎧 *Track 124*

Crystal: I'm just assigned to deal with the bid for the design of the Hsinchu Park.

克莉絲朵：我剛剛被指派去處理新竹公園設計的標案。

Nancy: Wow, that's awesome. This means the manager trusts your ability, so you are his designate.

南西：哇～真是太棒了！這意味著經理很信任你的能力所以你才能成為他的人選。

Crystal: I decided to resign for a better position, though. So I recommend you to the manager that he can assign this project to you.

克莉絲朵：但我已經為了更好的職位決定辭職了。所以我向經理推薦可以將這個計畫指派給你。

Nancy: What? You are leaving? How can I complete this project by myself without your help?

南西：什麼？你要離開了？沒有你的幫忙我要怎麼獨自完成這項計畫？

Crystal: Don't worry, Nancy. If you need instruction, you can still come to me. I know your ability is way beyond this.

克莉絲朵：南西，別擔心。如果你需要指導的話，你還是可以找我幫忙。我知道你的能力不只僅僅於此。

單字解析 零距離

❶ as 向、朝 **+ sign** 記號、標記

assign [ə`saɪn] 動 分派

延伸片語 **assign... to...** 將……分派給……

▶ The intern was assigned to the stockroom.
該實習生被派到倉庫工作。

Ch 3

Part 1

Part 2

Part 3

Part 4

表示行為、動作

❷ **de** 往下 ＋ **sign** 記號

design [dɪˋzaɪn] 勔 設計

延伸片語 **have designs on...** 對……存心不良；打……的主意

▶ Obviously the woman has designs on the rich old man.
那女人顯然在打那個有錢老人的主意。

• •

❸ **de** 往下 ＋ **sign** 記號 ＋ **ate** 進行一項行為

designate [ˋdɛzɪɡ͵net] 勔 指派

延伸片語 **the... designate** ……指定人選

▶ As the minister designate, John is a focal point wherever he goes.
身為部長的指定人選，約翰無論到哪裡都是眾人的焦點。

• •

❹ **re** 返、再 ＋ **sign** 標記

resign [rɪˋzaɪn] 勔 辭職

延伸片語 **resign oneself to one's fate** 聽天由命

▶ Mary lived a tough life but she never resigned herself to her fate. 瑪莉生活艱困，卻從不聽天由命。

延伸補充 自然學

☆ **signal**	記號的	名 訊號、暗號
☆ **cosign**	一起做標記	勔 聯合簽署保證
☆ **assignment**	被分派到的東西	名 作業

情境對話試水溫

🎧 Track 125

Linda: Can you show me how to activate this chemical reaction?

琳達：你能告訴我怎麼開始這化學反應嗎？

Daisy: Just drop this liquid into the vessel. As long as you see the pigments start to ciruclate, it's done.

黛西：只要把這液體滴入容器中。 只要你看到色素開始循環，就完成了。

Linda: And when should I take the record?

琳達：我應該什麼時候做紀錄？

Daisy: All you need to do is to concentrate on the density of the foams, and take notes when the foams begin to drop back down into the liquid.

黛西：你只需要專注在泡沫的密度，並在泡沫開始變回液體時記下來。

Linda: I see. Thank you so much. I remember this procedure's name is abbreivated as FBTD, right?

琳達：我懂了。 非常感謝你。 我記得這流程縮寫是FBTD，對吧？

Daisy: Yes. It's named after the complicated processes designed by professor Lee.

黛西：對。它以李教授設計的複雜過程命名。

Linda: I see. Thanks again. It's my pleasure to cooperate with you in this project.

琳達：我明白了。再次感謝。很高興在這個專案中與您合作。

單字解析零距離

1 **activ** 活躍的 **+** **ate** 動詞字尾，使成為行動

activate [ˈæktəˌvet] 動 活化；使……活潑

延伸片語 to activate a program 啟動程式

▶ You need to press this button to active this program.
你需要按這個按鈕來啟動這個程式。

. . . .

❷ circ 圓圈 **+ ul + ate** 動詞字尾，使成為行動

circulate [ˈsɝkjəˌlet] 🔟 循環；環行；傳播

延伸片語 **rumor circulates...** 謠言流傳

▶ The rumor circulates quickly right after the news report of the scandal. 這醜聞爆發後，謠言馬上就開始流傳。

. . . .

❸ con 共同 **+ centr** 中心 **+ ate** 動詞字尾，使成為行動

concentrate [ˈkɑnsɛnˌtret] 🔟 集中；聚集；集結

延伸片語 **to concentrate on** 專注於

▶ I ask myselft to concentrate on my job and not get influenced by the breakup. 我要求我自己專注於我的工作，不受失戀影響。

. . . .

❹ abbrevi 簡化 **+ ate** 動詞字尾，使成為行動

abbreviate [əˈbrivɪˌet] 🔟 縮短；使簡短

延伸片語 **abbreviate...to...** 將～縮短為～

▶ Margaret's friends often abbreviate her name to "Meg."
馬格麗特的朋友往往將她的名字縮短為梅格。

. . . .

❺ co 共同 **+ oper** 執行 **+ ate** 動詞字尾，使成為行動

cooperate [koˈɑpəˌret]

延伸片語 **to cooperate with** 和～合作

▶ Our teacher asked us to cooperate with the person sitting next to us. 我們老師要求我們和坐旁邊的人合作。

延伸補充 自然學

與 ate 同含義的字尾：act

☆ **retroact**　反 + 動詞字尾，使成為行動　　　　🔟 反作用力
☆ **react**　　 回、反 + 動詞字尾，使成為行動　　🔟 反應
☆ **transact**　交換的行動　　　　　　　　　　　🔟 交易

Chapter 4

Unit 126 根 anthrop 人類

情境對話試水溫

Jake: Hey, how's your project for the anthropology class going?

傑克：嘿，你的人類學報告做得如何？

Damian: Don't even talk about it. It's a selective course. A misanthrope like me doesn't want to do that project.

達米安：別提了。只是一堂選修。像我這樣厭世的人才不想做那種報告。

Jake: Please get ride of that misanthropy vibe. It's always interesting to see how human race evolves til now.

傑克：請拋開厭世的氛圍。其實觀察人類演變很有趣。

Damian: I know what you mean, but I guess I'm more fascinated with anthropomorphism. I mean, I don't particularly care about human beings, but I do like the human form.

達米安：我知道你的意思，但我想我更喜歡擬人論。我是說，我並不在乎人類演進，但我的確蠻喜歡人類形體。

Jake: I feel like you're a philanthropist to this school. Your tuition is basically paid for nothing. I guess you better transfer to the literature department.

傑克：感覺你是來學校做善事的，付的學費幾乎沒有學到東西。我想你還是轉到文學系吧。

單字解析零距離

① **anthrop** 人 + **ology** 名詞字尾，表示知識；學科

anthropology [ˌænθrəˈpɑlədʒɪ] 名 人類學

延伸片語 social anthropology 社會人類學

▶ My father is a famous professor in the field of social anthropology.
我爸爸在社會人類學領域是一位有名的教授。

❷ **mis** 厭惡 + **anthrop** 人 + **y** 名詞字尾

misanthropy [mɪˋzænθrəpɪ] 名 不願與人來往;厭世

延伸片語 the trait of misanthropy　厭世的特質

▶ Judging from the way he deals with people, I can tell the trait of misanthropy in his personality.
從他與人相處的方式來看,他本身就有厭世的特質。

❸ **anthrop** 人 + **o** + **morph** 形狀 + **ism** 名詞字尾,表示主義

anthropomorphism [ænθrəpəˋmɔrfɪzəm] 名 擬人論;擬人觀

延伸片語 the concept of anthropomorphism　擬人論的概念

▶ My English literature professor focuses solely on the concept of anthropomorphism in this class.
我的英國文學教授在這堂課完全著重在擬人化的概念。

❹ **phil** 愛 + **anthrop** 人 + **ist** 名詞字尾,表示人

philanthropist [fɪˋlænθrəpɪst] 名 慈善家

延伸片語 to pretend to be a philanthropist　假裝是慈善家

▶ Many politicians pretend to be philanthropists in order to win the votes.
很多政客為了贏得選票,都會假裝是慈善家。

❺ **mis** 厭惡 + **anthrop** 人 + **e** 名詞字尾,表示人

misanthrope [ˋmɪzənˌθrop] 形 厭世者;不願與人來往者

延伸片語 the mind of a misanthrope　厭世者心理

▶ A fun-loving person like me sometimes finds it hard to understand the mind of a misanthrope.
像我這樣樂天的人,有時實在很難理解厭世者的心理。

💡 延伸補充 自然學

☆ **anthropoid**　人 + 形容詞字尾,似……的　形 似人類的;類人的

Unit 127 根 ego 自我

情境對話試水溫

Track 127

Thomas: Nick is so egocentric. Were you there at the group discussion?

托馬斯：尼克真的很以自我為中心。你小組討論時在場嗎？

Charlie: No. What's wrong?

查理：不在，怎麼了？

Thomas: He wouldn't listen to others, and kept laughing at others' opinions. What an egomaniac.

托馬斯：他不聽別人的話，還只會嘲笑別人的意見。根本自大狂。

Charlie: But to say that he is an egoist also impliesthat he insists on his ideas and wouldn't compromise.

查理：但若說他是個自我主義者，也代表他堅持自己的想法且不會妥協。

Thomas: That's exactly what I'm saying. His egoism has made him a very annoying person and detestable to work with.

托馬斯：我就是這個意思。他的自我主義非常討人厭，而且讓人不想跟他合作。

Charlie: Well, somebody needs to challenge him and let him drop his ego. That's for sure.

查理：嗯，真該有人來磨磨他，讓他放下自尊了。

單字解析零距離

❶ ego 自我 **+ centric** 中心的

egocentric [ˌigoˈsɛntrɪk] 形 自我主義的

延伸片語 **egocentric speech** 自我中心言語

▶ Egocentric speech is an important phenomenon in children's development of speech and thinking.
自我中心言語是兒童言語和思維發展過程中的一個重要現象。

Ch 4

Part 1

表示人類、個人、社會

Part 2

Part 3

Part 4

❷ ego 自我 **＋ maniac** 名詞字尾，病態

egomaniac [ˌigoˈmenɪˌæk] **名** 極端自我主義者

延伸片語 an egomaniac 一個極端自我主義者

▶ Is your boss an egomaniac?
你的老闆是個極端自我主義者嗎？

- -

❸ ego 自我 **＋ ist** 名詞字尾，表示人

egoist [ˈigoɪst] **名** 自我中心者

延伸片語 an egoist 自我中心者

▶ He is an absolute egoist.
他是一個徹頭徹尾的利己主義者。

- -

❹ ego 自我 **＋ ism** 名詞字尾，表示主義

egoism [ˈigoˌɪzəm] **名** 自大；自我本位

延伸片語 ethical egoism 利己主義

▶ Some people think that ethical egoism is blooming in modern society.
有些人認為利己主義在當今社會正在蓬勃展現。

- -

❺ ego 自我

ego [ˈigo] **名** 自我；自我意識；自尊心

延伸片語 to have a high ego 自尊心很高

▶ Why have a high ego when he has already apologized?
他都已經道歉為什麼你還要擺高姿態？

延伸補充 自然學

☆ **ego**tistical 以自我為中心 **形** 自我中心的

 情境對話試水溫

🎧 *Track 128*

Patricia: You didn't attend the meeting in the morning. Let me tell you something. Our boss just called Mary impotent in front of everyone.	派翠西亞：你沒參加早上的會議。跟你說，老闆在所有人面前說瑪麗無能。
Sophie: What? Why?	蘇菲：什麼？為什麼？
Patricia: He straightforwardly said that Mary has no potential in being a salesperson.	派翠西亞：他直接了當地說，瑪麗沒有業務潛力。
Sophie: Well, that part is true. But I think Mary is a very potent team leader. She knows how to cheer people up. No one is omnipotent.	蘇菲：應該是在測試她吧。但我覺得瑪麗是非常有能力的團隊主管。她知道怎麼激勵人心。沒有人是全能的。
Patricia: But our boss focues solely on how much profit one can bring, and Mary doesn't do well in that aspect. We can't ignore that.	派翠西亞：但老闆完全只關心大家能為公司賺多少錢，瑪麗在這方面表現不好。 我們不能忽視這一點。
Sophie: That's true, but I think it has something to do with the new drug Mary is responsible for. Its potency has not even been tested out. How is she supposed to sell it?	蘇菲：說的也是，但我認為這與瑪麗負責的新藥有關。它的藥效甚至還沒有經過測試。那要她怎麼賣？

單字解析零距離

❶ **im** 不 ＋ **pot** 能力 ＋ **ent** 形容詞字尾，表示……的

impotent [ˈɪmpətənt] 形 使不上力的

Ch 4

Part 1

表示人類、個人、社會

Part 2

Part 3

Part 4

延伸片語 impotent rage 無濟於事的憤怒
▶ Calm down. Impotent rage cannot solve the problem.
冷靜下來。無濟於事的憤怒並無法解決問題。

❷ **pot** 能力 ＋ **ent** ……的 ＋ **ial** 形容詞字尾

potential [pə`tɛnʃəl] 名 潛能
延伸片語 dancing potential 跳舞的天份
▶ Lily has dancing potential, but she needs a teacher to train her. 莉莉有跳舞的天份，但她需要一位老師訓練她。

❸ **pot** 能力 ＋ **ent** 形容詞字尾

potent [`potnt] 形 有效的
延伸片語 potent tea 濃茶
▶ He drank a cup of potent tea in order to stay clear-headed.
他喝了一杯濃茶以保持頭腦清醒。

❹ **omni** 全 ＋ **pot** 能力 ＋ **ent** 形容詞字尾

omnipotent [ɑm`nɪpətənt] 形 萬能的
延伸片語 the Omnipotent 全能者（指上帝）
▶ They thanked the Omnipotent for giving them food and residence. 他們感謝上帝賜給他們食物與居所。

❺ **pot** 能力 ＋ **ency** 名詞字尾

potency [`potnsɪ] 名 力量
延伸片語 male potency 男性雄風
▶ He took a Viagra in order to recover his male potency.
他服了一顆威而剛以重振男性雄風。

延伸補充 自然學

☆ **pleni**potentiary　完全有能力的　形 有全權的
☆ **poten**tate　有能力的人　名 當權者
☆ **im**potence　不＋能力＋名詞字尾　名 無能

273

根 priv 私有、個人的

Regina: Hey, don't you know how to knock before you get in others' rooms? You are depriving my privacy!

芮吉娜：嘿，你不知道進別人房間前要先敲門嗎？你剝奪我的隱私了！

Ray: Oops, I will remember to do so next time. Lend me some money!

雷：喔，我下次會記得！借我一些錢！

Regina: Don't touch my purse! I haven't agreed to lend you some money, so leave my private belongings alone. Don't think you get the privilege to do whatever you want just because Mom spoils you. You need to show some respect.

芮吉娜：別碰我的錢包！我還沒答應要借你錢，所以把你的手從我的私人物品上拿開！別以為媽媽很寵你你就有特權做你想做的事。你要懂得尊重！

Ray: Alright! But we are siblings, why can I share your privy stuff?

雷：好吧！但我們是姊弟，為什麼我不能跟你分享你的私人物品？

Regina: It's not sharing! It's taking without others' consensus!

芮吉娜：你這不是分享！是沒經過別人同意就拿走！

單字解析零距離

1 de 去除 ＋ prive 私有、個人

deprive [dɪˋpraɪv] **動** 奪取……；使喪失

延伸片語 deprive of 剝奪

▶ The fact that his father died almost deprived him of his will to live.
他父親過世的事實讓他幾乎不想活了。

Ch 4

Part 1

表示人類、個人、社會

Part 2

Part 3

Part 4

❷ priv 個人 **＋ acy** 名詞字尾

privacy [ˋpraɪvəsɪ] 名 隱私

延伸片語 **right of privacy** 隱私權

▶ Everyone should respect another person's right of privacy.
每個人都應該尊重他人的隱私權。

- -

❸ priv 私有、個人 **＋ ate** 形容詞字尾

private [ˋpraɪvɪt] 形 私人的

延伸片語 **private school** 私立學校

▶ My sister goes to a private girls' high school.
我妹妹就讀於一間私立女子中學。

- -

❹ priv 個人 **＋ ilege** 指定、法律

privilege [ˋprɪvlɪdʒ] 名 特權

延伸片語 **diplomatic privilege** 外交特權

▶ Both ambassadors or envoys enjoy diplomatic privileges.
大使或是使節都享有外交特權。

- -

❺ priv 私有、個人 **＋ y** 形容詞字尾

privy [ˋprɪvɪ] 形 私人的

延伸片語 **be privy to...** 對……知情

▶ None of them is privy to the details of the contract.
他們之中沒有人知道合約的內容細節。

延伸補充 自然學

☆ **under**priv**ileged**	在享有特權的人下面	形 窮困的
☆ **priv**ileged	與個人有關之法律的	形 享特權的
☆ **priv**atization	私人化的	名 民營化

根 demo 人民

Ellie: Do you know that he is a democrat?

艾莉：你知道他是民主黨的嗎？

Mars: Of course. And it's quite obvious actually. He's all for democracy.

馬爾思：當然。而且其實很明顯。他超級擁抱民主。

Ellie: Well, what's so good about democracy anyway? Can we survive on a minimum basis under a democratic system?

艾莉：這樣啊，但民主說到底有什麼好啊？我們可以在民主制度下以最低限度活著嗎？

Mars: I'm not going to say that you're going to be super rich, but without human rights, which democracy protects, you won't even be able to "try to survive."

馬爾思：我不會說你會變得超有錢，但沒有人權，也就是民主所保障的東西，你大概連「試著生存」都不太可能辦得到。

Ellie: Is it that serious?

艾莉：這麼嚴重？

Mars: Just look at this demographic data, and you'll know.

馬爾思：就看看這張人口統計數據吧，你就會知道了。

Ellie: Wow... this is brutal. I hope all the countries get democratized.

艾莉：哇～這好殘忍。我希望所有的國家都可以民主化。

Mars: That's not necessarily helpful. The key point is the protection of the exertion of civil rights.

馬爾思：那並不一定有幫助。關鍵是人權行使的保護。

單字解析零距離

❶ demo 人民 **＋ crat** 支持某政體的人

Ch 4

Part 1

表示人類、個人、社會

Part 2

Part 3

Part 4

democrat [ˋdɛməˌkræt] 名 民主主義者
延伸片語 the Democrats 民主黨
▶ I'll always stay by the Democrats and vote for them.
我會始終支持民主黨並為他們投票的。

❷ **demo** 人民 ＋ **cracy** 統治
democracy [dɪˋmɑkrəsɪ] 名 民主
延伸片語 true democracy 真正的民主
▶ A true democracy allows free speech.
真正的民主是允許言論自由的。

❸ **demo** 人民 ＋ **crat** 支持某政體的人 ＋ **ic** 形容詞字尾
democratic [ˌdɪməˋkrætɪk] 形 民主的
延伸片語 democratic politics 民主政治
▶ How do you view the current democratic politics?
你如何看待當下的民主政治？

❹ **demo** 人民 ＋ **graph** 寫 ＋ **ic** 的
demographic [ˌdɪməˋgræfɪk] 形 人口統計學的
延伸片語 demographic data 人口資料、人口資料
▶ I need more demographic data, could you provide me more?
我需要更多的人口資料，你能給我嗎？

❺ **demo** 人民 ＋ **crat** 支持某政體的人 ＋ **ize** 化
democratize [dɪˋmɑkrəˌtaɪz] 動 使……民主化
延伸片語 democratize (a country) 使一個國家民主化
▶ Can Turkey help democratize the Middle East?
土耳其能幫助中東地區走向民主嗎？

延伸補充 自然學

demo的變化型：dem
☆ **endemic** 在人民之間的　　形 地方的
☆ **epidemic** 在人民中間的　　形 傳染的、流行的

情境對話試水溫　　　　　　　　　🎧 *Track 131*

Chloe:	The news says the government is going to enforce urban renewal in this area.	克羅伊：新聞說政府將在這個地區進行都更。
Charlotte:	Really? But I still see some habitants living here. Hasn't the government persuaded them to move?	夏綠蒂：真的嗎？但我仍然看到有些居民住在這裡。政府還沒說服他們搬走嗎？
Chloe:	They has. However, the inhabitants urged to preserve the heritage next door, and also renovate it, so it would be integrated more into the renewal project, not like an uninhabited house.	克羅伊：有啊！但這些居民要求要保存隔壁的遺跡，並且修復成不像沒人居住的房子，才更能讓遺跡融入都更計畫。
Charlotte:	That's true. But how did the government say?	夏綠蒂：說得沒錯，但政府怎麼回應呢？
Chloe:	The government and the construction company agreed, but they said the completion date would be delayed, so they would like to start the project immediately without thorough plan.	克羅伊：政府與建商都同意了，但他們說完工日期會延宕，所以在沒有完整規劃下便想立即開工。
Charlotte:	No wonder the residents still inhabit in here, those are mere words without a factual basis after all.	夏綠蒂：難怪這些居民仍然住在這裡，畢竟口說無憑。

Ch 4

Part 1

表示人類、個人、社會

Part 2
Part 3
Part 4

單字解析零距離

❶ habit 居住 **+ ant** 人

habitant ['hæbətənt] 名 居民、居住者

延伸片語 **the habitant farmhouse** 居民農舍

▶ These are the habitant farmhouses of old Quebec.
這些就是老魁北克時期的居民農舍。

- -

❷ in 裡面 **+ habit** 居住 **+ ant** 人

inhabitant [ɪn'hæbətənt] 名 居住者、居民、棲息者

延伸片語 **native inhabitant** 本地人

▶ The native inhabitants here have a different eating habit.
這裡的本地居民有著跟別人不一樣的飲食習慣。

- -

❸ un 沒有 **+ in** 內、裡面 **+ habit** 居住 **+ ed** 形容詞字尾

uninhabited [ˌʌnɪn'hæbɪtɪd] 形 無人居住的、無人跡的

延伸片語 **an uninhabited island** 一個無人居住的荒島

▶ The poor prince was banished to an uninhabited island.
可憐的王子被放逐到了一個無人居住的荒島上。

- -

❹ in 裡面 **+ habit** 居住

inhabit [ɪn'hæbɪt] 動 存在於、居住在

延伸片語 **inhabit in a city** 居住在城市

▶ More and more people choose to inhabit in cities.
有越來越多的人願意選擇居住在城市。

延伸補充自然學

✿ **habitable**	能夠居住的	形	可居住的
✿ **habitation**	居住的行為	名	居所、生活環境
✿ **habitat**	居住的地方	名	棲息地
✿ **cohabitation**	一起居住的行為	名	同居生活
✿ **cohabitant**	一起居住的人	名	同居人

情境對話 試水溫

Mark: You seem to be in a bad mood. Why?

馬克：你看起來心情很差，怎麼了？

Ying: Paul, the associate editor of TMS is one of my consociate members. We're trying to obtain the distribution right of a new brand in England. Paul is sociable, but recently I found out that he is such a social climber that only makes contact with wealthy people and clients. Whenever we have meetings, he dissociated himself from working.

瑩：TMS的副總編保羅是我的合夥人之一，我們正嘗試要代理一個英國品牌。保羅擅長交際，但我最近發現他只跟有錢人及客戶接觸，想往更高的社會階層爬。每次我們開會的時候，工作像是與他無關。

Mark: Maybe that's because there's a higher possibility the rich may invest your company?

馬克：也許是因為有錢人較有可能投資你們公司？

Ying: I don't know. He said that I'm antisocial because I never join their party in the bar. I guess he mistook anti-social with being efficient.

瑩：我不知道，他覺得我很不善交際因為我從不參加他們在酒吧的派對。但我想他大概搞不清楚反社交和做事有效率之間的差別吧。

 單字解析 零距離

1 anti 反 ＋ **soci** 交際 ＋ **al** 形容詞字尾

antisocial [ˌæntɪˋsoʃəl] 形 反社會的

延伸片語 an antisocial deed 反社會行為

▶ The boy's self-mutilation is obviously an antisocial deed.
男孩的自殘無疑是一種反社會行為。

Ch 4

Part 1

表示人類、個人、社會

Part 2

Part 3

Part 4

❷ as 向、朝 ＋ **soci** 交際 ＋ **ate** 使……成為

associate [əˋsoʃɪt] 勔 聯想 名 夥伴 形 副的

延伸片語 **associate professor** 副教授

▶ Dr. Lin is an associate professor of Anthropology in Harvard University. 林博士是哈佛大學的人類學副教授。

‧ ‧

❸ con 共同 ＋ **soci** 交際 ＋ **ate** 使……成為

consociate [kənˋsoʃɪet] 勔 聯合

延伸片語 **consociate member** 合夥人

▶ We were introduced to all the consociate members of his business. 他把我們介紹給他事業上的合夥人。

‧ ‧

❹ dis 不、否 ＋ **soci** 陪伴 ＋ **ate** 使……成為

dissociate [dɪˋsoʃɪet] 勔 分開

延伸片語 **dissociate oneself from...** 否認與……有關係

▶ All his friends dissociated themselves from him as soon as he was accused of a murder.
他一遭控謀殺，他所有的朋友便馬上撇清與他之間的關係。

‧ ‧

❺ soci 交際 ＋ **able** 能夠……的

sociable [ˋsoʃəbl̩] 形 善交際的

延伸片語 **a sociable chat** 社交性的談話

▶ Making new friends is hard. A delightful sociable chat is a good start. 交新朋友不難，一段愉快的社交談話就是個好開始。

‧ ‧

❻ soci 交際 ＋ **al** 形容詞字尾

social [ˋsoʃəl] 形 社會的

延伸片語 **social climber** 攀龍附鳳者、攀附權貴向上爬者

▶ A social climber like him won't give up the opportunity to marry a rich woman. 他那種攀龍附鳳的傢伙不會放棄娶有錢女人的機會。

延伸補充 自然學

☆ **sociology**	社會學科的	名 社會學
☆ **sociopolitical**	社會學 ＋ 政治的	形 社會政治的

Unit 133 根 serv(e) 服務、保留

情境對話試水溫

Track 133

William: Stop running. You need to conserve energy for the next race.
威廉：不要再跑了。你需要為下一場賽事保留體力。

Rebecca: It's okay. My mom has preserved some energy food for me.
瑞貝嘉：沒關係。我媽有替我保留一些能量食品。

William: Well, it's still safer to have some spirit in reserve.
威廉：這個嘛。還是留點精神比較保險。

Rebecca: I know. I just don't want to be in servitude for fame and all that.
瑞貝嘉：我知道。我只是不想要成為在名氣那類東西之下呈現被奴役的狀態。

William: But with all the hard work, you deserve the prizes.
威廉：但是你的辛勤值得那些獎賞。

Rebecca: Isn't owing up to one's heart enough?
瑞貝嘉：對得起自己不就夠了嗎？

單字解析零距離

1 con 共同 + **serve** 保存

conserve [kən`sɝv] 動 保存

延伸片語 **fruit conserve** 水果蜜餞

▶ The hostess served her guests with her homemade cranberry fruit conserve.
女主人為賓客端上她自製的小紅莓水果蜜餞。

Ch 4

Part 1

表示人類、個人、社會

Part 2

Part 3

Part 4

❷ pre 事前 **＋ serve** 保存

preserve [prɪˋzɝv] 動 保存

延伸片語 **preserve...from...** 保護某物免於……

▶ Salt preserves meat from rotting.
鹽能保存肉類，使其免於腐壞。

- -

❸ re 加強 **＋ serve** 保存

reserve [rɪˋzɝv] 動 保留

延伸片語 **in reserve** 儲用、儲備

▶ It is important to have some money in reserve.
有一些備用的錢是很重要的。

- -

❹ serve 服務 **＋ i ＋ tude** 名詞字尾

servitude [ˋsɝvəˏtjud] 名 奴役狀態

延伸片語 **in servitude** 被奴役

▶ These black people spent their lives in servitude.
這些黑人一輩子被奴役。

- -

❺ de 去除 **＋ serve** 服務

deserve [dɪˋzɝv] 動 應得（賞、罰）

延伸片語 **get what one deserve** 罪有應得

▶ To the satisfaction of everyone, the bully finally gets what he deserves.
那個惡棍總算罪有應得，真是大快人心。

Unit 134 根 **leg** 指定、法律

🎧 *Track 134*

💬 情境對話試水溫

Lily: There are some Taiwanese caught with illegal possession when they were trying to walk through the Japanese customs today.

莉莉：有些台灣人今天在過日本海關的時候被抓到擁有非法物品。

Marshall: Yeah, I heard of that. It's a large amount of gold, and might cause them serious criminal responsibilities.

馬歇爾：嗯，我聽說了。是大量的黃金，而且也許會有嚴重的刑責。

Lily: Isn't legal to bring the gold? Won't Taiwan delegate some officials to help them?

莉莉：攜帶黃金不是合法的嗎？台灣會指派一些官員去幫忙他們嗎？

Marshall: It's very severe to carry gold to Japan without declaration, so I don't think the officials will be sent. It's dishonor to use the privilege to cut down on the punishment after all. Those people would just be scapegoats; the real mastermind might get away from this.

馬歇爾：攜帶黃金到日本且不申報是很嚴重的，所以我認為不會派官員過去，畢竟使用特權去減刑是不光彩的。那些人只是代罪羔羊而已，主謀也許會逃過一劫。

Lily: Those people are silly to carry the gold just to earn quick money. They should have known the legality of the content of the luggage before saying yes.

莉莉：這些人為了快速賺錢實在是太愚蠢了，他們應該在答應之前早就要知道行李內容物的合法性。

單字解析零距離

❶ **il** 不、否 + **leg** 法律 + **al** 形容詞字尾

illegal [ɪ'lig!] 彫 違法的、非法的

Ch 4

Part 1

Part 2

表示規範、法律

Part 3

Part 4

延伸片語 illegal immigrant 非法移民
> There are a lot of illegal immigrants from Mexico in this town. 這個小鎮裡有許多來自墨西哥的非法移民。

. . . .

❷ leg 法律 **+ al** 形容詞字尾

legal ['ligḷ] **形** 合法的、正當的
延伸片語 legal holiday 法定假日
> You can't make us to work on legal holidays.
> 你不能強迫我們在法定假日上班。

. . . .

❸ de 源自某地 **+ leg** 指定、法律 **+ ate** 名詞字尾

delegate ['dɛləͺget] **動** 委託、委派
延伸片語 walking delegate 工會代表
> These workers prepared to complain to the walking delegate next week. 這些工人準備下星期向工會代表抱怨。

. . . .

❹ privi 個人 **+ leg** 指定、法律 **+ e**

privilege ['prɪvḷɪdʒ] **名** 特權、給……優待
延伸片語 executive privilege 行政官員豁免權（行政官員可拒絕出席法庭作證的特權）
> Mayor Jason was absent again; people said he always use executive privilege inappropriately.
> 傑森市長又缺席了，人們說他總是不當使用行政官員豁免權。

. . . .

❺ leg 法律 **+ ality** 名詞字尾

legality [lɪ'gælətɪ] **名** 合法性
延伸片語 legality of abortion 墮胎的合法性
> The legality of abortion is still controvertible.
> 墮胎的合法性依然很具爭議。

延伸補充自然學

☆ **legislate**	法律 + 動詞字尾	**名** 立法
☆ **legislature**	帶來法律的地方	**名** 立法機構
☆ **legislation**	關於法律的行為	**名** 法律的訂定

情境對話試水溫

🎧 *Track 135*

Andy: Have you seen that abnormal creature the biologists just brought in? It's enormous and horrifying!	安迪：你有看到那個生物學家們剛剛帶進來的畸形物種嗎？超大而且超嚇人的！
Marvin: Well, as a biologist yourself, you shouldn't be so definitive toward what's normal and what's subnormal.	馬文：這個嘛，你自己身為一名生物學家，不應該對於什麼是正常的以及什麼是不正常的有這麼清楚的分界。
Andy: I know, but that thing has this horrid face and body parts. It got on my nerves. It should at least have symmetrical eyes!	安迪：我知道，但是那個東西有超嚇人的臉和四肢。我覺得好不舒服。牠應該至少要有對稱的眼睛！
Marvin: Stop normalizing things you see. You'd be happier.	馬文：不要再把你看見的東西正常化了。你會開心一點。
Andy: Why are you always so calm?	安迪：你怎麼總是這麼冷靜？
Marvin: Because I'm open-minded.	馬文：因為我心胸開闊。

單字解析零距離

1 **ab** 離開 ＋ **norm** 規範 ＋ **al** 形容詞字尾

abnormal [æbˋnɔrml] 形 異常的

 **abnormal behavior** 異常行為

▶ Parents should be aware of any abnormal behavior of their children. 父母必須注意孩子們任何的異常行為。

② e 出 ＋ **norm** 規範 ＋ **ous** 形容詞字尾

enormous [ɪˈnɔrməs] 形 巨大的

延伸片語 **enormous expenses** 龐大的開支

▶ His slender salary couldn't afford the enormous medical expenses. 他微薄的薪水負擔不起這項龐大的醫藥費。

③ **norm** 規範 ＋ **al** 形容詞字尾

normal [ˈnɔrml̩] 形 正常的

延伸片語 **normal school** 師範學校

▶ He goes to a normal school because he wants to become teacher. 因為想當老師，所以他上師範學校。

④ **sub** 在～之下 ＋ **norm** 規範 ＋ **al** 形容詞字尾

subnormal [sʌbˈnɔrml̩] 形 不及正常的

延伸片語 **subnormal intelligence** 智力偏低

▶ It's quite rude to call a person of subnormal intelligence aretarded.
以白痴稱呼一個智力偏低的人是相當無禮的行為。

⑤ **norm** 規範 ＋ **al** ……的 ＋ **ize** 使～成為

normalize [ˈnɔrml̩ˌaɪz] 動 使……正常化

延伸片語 **normalize deviant behavior** 導正偏差行為

▶ The guidance counselor is trying to normalize deviant behavior of the boy.
輔導老師試圖導正男孩的偏差行為。

延伸補充 自然學

| ☆ **norm** | 規範 | 名 基準 |
| ☆ **enormity** | 超出規範外的 | 名 極大 |

根 **polit** 政治

🎧 *Track 136*

💬 **情境對話**試水溫

George: It's very impolitic of this politician to do this. He just ruined his career.

喬治：這政客做這件事真是不智之舉，根本就毀了他的職業生涯。

Ava: Why? Politics is very complex and unpredictable. You never know.

伊娃：為什麼？政治很複雜又很難預測，你永遠都摸不透。

George: That may be true, but I still think there are some basic political guidelines to follow. Otherwise, there won't be any department of political science.

喬治：是沒錯，但我認為還是有些基本政治的準則可以遵循，否則就不會有政治系存在。

Ava: You mean there's still a fine line of what is politic to do in terms of one's political development.

伊娃：你是指，以個人的政治發展來說，仍然有一條精準界線規範什麼是策略性的做法？

George: Yes. And it's never too late for a politician to apologize!

喬治：是呀，而且政客道歉永遠不嫌晚！

⚡ **單字解析**零距離

❶ **im** 不 ＋ **polit** 政治 ＋ **ic** 形容詞字尾，表示屬於……的

impolitic [ɪm`pɑlətɪk] 形 失策的；不當的

延伸片語 **an impolitic approach to...** 處理……的方法失策

▶ How the government suppressed the riot was an impolitic approach to address this sensitive issue.
政府鎮壓此次暴動的方式是處理敏感議題的不當舉動。

Ch 4

Part 1

Part 2

表示規範、法律

Part 3

Part 4

❷ **polit** 政治 ＋ **ic** 與……相關的 ＋ **ian** 名詞字尾，表示人

politician [ˌpɑləˈtɪʃən] 名 政客

延伸片語 **politician's lies** 政客的謊言

▶ People are getting sick of those politicians' lies.
人民已經越來越厭倦那些政客的謊言了。

. . . .

❸ **polit** 政治 ＋ **ics** 名詞字尾，學科

politics [ˈpɑlətɪks] 名 政治學

延伸片語 **party politics** 政黨政治

▶ Taiwan is a country of party politics.
台灣是一個政黨政治的國家。

. . . .

❹ **polit** 政治 ＋ **ical** 形容詞字尾，表示與……相關的

political [pəˈlɪtɪkl] 形 政治的；政治上的；政黨的；黨派的

延伸片語 **political parties** 政黨

▶ They are the two main political parties in this country.
他們是這國家的兩大政黨。

. . . .

❺ **polit** 政治 ＋ **ic** 形容詞字尾，表示與……相關的

politic [ˈpɑlətɪk] 形 精明的

延伸片語 **body politic** 全體人民；國家

▶ It is their ambition to make themselves into a sovereign and independent body politic.
成為一個主權獨立的國家是他們的夙願。

💡 延伸補充 **自然學**

polit的變化型：polic、polis

☆ **policy** 具政治性質的事 名 政策

☆ **metropolis** 如母親一般的都市 名 首都

☆ **necropolis** 充滿屍體的城市 名 大墓地

☆ **police** 與政治相關的人 名 警察

Unit 137 根 domin 統治

💬 情境對話試水溫

Laura: I just read a piece of news article. It says that even though the country has a new domineering dictator, with lack of experience, a new kind of virus begins to predominate its principal cities.	蘿拉：我剛看一篇新聞說這國家有了新的一位囂張跋扈的獨裁者，但因為沒經驗，一種新的「毒瘤」占領了首都。
Daniel: Oh, you mean the infamous military rebel. I wouldn't be surprised, though. The domination is basically illegal. He "buys" the country with guns.	丹尼爾：哦，你是指那些無恥的叛軍，但我不意外。這種統治基本上是非法的，是用槍支「買下」這個國家。
Laura: That's a very precise way to put it. The public doesn't want him and his crew to dominate their precious land. I hope his presidency can end soon.	蘿拉：這是很精確的解釋。民眾不想要他的團隊來統治他們寶貴的土地。希望他的總統任期能盡快結束。
Daniel: I'm very pessimistic about this. He is now in a dominant position in the country's political and economical status.	丹尼爾：我覺得不樂觀。他目前在該國的政治和經濟方面正處於主導的地位。
Laura: Let's pray for the people then.	蘿拉：讓我們為那些人祈禱吧。

⚡ 單字解析零距離

1 domin 統治 ＋ **eer** 名詞字尾，表示人

domineer [ˌdɑməˈnɪr] 動 跋扈

Ch 4

Part 1

Part 2

Part 3

Part 4

表示規範、法律

延伸片語 **domineer over** 跋扈、高聳

▶ The new manager tried to domineer over everyone.
新經理試圖對每個人都專橫跋扈。

- - -

2 **pre** 前、先 ＋ **domin** 統治 ＋ **ate** 動詞字尾，表示行動

predominate [prɪˈdɑmənet] 動 佔主導地位

延伸片語 **predominate over** 統治、支配、佔優勢

▶ Knowledge will always predominate over ignorance.
知識總是會勝過無知。

- - -

3 **domin** 統治 ＋ **ation** 名詞字尾，表示行為

domination [dɑməˈneʃən] 名 支配

延伸片語 **world domination** 統治世界

▶ This failure would put an end to his dream of world domination.
這次失敗將結束他主宰世界的夢想。

- - -

4 **domin** 統治 ＋ **ate** 動詞字尾，表示行動

dominate [ˈdɑmənet] 動 統治、支配

延伸片語 **dominate over** 統治、支配

▶ He was dominating over the party at one time.
他曾一度在黨內有支配地位。

- - -

5 **domin** 統治 ＋ **ant** 形容詞字尾，表示……狀態的

dominant [ˈdɑmənənt] 形 統治狀態的

延伸片語 **the dominant partner** 舉足輕重的合夥人

▶ Don't you know him? He is the dominant partner of the company. 你不認識他嗎？他是公司中舉足輕重的合夥人。

延伸補充 自然學

domin的變化型：dom

☆ **domestic**	與房屋有關的	形 家庭的；國內的
☆ **domain**	與房屋、人有關的	名 領地
☆ **domicile**	房屋 ＋ 統計的單位	名 住所

291

根 reg 命令、統治

情境對話試水溫

🎧 **Track 138**

Tom: This lesson is about how the regicide affected the economy of the main economic regions of this country back in 1860s.	湯姆：這一課是有關1860年代弒君對這國家經濟區域的影響。
Eve: So, poverty, epidemics, and famine were basically regular phenomenon.	伊芙：所以，貧窮、傳染病和飢荒基本上都很常見。
Tom: Correct.	湯姆：沒錯。
Eve: Had not regional administration done anything?	伊芙：地方的政府沒有發聲嗎？
Tom: They were all controlled by the regal powers, who were only focusing on the expansion of oversea colonies.	湯姆：他們都被皇室的權力掌控，只在乎擴展海外殖民地。
Eve: I see. I was glad I wasn't born in that era.	伊芙：我懂了。好險我沒有出生在那個年代。

單字解析零距離

1 reg 統治 ＋ **i** ＋ **cide** 名詞字尾，表示殺

regicide [ˈrɛdʒəˌsaɪd] **名** 弒君

延伸片語 **be charged with regicide** 被控弒君罪

▶ I can't believe that Sam was charged with regicide.
我不敢相信山姆被控犯了弒君罪。

Ch 4

Part 1

Part 2

Part 3

Part 4

表示規範、法律

2 **reg** 統治 ＋ **ion** 名詞字尾

region [ˋridʒən] 名 地域

延伸片語 **in the region of** 大約、差不多

▶ This designer handbag costs in the region of US$3,000.
這個設計師名牌包大概要三千美元左右。

- -

3 **reg** 統治 ＋ **ular** 形容詞字尾，表示有⋯⋯性質的

regular [ˋrɛgjələ] 形 規律的

延伸片語 **regular script** 楷書

▶ Most of his manuscripts were written in running script rather than regular script.
他大部分的手稿是以草書而非楷書書寫。

- -

4 **reg** 統治 ＋ **ion** 關係 ＋ **al** 形容詞字尾

regional [ˋridʒən!] 形 區域性的

延伸片語 **regional committee** 地區委員會

▶ The regional committee this year will be held in the beginning of July.
今年的地區委員會將在七月初舉行。

- -

5 **reg** 統治 ＋ **al** 形容詞字尾

regal [ˋrig!] 形 王室的

延伸片語 **regal attire** 帝王服飾

▶ The king looked quite awe-inspiring in regal attire.
身穿帝王服飾的國王看起來十分威嚴。

💡 延伸補充 **自然學**

☆ **irregular**   不聽命令的   形 不規律的

☆ **regulator**   統治的物   名 調節器

尾 ia 疾病、病痛

Kathy: Are you okay? You look so pale.	凱西：你還好嗎？你看起來好蒼白。
Betty: I suffered from severe insomnia recently, and I also just recovered from pneumonia. The world is not treating me well these days.	貝蒂：我最近嚴重失眠，而且我肺炎才剛好。最近真是衰事連連。
Kathy: Oh my god. And you seem a bit edgy. Any hysteria symptoms?	凱西：我的天。而且你看起來有點暴躁。有任何情緒激動的症狀嗎？
Betty: Yes, it's coming from paranoia. My doctor said that I need to quit my job and take at least half a year's rest.	貝蒂：有，是來自於偏執症。我的醫生說我需要辭職然後至少休息半年。
Kathy: You really should do so. Please regain your health as soon as possible!	凱西：你真的應該這麼做。請盡快恢復健康！

單字解析零距離

❶ insom 失眠 **＋ ia** 疾病

insomnia [ɪnˋsɑmnɪə] 名 失眠

延伸片語 **learned insomnia** 學習性失眠

▶ Patients with learned insomnia are anxious about not being able to fall asleep.
學習性失眠的患者會憂慮自己無法入睡。

表示疾病、學說、紀錄

2 **pneumon** 肺的 **＋ ia** 疾病

pneumonia [nju`monjə] 名 肺炎

延伸片語 atypical pneumonia 非典型肺炎

▶ The woman was diagnose with atypical pneumonia.
女子被診斷患了非典型肺炎

3 **hyster** 歇斯底里 **＋ ia** 疾病

hysteria [hɪs`tɪrɪə] 名 歇斯底里

延伸片語 in hysteria 歇斯底里症發作

▶ She started screaming and weeping uncontrollably in hysteria.
歇斯底里症發作時，她會開始無法控制地尖叫和哭泣。

4 **parano** 偏執狂的 **＋ ia** 疾病

paranoia [ˌpærə`nɔɪə] 名 妄想症、偏執症

延伸片語 border on paranoia 近乎偏執

▶ Julia's passion for photography borders on paranoia.
茱莉亞對攝影的熱愛近乎偏執。

延伸補充自然學

☆ **dyspeps**ia　　消化不良的＋病痛　　名 消化不良

☆ **malar**ia　　瘧疾的＋疾病　　名 瘧疾

情境對話試水溫 Track 140

Ellen: I bumped into Ricky's mom yesterday, and she told me that Ricky has got into the Athletics Hall of Fame in his school.

艾倫：我昨天遇到瑞奇的媽媽，她說瑞奇進入了他學校的體育名人堂。

Robert: Her son is also a senior, right?

蘿伯：他兒子也是高三生，對吧？

Ellen: Yes, and he is deciding his major now. It could be economics, electronics, statistics, and applied mathematics.

艾倫：對，現在正在從經濟學系、電子系、統計學系，以及應用數學系中挑主修。

Robert: That's cool. What about OUR son?

蘿伯：真棒！那我們的兒子呢？

Ellen: Computer engineering. He is confident that he could get the admission.

艾倫：電子工程系。他很有自信能拿到入學許可。

Robert: ...He is so positive. I never see him studying or preparing for his application packet. We should use some tactics to encourage him to get well-prepared for the upcoming interviews.

蘿伯：……他好樂觀，我從沒看過他讀書或準備申請資料，我們應該採取戰略鼓勵他在即將到來的面試裡做好準備。

Ellen: Don't worry. Let's just be supportive of him.

艾倫：別擔心，我們全力支持他就夠了。

單字解析零距離

① **athle** 競賽 ＋ **t** ＋ **ics** 學科、學術

athletics [æθˋlɛtɪks] 名 體育運動

延伸片語 **athletics meet** 運動會

▶ The athletics meet is held once every year. 運動會一年舉行一次。

② **econom** 經濟 **+ ics** 學科、學術

economics [ˌikəˋnamɪks] 名 經濟

延伸片語 **home economics** 家政學；家庭經濟學

▶ In the past, home economics was a required course for girls in high school. 家政課過去是女生在高中時的必修課。

③ **electron** 電子 **+ ics** 學科、學術

electronics [ɪlɛkˋtranɪks] 名 電子學科

延伸片語 **physical electronics** 物理電子學

▶ Joseph will attend the school of physical electronics this summer. 約瑟夫今年夏天就要進那間物理電子學院就讀了。

④ **mathemat** 數學 **+ ics** 學科、學術

mathematics [ˌmæθəˋmætɪks] 名 數學

延伸片語 **applied mathematics** 應用數學

▶ Oliver has been a professor of applied mathematics for many years. 奧立佛已擔任應用數學教授多年。

⑤ **stat** 站立 **+ ist + ics** 學科、學術

statistics [stəˋtɪstɪks] 名 統計學

延伸片語 **vital statistics** 生命統計；人口動態統計

▶ According to the vital statistics, the birthrate in this country is declining rapidly.
根據人口動態統計，這個國家的出生率正在快速下降中。

⑥ **tact** 接觸 **+ ics** 學科、學術

tactics [ˋtæktɪks] 名 策略、戰術

延伸片語 **scare tactics** 恐嚇戰術

▶ The government used scare tactics to encourage their youngsters to go into the army. 政府用恐嚇戰術鼓勵年輕人參軍。

Unit 141 尾 ism 主義、學說

💬 情境對話 試水溫

Eric: Bob has been working on terrorism issues for weeks. Some said that terrorism has something to do with racism and radicalism. People, following radicalism and communism, claim that social conservatism slows down the advancement of a country. That's why some of them take extreme actions.

艾瑞克：鮑柏正鑽研恐怖主義議題好幾週了，有些人說恐怖主義與種族主義、激進主義有關。激進主義與共產主義的追隨者主張社會保守主義會延遲國家的進步，這也是為什麼有一部分的人採取極端的手段。

Jay: Wait...You mean Bob is now in international news department? He was studying Darwinism last month for his report. Transferring to international news department should be really challenging!

杰：等等，你是說鮑柏現在在國際新聞組嗎？他上個月還在為了報告研究達爾文學說耶！調任到國際新聞組是很大的挑戰！

Eric: Being a journalist is never easy!

艾瑞克：當記者本來就不是簡單的事！

⚡ 單字解析 零距離

❶ commun 共同 **＋ ism** 主義

communism [ˈkɑmjʊˌnɪzəm] 名 共產主義

延伸片語 religious communism 宗教共產主義

▶ Social conservatism is believed to obstruct a country from progress. 社會保守主義被視為國家進步的阻礙。

❷ conservat 保守 **＋ ism** 主義

Ch 4

Part 1

Part 2

Part 3

表示疾病、學説、紀錄

Part 4

conservatism [kən`sɝvəˌtɪzəm] 名 保守主義

延伸片語 **social conservatism** 社會保守主義

▶ Some believe that social conservatism will obstruct the advancement of a country.
有些人認為社會保守主義會阻礙國家的進步。

· ·

❸ **Darwin** 達爾文 ＋ **ism** 學説

Darwinism [`dɑrwɪnˌɪzəm] 名 達爾文學説

延伸片語 **social Darwinism** 社會達爾文主義

▶ In my opinion, social Darwinism is a theory based on racial discrimination. 在我看來，社會達爾文主義是個以種族主義為基礎的理論。

· ·

❹ **rac(e)** 種族 ＋ **ism** 主義

racism [`resɪzəm] 名 種族歧視

延伸片語 **environmental racism** 種族歧視的環境政策

▶ The Third World should stand against environmental racism and reject hazardous waste from advanced countries.
第三世界應該反抗種族歧視的環境政策，並拒絕接受先進國家的有害廢棄物。

· ·

❺ **radical** 徹底的 ＋ **ism** 主義

radicalism [`rædɪklˌɪzəm] 名 激進主義

延伸片語 **campus radicalism** 校園激進主義

▶ The raising campus radicalism starts to worry the government.
不斷升高的校園激進主義開始讓政府感到擔憂了。

· ·

❻ **terror** 恐怖 ＋ **ism** 主義

terrorism [`tɛrəˌrɪzəm] 名 恐怖主義

延伸片語 **consumer terrorism** 消費者恐怖主義

▶ He was suspected to use consumer terrorism to extort money from the manufacturer. 他涉嫌利用消費者恐怖主義向製造商勒索。

💡 延伸補充**自然學**

☆ **feminism**	女性的主義	名 女權運動
☆ **nationalism**	國家的主義	名 民族主義

尾olgy 研究、學科

情境對話試水溫

🎧 *Track 142*

Linda: Have you decided on what to major? I assume it's still anthropology?

琳達：你決定好要主修什麼了嗎？我猜是人類學？

Lily: No. After I've done my research, I found out even though anthropology is related to the study of human beings, I'm more interested in archaeology. I like discovering what human being have done before. What about you?

莉莉：不。在我做完功課之後，我發現雖然人類學和人類的研究相關，但我還是對考古學比較有興趣，我喜歡去挖掘人類以前做過的事。你呢？

Linda: Opposite to yours, my passion is in animals. So, I've decided to study as a vet, and minor in zoology. Hopefully, I can work in a zoo after I graduate.

琳達：和你相反，我的熱情在於動物。所以，我決定要學習當一名獸醫，然後副修動物學。希望我可以在畢業後於動物園內工作。

William: Why didn't you guys ask mine? I decided to study in phenomenology because I'm interested in both human beings and animals! I'm going to study every phenomenon I see!

威廉：為什麼你們不問我的？我決定去念現象學，因為我對於人類和動物都很有興趣！我要去鑽研我所見到的每一個現象！

Linda and Lily: That's why we didn't ask you.

琳達和莉莉：這就是為什麼我們不問你。

單字解析零距離

1 **anthrop** 人類 + **ology** 學科

表示疾病、學說、紀錄

anthropology [ˌænθrəˈpɑlədʒɪ] 名 人類學

延伸片語 modern anthropology 現代人類學

▶ Claude Lévi-Strauss is the father of modern anthropology.
克勞德·李維-史陀是現代人類學之父。

❷ **archaeo** 古老的 ＋ **ology** 學科

archaeology [ˌɑrkɪˈɑlədʒɪ] 名 考古學

延伸片語 the methods of archaeology 考古學手法

▶ The team decided to employ the methods of archaeology to explore this issue.
這個團隊決定使用考古學的方法來探討這個議題。

❸ **zoo** 動物 ＋ **logy** 學科

zoology [zoˈɑlədʒɪ] 名 動物學

延伸片語 the study of zoology 動物學的研究

▶ Surprisingly, the study of zoology can actually help us understand human evolution better.
令人驚訝的是，動物學的研究其實可以幫助我們更深入瞭解人類演化。

❹ **phenom** 現象 ＋ **en** ＋ **ology** 學科

phenomenology [fəˌnɑmɪˈnɑlədʒɪ] 名 現象學

延伸片語 the profundity of phenomenology 現象學的深奧

▶ Many graduate students are greatly confounded by the profundity of phenomenology.
許多研究生對現象學的奧義感到困惑不已。

延伸補充 自然學

✩ **astrology**	星星的 ＋ 學科	名 占星學
✩ **biology**	生物的 ＋ 學科	名 生物學
✩ **psychology**	心理的 ＋ 學科	名 心理學
✩ **sociology**	社會的 ＋ 學科	名 社會學
✩ **genealogy**	種族 ＋ 學科	名 家譜

尾 stasis 停滯狀態

情境對話試水溫

Professor:	Okay, to conclude, thermostasis is the regulation of temperature.	教授：好的，做個結論，體溫恆定就是溫度的調節。
Lee:	Which means that there are organs maintaining the homeostasis of the body?	李：也就是説，有許多器官會維持身體內的動態平衡？
Professor:	Thermostasis regards specifically with temperature.	教授：體溫恆定特指溫度。
Lee:	I see. But what if there's a sort of metastasis, and the organ loses its function?	李：我懂了。那如果突然出現了轉移，然後器官失去作用了呢？
Professor:	Then it may lead to symptoms like haemostasis failure and so on.	教授：那就會導致像是止血失敗這樣的症狀。
Lee:	Thank you so much for your explanation!	李：謝謝您的解釋！

單字解析零距離

❶ thermo 熱 ＋ **stasis** 停滯狀態

thermostasis [ˈθɜmoˈstesɪs] 名 體溫恆定

延伸片語 the process of thermostasis 體溫恆定過程

▶ We can observe the prcocess of thermostasis in mammals from a biological lens.
我們可以透過生物學的角度來觀察哺乳類動物中體溫恆定的過程。

Ch 4

Part 1

Part 2

Part 3

表示疾病、學說、紀錄

Part 4

❷ **homeo** 相同的 + **stasis** 停滯狀態

homeostasis [ˌhomɪəˈsteɪsɪs] 名 體內平衡

延伸片語 **to maintain one's homeostasis** 維持體內平衡

▶ Meditation and exercise is said to be beneficical to maintain one's homeostasis.
冥想和運動被認為對維持一個人的體內平衡有所益處。

• •

❸ **meta** 改變 + **stasis** 停滯狀態

metastasis [məˈtæstəsɪs] 名 轉移

延伸片語 **cancer cell metastasis** 癌細胞轉移

▶ Cancer cell metastasis is considered as the sign of irreversible deterioration of one's health.
癌細胞轉移被視為是患者健康無法恢復的惡化。

• •

❹ **haemo** 血 + **stasis** 停滯狀態

haemostasis [heməˈsteɪsɪs] 名 止血

延伸片語 **haemostasis failure** 止血失敗

▶ Unfortunately, his father died of haemostasis failure.
不幸的是，他的父親死於止血失敗。

 延伸補充 自然學

☆ **epistasis**　　　往上的 + 停止狀態　　名 上位作用

尾 ant　做某事的人

Interviewer: There are a lot of job applicants for this vacancy, so why do you think we should hire you?	面試官：這個職缺有非常多求職者，請問你覺得為什麼我們應該僱用你呢？
Interviewee: First, I'm an British immigrant, so my English fluency is without a doubt. Also, I'm an active participant in all kinds of career lessons, which means I know what I want and I can achieve it quickly and thoroughly. With all these qualities, I think I'm a perfect match as a personal assistant of the manager.	面試者：首先，我是英國移民，所以我的英文程度是無庸置疑的。再者，我是位積極參加各種職業課程的人，說明了我知道我自己要什麼，而且我可以快速、完整地達成。有了這些特質，我想我是最適合成為總經理特助的人。
Interviewer: Indeed, you have the qualities we are looking for, but we want the inhabitant with permanent visa. I doubted you have obtained one.	面試官：沒錯，你有我們所需要的特質，但我們也需要擁有永久居留證的居民，我想知道你是否有了居留證？
Interviewee: Don't worry about my visa. I'm applying for dependent visa, so soon I'll be able to work legally.	面試者：請別擔心，我目前正在申請依親簽證，所以我很快就能合法工作了。
Interviewer: Okay, understood. So this is it. We will inform you the result ASAP. Thank you for your time.	面試官：好，了解了！今天就到這裡，我們會盡快通知你面試結果，謝謝你撥冗參加。

 單字解析零距離

❶ applic 申請 ＋ **ant** 做某事的人

Ch 4

Part 1

Part 2

Part 3

Part 4

表示職業、身份、性別

applicant [ˈæpləkənt] 名 申請者

延伸片語 **job applicant** 求職者

▶ More than 3,000 job applicants crowded into the site of the recruiting seminar. 超過三千名求職者湧入徵才說明會會場。

❷ **immigr** 移入 ＋ **ant** 做某事的人

immigrant [ˈɪməgrənt] 名 （從外地移入的）移民

延伸片語 **illegal immigrant** 非法移民

▶ Those illegal immigrants were sent back to their own countries. 那些非法移民已被遣返回國。

❸ **particip** 參與 ＋ **ant** 做某事的人

participant [pɑrˈtɪsəpənt] 名 參加者

延伸片語 **participant observation** 參與觀察法

▶ The sociologist used participant observation as his research strategy. 該社會學家以參與觀察法作為他的研究策略。

❹ **assist** 協助 ＋ **ant** 做某事的人

assistant [əˈsɪstənt] 名 助理、助手

延伸片語 **personal assistant** 私人秘書；私人助理

▶ In our office, only managers can have personal assistants. 在我們公司，只有經理才能擁有私人助理。

❺ **inhabit** 居住 ＋ **ant** 做某事的人

inhabitant [ɪnˈhæbətənt] 名 居住者、居民

延伸片語 **indigenous inhabitant** 原住民

▶ Indians were the indigenous inhabitants of the American continent. 印地安人是美洲大陸的原住民。

延伸補充自然學

與 ant 近義的字尾：ar

☆ **beggar** 　　　　乞討的人 　　　　名 乞丐

☆ **scholar** 　　　　研究學術的人 　　　名 學者

尾 er 從事……的人

💬 情境對話試水溫

Cathy: Congrats, Lena! Now that you've completed the goals other people set for you, make sure that you have a list of your own. So what do you want to do?

凱西：麗娜，恭喜你！既然你已經完成了別人為你訂定的目標，現在就為自己列一份想要完成的清單吧。你想做什麼？

Lena: Well, my major is finance, so the perfect match may be a banker. However, I want to turn loose the wonders of the creative imagination on commercials. So I really want to be in an advertising company, wowing those advertisers.

麗娜：嗯···我的主修是財金，所以我想銀行家可能最適合吧！但我想要發揮創意在電視廣告上，所以我真想進廣告商，驚艷那些廣告客戶。

Cathy: That's awesome! As long as it's what you want to do, just stick with it. I can be your personal trainer to teach you how to be interviewed.

凱西：那很棒呀！只要是你想做的事，就堅持下去！我可以當你的私人訓練官，教你如何面試。

Lena: Thanks a lot! Probably we can do role play. How about you being the employer as well as the interviewer? I think you have more experiences than me, so you can definitely help me answer those questions and figure out what I should care about at workplace.

麗娜：真是謝謝你！也許我們可以做角色扮演，那你當雇主兼面試官好嗎？我想妳比我更有經驗，所以你一定可以幫助我回答那些問題，而且讓我釐清職場上我需注意的事項。

Cathy: Sure, let's start!

凱西：當然！那我們開始吧！

⚡ 單字解析零距離

❶ **bank** 銀行 ＋ **er** 從事……的人

banker [ˋbæŋkɚ] 名 銀行員

延伸片語 **successful merchant banker** 成功的工商銀行家

▶ It is hard to believe that this successful merchant banker was formerly a bank clerk.
很難相信這個成功的工商銀行家原來只是個銀行職員。

· ·

❷ **advertis** 廣告 ＋ **er** 從事……的人

advertiser [ˋædvɚˌtaɪzɚ] 名 廣告刊登者

延伸片語 **commercial advertiser** 刊登商業廣告者

▶ All the commercial advertiser want is to increase consumption of his products. 那個廣告業主要的就是增加他的產品銷售量。

· ·

❸ **train** 訓練 ＋ **er** 從事……的人

trainer [ˋtrenɚ] 名 訓練家

延伸片語 **personal trainer** 私人教練

▶ His personal trainer suggested that he have aerobic weight training once every week.
他的私人教練建議他每週做一次有氧重量訓練。

· ·

❹ **employ** 僱用 ＋ **er** 從事……的人

employer [ɪmˋplɔɪɚ] 名 雇主

延伸片語 **employer of choice** 最佳雇主

▶ My company has been selected as the employer of choice of this year. 我服務的公司被選為今年最佳雇主。

· ·

❺ **interview** 面試 ＋ **er** 從事……的人

interviewer [ˋɪntɚˌvjuɚ] 名 負責面試者、負責接見的人

延伸片語 **telephone interviewer** 電話調查員

▶ She chose to be a telephone interviewer so that she could work from home. 她選擇做一名電話調查員，如此一來她才能夠在家工作。

💡 延伸補充 **自然學**

er 的變化型：eer

☆ **charioteer**　　　　開戰車的人　　　　名 戰車駕駛

☆ **mountaineer**　　　從事登山的人　　　名 登山客

Unit 146 尾 ee 做……動作者

情境對話試水溫

Track 146

Harry: The nominee for the Presidency, Charles, proposed that he will found organizations to deal with the massive refugees problems.

哈利：被提名總統候選人查爾斯提出他將設置機構以解決巨量的難民問題。

Tina: Charles started from a normal government employee, and was an adoptee. He worked quite hard to have high social position.

堤娜：查爾斯從基層公務員做起，出身是個被收養的孩子，他拼命努力才有今天的社會地位。

Harry: My coordinator once had an exclusive interview with him and I was there as a trainee. He, as an interviewee, got well-prepared for the content and familiar with all the government's policies. I was so impressed by his intelligence and humbleness!

哈利：我組長曾經獨家採訪過他，我當時作為菜鳥也在現場。他作為一位受訪者，內容準備周全，且對於政府政策相當了解，我當時對於他的才智及謙遜的印象深刻！

單字解析零距離

❶ **ad** 朝向 ＋ **opt** 選擇 ＋ **ee** 做……動作者

adoptee [əˌdɑpˋti] 名 被收養的人

延伸片語 abused adoptee 受虐的被收養人

▶ The social workers found that the missing boy was actually an abused adoptee.
社工發現那個失蹤的男孩原來是個受虐的養子。

Ch 4

Part 1
Part 2
Part 3
Part 4

表示職業、身份、性別

❷ em 向內 ＋ **ploy** 摺疊 ＋ **ee** 做……動作者

employee [ˌɛmplɔrˋi] 名 受雇者；員工

延伸片語 **government employee** 公務員；政府雇員

▶ It is believed that government employees benefit from better welfare. 大家都認為公務員的福利比較好。

❸ inter 兩個之間 ＋ **view** 觀看 ＋ **ee** 做……動作者

interviewee [ˌɪntɚvjuˋi] 名 被面試者；被面談的人

延伸片語 **a tactful interviewee** 老練的受訪者

▶ You can tell that he is a tactful interviewee by his evasive answers. 你從他避重就輕的回答就能知道他是個老練的受訪者。

❹ nomin 名字 ＋ **ee** 做……動作者

nominee [ˌnɑməˋni] 名 被提名者

延伸片語 **nominee for the Presidency** 被提名的總統候選人

▶ It is rumored that Jack will be the nominee for the Presidency of the political party. 謠傳傑克將會是該黨提名的總統候選人。

❺ re 返回 ＋ **fug** 逃離 ＋ **ee** 做……動作者

refugee [ˌrɛfjuˋdʒi] 名 災民

延伸片語 **political refugee** 政治難民

▶ Those political refugees went to the British Embassy for asylum. 那些政治難民到英國大使館去請求庇護。

❻ train 訓練 ＋ **ee** 做……動作者

trainee [treˋni] 名 受訓的人

延伸片語 **graduate trainee** 企業見習生；儲備幹部

▶ It is ridiculous that Mr. Chen took on the lad as a graduate trainee. 陳先生竟然雇用那個小夥子做儲備幹部，真是太可笑了。

情境對話試水溫

🎧 Track 147

Chris: The news reported that feminists around the world condemned ISIS altogether, for they kidnapped numerous girls and caused them to endure huge pain mentally and physically.

克里斯：新聞說世界各地的女權主義者同聲譴責伊斯蘭國，因為他們綁架很多女性，讓她們身心承受極大的痛苦。

Scarlet: ISIS is so hopelessly inhumane that condemnation does no harm to them. According to psychologists, those terrorists do such thing from the longing for group recognition, and also show the world how mighty they are.

史嘉蕾：伊斯蘭國真是無可救藥地殘忍，所以譴責對他們來說不痛不癢的。根據心理學家指出，恐怖份子做出這種行為是出自於渴望團體認可，並且也讓全世界看到他們多強大。

Chris: However, the journalist also said the U.S. is soon going to take the next action to keep those people from persecution since their chemists from The States have invented new kinds of powerful chemical weapons against ISIS. So I think this war is about to end.

克里斯：但是新聞記者也說美國即將有下一步行動使那些人免於迫害，因為美國的化學家研發出新種強大的生化武器。所以我想戰爭很快就會結束了。

Scarlet: I hope so. May all the victims receive redemption soon.

史嘉蕾：我也希望，願那些受害者很快就能得到救贖。

 單字解析零距離

❶ **femin** 女性 ＋ **ist** 某主義或信仰的遵守者

feminist [ˈfɛmənɪst] 名 支持男女平權者

延伸片語 feminist consciousness 女權意識

Ch 4

Part 1

Part 2

Part 3

Part 4

表示職業、身份、性別

▶ The awakening of feminist consciousness encourages resistance against chauvinism.
女權意識的覺醒鼓勵對沙文主義的對抗。

❷ **psycholog** 心理學 ＋ **ist** 從事……者

psychologist [saɪˋkalədʒɪst] 名 心理學家

延伸片語 criminal psychologist 犯罪心理學家

▶ According to the criminal psychologist, the intention of the murder was betrayal. 根據犯罪心理學家的說法，謀殺意圖是出於背叛。

❸ **terror** 恐怖 ＋ **ist** 某主義或信仰的遵守者

terrorist [ˋtɛrərɪst] 名 恐怖份子

延伸片語 terrorist attack 恐怖攻擊

▶ Thousands of people were killed in the terrorist attacks occurred in 2001.
數以千計的人死於 2001 年的恐怖攻擊事件。

❹ **journal** 日誌、日報 ＋ **ist** 從事……者

journalist [dʒɝnəlɪst] 名 新聞記者

延伸片語 a freelance journalist 文章自由撰稿人

▶ As a freelance journalist, you can work at your own pace freely.
身為一位文章自由撰稿人，你可以自由地依照自己的步調工作。

❺ **chem** 化學 ＋ **ist** 從事……者

chemist [ˋkɛmɪst] 名 化學家

延伸片語 dispensing chemist 藥劑師

▶ It's important to have a certificated dispensing chemist to fill the prescription for you.
找合格的藥劑師幫你按處方配藥是很重要的。

延伸補充 自然學

與 ist 近義的字尾：-ster、-logist

☆ **old**ster　　　　老的人　　　　　　名 老人
☆ **dermato**logist　皮膚 ＋ 專科人士　　名 皮膚科專家

尾 ess 女性

Track 148

情境對話試水溫

Chloe: Harper won the Best Leading Actress Award! She is so sweet!

克羅伊：哈波贏得了最佳女主角獎！她真的好甜美哦！

Olivia: Really!? I love her so much! She not only cares about public issues but also devoted herself to charities.

歐莉薇亞：真的嗎？！我也超愛她！她不只關心社會議題，也經常致力於慈善團體。

Chloe: She is exactly a noble and elegant princess. She is the only heiress to his dad's company, but she is never domineering or looks down on anyone.

克羅伊：她真的是高貴優雅的公主，她是她父親公司的唯一女性繼承人，但她從不盛氣凌人或瞧不起人。

Olivia: Unlike me, just a waitress in a small restaurant. I would rather be an air hostess because at least I could travel to different countries.

歐莉薇亞：不像我，就只是個小餐廳的女服務生，我還寧可自己是空服員咧，至少可以到不同國家旅行。

Chloe: Once you become a stewardess, foreign travel will lost its glamour for you.

克羅伊：一旦你變成空服員，出國旅遊對你而言就會失去吸引力啦！

單字解析零距離

1 actr 演員 ＋ **ess** 女性

actress [ˈæktrɪs] 名 女性演員

延伸片語 **leading actress** 女主角

▶ Her ambition is to win the Best Leading Actress Award this year.

她志在贏得今年的最佳女主角獎。

❷ heir 繼承人 ＋ **ess** 女性

heiress [ˈɛrɪs] 名 女性的繼承人

延伸片語 **a heiress to...** ……的女繼承人

▶ His only daughter is going to be the heiress to this company.
他的獨生女將成為這間公司的繼承人。

. . . .

❸ host 主人 ＋ **ess** 女性

hostess [ˈhostɪs] 名 女主人

延伸片語 **air hostess** 空中小姐

▶ The air hostess served me with a cup of coffee.
空中小姐端了一杯咖啡給我。

. . . .

❹ princ 貴族 ＋ **ess** 女性

princess [ˈprɪnsɪs] 名 公主

延伸片語 **crown princess** 王妃

▶ It was Diana's dream to be the crown princess when she was a girl. 當黛安娜還是個女孩時，成為王妃是她的夢想。

. . . .

❺ steward 服務員 ＋ **ess** 女性

stewardess [ˈstjuwədɪs] 名 （飛機、船）女服務生

延伸片語 **airline stewardess** 航空公司空姐

▶ It is heard that airline stewardesses of Asia are all very mild and sweet. 聽說亞洲的航空公司女服務員都非常溫和甜美。

. . . .

❻ waitr 侍者 ＋ **ess** 女性

waitress [ˈwetrɪs] 名 女服務生

延伸片語 **cocktail waitress** 酒吧女招待

▶ The man asked for a Bloody Mary from the cocktail waitress.
男子向酒吧女招待要了一杯血腥瑪莉。

延伸補充 自然學

與 ess 近義的字尾：-ine

| ☆ **chorine** | 女性的歌舞團員 | 名 歌舞團女團員 |
| ☆ **heroine** | 女性的英雄 | 名 女英雄 |

尾 hood 身份、時期

情境對話試水溫

🎧 *Track 149*

William: Have you seen the movie "Boyhood"?

威廉：你看過「年少時代」這部電影嗎？

Marvin: Directed by Richard Linklater? Of course!

馬文：李察‧林克雷特執導的那部？當然有！

William: How do you like it? I must say I love how the director portrays the transition from childhood and adulthood. The subtle and inevitable feelings that we have during the adolescence are nicely filmed.

威廉：你覺得怎麼樣？我很喜歡導演詮釋童年跟成年中間的轉換。青春期時那微妙又必然的感受都拍得很好。

Marvin: I agree. I love it, too. It shows various kinds of "likelihood" that one may encounter on the path to future.

馬文：沒錯，我也很愛。表現出在未來路上會遇到的各種「可能性」。

William: It's all about choosing an ideal identity and making efforts to achieve it.

威廉：就是選擇一個你理想中的目標，然後努力去達成。

Marvin: And when one enters into parenthood, everything will gain new meanings. Life is certainly a transformative circle.

馬文：而當一個人成為父母時，一切都擁有新的意義。人生就是一個充滿變化的循環。

單字解析零距離

❶ boy 少年 ＋ **hood** 時期

boyhood [ˋbɔɪhʊd] 名 （男性的）童年，少年時代

延伸片語 since boyhood 從年少時期

▶ I've been fascinated with car models since boyhood.
我從年少時期就很喜歡模型車。

314

Ch 4

Part 1

Part 2

Part 3

Part 4

表示職業、身份、性別

❷ child 兒童 **＋ hood** 時期

childhood [ˋtʃaɪldˌhʊd] 名 幼年時期；童年時期

延伸片語 **childhood memories** 童年回憶

▶ I grew more and more attached to childhood memories as I became older. 隨著年紀增長，我越來越依戀童年回憶。

❸ adult 成人 **＋ hood** 時期

adulthood [əˋdʌltˌhʊd] 名 成年（期）

延伸片語 **to reach adulthood** 進入成人期

▶ Having the shoulders to take on responsibility is what's usually considered as reaching adulthood.
當你能夠有肩膀負起責任時，通常就代表你已進入成人期了。

❹ likeli 可能的 **＋ hood** 時期

likelihood [ˋlaɪklɪˌhʊd] 名 可能；可能性

延伸片語 **in all likelihood** 很有可能

▶ In all likelihood, he is going to drop out of school.
他很有可能會休學。

❺ parent 雙親 **＋ hood** 時期

parenthood [ˋpɛrəntˌhʊd] 名 父母身分；雙親立場

延伸片語 **planned parenthood** 計畫生育

▶ With low salary and economic downturn, planned parenthood is less common now. 隨著低薪跟經濟衰退，越來越少人在計畫生育。

延伸補充自然學

☆ **girl**hood	少女＋時期	名 少女時代，少女時期
☆ **mother**hood	母親＋時期	名 母性；母親的身分
☆ **liveli**hood	生活＋時期	名 生活；生計
與 hood 近義的字尾：dom		
☆ **star**dom	明星＋地方；領域	名 名演員的身分；明星界
☆ **martyr**dom	烈士；殉難＋地方；領域	名 殉難；殉教；受難

315

尾 aholic, oholic, holic 嗜～者、對～上癮者

情境對話試水溫

🎧 *Track 150*

Beth: Look what you just bought…you're such a shopaholic.	貝絲：看看你剛買的東西……真是個購物狂。
Adam: That's because you're a workaholic and have no time to spend with me.	亞當：還不是因為你是工作狂，都沒時間陪我。
Beth: What an excuse me. Last time, when we went to Italy, you turned into an alcoholic again and bought several cases of red wine and transported them by air!	貝絲：好一個藉口。上次我們去義大利，你又變酒鬼，買了好幾箱紅酒，還空運回來！
Adam: What about you? When we went to England, you transformed into an unbelievable bookaholic and tried to purchase a whole bookshelf of English literature!	亞當：那你呢？我們去英國時，你變一個莫名其妙的嗜書狂，還想買下一整櫃的英國文學！
Beth: FINE. I'm done arguing. I need to charge my phone now.	貝絲：好了，吵夠了。我現在手機要充電。
Adam: Now we have something in common. We two are both chargeaholic!	亞當：現在我們終於有共同點。我們兩個都是充電狂！

單字解析零距離

❶ **shop** 購物 ＋ **aholic** 對～上癮者

shopaholic [ˌʃɑpəˈhɔlɪk] 名 購物狂；購物成癖的人

延伸片語 to become a shopaholic 變成購物狂

Ch 4

Part 1

Part 2

Part 3

Part 4

表示職業、身份、性別

▶ I have no idea why she suddenly became a shopaholic.
我不知道她為什麼突然間變成購物狂。

⋯⋯⋯⋯⋯⋯⋯⋯⋯⋯⋯⋯⋯⋯⋯⋯⋯⋯⋯⋯

❷ work 工作 **+ aholic** 對～上癮者

workaholic [ˈwɝkəˈhɑlɪk] 名 工作第一的人；專心工作的人；工作狂

延伸片語 **to grow into a workaholic** 成為工作狂

▶ With all the financial burden, he grew into a workaholic unwillingly. 在經濟負擔之下，他不得已而成為工作狂。

⋯⋯⋯⋯⋯⋯⋯⋯⋯⋯⋯⋯⋯⋯⋯⋯⋯⋯⋯⋯

❸ alc 酒精 **+ oholic** 對～上癮者

alcoholic [ˌælkəˈhɔlɪk] 名 酒精中毒病人；嗜酒者

延伸片語 **to dislike alcoholic** 不喜歡酒鬼

▶ My mother dislikes alcoholic, for her father was one and he ruined her childhood.
我媽媽不喜歡酒鬼，因為我爺爺就是酒鬼且毀了她童年。

⋯⋯⋯⋯⋯⋯⋯⋯⋯⋯⋯⋯⋯⋯⋯⋯⋯⋯⋯⋯

❹ book 書 **+ aholic** 對～上癮者

bookaholic [ˌbʊkəˈhɑlɪk] 名 讀書迷；藏書狂；書癡

延伸片語 **to turn into a bookaholic** 變成書呆子

▶ She turned into a bookaholic after she met a group of educated professors.
當她遇到一群學識淵博的教授時，就會變成一個愛書者。

⋯⋯⋯⋯⋯⋯⋯⋯⋯⋯⋯⋯⋯⋯⋯⋯⋯⋯⋯⋯

❺ charge 充電 **+ aholic** 對～上癮者

chargeaholic [tʃɑrdʒəˈhɔlɪk]

延伸片語 **to stop being a chargeaholic** 別再一直幫手機充電

▶ Can you stop being a chargeaholic? There's just no place for you to charge your phone!
你可以不要再一直找地方充電了嗎？沒有地方給你充電了！

💡 延伸補充 自然學

☆ **chocoholic** 巧克力 + 癮 名 嗜食巧克力者

☆ **sugarholic** 糖 + 癮 名 嗜吃糖的人

Chapter 5

情境對話 試水溫

🎧 *Track 151*

Alice: Did you hear the news that almost ten children had been abducted soley in this year around the neighborhood?

愛莉絲：你有看到新聞報導嗎？說單單今年就有快十個孩童在這社區附近被綁架。

Paige: What? That's way too abnormal. How did the government respond to this?

姵姬：什麼？這太反常了吧。政府怎麼回應此事？

Alice: You know, authorities concerned started to abnegate responsibilities.

愛莉絲：你知道的，相關單位開始推卸責任。

Paige: Imaging if these kids get any physical abuses…

姵姬：想像一下如果這些孩子受到什麼肢體虐待……

Alice: I know right? That's why I always say "Do not abstain from voting." Electing a responsible politician is extremely important.

愛莉絲：真的！這就是為什麼我總是說「不要放棄投票的權力」。選出一個負責任的政治人物是非常重要的。

Paige: I guess politics is just too abstract for many people. They have no idea that it affects all aspects of our lives. You see, making money matters the most to them.

姵姬：我猜政治對許多人來說都太抽象了。他們無法理解其會影響到我們生活的所有面向。你看，賺錢對他們來說比較重要。

Alice: And now they are groaning about how the governement did nothing. Funny.

愛莉絲：然後現在他們在抱怨政府什麼都沒做。真好笑。

單字解析 零距離

① ab 離開 ＋ **duct** 引導

abduct [æbˋdʌkt] 動 拐騙

延伸片語 abduct a child 誘拐孩童

▶ The man was caught for attempting to abduct a child.
那個男人因為企圖誘拐孩童而被逮捕。

· ·

② **ab** 離開 ＋ **neg** 否定 ＋ **ate** 動詞字尾

abnegate [ˋæbnɪˌget] 動 放棄（權力等）

延伸片語 abnegate responsibility 推卸責任

▶ It's a shame that units concerned all tried to abnegate their responsibilities. 相關單位全都想推卸責任，真是讓人遺憾。

· ·

③ **ab** 相反 ＋ **norm** 常態 ＋ **al** 形容詞字尾

abnormal [æbˋnɔrml̩] 形 不規律的、反常的

延伸片語 abnormal behavior 異常行為

▶ Parents should be aware of any abnormal behavior of their children. 父母必須注意孩子們任何的異常行為。

· ·

④ **ab** 相反 ＋ **use** 使用

abuse [æˋbjus] 動 虐待

延伸片語 drug abuse 濫用毒品

▶ They couldn't believe that their son would descend to drug abuse. 他們無法相信他們的兒子竟然會墮落到濫用毒品這個地步。

· ·

⑤ **ab** 離開 ＋ **s** ＋ **tract** 拉

abstract [ˋæbstrækt] 形 抽象的

延伸片語 in the abstract 抽象地；理論上

▶ I like flowers in the abstract, but I can't stand the smell of Perfume Lily. 理論上來說我是喜歡花的，但是我無法忍受香水百合的花香。

延伸補充 自然學

與 ab 同含義的字首：abs

☆ **abscond**　　悄悄離開　　　動 潛逃

☆ **abstruse**　　離開＋推　　　形 難懂的

首 mis 錯誤、無、缺乏

情境對話 試水溫

🎧 *Track 152*

Alice: Don't misunderstand me. That's now that I meant.	愛莉絲：不要誤解我。我不是那個意思。
Natalie: Well, your misbehavior has already led to the mistrust between us. Don't blame me.	娜塔莉：這個嘛，但是你的不當行為已經造成我們兩個之間相互不信任了。不要怪我。
Alice: Who doesn't make mistakes? Why are you so harsh on the people around you?	愛莉絲：誰不會犯錯？為什麼你要對身邊的人這麼苛刻？
Natalie: And I'm supposed to be okay when people also laugh at my misfortunes?	娜塔莉：然後人們嘲笑我的不幸，我就應該要覺得沒事？
Alice: Of course not! It's just that you're so defensive. It makes it hard for us to be near you.	愛莉絲：當然不是！只是你太保護自己了。這讓我們很難親近你。
Natalie: Real friends should know who I truly am, though.	娜塔莉：但是真正的朋友應該要知道我真正的樣子。

單字解析 零距離

1 **mis** 錯誤 ＋ **understand** 了解

misunderstand [ˌmɪsʌndɚˋstænd] 動 誤解

延伸片語 **misunderstand one's good intention** 誤解某人的好意

▶ They misunderstood his good intention just because he looked scary. 就因為他看起來很嚇人，他們就誤解了他的好意。

2 **mis** 錯誤 ＋ **take** 拿取

mistake [mɪˋstek] 動 弄錯、誤認為 名 錯誤

延伸片語 **to make mistakes** 犯錯

▶ We all make mistakes. Don't be too hard on yourself.
我們都會犯錯。不要對自己太苛刻。

· ·

3 **mis** 錯誤 ＋ **be** 使…… ＋ **hav** 擁有 ＋ **ivor** 名詞字尾

misbehavior [ˌmɪsbɪˋhevjɚ] 名 不正當的行為

延伸片語 **the consequences of misbehavior** 不當行為的後果

▶ Adults or children, we all need to face the consequences of
misbehavior.
不管是成人還是孩童，我們都需要面對不當行為的後果。

· ·

4 **mis** 沒有 ＋ **trust** 信任

mistrust [mɪsˋtrʌst] 動／名 不信任

延伸片語 **the mistrust between A and B** A 和 B 之間的不信任

▶ I can sense the hostile mistrust between these two parties.
我可以感覺到這兩個黨派對於彼此充滿敵意的不信任。

· ·

5 **mis** 錯誤 ＋ **fortun** 命運 ＋ **e**

misfortune [mɪsˋfɔrtʃən] 名 不幸；惡運

延伸片語 **a great deal of misfortune** 厄運連連

▶ That actor suffered a great deal of misfortune and was seen
begging on the street last month.
這名演員厄運連連，上個月還被人看見在街上乞討。

💡 延伸補充**自然學**

與 mis 同含義的字首：dys

☆ **dysgenics** 　　　錯誤的基因　　　　名 劣生學

☆ **dysgraphia** 　　　錯誤＋書寫　　　　名 書寫障礙

Unit 153 首 un 無、不

情境對話試水溫

🎧 *Track 153*

Nancy: My mom underwent a major operation due to an unfortunate car accident last week.

南西：我媽上週因一場不幸的車禍，進行了一場大手術。

Terry: I'm so sorry to know that. Is her condition improving?

泰瑞：我很遺憾，情況有好轉嗎？

Nancy: It's still unstable. She needs to be kept in the hospital for days on observation status.

南西：還是很不穩定，必須待在醫院觀察幾天。

Terry: It takes unbounded patience and energy to looking after a patient.

泰瑞：照顧病人需要有無盡的耐心和精力。

Nancy: Kevin and I take turns to stay at the hospital with her. It's undeniable that Kevin is quite helpful. He helps undress my mom's sutured wound, apply ointment, and check the details with doctors every day. It all seems unreal, like a nightmare.

南西：我跟凱文輪流待在醫院，不可否認的是凱文真的很幫忙，他每天都幫忙拆開縫線繃帶，再塗上藥膏，並且跟醫生確認細節。這一切都像噩夢好不真實。

Terry: Take care. Don't wear yourself out.

泰瑞：照顧好自己，別累壞了。

單字解析零距離

1 un 無 ＋ bound 界限 ＋ ed 形容詞字尾

unbounded [ʌn'baʊndɪd] 形 無盡的

延伸片語 with boundless energy 精力旺盛

▶ It is tiring to play with children with boundless energy.
和精力旺盛的孩子們玩，是一件很累人的事情。

- -

2 un 不 **+ den(y)** 否定 **+ i + able** 形容詞字尾，表能力

undeniable [ˌʌndɪˈnaɪəbl] 形 不可否認的

延伸片語 **an undeniable fact** 不可否認的事實

▶ Whatever your reason is, that you stole the money is an undeniable fact.
不論你的理由是什麼，你偷了錢是一個不可否認的事實。

- -

3 un 無 **+ dress** 衣著

undress [ʌnˈdrɛs] 動 脫衣服

延伸片語 **in a state of undress** 在裸體的狀態下

▶ It is embarrassing to meet my future mother-in-law in a state of undress. 在裸體的狀態下見到我未來的丈母娘，真是太尷尬了。

- -

4 un 不 **+ fortun** 命運 **+ ate** 形容詞字尾

unfortunate [ʌnˈfɔrtʃənɪt] 形 不幸的、衰的

延伸片語 **the unfortunate** 不幸的人

▶ She spent her whole life helping the unfortunates.
她窮盡一生都在幫助不幸的人們。

- -

5 un 不 **+ real** 真實

unreal [ʌnˈril] 形 不真實的

延伸片語 **unreal entities** 虛幻的實體

▶ To scientists, zombies and vampires are both unreal entities.
對科學家來說，殭屍和吸血鬼都是虛幻的東西。

- -

6 un 不 **+ sta** 穩固 **+ ble** 形容詞字尾，表能力

unstable [ʌnˈstebl] 形 動盪的、不牢靠的

延伸片語 **emotionally unstable** 情緒不穩定

▶ He has been emotionally unstable since his father died.
自從他父親死後，他便一直處於情緒不穩定的狀態。

情境對話試水溫

🎧 *Track 154*

Danny: I heard that Mia had been discharged from the mental hospital, but not yet returned to work. She is incapable of doing anything now.	丹尼：聽說米亞從精神病院出院了，但還沒回到工作崗位上，她現在無法自理。
Joey: I once witnessed her talking to an empty space, like there's an invisible person standing in front of her.	喬伊：我曾目睹她對著空氣說話，好像她面前站了一個隱形的人一樣。
Danny: She shouldered too many responsibilities. She was indeed an incredible partner, but working with her was quite stressful.	丹尼：她承擔太多責任，她的確是個很棒的夥伴，但和她共事也真的很有壓力。
Joey: True. She was a perfectionist, and could always spot teeny-tiny flaws.	喬伊：真的。她是個完美主義者，總是能發現超級細微的瑕疵。
Danny: Her rapid-fire calls also drove me insane. It's inappropriate to bother others after work, isn't it? Plus, it was 2 a.m. when she called me.	丹尼：她的奪命連環電話也把我逼瘋！下班後還打擾別人是很不恰當的吧！而且，她是半夜兩點打給我。
Joey: So did you pick up the phone?	喬伊：那你有接電話嗎？
Danny: Yes, I did. However, all she said was entirely incoherent and made no sense.	丹尼：有啊，但那時候她講的內容已經毫無條理且不合理……

單字解析零距離

❶ **in** 不＋**ap** 朝向＋**propri** 適當的＋**ate** 形容詞字尾

inappropriate [ˌɪnəˈprɔprɪɪt] 形 不適當的

延伸片語 **inappropriate behavior** 不當行為

▶ Clamoring in a public place is an inappropriate behavior.
在公共場所大聲叫嚷是不當的行為。

- -

❷ in 無 **+ cap** 頭 **+ able** 形容詞字尾，有……能力的

incapable [ɪnˋkepəbl] 形 無能的
延伸片語 **incapable of...** 沒能力做……

▶ Jeff is incapable of doing anything without his wife.
老婆不在，傑夫什麼事也做不了。

- -

❸ in 不 **+ co** 一起 **+ her** 黏合 **+ ent** 形容詞字尾

incoherent [ˌɪnkoˋhɪrənt] 形 無條理的、不一致的
延伸片語 **incoherent with grief** 悲傷地語無倫次

▶ I could hardly understand what he was talking about because
he was incoherent with grief.
我不知道他在說什麼，因為他悲傷地語無倫次了。

- -

❹ in 不 **+ cred** 信任 **+ ible** 形容詞字尾

incredible [ɪnˋkrɛdəbl] 形 極驚人的、令人難以置信的
延伸片語 **at incredible speed** 以驚人的速度

▶ The racer broke the world record at incredible speed.
該賽車手以驚人的速度破了世界紀錄。

- -

❺ in 無 **+ sane** 頭腦清楚的

insane [ɪnˋsen] 形 瘋狂的
延伸片語 **drive someone insane** 讓某人惱火、使人受不了

▶ His stubbornness drives everybody insane. 他的頑固把所有人都搞瘋了。

- -

❻ in 不 **+ vis** 看 **+ ible** 形容詞字尾，可以……的

invisible [ɪnˋvɪzəbl] 形 看不見的、隱形的
延伸片語 **invisible earnings** 無形收益

▶ The flourishing tourism industry has brought in a huge amount
of invisible earnings. 蓬勃的觀光產業帶來了大筆的無形收益。

情境對話試水溫

🎧 *Track 155*

Doris: I had tons of sweets to counteract the depression after being dumped by my ex. However, it caused countereffect because I gained 6 kilograms.

朵莉絲：被我前男友甩了之後為了對抗憂鬱我吃了一大堆甜食，但造成了反效果，一個月胖六公斤。

Eva: Dear, you'd better take an emergency countermeasure. Our bestie's wedding is right on the corner! You'll be the bridesmaid, right?

伊娃：親愛的，你最好採取緊急措施就好了，我們好友的婚禮就要到了，你是伴娘對吧？

Doris: Yes. I just learned one way to banish bingo wings. First, fully stretch your arms out and slowly perform as many counterclockwise circles as you could …

朵莉絲：對啊！我現在學了一招可以消滅蝴蝶袖。首先，你要先延展你的手臂，然後慢慢地以順時針方向畫圓⋯⋯

Eva: Thank you, but I prefer starving myself to working out. Working out could kill me. I provide a counterexample against the saying: Exercising makes people happy.

伊娃：好的謝謝。但我寧願挨餓也不想健身，運動根本是要我的命！我就是這句話的反例：運動使人快樂。

Doris: Haha! You and my sister are exact counterparts in terms of personality!

朵莉絲：哈！你跟我妹個性簡直一模一樣。

單字解析零距離

1 counter 反、對抗 **＋ act** 起作用

counteract [ˌkaʊntəˈækt] 動 反抗、抵銷

延伸片語 counteract depression 對抗憂鬱

▶ Many people thought alcohol could counteract depression, but the truth is—it can't.
很多人認為酒精能夠對抗憂鬱，但事實是——不行。

② counter 反 + effect 作用、影響

countereffect [ˌkauntɚˈfɛkt] **名** 反效果

延伸片語 have a countereffect on... 對⋯⋯起反效果

▶ This kind of diet pill actually has a coutereffect on weight loss.
這種減肥藥事實上對減重有反效果。

③ counter 反 + example 例子

counterexample [ˌkauntɚɪgˈzæmpl̩] **名** 反例

延伸片語 counterexample-guided 反例引導

▶ Professor Smith's counterexample-guided teaching style is popular with the students.
史密斯教授反例引導的教學風格深受學生歡迎。

④ counter 反 + clockwise 順時針方向的

counterclockwise [ˌkauntɚˈklɑkˌwaɪz] **形** 逆時鐘的

延伸片語 counterclockwise direction 逆時鐘方向

▶ It rotated around the pillar in a counterclockwise direction.
它以逆時針方向繞著柱子旋轉。

⑤ counter 對抗 + measure 方法

countermeasure [ˈkauntɚˌmɛʒɚ] **名** 對策、反抗手段

延伸片語 emergency countermeasure 緊急應變措施

▶ The hospital took an emergency countermeasure to combat the spread of Superbug.
醫院採取緊急應變措施以防止超級細菌的傳播。

⑥ counter 相對 + part 部分

counterpart [ˈkauntɚˌpart] **名** 配對物、對應的人或物

延伸片語 overseas counterpart 境外同業

▶ Peter is in charge of business with their overseas counterparts.
彼得負責處理境外同業往來之業務。

首 de 解除、反轉

🎧 *Track 156*

情境對話試水溫

Mandy:	It is said that as long as you decode this program, engineers no long have to debug anymore.	蔓蒂：據説，只要將這個程式解碼，工程師們就不再需要排除程序故障了。
Marco:	Really? Then the whole industry will decompose and transform into a news structure!	馬可：真的嗎？那整個產業就會分解了，並轉變成新的架構了。
Mandy:	It's actually not a bad thing. We can decontaminate some of the hidden rules in this field.	蔓蒂：這不全然是壞事。我們可以把這個產業的一些潛規則都清除掉。
Marco:	What do you mean?	馬可：什麼意思？
Mandy:	Remember the engineer who was paid a great sum of money to help his boss' enemy with the debugging of a new program? They made a fortune at the end.	蔓蒂：記得那個被付大把鈔票去幫他老闆的敵人移除新程式故障的那個人嗎？他們最後發了大財。
Marco:	Wow. He surely defamed himself.	馬可：哇，他的是讓自己臭名遠播了。
Mandy:	You bet.	蔓蒂：沒錯。

 單字解析零距離

❶ **de** 解除 ＋ **code** 密碼

　decode [`dɪ`kod] 勔 解碼

　延伸片語 **decode Morse Code** 破解摩斯密碼

▶ We need someone to decode Morse Code in order to understand the message.
我們需要一個會破解摩斯密碼的人，以明白訊息的內容。

❷ **de** 解除＋**bug** 蟲子

debug [dɪˋbʌg] 動 除去故障

延伸片語 debug command　除錯指令

▶ You can use the debug commands to remove conditional breakpoints. 你可以利用除錯指令移除條件斷點。

❸ **de** 解除＋**com** 共同＋**pose** 放置

decompse [ˌdɪkəmˋpoz] 動 分解、腐敗

延伸片語 decompose ... into　將……分解為……

▶ The bacteria can decompose organic matter into water and carbon dioxide. 細菌會將有機物分解為水和二氧化碳。

❹ **de** 解除＋**con** 一起＋**tamin** 接觸＋**ate** 動詞字尾

decontaminate [ˌdɪkənˋtæməˌnet] 動 淨化、去汙

延伸片語 decontaminate oneself　自我淨化

▶ If you accidentally eat the cockroach killer, decontaminate yourself by drinking a large amount of water and go to a doctor immediately.
若誤食蟑螂藥，喝大量清水做自我淨化，並立刻就醫。

❺ **de** 解除＋**fame** 名聲

defame [dɪˋfem] 動 破壞名聲

延伸片語 defame someone with...　以……破壞某人的名聲

▶ It is nasty of him to defame the actress with a candid picture.
他以一張偷拍照片破壞那名女星的名聲，實在很齷齪。

延伸補充 自然學

與 de 近義的字首：dis、un

☆ **disarm**　　　　　除去裝備　　　　　動 解除武裝

☆ **unfold**　　　　　反轉＋折疊　　　　動 展開

情境對話試水溫

🎧 *Track 157*

CEO: I just finished the board meeting today. Half of the board members disagreed with my proposal of the harbor BOT in downtown. They thought there are more disadvantages than advantages.

執行長：今天我剛開完董事會，過半的董事不同意我的市鎮港口BOT提案，因為他們認為弊大於利。

CEO's wife: What's the main reason why they disapproved? Perhaps we can hold another meeting to propose this issue again and let everybody talk it over.

執行長夫人：你覺得造成他們不贊成的主因是什麼？也許我們可以再舉行一場會議，大家提出討論。

CEO: The main reason was I couldn't clarify the financial report CFO integrated because it's so rough that I need to disclose more details to the board members to set their mind at rest and believe in our financial situation.

執行長：主要是因為我無法解釋財務長所整合的財務報告。因為報告太粗略了，我必須揭露更多的財務細節讓董事們安心並相信我們的財務狀況。

CEO's wife: Honey, I know you can nail it. Just make sure everything is crystal clear; therefore, they will discover that this proposal can make them billionaires.

執行長夫人：親愛的，我相信你可以做到的！只要你能確保每件事都是清晰明瞭的，他們將會發現這項提案會讓他們成為億萬富翁的！

單字解析零距離

1 **dis** 相反 ＋ **agree** 同意

disagree [ˌdɪsəˈgri] 動 不同意、意見相左

延伸片語 disagree with... （食物）對……不適宜

▶ Milk disagrees with people with lactose intolerance.
有乳糖不耐症的人不能喝牛奶。

· ·

❷ **dis** 缺乏 ＋ **ad(v)** 朝向 ＋ **ant** 前面 ＋ **age** 名詞字尾

disadvantage [ˌdɪsədˈvæntɪdʒ] 名 劣勢

延伸片語 to one's disadvantage 對某人不利

▶ Lack of English communication capability will be your disadvantage.
缺乏英語溝通能力將對你不利。

· ·

❸ **dis** 不 ＋ **ap** 朝向 ＋ **prov(e)** 證實

disapprove [ˌdɪsəˈpruv] 動 不贊同

延伸片語 disapprove of... 不同意……

▶ Jenny disapproves of working overtime.
珍妮不喜歡加班。

· ·

❹ **dis** 不 ＋ **close** 關閉

disclose [dɪsˈkloz] 動 顯露出

延伸片語 disclose...to someone 對某人洩漏……

▶ Do not disclose the password of your ATM card to anyone.
不要對任何人洩漏你的提款卡密碼。

· ·

❺ **dis** 不 ＋ **cover** 遮蔽

discover [dɪsˈkʌvɚ] 動 發現、發覺

延伸片語 discover the existence of... 發現……的存在

▶ The man didn't discover the existence of his child until now.
男人一直到現在才發現他孩子的存在。

💡 延伸補充 自然學

與 dis 近義的字首：de-

☆ **de**hydrate　　　　除去 ＋ 使充滿水　　　動 脫水

☆ **de**frost　　　　　除去 ＋ 冰霜　　　　　動 除霜

根  neg 否定

💬 情境對話試水溫

Sandy: Why do you always negate my opinions?

姍蒂：你為什麼總是要否定我的想法？

Mark: I didn't. I just neglect them.

馬克：我沒有。我只是無視它們。

Sandy: And the reasons are?

姍蒂：那理由是？

Mark: They are so negative that they become instantly neglectable. Trust me. If you bring them up in the meeting, you will be considered abnegating your responsibilities for the project. They'll think you're just lazy to come up with better ideas.

馬克：因為它們太過負面，以至於它們立刻得以被忽視。相信我，如果你在會議中提起這些想法，你會被認為在推卸專案的責任。他們會覺得你太懶所以無法想出更好的點子。

Sandy: That doesn't make sense. I do think my proposals are good ones.

姍蒂：那不合理。我認為我的提案都蠻好的。

Mark: Well, maybe you should learn more from me.

馬克：這個嘛，也可以你該多向我學學。

Sandy: Okay…

姍蒂：好喔……

單字解析零距離

❶ neg 否定 ＋ **ate** 使……成為

negate [nɪ`get] 動 否定

延伸片語 **negate a contract** 合約無效

▶ That he lied about his age negated the contract.
他謊報年齡使得合約無效。

② neg 否定 ＋ lect 挑選

neglect [nɪgˋlɛkt] 動 忽視

延伸片語 neglect one's duty　怠忽職守

▶ He was fired for neglecting his duty.
他因怠忽職守而被開除。

- -

③ neg 否定 ＋ ative 形容詞字尾

negative [ˋnɛgətɪv] 形 負面的

延伸片語 negative thought　負面思維

▶ Don't let your negative thoughts influence your life.
別讓負面思維左右你的人生。

- -

④ neg 否定 ＋ lect 挑選 ＋ able 能夠的

neglectable [nɪgˋlɛktəbl] 形 可忽視的

延伸片語 neglectable duty　不重要的職務

▶ Some people think that an assistant manager is a neglectable duty, but it's not.
有些人認為助理是不重要的職務，其實不然。

- -

⑤ ab 離開 ＋ neg 否定 ＋ ate 使……成為

abnegate [ˋæbnɪˏget] 動 放棄（權力）

延伸片語 abnegate responsibility　推卸責任

▶ It's a shame that units concerned all tried to abnegate their responsibilities.
相關單位全都想推卸責任，真是讓人遺憾。

延伸補充 自然學

☆ **negation**	否定 ＋ 名詞字尾	名 否定
☆ **negligible**	能夠否定的	形 可被忽略的
☆ **abnegator**	離開 ＋ 否定 ＋ 人	名 放棄的人

335

Part1

Unit 159 首 anti 反對、對抗

情境對話試水溫

🎧 *Track 159*

Kate: I want to buy that anti-aging night cream I just saw, but it's so expensive.

凱特：我想買剛剛看到的抗老晚霜，但它太貴了。

Ellen: I thought an antisocial person like you are not into commercial product.

艾倫：我以為像你這樣的反社會人士對這種商品都沒興趣。

Kate: I went to an anti-war march, and you consider me as antisocial. I guess your intuition was paid for nothing.

凱特：我參加反戰遊行，你就認為我是反社會的。你的直覺很爛。

Ellen: Well, you just seem to have this antipathy toward everything! Don't blame me for saying that. I don't mean to be rude. You know me.

艾倫：嗯，你似乎對所有事情都會有這種反感！別怪我這樣講，我不是刻意對你不禮貌，你懂的。

Kate: I get it. I've heard this sort of description of me quite frequently. I have antibody now. But just to be clear, I'm not antisocial! I still love hanging out with people.

凱特：我知道。這種話我常聽到。我現在有抗體，但還是澄清一下，我不反社會！我還是喜歡和朋友們一起出去玩。

Ellen: Yeah, the antisocial ones.

艾倫：對呀，跟反社會的朋友。

單字解析零距離

1 **anti** 反對；對抗 ＋ **soci** 群體 ＋ **al** 形容詞字尾

antisocial [ˌæntɪˈsoʃəl] 形 反社會的

延伸片語 an antisocial personality 反社會人格

336

▶ She has an antisocial personality. You can encourage her more often. 她有反社會人格，你可以多鼓勵她。

- -

❷ anti 反對；對抗 **+ ag(e)** 年齡 **+ ing** 形容詞字尾

anti-aging [ˌæntɪˈedʒɪn] 形 抗老化的

延伸片語 **anti-aging skincare products** 抗老護膚產品

▶ I use anti-aging skincare products daily.
我每天都用抗老的護膚產品。

- -

❸ anti 反對 **+ war** 戰爭

anti-war [ˌæntɪˈwɔr] 形 抗戰的

延伸片語 **an anti-war campaign** 反戰爭遊行

▶ My father asked the whole family to participate in an anti-war campaign tomorrow. 我爸爸要求全家人都去參加明天的反戰爭遊行。

- -

❹ anti 反對 **+ path** 感覺 **+ y** 名詞字尾

antipathy [ænˈtɪpəθɪ] 名 反感、厭惡

延伸片語 **an antipathy against** 對～的反感

▶ The statement is fundamentally a gender antipathy against LGTBQA communities. 那則聲明根本就只是在表達對同志文化的反感。

- -

❺ anti 對抗 **+ body** 體

antibody [ˈæntɪˌbɑdɪ] 名 抗體

延伸片語 **to (not) have antibody** （沒）有～的抗體

▶ Unfortunately, this patient does not have enough antibody to protect himself against the disease.
不幸地，這患者沒有足夠抗體來應付這個疾病。

💡 延伸補充 自然學

☆ **antivirus**　　反對＋病毒　　　　　　　形 防毒的；抗毒的

☆ **antibiotic**　　反對＋生命＋形容詞字尾　形 【生】抗生的，抗菌的

contra 反對、對抗、相反

🎧 *Track 160*

Allen: Wow. Today is the forth anniversary of that peace demonstration I went to.

艾倫：哇。今天我去過的那場和平示威滿四周年的日子。

Ray: I was there too!

雷：我當時也有去！

Allen: What a coincidence! Did you have fun? I made lots of like-minded friends there.

艾倫：這麼巧！你玩的開心嗎？我在那裡交了很多志同道合的朋友。

Ray: No. On the contrary, I argued with lots of people. I noticed that some of them actually contradicted themselves. They didn't want missiles, and they didn't want democracy, too.

雷：沒有。相反地，我跟很多人吵架。我發現其中一些人很矛盾。他們不要戰爭，也不要民主。

Allen: What do you mean?

艾倫：什麼意思？

Ray: Their beliefs were in contrast against one another. I was super confused by the contradictions.

雷：他們的信仰彼此相牴觸。這些矛盾真的讓人很不解。

Allen: Tell me about it. Let's just stick to truth and steer away from all contradictory stuff in life.

艾倫：這還用說。我們只要堅持真相，避開這些生活中矛盾的東西。

單字解析零距離

❶ **contra** 相反＋ **ry** 形容詞字尾

contrary [ˈkɑntrɛrɪ] 形 相反的 名 相反（的事物）

延伸片語 **on the contrary...** 相反地

▶ On the contrary, my parents were not satisfied with my grades at all. 相反地，我爸媽完全不滿意我的成績。

- -

❷ contra 相反 **+ dict** 説

contradict [͵kɑntrəˋdɪkt] **動** 與～矛盾

延伸片語 to contradict oneself　自相矛盾

▶ Do you know that you are contradicting yourself by not behaving in accordance with your words?
你知道你現在自相矛盾嗎？完全言行不一。

- -

❸ contra 相反 **+ st**

contrast [ˋkɑn͵træst] **名** 對比；對照

延伸片語 in contrast with　形成對比

▶ Her brilliant performance is in stark contrast with his.
她精湛的表演跟他的形成強烈對比。

- -

❹ contra 相反 **+ dict** 説 **+ ion** 名詞字尾

contradiction [͵kɑntrəˋdɪkʃən] **名** 矛盾

延伸片語 a contradiction between A and B　A與B之間的矛盾

▶ There's a great contradiction between her current testimony and her previous one. 她目前的證詞與先前的相互矛盾。

- -

❺ contra 相反 **+ dict** 説 **+ ary** 形容詞字尾

contradictory [͵kɑntrəˋdɪktərɪ] **形** 矛盾的

延伸片語 be contradictory to　與～相矛盾

▶ What is absurd is that the president's statement is contradictory to the vice president's. 荒謬的是，總統與副總統的説法互相矛盾。

延伸補充 自然學

與 contra- 近義的字首：contro

☆ **controversial**	相反 + 轉 + 形容詞字尾	**形** 具爭議性的
☆ **controversy**	相反 + 轉 + 名詞字尾	**名** 爭議

根 fort 強壯、強力

💬 情境對話試水溫

Mavis: Vera, do you have a moment?	梅薇絲：薇拉，可以跟你借步說話嗎？
Vera: Sure, what's going on?	薇拉：當然，怎麼了嗎？
Mavis: My grandfather was rushed to the hospital this morning for unknown acute discomfort. Can I take half day off and ask you to cover for me?	梅薇絲：我爺爺今早因為不明的急性不適被送進醫院了。我可以請半天假並請你當我的代理人嗎？
Vera: Absolutely. Is he fine?	薇拉：好啊，他還好嗎？
Mavis: He's still under checkup, but the doctor has injected some analgesic to comfort him. In spite of this, my mom said he still tried to joke around relieving her intensity.	梅薇絲：他仍然在進行檢查，但醫生有幫他注射一些鎮痛劑讓他舒服一點，儘管如此，我媽媽說他還在開玩笑，試著舒緩她的緊張情緒。
Vera: It's hard to see someone old like your grandfather suffer from the pain with fortitude.	薇拉：看著像爺爺這麼老的人堅毅地忍受著痛苦，真是讓人心疼。
Mavis: Exactly, I just hope the doctor makes efforts to soothe his pain and find the cause.	梅薇絲：對呀，我只希望醫生能盡力舒緩他的不適並找出原因。

⚡ 單字解析零距離

❶ **dis** 不 ＋ **com** 一起 ＋ **fort** 強壯、強力
discomfort [dɪsˈkʌmfət] 名 不舒適
延伸片語 the discomforts of travel 旅途的困苦

▶ The discomforts of travel made him fall asleep fast.
旅途的困苦使他很快睡著了。

∙∙∙

❷ com 一起 **+ fort** 強壯、強力

comfort [`kʌmfət] **動** 安慰

延伸片語 **words of comfort** 安慰的話

▶ Why didn't you say some words of comfort to her at that time?
那時候你為什麼不對她說些安慰的話呢？

∙∙∙

❸ fort 強壯 **+ i + tude** 表狀態

fortitude [`fɔrtətjud] **名** 堅毅

延伸片語 **with fortitude** 毅然

▶ Emma bore the pain with great fortitude.
愛瑪以巨大的毅力忍受了痛苦。

∙∙∙

❹ ef 出 **+ fort** 強力

effort [`ɛfət] **名** 努力

延伸片語 **without effort** 輕鬆地、輕易地

▶ You won't pass the exam without effort.
你不會輕鬆地通過這個考試的。

延伸補充 自然學

☆ fort	強力堅固之所	名 要塞

根 firm 堅定、強壯的

情境對話試水溫

Track 162

Jessica:	Have you confirmed the source of the news?
Madison:	Not yet, so I can't affirm the falsity of his statement right now.
Jessica:	Well, you'd better hurry. People are worried about the mentally-ill patient who just escaped from the infirmary. He is said to have several major criminal records.
Madison:	I know, but the person who got me this scoop is infirm of telling me the name of the patient. He changed his mind all of a sudden.
Jessica:	Just try to get a confirmative answer from him. You can do it.
Madison:	All right. I'll try.

潔西卡：你有確認新聞的來源了嗎？

麥迪遜：還沒，所以我現在還無法確認他的證詞的真偽。

潔西卡：嗯，你最好快一點。大眾很擔心那個從醫院逃出來的心理不正常的病人。據說他有幾項重大犯罪紀錄。

麥迪遜：我知道，但是給我這個秘辛的人對於要不要告訴我病人姓名也很優柔寡斷。他突然就改變心意了。

潔西卡：就是試著從他那邊得到確定的答案。你可以的。

麥迪遜：好吧，我試試看。

單字解析零距離

① **con** 共同 ＋ **firm** 堅定、強壯的

confirm [kənˋfɝm] **動** 證實、確認

延伸片語 confirm a rumor 證實流言的真假

▶ I think no one can confirm those rumors now.
我認為現在沒人能證實那些流言的真假了。

0.0001

② af 朝向 ＋ **firm** 堅定的

affirm [ə`fɜm] 動 確認

延伸片語 affirm the statement 肯定說法

▶ We affirm the statement to be true.
我們肯定這種說法是對的。

- -

③ in 不 ＋ **firm** 堅定、強壯的 ＋ **ary** 地方

infirmary [ɪn`fɜmərɪ] 名 醫院

延伸片語 Royal Infirmary 皇家醫院

▶ The princess will certainly go to the Royal Infirmary when she gets ill.
公主生病的時候當然要去皇家醫院。

- -

④ in 不 ＋ **firm** 堅定的

infirm [ɪn`fɜm] 形 優柔寡斷的

延伸片語 infirm of purpose 意志力薄弱的、優柔寡斷的

▶ Tony is so infirm of purpose that he can not give us any good advice.
湯尼這個人優柔寡斷，他給不了我們任何好的建議。

- -

⑤ con 共同、聚合 ＋ **firm** 堅定的 ＋ **ative** 形容詞字尾

confirmative [kən`fɜmətɪv] 形 確定的

延伸片語 confirmative answer 確定的答案

▶ Dolly has a confirmative answer in her mind.
在多麗的心中有個確定的答案了。

延伸補充自然學

☆ **affirmable**	斷言 + 形容詞字尾	形 可斷言的
☆ **infirmity**	不強壯的 + 名詞字尾	動 虛弱

首 hetero, homo
不同的、相同的

💬 情境對話試水溫

🎧 *Track 163*

Harry: Do you know that Jack is homosexual?	哈利：你知道傑克是同性戀嗎？
Mandy: Yes, I know. And then?	蔓蒂：是的，我知道。然後呢？
Harry: Nothing. I just thought he is heterosexual. He's super attractive! Actually, his friends are all good-looking.	哈利：沒什麼。我只是以為他是異性戀。他超帥的！事實上，他的朋友都很帥。
Mandy: Homogeneous people hang out together.	蔓蒂：同性質的人都會混在一起的。
Harry: That's why a heterodox like you will never be part of his social circle. Haha!	哈利：這就是為什麼像你這樣的異端份子不會出現在他的社交圈。哈哈！
Mandy: As if you're not friends with me.	蔓蒂：講得好像你不是我朋友一樣。

單字解析零距離

1 homo 相同的 **+ sexual** 性的

homosexual [ˌhomə`sɛkʃʊəl] 形 同性戀的 名 同性戀者

延伸片語 **homosexual communities** 同性戀社群

▶ On the contrary, homosexual communities are very open-minded.
相反的是，同性戀社群是非常開明的。

❷ hetero 不同的 **+ sexual** 性的

heterosexual [ˌhɛtərəˋsɛkʃʊəl] 形 異性戀的 名 異性戀者

延伸片語 **heterosexual species** 異性戀物種

▶ On planet earth, heterosexual species are the majorities.
在地球上，異性戀的物種佔絕大多數。

- -

❸ homo 相同的 **+ gene + 起源 + ous** 形容詞字尾

homogeneous [ˌhoməˋdʒɪnɪəs] 形 同質的

延伸片語 **a homogeneous group** 同質性組織

▶ The supporters of the political party do not belong to, surprisingly, a homogeneous group.
令人驚訝的是，這個政黨的支持者並不屬於同一性質的組織。

- -

❹ hetero 不同的 **+ dox** 信仰

heterodox [ˋhɛtərəˌdɑks] 形 異端的

延伸片語 **a heterodox idea** 非正統的想法

▶ This is such a heterodox idea. I won't accept it.
這真是個太異端的想法了。我不能接受。

延伸補充 自然學

與 homo 近義的字首：iso-

☆ **isobar**	相同 + 壓力	名 等壓線
☆ **isotope**	相同 + 位置	名 同位素
☆ **isotherm**	相同 + 溫度	名 等溫線

根 crypt 隱密的

Track 164

情境對話試水溫

Joe: I heard that the archaeologists found a cryptogram on the hidden crypt of the museum!

喬：我聽說考古學家們在博物館一個隱藏的地窖裡面找到了一段密文！

Oscar: Really? Have they decrypted the words?

奧斯卡：真的嗎？那他們有解密文字了嗎？

Joe: Not yet. They were written in an extinct language. A professional cryptographer is needed to solve the puzzle.

喬：還沒。他們是使用一種絕跡的語言寫的。他們需要一名專業的解碼者來解開這個謎題。

Oscar: But if it turns out that the message was "Happy Birthday," then it would be another waste of time trying to know why they encrypted the letters.

奧斯卡：但是如果後來發現，他們寫的訊息是「生日快樂」，那不就很浪費時間知道他們為什麼要將文字譯成密碼嗎？

Joe: You surely know how to be a joy killer.

喬：你真的很懂得掃興。

單字解析零距離

① **en** 使 ＋ **crypt** 隱藏、祕密

encrypt [ɛnˋkrɪpt] 動 譯成密碼

延伸片語 to encrypt messages 將訊息譯成密碼

▶ Don't worry. We will encrypt the messages to protect your privacy.
別擔心。我們會將訊息譯成密碼來保護你的隱私。

❷ crypt 隱藏、祕密

crypt [krɪpt] 名 地下室

延伸片語 **to be hidden in a crypt** 藏在地下室

▶ The antique has been hidden in a crypt for more than 100 years.
這個骨董被藏在地下室超過一百年。

- -

❸ crypt 隱藏、祕密 **+ o + gram** 書寫、紀錄

cryptogram [ˈkrɪptəˌgræm] 名 密碼；密文

延伸片語 **to receive a cryptogram** 收到密文

▶ The general received a cryptogram and was trying to decode it.
將軍收到了一封密文，並試著要解碼。

- -

❹ de 除去 **+ crypt** 隱藏、祕密

decrypt [diˈkrɪpt] 名 解碼；譯文

延伸片語 **to decrypt a code** 解碼

▶ All the professionals gathered in the room, trying to decrypt the code.
所有的專家都聚集在房間裡，試著解開密碼。

- -

❺ crypt 隱藏、祕密 **+ o + graph** 紀錄 **+ er** 名詞字尾，表示人

cryptographer [krɪpˈtagrəfɚ] 名 譯碼者

延伸片語 **to study as a cryptographer** 學習成為譯碼者

▶ My brother is now under internship and studies as a cryptographer.
我的哥哥現在正在實習並學習成為譯碼者。

延伸補充**自然學**

☆ **cryptic**　　密碼 + 形容詞字尾　　形 隱密的；如謎一般難解的

根 plen, plete

滿的、填滿

💬 情境對話試水溫

🎧 *Track 165*

Bree:	Have you completed the project on the growing condition of the new seeds?	布里：你完成那個紀錄新種子生長的專題了嗎？
Adam:	Not yet. All the candidate lands were found to be all ready depleted.	亞當：還沒，所有適合的土都已經用盡了。
Bree:	Really? I thought your program provided a plentiful of choices.	布里：真的嗎？我以為你有很多選擇。
Adam:	Only three this year. And the completion of the report needs to made by next week. I'm doomed.	亞當：今年只有三個，報告要在下週前完成，我完蛋了。
Bree:	Don't worry. I have plenty of other materials you may want. Want to check them out?	布里：別擔心，我還有很多你可能想要的材料，想看看嗎？
Adam:	Of course. Thanks a lot!	亞當：好啊，非常感謝！

 單字解析零距離

❶ **com** 完全 + **plete** 填滿

complete [kəm`plit] 勵 完成

延伸片語 **to complete a project** 完成專題

▶ Our demanding professor asked us to complete the project on time.
我們那嚴格的教授要求我們準時完成這項專題。

• •

② de 除去 + plete 填滿

deplete [dɪ`plit] 動 耗盡、用盡

延伸片語 to deplete resources 消耗……的資源

▶ We are dying soon because we never stop the speed to deplete all the resources on earth.
我們就快滅亡了，因為我們從不停止消耗地球資源的速度。

- -

③ plen 滿的 + ti + ful 形容詞字尾

plentiful [`plɛntɪfəl] 形 許多的

延伸片語 a plentiful of 很多種……

▶ We saw a plentiful of fresh fruits in the garden.
我們在花園裡看見很多種新鮮水果。

- -

④ com 完全 + plet 填滿 + ion 名詞字尾

completion [kəm`pliʃən] 名 完成

延伸片語 to be near completion 即將完工

▶ The construction is finally now near completion.
這個建設現在終於即將完工。

- -

⑤ plen 滿的 + ty 名詞字尾

plenty [`plɛntɪ] 名 許多

延伸片語 plenty of... 多種……

▶ Our teacher wanted us to use as plenty of natural elements as possible in our artwork.
我們老師想要我們的美術作品盡可能地用多種天然元素。

延伸補充 自然學

☆ **depletion**　　去除＋填滿＋名詞字尾　　名 耗盡

☆ **plenilune**　　滿＋月亮　　名 滿月

Unit 166 根 nov 新的

🎧 *Track 166*

💬 情境對話試水溫

Mason:	Your house is so beautifully renovated. You're always innovative in interior design!	梅森：你的家裡裝修得好漂亮。在室內設計方面你總是很具創新性！
Ava:	Well, thanks to some other novel ideas contributed by my husband. He helped a lot.	艾娃：這個嘛，多虧我老公貢獻的一些新點子。他幫了很多。
Mason:	Right, your husband. A novelist, right?	梅森：對，你的老公。小說家，對吧？
Ava:	Yes, he just published a novel recently. It's called Utopia.	艾娃：對的，他剛出了新的小說。叫做《烏托邦》。
Mason:	I'll surely check it out. By the way, can you kindly ask him how a novice in writing, like me, gets to establish herself as a novelist?	梅森：我一定會去看看的。對了，你可以問問他像我這樣的寫作新手要怎麼像他一樣成為一名小說家嗎？
Ava:	I'll ask him, but I know his answer will be never stop writing.	艾娃：我會問他，但我想他的答案會是永遠不要停止寫作。

⚡ 單字解析零距離

❶ re 再 ＋ nov 新的 ＋ ate 動詞字尾

renovate [ˈrɛnəˌvet] 動 裝修；重新改善

 延伸片語 to renovate the house 裝修房子

▶ My parents said that they wanted to renovate the house because the paints were beginning to peel off.
我的父母說他們想要裝修房子，因為油漆開始脫落了。

❷ **in** 進入＋ **nov** 新的＋ **a** ＋ **tive** 形容詞字尾

innovative [`ɪnoˌvetɪv] 形 創新的

延伸片語 an innovative idea 一個創新的點子

▶ The architect brought up an innovative idea and won unanimous approval.
這名建築師想到了一個創新的點子，且贏得了一致的認同。

. . . .

❸ **nov** 新的＋ **el** 名詞／形容詞字尾

novel [`nɑvl] 名 小説 形 新奇的

延伸片語 to write a novel 寫小説

▶ In my spare time, I always try to write a novel. I fail everytime, though.
在閒暇時間，我總是會試著寫小説。不過我每次都失敗。

. . . .

❹ **novel** 小説＋ **ist** 表示人

novelist [`nɑvlˌɪst] 名 小説家

延伸片語 to aspire to be a novelist 志願當一名小説家

▶ I aspire to be a novelist like Jane Austen whe I grow up.
我志願在長大當一名像珍‧奧斯丁那樣的小説家。

. . . .

❺ **nov** 新的＋ **ice** 名詞字尾

novice [`nɑvɪs] 名 新手；菜鳥

延伸片語 to be complicated for novices 對新手來説很複雜

▶ This task is way too complicated for novices.
這項任務對新手來説太過複雜了。

延伸補充 自然學

| ☆ **innovate** | 進入＋新的＋動詞字尾 | 動 創新 |
| ☆ **novelty** | 新的＋名詞字尾 | 名 新奇（的事物） |

情境對話試水溫

🎧 *Track 167*

Eva: Do you know that the prototype of the protagonist in this movie is the proto-human?	伊娃：你知道這部電影中主角的原型其實是原始人嗎？
Laura: How come?	勞拉：怎麼會？
Eva: Remember the scenes when he wandered around alone on the moor and caught animals with his bare hands? He ate them raw, and used their skins as shelters.	伊娃：還記得當他獨自在沼地上遊蕩並赤手抓住動物的場景嗎？他直接生吃這些動物，再穿他們的毛皮。
Laura: Oh…that makes sense. But I thought it was because he broke the protocol and had to be exiled?	勞拉：哦……聽起來合理，但我以為是因為他違反規定才不得不被流放。
Eva: That's part of the reasons. But mainly, it was because he lived in a very primordial era comparatively.	伊娃：這是其中之一的原因，但主要是因為他本來就生活在一個比較原始的時代。
Laura: However, if he didn't break the rules, he could at least live with other nomads.	勞拉：但是，如果他沒有違反規定，他至少可以與其他游牧民生活在一起。
Eva: Fine. The movie is open for interpretations.	伊娃：好吧，這電影就是讓大家自由詮釋。

單字解析零距離

❶ **proto** 原初的 ＋ **type** 形式

prototype [ˈprotəˌtaɪp] 名 原型

延伸片語 **a prototype of a machine** 機器的原型

▶ Our boss asked me to transport the prototype of a machine to our client.
老闆要求我們把機器原型運送給客戶。

· ·

❷ **proto** 原初的 ＋ **agon** 動作 ＋ **ist** 人

protagonist [proˈtæɡənɪst] 名 主角

延伸片語 **to act as a protagonist** 當主角

▶ This young actress expressed her desire to act as a protagonist in the upcoming film.
這位年輕的女演員表現出她想在接下來這部影片當主角的渴望。

· ·

❸ **proto** 原初的 ＋ **col** 集合

protocol [ˈprotəˌkɑl] 名 協議

延伸片語 **according to the protocol** 根據協議

▶ All the countries needed to reduce marine waste according to the protocal.
根據協議，所有國家都必須減少海洋資源的浪費。

· ·

❹ **proto** 原初的 ＋ **human** 人類

proto-human [ˈprotoˈhjumən] 名 早期原始人

延伸片語 **the proto-human stage** 原始人階段

▶ Electricity was not yet invented in the proto-human stage.
原始人階段時還沒有發明電力。

延伸補充 自然學

與 proto- 近義的字首：arche、arch

☆ **archetype** 最早的型態 名 原型
☆ **arch-enemy** 主要的敵人 名 大敵

根 pur(e) 純淨

🎧 *Track 168*

💬 情境對話試水溫

Derek: The Burmese purists tried to maintain ethnic purity, so they used the uprising by ARSA as an excuse to send troops to suppress the rebel army.

德瑞克：緬甸的純粹主義者為了維持種族統一性，利用若開羅興亞救世軍的暴動為藉口發動軍隊剿匪。

Jacky: I saw the news that there were over 1000 casualties and 700,000 Rohingya people were forced to leave their home.

傑奇：我看到新聞報到有超過1000人死亡、七十萬人被迫離開家園。

Derek: It has attracted the attention worldwide. But the Burmese authorities denied they were purifying the ethnicity.

德瑞克：全世界都已經在關注這件事，但緬甸官方否認他們是在淨化種族。

Jacky: Shame on them. They are inhumane and dishonest people with impure thoughts, they want to eliminate those Rohingya people by all means.

傑奇：他們太無恥了。他們是有著壞念頭、無良又不誠實的一群人且想盡辦法要除掉羅興亞人。

⚡ 單字解析零距離

❶ pur 純淨、清 ＋ **ist** 人

purist [ˈpjʊrɪst] 名 純粹主義者

延伸片語 purist movement 純化運動

▶ The followers of the art purist movement refuse to be characterized as any types of artists.
藝術純化運動的支持者拒絕被歸類為任何一類的藝術家。

② **pur** 純淨 ＋ **ity** 名詞字尾

purity [ˈpjʊrətɪ] 名 純潔、純淨

延伸片語 **ethnic purity** 民族統一性、種族純化

▶ To maintain ethnic purity, they forbid mixed marriages.
為了維護民族統一性，他們禁止異族聯姻。

③ **pur** 純淨 ＋ **ify** 使……化

purify [ˈpjʊrəˌfaɪ] 動 淨化

延伸片語 **purify water** 淨水

▶ This machine is invented to purify water.
這機器是發明來淨水的。

④ **im** 不 ＋ **pure** 純淨

impure [ɪmˈpjʊr] 形 不純的

延伸片語 **impure thoughts** 壞念頭

▶ The man came up with some impure thoughts while he saw the scantily-clad girl.
男人看到那個穿著清涼的女孩就起了壞念頭。

延伸補充自然學

☆ **puritan**	信奉純淨學說的人	形 清教徒的
☆ **purge**	使……純淨	動 潔淨
☆ **expurgate**	為潔淨把事物向外除	動 刪除；修訂

尾 less 不能……的、沒有……的

情境對話試水溫

Ada: After being a mother, I have countless things to worry about.

艾達：當媽之後，我必須擔心好多事情。

Mavis: Why do you say that?

瑪菲斯：你怎麼這麼說？

Ada: Well, first, it's my husband. He is senseless about when he is needed to deal with the baby. I feel so helpless sometimes.

艾達：嗯，第一，就是我老公。他不知道他何時需要去處理小孩，我有時覺得超無助的。

Mavis: It sounds really frustrating. What else?

瑪菲斯：這聽起來真的很令人沮喪，還有其他的嗎？

Ada: Then, being a mother means you have much more responsibilities. I can't be reckless whenever I make a decision. You don't want to see it turns out to be a mistake to affect your kid's life in the future.

艾達：當一個媽媽意味者妳的責任更多，下決定時不能太魯莽。你不會在未來想看到這個決定是錯誤的，而影響小孩的一生。

Mavis: Motherhood sounds like a real tough job. However, it's useless to worry that much now. Hang in there. I'll be by your side.

瑪菲斯：媽媽聽起來就是個困難的工作，但現在去擔心這些根本沒用，撐著點，我會陪著你的。

單字解析零距離

❶ **count** 計算 ＋ **less** 不能……的

countless ['kauntlɪs] 形 數不完的

延伸片語 countless reasons 無數的理由

▶ There are countless reasons why I can't marry you.
我不能跟你結婚的理由多得不勝枚舉。

··

❷ sense 感知 **＋ less** 沒有……的

senseless [ˈsɛnslɪs] 形 無知的、不醒人事的

延伸片語 senseless act 毫無意義的行為

▶ Arguing with such an unreasonable person is a senseless act.
跟一個不講理的人爭執是毫無意義的行為。

··

❸ help 幫助 **＋ less** 沒有……的

helpless [ˈhɛlplɪs] 形 無助的、無奈的

延伸片語 as helpless as a baby 像孩子一樣無助

▶ Being robbed, he sat on the roadside as helpless as a baby.
遭到搶劫的他，像個孩子一樣無助地坐在路邊。

··

❹ reck 顧慮 **＋ less** 沒有……的

reckless [ˈrɛklɪs] 形 不顧後果的、魯莽的

延伸片語 reckless driver 魯莽的駕駛

▶ The traffic cop stopped the truck and wrote the reckless driver a ticket.
交通警察攔下卡車，並且給那魯莽的駕駛開了張罰單。

··

❺ use 使用 **＋ less** 不能……的

useless [ˈjuslɪs] 形 沒用的

延伸片語 be useless at... 不擅長……

▶ Carl is smart, but he is totally useless at sports.
卡爾很聰明，但他完全不擅長運動。

⚡ 延伸補充 自然學

與 less 近義的字尾：-free

☆ **rent-free**　　　不用地租的　　　形 免地租的

☆ **duty-free**　　　不用稅租的　　　形 免稅的

Unit170 尾 ful 充滿……的

情境對話 試水溫

TV host: Today we have a guest with us for the show, whom we are all respectful to. He is a philanthropist, and also a life fighter. Let's welcome Shane Ke!	主持人：今天我們邀請到一位來賓參與我們節目，他受到了大眾的尊敬，他是一位慈善家，更是一位生命鬥士。讓我們歡迎柯沙恩！
Shane: Thanks, Miss Lin. Hello, everyone.	沙恩：謝謝，林小姐！大家好！
TV host: Shane, can you tell me how to deal with your emotions when you learned you had to have your left arm amputated?	主持人：沙恩，可以告訴我們當你得知你必須截肢掉左手，你是如何排解自己的情緒的呢？
Shane: Well...at first, I'm really resentful for everything and everyone. Therefore, everyone is leaving me except my wife, Angela. She is still careful of me physically and mentally. I'm very appreciative of her.	沙恩：嗯……一開始，我對每件事、每個人都充滿怨恨，所以每個人都離開了我，除了我的妻子，安琪拉。無論心靈上或身體上她仍然對我很照顧。我真的非常感謝她！
TV host: Then how did you make it through?	主持人：那之後你怎麼熬過的呢？
Shane: I turned to the hypnotherapy and Buddhism, and I found a peaceful land in my mind. Both are really useful. As a result, I decided to give back to the society to help more people.	沙恩：我後來接觸了催眠及佛教，我找到了心靈的一片淨土。兩者都非常有用。所以我決定要回饋社會盡一分心力。

單字解析 零距離

❶ re 回 **＋ spect** 看 **＋ ful** 充滿……的

respectful [rɪˈspɛktfəl] 形 尊敬的、恭敬有禮的

延伸片語 **respectful behavior** 尊敬他人的行為

▶ Look at people in the face while they're talking to you is a respectful behavior. 當別人跟你説話時，直視對方是尊敬他人的行為。

- -

❷ **re** 一再 ＋ **sent** 感覺 ＋ **ful** 充滿……的

resentful [rɪˈzɛntfəl] 形 怨恨的

延伸片語 **be resentful at...** 對某事感到氣憤

▶ Everyone was resentful at the unfair judgement.
所有人都對不公平的判決感到氣憤。

- -

❸ **care** 照顧 ＋ **ful** 充滿……的

careful [ˈkɛrfəl] 形 細心的、小心的

延伸片語 **careful with money** 不亂花錢

▶ Even he is a millionaire, he is careful with money.
即使他是百萬富翁，花錢也是很精打細算。

- -

❹ **peace** 和平 ＋ **ful** 充滿……的

peaceful [ˈpisfəl] 形 和平的、平靜的

延伸片語 **peaceful time** 和平時期

▶ The Zhenguan Reign Period was a peaceful time in Tang Dynasty. 貞觀在位期間是唐朝的一個和平時期。

- -

❺ **use** 作用 ＋ **ful** 充滿……的

useful [ˈjusfəl] 形 有用的

延伸片語 **be useful to someone** 對某人有幫助

▶ A flashlight can be very useful to you when there is a power failure. 手電筒在停電的時候是非常有幫助的。

- -

❻ **taste** 品味 ＋ **ful** 充滿……的

tasteful [ˈtestfəl] 形 高雅的、優美的

延伸片語 **a tasteful style** 高雅格調

▶ The interior designer decorated his own apartment in a tasteful style. 這位室內設計師以高雅的格調裝潢自己的公寓。

Unit 171 尾 able 可……的、能夠……的

情境對話試水溫

Katherine: I'm so sorry for your loss, Michael. It's inevitable for everyone to go through this, but I believe God has led your grandfather to a better place.

凱薩琳：麥可，我很遺憾你的爺爺逝世了。對每個人來說這是必經之路，但我相信上帝已經帶領他去了更好的世界。

Michael: Thanks, K. He is such an adorable person for his integrity. He lived a full life and was an inspiration to me and many others.

麥可：謝了，凱。因為他的誠實正直，他是如此的受人敬愛。他已經活得很精彩，而且也是我及大家的榜樣。

Katherine: Totally. He is a formidable second lieutenant to the soldiers, but also a amiable old man to every acquaintance. He is free from the changeable state of the illness now.

凱薩琳：沒錯，對於士兵來說，他是為可畏的少尉，但對於每位熟人來說，他也是親切的老人。他現在已經不受多變的病情而困擾了。

Michael: Exactly, it's so honorable to have him as my PaPa.

麥可：是的，我很榮幸有他當我的爺爺。

單字解析零距離

❶ in 不 **+ evit** 避免 **+ able** 能夠……的

inevitable [ɪnˈɛvətəbl] 形 無法避免的、必然的

延伸片語 inevitable result 必然的結果

▶ Their divorce is an inevitable result of his infidelity.
他們會離婚是他的不忠所造成的必然結果。

2 ador 可愛、敬重 ＋ **able** 可……的

adorable [əˋdorəbl] 形 可人的、可愛的

延伸片語 **be adorable for...** 因……而令人崇敬

▶ His grandfather is adorable for his integrity.
他的祖父因誠實正直而受人敬愛。

- -

3 formid 可怕的 ＋ **able** 可……的

formidable [ˋfɔrmɪdəbl] 形 可畏的

延伸片語 **formidable opponent** 勁敵

▶ He is a formidable opponent who shouldn't be underestimated.
他是一個不容小覷的勁敵。

- -

4 ami 愛好、朋友 ＋ **able** 可……的

amiable [ˋemɪəbl] 形 和藹可親的、厚道的

延伸片語 **in an amiable mood** 心情好的

▶ She was rarely in an amiable mood, and generally either irritable or sullen. 她很少心情好，而且常常不是暴怒就是陰鬱。

- -

5 change 變更 ＋ **able** 能夠……的

changeable [ˋtʃendʒəbl] 形 不定的、善變的

延伸片語 **changeable climate** 多變的氣候

▶ I can never get used to the changeable climate in London.
我永遠也無法習慣倫敦多變的氣候。

- -

6 honor 榮譽 ＋ **able** 可……的

honorable [ˋɑnərəbl] 形 光榮的、高貴的

延伸片語 **honorable mention** 榮譽獎

▶ You should be proud of yourself for getting the honorable mention. 得到榮譽獎，你應該以自己為榮。

延伸補充 自然學

able 的變化型：-ible

☆ **conductible** 能夠傳導的 形 可傳導的

☆ **seducible** 誘惑的 形 易受誘惑的

尾 proof 防止……的

情境對話 試水溫

Mark: Do you know that this glass is bulletproof?	馬克：你知道這玻璃是防彈的嗎？
Daisy: Of course. I also know that it's a perfect material for glass windows because it's also soundproof and heatproof.	黛西：當然，我也知道它是製作玻璃窗的完美材料，因為它隔音又耐熱。
Mark: Well, those are common qualities of windows, though.	馬克：嗯，那些是窗戶的基本品質。
Daisy: How about rustproof? That's worth telling.	黛西：那防銹怎麼樣？這值得討論一下。
Mark: What kind of glass rusts? You may as well tell me it's waterproof.	馬克：哪種玻璃會生鏽啊？你乾脆說它防水好了。
Daisy: Uhm… you're right! It's waterproof!	黛西：恩……對欸！它防水！
Mark: Oh my god.	馬克：我的老天。

單字解析 零距離

① bullet 子彈 **＋ proof** 防止的

bulletproof [ˈbʊlɪtˌpruf] 形 防彈的

延伸片語 **bulletproof vest** 防彈背心

▶ All security guards are equipped with bulletproof vests.
所有安全警衛都裝備有防彈背心。

❷ sound 聲音 ＋ **proof** 防止的

soundproof [ˈsaʊndˌpruf] 形 防噪音的、隔音的

延伸片語 **soundproof room** 隔音房間

▶ I always practice playing drums in the soundproof room so as not to disturb others.
我總是在隔音房間內練習打鼓，免得打擾到別人。

❸ heat 熱度 ＋ **proof** 防止的

heatproof [ˈhitpruf] 形 抗熱的

延伸片語 **heatproof glass** 耐熱玻璃

▶ The water pitcher is made of heatproof glass.
這個水壺是以耐熱玻璃製成的。

❹ rust 銹蝕 ＋ **proof** 防止的

rustproof [ˈrʌstˌpruf] 形 不銹蝕的

延伸片語 **rustproof paint** 防銹漆

▶ He repainted the room with rustproof paint.
他以防銹漆為房間重新上漆。

❺ water 水 ＋ **proof** 防止的

waterproof [ˈwɔtɚˌpruf] 形 防水的

延伸片語 **waterproof coat** 防水外套；雨衣

▶ You'd better wear your waterproof coat because it's very likely to rain.
今天很可能會下雨，你最好穿著防水外套。

延伸補充自然學

| ☆ **foolproof** | 防止愚鈍的 | 形 相當簡單的 |
| ☆ **shockproof** | 防止震動的 | 形 防震的 |

Unit 173 尾 ish 像……般的

Track 173

情境對話試水溫

Leo: My mom is so childish. She kept saying that I now look boyish with this haircut.	里歐：我媽媽好幼稚，她一直說我現在髮型很像小男孩。
Marco: Haha. She's just worried that you may seem more bookish than before. Remember the last time she said you look nerdy?	馬可：哈哈，她只是擔心你變得像書呆子。還記得上次她說你看起來很像書呆子嗎？
Leo: Well, I'd rather be bookish than foolish. Look at my brother. He plays mobile games all the time.	里歐：嗯，我寧願像書呆子而不是笨蛋，看看我弟弟，他只會一直打手遊。
Marco: Let's just be objective. Maybe he does read and study when you're not around.	馬可：我們客觀一點，也許你不在的時候他也會看書跟學習。
Leo: Fine. Then it's better to look bookish than snobbish, like my sister. She always thought she's better everyone else just because she is rich.	里歐：好吧，那也好過像我妹一樣，看起來很自大。她總認為她比其他人更好，因為她很有錢。
Marco: That's true.	馬可：那是真的。

單字解析零距離

❶ boy 男孩 **+ ish** 形容詞字尾，像……般的

boyish [ˈbɔɪʃ] 形 男孩子氣的

延伸片語 **to look boyish** 看起來男孩子氣

▶ My younger sister looks boyish but also cute.
我妹妹看起來很孩子氣但是很可愛。

② **book** 書籍 ＋ **ish** 形容詞字尾，像……般的

bookish [ˋbʊkɪʃ] 形 書呆子的；學究的

延伸片語 **to seem bookish** 看起來像書呆子

▶ Wearing a pair of glasses, I now seem bookish than ever.
一戴上眼鏡，我看起來比以前像書呆子。

・・・・・・・・・・・・・・・・・・・・・・・・・・・・・

③ **child** 孩童 ＋ **ish** 形容詞字尾，像……般的

childish [ˋtʃaɪldɪʃ] 形 孩子的；幼稚的

延伸片語 **a childish behavior** 幼稚的行為

▶ Do you know that a childish behavior like that may cause you troubles? 你知道像那樣幼稚的行為可能會讓你惹上麻煩嗎？

・・・・・・・・・・・・・・・・・・・・・・・・・・・・・

④ **fool** 傻瓜 ＋ **ish** 形容詞字尾，像……般的

foolish [ˋfulɪʃ] 形 愚蠢的

延伸片語 **a foolish thing** 愚蠢的事情

▶ Please promise me you don't do a foolish thing like this ever again. 請答應我你不會再做這種愚蠢的事情。

・・・・・・・・・・・・・・・・・・・・・・・・・・・・・

⑤ **snob** 勢利的人 ＋ **ish** 形容詞字尾，像……般的

snobbish [ˋsnɑbɪʃ] 形 勢利的

延伸片語 **to be snobbish about** 對……很講究

▶ The rich family is very snobbish about cheap hotels.
這有錢人家很講究便宜的飯店。

🔋 延伸補充 自然學

與 ish 近義的字尾：like

☆ **chidlike**	孩子 ＋ ……般的	形	像孩子一般的
☆ **dreamlike**	夢 ＋ ……般的	形	像夢一般的
☆ **businesslike**	商業 ＋ ……般的	形	商業般的

情境對話試水溫

Track 174

Will: The man in the black shirt was caught putting an explosive in front of the fountain. When the police arrived, he resisted and sprayed corrosive liquids to people around him.

威爾：穿著黑色上衣的男子被抓到在噴泉前放置爆炸物，警方抵達時，他拒絕被捕還朝著身旁民眾噴射腐蝕性液體。

Lillian: It was Sunday! Lots of people gathered in that square!

莉莉安：那天是星期日！很多人聚集在那個廣場！

Will: Fortunately, no one got injured. The man confessed that he was afflicted with an infective disease. He didn't want to be the only one suffering in this world.

威爾：幸運的是那天沒人受傷，那男子坦承他染上了傳染性的疾病，他不想要這世界上只有他一人在承受痛苦。

Lillian: Thank God! His vicious plan was just an abortive attempt.

莉莉安：謝天！他邪惡的計畫失敗了！

Will: Big thanks to the police. Their efficiency and performance were so impressive! They stuck to their respective duties and saved the day.

威爾：特別感謝員警，他們的效率及表現都讓人印象深刻！他們每人堅守各自的崗位，化解了危機。

單字解析零距離

❶ abort 流產 ＋ **ive** 有……傾向的

abortive [ə'bɔrtɪv] 形 流產的

延伸片語 **abortive attempt** 嘗試失敗

▶ Their first uprising against the government was an abortive attempt. 他們第一次的反政府起義失敗了。

2 **cor** 共同 ＋ **ros** 腐蝕 ＋ **ive** 有⋯⋯性質的

corrosive [kə`rosɪv] 形 侵蝕的

延伸片語 corrosive injury 腐蝕性傷害

▶ Ingestion of pesticides will cause corrosive injury to gullet and stomach. 吞食農藥將對食道及胃造成腐蝕性傷害。

. . . .

3 **ex** 向外 ＋ **plos** 大聲響 ＋ **ive** 有⋯⋯傾向的（此表名詞）

explosive [ɪk`splosɪv] 形 爆炸性的

延伸片語 plastic explosive 塑膠炸藥

▶ The police tried to stop the man from detonating the plastic explosive. 警方試圖阻止男子引爆那枚塑膠炸藥。

. . . .

4 **im** 使 ＋ **press** 放置 ＋ **ive** 有⋯⋯性質的

impressive [ɪm`prɛsɪv] 形 使人印象深刻的

延伸片語 impressive movie 感人的電影

▶ The Titanic is by far the most impressive movie that I have ever seen. 鐵達尼號是目前我所看過的電影中，最令我印象深刻的一部。

. . . .

5 **in** 使 ＋ **fect** 做 ＋ **ive** 有⋯⋯傾向的

infective [ɪn`fɛktɪv] 形 有傳染力的

延伸片語 anti-infective drug 抗感染物

▶ The man took the anti-infective drug so as to prevent the infectious disease. 男子服用抗感染物以預防傳染病。

. . . .

6 **re** 再 ＋ **spect** 看 ＋ **ive** 有⋯⋯性質的

respective [rɪ`spɛktɪv] 形 各別的

延伸片語 respective duties 各自的工作崗位

▶ Everyone returned to their respective duties right after the meeting. 所有人在開完會後隨即回到各自的工作崗位上。

💡 延伸補充 **自然學**

| ☆ **imaginative** | 想像 ＋ 有⋯⋯性質的 | 形 具想像力的 |
| ☆ **talkative** | 說話 ＋ 有⋯⋯性質的 | 形 話多的 |

尾 ability 具有……性質、可……性

情境對話試水溫

Molly: I always thought that I have the capability to deal with all the difficulties in life, but it turns out that I have to face my own vulnerability first.

莫莉：我總是以為我有那個能力去面對生命中的所有難題，但是事實是，我必須先面對自身的脆弱。

Andie: Of course. And you have to remember that the inevitability to confront oneself is the same as the negotiability of life. While you think something is impossible to change, think about how you always go back to your own history.

安迪：當然。而且你要記得的是，面對自己的必然性和生命的可協調性是一樣的。當你認為某件事不可能被改變的時候，想想你是如何總是回到自己的歷史。

Molly: What do you mean by history?

莫莉：你指的歷史是什麼意思？

Andie: The sedimentation of your past experiences. The attainability of certain memories will help you cope with life.

安迪：你過往經驗的沉澱。某些回憶的可取得性會幫助你面對生命。

Molly: That's deep. Thanks!

莫莉：好深奧。謝謝！

單字解析零距離

❶ **cap** 拿取 ＋ **ability** 具有……性質

capability [ˌkepəˈbɪlətɪ] 名 能力、才能

延伸片語 the capability of doing... 做某事的才能

▶ We're looking for someone who has the capability of managing a branch office.
我們在徵求擁有管理一間分公司能力的人才。

2 **vulner** 弱點 ＋ **ability** 具有……性質

vulnerability [ˌvʌlnərəˈbɪlətɪ] 名 罩門、弱點

延伸片語 critical vulnerability 嚴重漏洞

▶ Unrestrained gun trade is a critical vulnerability of the public security in that country. 不限制槍枝交易是該國治安的嚴重漏洞。

3 **in** 不 ＋ **evit** 避免 ＋ **ability** 具有……性質

inevitability [ˌɪnɛvətəˈbɪlətɪ] 名 不可逃避性、必然性

延伸片語 inevitability of life 生命的必然性

▶ To go through birth, aging, illness and death is the inevitability of life. 經歷生老病死是生命必然之事。

4 **negoti** 協商 ＋ **ability** 具有……性質

negotiability [nɪˌgoʃɪəˈbɪlətɪ] 名 可協商性

延伸片語 lack of negotiability 缺乏協商性

▶ My mother doesn't like shopping online because of its lack of negotiability. 我媽媽不喜歡線上購物，因為線上購物不能議價。

5 **attain** 獲得 ＋ **ability** 具有……性質

attainability [əˌtenəˈbɪlətɪ] 名 可獲得、可達到

延伸片語 attainability of drug 毒品可得性

▶ It is reported that the attainability of drugs is increasing on campus. 據報導，在校園內越來越容易取得毒品了。

延伸補充 自然學

ability 的變化型：-ibility

☆ **access**ibility	可接近性的	名 容易接近、可親
☆ **edib**ility	食用＋具有……性質	名 可食性
☆ **flexib**ility	彎曲＋可……性	名 彈性、靈活度
☆ **possib**ility	可能＋可……性	名 可能性

尾 ship 狀態、身分、關係

💬 情境對話試水溫　　　　　　　　　　🎧 *Track 176*

Ava: I heard that you participated in the National High School Skills Competition and won the championship.	艾娃：聽說你參加了全國高中職的技藝競賽而且還得了冠軍。
Liam: Yes, I'm so blessed to win this competition, so I can obtain the scholarship for the university.	連恩：對呀！我好幸運贏得這場比賽，這樣我就能得到大學的獎學金了。
Ava: That's a big amount of money. What a wonderful prize!	艾娃：那是很大一筆錢耶！好棒的獎品！
Liam: Thanks, this honor doesn't all belong to me. I also appreciated that Byron always practiced with me so that I could be so familiar with the contest.	連恩：謝啦！但這榮譽不全然屬於我的，我也要謝謝拜倫總是陪我練習，所以我才能對比賽如此熟悉。
Ava: He is such a good friend that your friendship will be everlasting.	艾娃：他是這麼好的朋友，你們的友情必定長存。
Liam: I hope so. I also hope I will be able to obtain the ownership of the franchise mechanics shop, and be an outstanding mechanic in the future.	連恩：但願如此，我也希望未來我能取得連鎖修車廠的經營權，並成為傑出的技師。

⚡ 單字解析零距離

❶ champ 平原 **＋ ion** 名詞字尾 **＋ ship** 身分

championship [ˈtʃæmpɪənˌʃɪp] **名** 冠軍

延伸片語 Women's Championships 女子錦標賽

▶ They are practicing very hard in order to win the Women's Volleyball Championships.
為了贏得女子排球錦標賽她們努力練習。

- -

❷ **scholar** 學術的 ＋ **ship** 狀態

scholarship [ˈskɑləˌʃɪp] 名 獎學金；學識
延伸片語 sports scholarship 體育獎學金

▶ Jerry goes to a nice university on the sports scholarship.
傑瑞靠這份體育獎學金在一間不錯的大學就讀。

- -

❸ **friend** 朋友 ＋ **ship** 關係

friendship [ˈfrɛndʃɪp] 名 友情
延伸片語 everlasting friendship 永恆的友誼

▶ I am impressed with the everlasting friendship between my father and Uncle Jack.
我父親與傑克叔叔長存的友誼讓我很感動。

- -

❹ **own** 擁有 ＋ **er** ……的人 ＋ **ship** 狀態、身分

ownership [ˈonəʃɪp] 名 擁有者；所有權
延伸片語 public ownership 公有制；國家所有制

▶ Power industry still remains in public ownership in this country.
電力工業在這國家仍維持國家所有制。

💡 延伸補充 自然學

☆ **fellowship**	夥伴的關係	名 夥伴關係
☆ **sportsmanship**	運動家的狀態	名 運動家精神
☆ **kinship**	家族的關係	名 血緣關係
☆ **citizenship**	公民的身分	名 公民身分

Unit 177 尾 age 狀況、行為、數量、性質

情境對話試水溫

Gillian: Elena is one of the survivors of the airline incident. Her husband died in the air crash. The police are checking the plane breakage, and try to find the flight recorder from the plane wreckage to see the CVR, mileage from FDR, and other details.

吉莉安：伊蓮娜是那場空難其中一位生還者，而她丈夫死於那場空難，警察正在機身壞損，並從飛機殘骸中找尋飛航記錄器，確認座艙通話記錄器、飛航紀錄器裡的里程，以及其他細節。

Adam: Jenny and I went to the hospital to visit her yesterday. She was almost covered with the bandage and pipes.

亞當：我跟珍妮昨天去醫院探視伊蓮娜，她幾乎全身都被繃帶和管子覆蓋。

Gillian: Elena and her husband had a lovely and happy marriage. They are aligned with each other's soul and just meant to be.

吉莉安：伊蓮娜和他丈夫有很美滿的婚姻，他們靈魂契合註定要和彼此在一起。

Adam: It will definitely be a long way for her to get recovery from sorrow.

亞當：要她從傷痛中復原勢必是條漫漫長路。

單字解析零距離

❶ band 用帶捆 ＋ **age** 狀態

bandage [ˈbændɪdʒ] 名 繃帶、束縛

延伸片語 **bandage up** 包紮起來

▶ The nurse bandaged up his injured arm roughly.
護士粗魯地將他受傷的手臂包紮起來。

❷ mile 公里的 ＋ **age** 數量

mileage [ˋmaɪlɪdʒ] 名 里程數

延伸片語 **low mileage** 低里程數

▶ He bought a small used car with low mileage.
他買了一輛總里程數低的小車。

‧‧‧

❸ **marri** 結婚 ＋ **age** 行為

marriage [ˋmærɪdʒ] 名 婚姻

延伸片語 **marriage bureau** 婚姻介紹所

▶ Thanks to the marriage bureau, my 45-year-old aunt finally found her Mr. Right.
感謝婚姻介紹所，讓我那四十五歲的姑姑終於找到她的真命天子。

‧‧‧

❹ **break** 毀壞的 ＋ **age** 狀態

breakage [ˋbrekɪdʒ] 名 壞損

延伸片語 **accidental breakage** 意外損害

▶ Any accidental breakage should be paid for.
任何意外損害都必須賠償。

‧‧‧

❺ **wreck** 失事 ＋ **age** 狀況

wreckage [ˋrɛkɪdʒ] 名 （飛機、船等）失事、遭難

延伸片語 **plane wreckage** 飛機殘骸

▶ The rescuers had to drag out the dead bodies of the victims from the plane wreckage.
救難人員必須從飛機殘骸中將罹難者的遺體拉出來。

‧‧‧

❻ **us** 使用 ＋ **age** 行為

usage [ˋjusɪdʒ] 名 使用方法

延伸片語 **ill-usage** 錯誤使用；濫用

▶ The damage to this machine is apparently caused by ill-usage.
這機器的損壞明顯是因為使用錯誤所造成。

延伸補充 自然學

☆ **shortage**　　短少的狀態　　名 短缺

☆ **appendage**　　附加的性質　　名 附加物

Unit 178 尾 ance 性質、狀態

🎧 *Track 178*

情境對話試水溫

Steven: Have you seen the news? Ivy is going to marry one of the richest businessman in Taiwan, and there will be a large attendance.

> 史蒂芬：你看到新聞了沒？艾薇即將跟台灣首富之一結婚了，而且很多有頭有臉的人物都會出席這場婚禮。

Ricky: Yes, I have. The wedding is totally an extravagance. The side-street news even reveals that Ivy is quite picky on the fragrance of the wedding venue. Who cares about what kind of aromatic they use?

> 瑞奇：我看到了啊！這婚禮根本就是鋪張，小道消息還指出艾薇很挑剔婚禮場地的香氣。到底誰在乎他們用哪牌的芳香劑了？

Steven: That's absolute nonsense. That businessman is indeed in ignorance of how miserable his life will be after marriage.

> 史蒂芬：真是太扯了，這位富商完全不知道他婚後的生活會是怎樣悲慘。

Ricky: Exactly. Also, there's a gossip that Ivy originally showed reluctance to the marriage, so the man doubled the bride-price to please her. If only I were very rich, I would also agree on everything!

> 瑞奇：沒錯，而且還有八卦指出當初艾薇不願接受這件婚事，所以富商把禮金加倍來討好她。如果我也這麼有錢，什麼我都嘛答應！

Steven: Dream on.

> 史蒂芬：少做白日夢了！

單字解析零距離

❶ **attend** 參加 ＋ **ance** 狀態

attendance [əˈtɛndəns] 名 參加、出席

延伸片語 perfect attendance　全勤

▶ The only perfect attendance award of this semester goes to Amy. 這學期唯一一個全勤獎的得獎人是艾咪。

- -

❷ **extra** 超出 ＋ **vag** 漫遊 ＋ **ance** 狀態

extravagance [ɪkˋstrævəgəns] 名 鋪張、浪費

延伸片語 live a life of extravagance　過著鋪張浪費的生活

▶ It is unbelievable that she lives a life of extravagance by borrowing. 真不敢相信她竟靠借貸過著鋪張浪費的生活。

- -

❸ **fragr** 芳香的 ＋ **ance** 性質

fragrance [ˋfregrəns] 名 芳香、香氣

延伸片語 flower fragrance　花香

▶ The whole room is filled with flower fragrance.
整個房間充滿了花香。

- -

❹ **ignor** 忽視 ＋ **ance** 狀態

ignorance [ˋɪgnərəns] 名 忽視、忽略

延伸片語 in ignorance of...　對……不知情

▶ It is sad that the old man is in complete ignorance of his son's death. 令人悲傷的是，老人對兒子的死一無所知。

- -

❺ **reluct** 不情願的 ＋ **ance** 狀態

reluctance [rɪˋlʌktəns] 名 不甘願、勉強

延伸片語 show reluctance to do...　不願做某事

▶ Mary showed reluctance to lend Peter any money.
瑪莉表示不願意借彼得任何一毛錢。

🔋 延伸補充 **自然學**

與 ance 近義的字尾：cy、sy

☆ **accuracy**　準確的性質　　　名 正確性

☆ **idiosyncrasy**　個人的習性　　　名 特質

Unit 179 尾 ence 行為、狀態

情境對話試水溫

David: Wenny accused the housekeeper of T Hotel stealing her diamond ring, and had firmly insistence to have access to all surveillance cameras.

大衛：溫妮指控T飯店的房務人員偷了她的鑽戒，她堅持調閱所有監視器。

Tim: The housekeeper stole the ring?

提姆：房務人員偷了戒指？

David: She tried to prove her innocence, but in vain. The surveillance camera showed that she was the only one entering Wenny's room. They all confronted in a tense ambience.

大衛：她嘗試證明自己的清白但徒勞無功，監視器顯示她是唯一進入溫妮房間的人，對質的氛圍很緊張。

Tim: Wasn't that Wenny's engagement ring?

提姆：那是溫妮的訂婚戒指吧？

David: Yes. The manager apologized for the negligence and promised to compensate for the loss.

大衛：是，經理對於他們的疏失道歉並且承諾賠償。

Tim: Wenny always acts with prudence, how could she put the costly ring in the room?

提姆：溫妮做事一向謹慎啊，怎麼會把昂貴的戒指放在房裡？

David: Losing a ring is not that big deal. It seemed like providence that the hotel was on fire the day after Wenny checked out!

大衛：弄丟戒指是小事。像是上天保佑一樣，溫妮退房的隔天，飯店發生大火！

單字解析零距離

❶ ambi 周圍 **+ ence** 狀態

ambience [ˈæmbɪəns] 名 周圍氣氛

延伸片語 **dining ambience** 用餐氣氛

▶ We enjoyed the relaxed dining ambience at the homey Italian restaurant. 我們喜歡那間家庭式義大利餐廳裡輕鬆的用餐氣氛。

❷ **in** 不 + **noc** 傷害 + **ence** 狀態

innocence [ˈɪnəsns] 名 無辜、清白
延伸片語 **prove one's innocence** 證明一個人的清白

▶ There is no sufficient evidence to prove his innocence.
沒有足夠的證據能證明他的清白。

❸ **in** 使 + **sist** 使站立 + **ence** 行為

insistence [ɪnˈsɪstəns] 名 堅持　延伸片語 **insistence on...** 對……的堅持

▶ They called a hunger strike to show their insistence on the removal of the president. 他們發起絕食抗議，以表示他們對罷免總統的堅持。

❹ **neglig** 忽略 + **ence** 行為

negligence [ˈnɛɡlɪdʒəns] 名 疏失
延伸片語 **contributory negligence** 共同過失

▶ The plaintiff cannot get the indemnity he requested for contributory negligence. 原告因共同過失而無法拿到他要求的賠償金。

❺ **pro** 預先 + **vid** 看 + **ence** 狀態

providence [ˈprɑvədəns] 名 遠見、天命
延伸片語 **act of providence** 不可抗力的天災

▶ The tsunami that killed 500 people ten years ago was deemed an act of providence.
十年前那場使五百人喪生的海嘯被視為不可抗力的一場天災。

❻ **prud** 正經 + **ence** 狀態

prudence [ˈprudṇs] 名 慎重　延伸片語 **act with prudence** 謹慎行事

▶ We must act with prudence so as not to leak out any information. 我們務必謹慎行事，以免走漏任何風聲。

377

情境對話試水溫

🎧 *Track 180*

Bill: The city government provided subsidization for enterprise as an encouragement to build factories in this area.

比爾：市政府為企業提供補助，作為他們在這區設建工廠的鼓勵。

Jam: The policy was for local development. However, most residents felt resentment at the industrial pollution the factories had caused the discharge of sewage, soot emi, such as ssion, noise pollution, etc.

詹姆：這個政策原本是為了地區發展，但多數居民因工廠造成的工業污染而感到不滿，像是廢水排放、廢氣排放、噪音汙染等等。

Bill: The residents even led a protest movement against the city government and enterprises involved. They asked the enterprises to make renouncement and stop operations of all authorized manufacturing factories.

比爾：居民甚至針對政府及涉及的企業發起抗議活動，他們要求企業停止運作所有未經授權的製造業工廠。

單字解析零距離

❶ **en** 使…… + **courage** 鼓勵 + **ment** 行為

encouragement [ɪnˋkɝɪdʒmənt] 名 獎勵、鼓勵

延伸片語 **negative encouragement** 消極鼓勵

▶ Experts believe that physical punishment is a negative encouragement to students.
專家認為體罰對學生來說是消極鼓勵。

2 develop 發展 ＋ ment 行為

development [dɪˈvɛləpmənt] 名 發展、進步

延伸片語 personality development 人格發展

▶ Home education can greatly influence one's personality development. 家庭教育對一個人的人格發展影響甚鉅。

- -

3 govern 統治 ＋ ment 行為

government [ˈɡʌvɚnmənt] 名 政府

延伸片語 tyrannical government 專制政府

▶ They are scheming an uprising to overthrow their tyrannical government. 他們正在計畫一場起義，以推翻他們的專制政府。

- -

4 move 移動 ＋ ment 行動

movement [ˈmuvmənt] 名 動作、行動

延伸片語 bowel movement 排便

▶ Regular exercise and fiber intake can improve bowel movement. 規律運動及攝取纖維能促進排便。

- -

5 re 回 ＋ nounce 說 ＋ ment 行為

renouncement [rɪˈnaʊnsmənt] 名 放棄、拒絕

延伸片語 right of renouncement 解除權

▶ His attorney suggested that he exercise the right of renouncement and rescind the contract.
他的律師建議他行使解除權，撤銷合約。

- -

6 re 一再 ＋ sent 情感 ＋ ment 行為

resentment [rɪˈzɛntmənt] 名 仇恨、怨恨

延伸片語 resentment against 對……感到憤慨

▶ The residents felt resentment against the industrial pollution caused by the factory. 居民對工廠造成的工業污染感到很憤慨。

尾 **ness** 性質、狀態

情境對話試水溫

🎧 *Track 181*

Jordan: A business genius should have the awareness of future trends.

喬登：一名商業天才需要知道未來趨勢。

Donnie: Well... So far, you have had one trait to start your career in Rothschild. What else?

唐尼：嗯……你已經擁有了一項可以開始在羅斯柴爾德工作的特質。還有呢？

Jordan: When you are about to persuade the potential customers, you should maintain the conciseness of the conversation, and impress them with accuracy and efficiency.

喬登：當你要說服潛在客戶時，你要維持對話簡潔，用精準度和效率讓他們印象深刻。

Donnie: Um, it gets more interesting now.

唐尼：嗯……越來越有趣了呢。

Jordan: What's more, you should talk with happiness in your eyes to let them know those penny stocks are really promising. Last but not least, you should always show kindness.

喬登：而且你應該要非常愉悅地告訴他們這支跌破面值股票是真的很有前景。最後，你要總是表達善意。

Donnie: Okay, I'm really looking forward to your performance in our company now.

唐尼：好，我現在真的很期待你未來在公司的表現。

單字解析零距離

❶ **busi** 商業 ＋ **ness** 性質

business ['bɪznɪs] 名 商業、生意

延伸片語 **out of business** 停業；歇業

▶ TThe restaurant has been out of business since last month.
那間餐廳自上個月起已經停業了。

- -

② **aware** 覺察 ＋ **ness** 狀態

awareness [ə`wɛrnɪs] 名 認知、覺察

延伸片語 eco-awareness 環保意識

▶ The ecologist gave a speech to promote eco-awareness.
該生態學家做了一場推動環保意識的演講。

- -

③ **con** 共同 ＋ **cise** 切 ＋ **ness** 性質

conciseness [kən`saɪsnɪs] 名 簡明、簡單

延伸片語 conciseness of expression 言簡意賅

▶ A good essay should be a balance between conciseness of expression and adequate information.
一份好的報告應該在言簡意賅及充分訊息中取得平衡。

- -

④ **happi** 快樂 ＋ **ness** 狀態

happiness [`hæpɪnɪs] 名 快樂、愉悅

延伸片語 in great happiness 非常愉快地

▶ The couple is preparing for their wedding in great happiness.
這對情侶正非常愉快地籌備他們的婚禮。

- -

⑤ **kind** 仁慈 ＋ **ness** 性質

kindness [`kaɪndnɪs] 名 仁慈、友好

延伸片語 kill someone with kindness 寵壞某人

▶ Stop spoiling your son. You're going to kill him with kindness.
別在溺愛你兒子了。寵他就是害了他。

延伸補充自然學

| ☆ **empti**ness | 空的狀態 | 名 空虛 |
| ☆ **swift**ness | 快捷的狀態 | 名 敏捷 |

尾 tion, sion
行動、狀態

🎧 *Track 182*

情境對話試水溫

Linda: I think this revolution has already caused too many social confrontations. It has to end.

琳達：我認為這場革命已經導致太多的社會衝突，它必須要結束。

Kevin: Well, on the bright side, tensions are actually good things. They make people reflect and contemplate on the situation they're facing.

凱文：嗯，從好的方面來說，緊張的局勢其實是好事，它使人們深省並思考他們所面臨的情況。

Linda: True. But it has led to the isolation of minorities from the general public. A strategic decision needs to be made.

琳達：沒錯，但它害得少數族群被大眾孤立，必須要做出決策了。

Kevin: So, you're saying that the government should suppress the civil action?

凱文：所以，你是說政府應該禁止公民運動？

Linda: No. I'm trying to say that the movement has crossed the boundaries.

琳達：不，我是覺得這場運動已經逾矩了。

單字解析零距離

❶ **con** 共同 ＋ **front** 正面的 ＋ **ation** 行動

confrontation [kɑnfrʌnˈteʃən] 名 衝突、對抗

延伸片語 a confrontation with 和……對峙

▶ The activistis were now in a confrontation with the government.
激進分子現在正與政府對峙。

表示狀態、情況

② **tens** 拉 ＋ **ion** 狀態

tension ['tɛnʃən] 名 緊張、緊繃

延伸片語 the tension between A and B　A和B之間的緊張氛圍

▶ It's not difficult to detect the tension between Marco and Mars.
我們不難察覺到馬可跟馬爾斯之間的緊張氛圍。

③ **i** ＋ **sol** 唯一 ＋ **ation** 狀態

isolation [ˌaɪsl̩ʼeʃən] 名 孤立、隔離

延伸片語 feelings of isolation　孤獨感

▶ Reaching mid-life, Alice keeps having feelings of isolation.
艾麗絲到了中年後，一直覺得很孤獨。

④ **de** 除去 ＋ **cis** 切除 ＋ **ion** 行動

decision [dɪˈsɪʒən] 名 決定、判斷

延伸片語 to make a decision　做決定

▶ In life, we are constantly forced to make decisions.
人生中，我們經常被迫做出決定。

⑤ **act** 行動 ＋ **ion** 行動

action ['ækʃən] 名 行動、行為

延伸片語 to take action　採取行動

▶ Facing this dire situation, I have to take action to protect myself.
面臨這種緊迫的局面，我必須要採取行動來保護我自己。

延伸補充自然學

| ☆ **persuasion** | 通過 ＋ 柔順的 ＋ 行動 | 名 說服 |
| ☆ **ambition** | 繞周圍走 ＋ 狀態 | 名 野心 |

原來如此 系列 E209

第一本英文會話╳例句╳情境分類的
字根字首字尾大全

一次掌握多種用法，學習節奏與效率都一氣呵成！

作　　者	吳悠（Giselle）◎著
顧　　問	曾文旭
社　　長	王毓芳
編輯統籌	耿文國、黃璽宇
主　　編	吳靜宜、姜怡安
執行主編	李念茨
執行編輯	陳儀蓁
封面設計	西遊記裡的豬
美術編輯	王桂芳、張嘉容
法律顧問	北辰著作權事務所　蕭雄淋律師、幸秋妙律師

初　　版	2019年10月
出　　版	捷徑文化出版事業有限公司
電　　話	（02）2752-5618
傳　　真	（02）2752-5619
地　　址	106 台北市大安區忠孝東路四段250號11樓-1

定　　價	新台幣420元／港幣140元
產品內容	1書

總 經 銷	采舍國際有限公司
地　　址	235 新北市中和區中山路二段366巷10號3樓
電　　話	（02）8245-8786
傳　　真	（02）8245-8718

港澳地區總經銷	和平圖書有限公司
地　　址	香港柴灣嘉業街12號百樂門大廈17樓
電　　話	（852）2804-6687
傳　　真	（852）2804-6409

▶本書圖片由 Shutterstock圖庫、123RF圖庫提供。

▌捷徑 Book站

現在就上臉書（FACEBOOK）「捷徑BOOK站」並按讚加入粉絲團，
就可享每月不定期新書資訊和粉絲專享小禮物喔！
http://www.facebook.com/royalroadbooks
讀者來函：royalroadbooks@gmail.com

國家圖書館出版品預行編目資料

第一本英文會話╳例句╳情境分類的字根字首
字尾大全 / 吳悠著 . -- 初版 . -- 臺北市：捷徑文
化，2019.10
　　面；　公分

ISBN 978-957-8904-81-1(平裝)

1. 英語 2. 讀本

805.18　　　　　　　　　　　　108007995